AF430362

THE CLOCKWORK HEART

OF MAGIC: BOOK TWO

T. ARIYANNA

Copyright © 2018, 2023 by T. Ariyanna

All rights reserved.

No part of this book may be reproduced in any form or by any electronic or mechanical means, including information storage and retrieval systems, without written permission from the author, except for the use of brief quotations in a book review.

PROLOGUE

19 Years Earlier

The Towers of Centric loomed over all of Lontorra, serving as a constant reminder of the world they oversaw. Though their shadows could reach even the most secluded of locales of this land, its magical influence had a far more disappointing effect. Humans had overthrown the majority of Lontorra's populace, but not through force. By surrender. Rather than cause the destruction of their shared land, the magical creatures opted for peace, and so they shut themselves into hiding. The Mages, the most hated and feared of those the humans opposed, made a true home for themselves in the very center of Lontorra, and it was there that anger fermented for some, and they watched, stifled by their suffering, as the world around them coped with the change. They watched from the safety of their Towers for the chance to strike back.

A man and woman sat in silence for hours, peering out of

the balcony of Talgrin, the greatest and most esteemed Tower in all of Centric. The small room was cramped, filled with plush furniture and vibrant colors. The rug beneath their feet resembled the ocean in both its magnificent waves of blue, and the cool water that lapped at the walls. A large ottoman sat just under the window, and the lush cushions soaked up the warmth from the setting sun. The base of the seat was ancient, depicting a battle between a large cat jumping gracefully, and a mighty beast with beautiful wings and a perfectly sharpened beak. Ribbons of crystals hung from the ceiling, gathering any stray light and reflecting it in rainbows across the surprisingly barren walls. The glimmers of sunlight danced around each other, swaying to a tune the ribbons played on the passing breeze.

The sleeves of the woman's velvet gown draped over the ledge elegantly, folding in on itself. She tapped her bare toes against the magic rug, and the water licked at her bare skin. She was no older than eighteen, but had seen so much tragedy in her short life that she hadn't any vitality left in her.

The man was only two years older, though he hadn't even begun to mature yet. Not in the ways that should be normal, at least. He remained a spoiled prince, heavily equipped with a wide assortment of threats, taunts, and punishments for any that displeased him. He excelled in creativity, yet surprisingly lacked in general intelligence. The woman thought it just a side effect of royalty, though the same could never be said for the man's father.

Centric below them was bustling, busy and populated as ever. A man was trying desperately to sell his wares, screaming about magical lamps at the top of his lungs, and swearing to an unknown god that he had found a carpet that could fly. His voice was the only one that held enough force and power to reach the tops of the Towers, but it also held a great sorrow.

Theresa leaned over the sill of the window to find the source of the voice. He was parked not far away, but he sat in shadows. As he lunged for another passerby, she thought his skin looked blue. *Preposterous. There haven't been any Droll in Centric for ages.*

The man pressed up against her side, curious in what had caught her attention. He tilted his head and scoffed at the poor man begging for acknowledgement. He raised his left hand, a sinister green glow already emanating from his palm.

Theresa snatched his hand before he could make his move. The magic that sparked from within stung her, but she had long ago grown accustomed to the pain.

"Don't, Crestyss. He spouts nothing more than the foolishness of children's stories. A poor old man with nothing left needs not your punishment. Please."

Crestyss glared at her a moment, but his expression softened before she could say any more. The man below them, seemingly knowing the danger he had been in, was now packing up his wares. As Theresa watched him, the rug he claimed to be magical fell over, knocking a vase to the floor. It shattered all around, scattering into the streets. The man bent over the rug, screaming profanities at it before regaining his composure and using a simple spell to undo the damage. With the man's attention diverted, Theresa almost thought she saw the rug actually move.

Before she could convince herself it had been just a trick of the eye, the mat unrolled suddenly, whacking against the man's legs. He whirled on the rug, but he didn't yell again. His shoulders sagged and he rolled the rug back up. Within minutes everything was packed, and the man was gone, a great weight on his shoulders.

With her distraction gone, Theresa turned to find Crestyss gazing at her intently. She dared herself to question him, but the proper words wouldn't come to her. His stare was inquisitive, and she was spared the feat of speaking her mind. The door burst open, and a man barely older than herself marched inside.

"Young Master Crestyss! I have the report on your father's meeting with the humans," Jenta said, breathless as he came into the room.

He stopped suddenly and gave a sloppy bow. Theresa glanced to Crestyss, worried it would offset his temper. He scowled at the young servant of his, and waved his hand to dismiss the bow.

"What of the reports? Is father not going to announce it to the world himself as he always does?" Crestyss turned away, disgusted. He picked at his nails absentmindedly, but Theresa could tell he was on edge by the way he tensed and relaxed his jaw repeatedly.

"My condolences, sir. I hate to bring news such as this, but I'm afraid your father is no longer alive in order to pass the news along. The humans assassinated him, but left his subordinate alive to convey their demands to us."

Crestyss froze at the words, but his emerald eyes flashed. Theresa looked away anxiously, awaiting his response. "And what might their demands be?" he asked slowly. It was obvious that he was guarding his thoughts, picking his words and reactions very carefully. There was nothing more terrifying than when Crestyss was cautious, not even when his anger flared.

"They wish to be left alone, completely. They will allow us to survive within the confines of Centric, but should we try to interfere with 'their world' any further, they claim that they will exterminate us all." Jenta sounded worried, and Theresa eyed him carefully. He was a scrawny young man who had yet to fully control his magic. His spellbook often hid from him, and he lacked the drive to search for it, and it gave him very few opportunities to practice with his magic.

Though Jenta idolized Crestyss, he could not read him like Theresa had grown to. After years of being by his side, she thought she knew him better than he knew himself, but he always found new ways to scare her. It was this uncertainty that kept her quiet, along with the fear of retaliation should she speak out of place.

"So father's dead, then. I assume I'll be forced to take his place," Crestyss mused aloud, his joy leaking into his tone.

"The Magicern has yet to convene on the subject, but I have no doubts that they will come to that conclusion," Jenta replied, looking slightly uneasy. He shifted his weight until he caught Crestyss' attention, and froze. "There was one other thing, sir."

"Well, out with it then," Crestyss snapped, glaring at Jenta.

"The humans have sent a sort of present for you. The weapon that was your father's undoing, they requested that it be brought to you." Jenta pulled his satchel into view, and took a lump of cloth from it. He handed it to Crestyss swiftly, clearly uncomfortable with it in his possession.

Crestyss snatched the object from his hands, and unwrapped it with sharp movements. Kept within it was a thick, bent hunk of metal slightly bigger than his hand. It had no blades or prongs, no clear indication that it was a weapon, but it gave Theresa a sense of malice to look at it.

Crestyss gripped the object as easily as he did anything else, he fingers curling around the leather handle without hesitation. He smiled wickedly as he stared into the muzzle of the thing.

"They called it a gun, sir. The humans claimed to have

made it themselves, but that can't be possible, can it? 'A weapon of mass murder,' they called it," Jenta said, eyeing the gun with caution.

Crestyss flipped a lever, and the body of the gun fell to the side, revealing six holes in a circle. "It's missing a few pieces. What a shame. Seems the humans aren't as stupid as we thought. Especially if they were able to create something out of Mage technology."

"Mage technology?" Theresa asked, finally provoked to speak.

Crestyss glanced at her and flashed another triumphant smile. He had finally incited a reaction from her. "Yes. This is clearly our work, but the humans somehow managed to get a hold of it. I wonder how that could have happened." Crestyss ran his fingers along the length of the gun, studying every inch of it.

Theresa looked away from him, terrified at the undertone of a secret in his voice. *What is he up to now? He couldn't possibly be-*

"What are you planning for your first action as head of the Magicern, sir?" Jenta asked, breaking Theresa from her thoughts.

"Hmm. I honestly haven't given it much thought. A lot has happened in such short a time, I'm not sure how to process it all right now. I suppose some sort of retaliation is in need for the humans. They are not the top of the food chain in this world, not by a long shot. But we haven't the forces for an outright attack. We must use cunning, strategy, and I fear a great deal of patience. We'll leave them be for now, allow them their false sense of security, but from here on out, we shall plan their destruction. Have you any suggestions, Theresa?"

Theresa gasped as he addressed her. He stared at her with a fierce and threatening look. She turned away from him, her face growing hot from the anxiety his stare brought upon. Her gut twisted and her heart nearly pounded out of her chest, his gaze boring holes into her. *Why must he bring about such strong reactions in me?* she thought furiously as she struggled to regain her mentality.

With his intense stare urging her on, she scanned her mind quickly. She thought first of the stories of the ancients, when war was more common than peace. One such story stuck in her mind, a legend of the greatest warriors that had been laid to rest in abandoned coves beneath the whole of Lontorra. The story, as incredible as it was, suggested that they had been preserved, stored in all their glory until they were again needed. The most likely truth to the tale was that the coves were their tombs, but it still implies that they are down there. And if the story was to be believed to any degree, they could be resurrected.

Theresa glanced up at Crestyss, and fear filled her again. His light green eyes shown so brightly, so maliciously, that there was no way he didn't want to bring about a war. She was certain that it had all been his doing, the creation of the weapon and the execution of his own father, had all been for his own gain.

She swallowed a lump in her throat, warring with herself. She thought back to her parents, murdered before her eyes ten years ago. They had been skilled healers that traveled all throughout Lontorra, even to the humans. She herself had developed an impressive amount of skill at her young age of eight.

They had been welcomed by all, rejoiced as saviors even. But the humans had attacked without warning, killing them both in cold blood. She was alive only thanks to Crestyss and his father, arriving just in time to frighten the humans away.

They had taken her in, and she couldn't remember a single day without Crestyss since.

How did they know to come for help? They barely travel outside of Centric, could it really be coincidence that they found me, helpless and staring down my own death? Could Crestyss- Could he have been this conniving at so young?

She shook the doubts from her head. They were her heroes, she owed everything to them. Crestyss especially had helped her through her sorrow and depression that followed her loss. He had saved her life more times than she could count, mostly from herself. The humans had caused all of the ruin in her life, had twisted and bruised her. She owed them nothing.

"There is a legend of the greatest warriors the world has ever seen, kept dormant just beneath our feet. They could be dead, but the story could be true. If we could harness enough power, enough magic, we could bring them to our aid. We could raise up an unstoppable army, and take back Lontorra for ourselves, and for our ancestors. We could rid this world of humans, forever," she said finally, emotionless.

Crestyss leaned back and clapped his hands together. "I can't tell you how happy I am to hear you say that, Theresa! What joy that we would have exactly the same plan, down to the wire. And together, it can become reality. I'm so over-whelmed, I'm nearly compelled to say that I love you! How ridiculous, that such a thing as impending doom of an entire species can bring two souls together like this."

Theresa turned to him in shock. The gleam in his eyes was that of a hunter staring down his prey. No, it was that of a boy, torturing a small animal he had trapped. Theresa had seen that from him far too much, the joy he had when he had brought her a small creature who's legs he had broken. It was then that she realized the story she had recalled had been the same one he had read to her every night for the first few years she had been with him. It was the same that they had played as children, pretending they were the world's best soldiers.

It was then that she realized he had broken her legs, her will to escape. She was trapped by him, as she had been from the very beginning. She was his slave, and she was performing exactly as he had planned.

CHAPTER 1

Kaitlyn

Kaitlyn sat against the wall of the dungeon. The woman had healed the wounds on her back easily, but her muscles ached with every movement. The pressure of leaning against the wall threatened to split her skin back open, and she sat forward slowly. A knotted, bloody braid was caught in her hands, and she tugged at it nervously. She watched the woman and the *thing* in the room as they argued, knowing that if she looked away from them, her eyes would be drawn to the last thing she wanted to see.

Arion's dead body.

The woman, Theresa, had replaced his heart, but the image of it was ingrained in her mind. She shook her head violently to rid herself of the thought. Ignoring the sound of the blood that splattered from her hair, she forced herself to focus on the conversation before her. It wasn't much better, but it was a distraction, at least.

"Why aren't you worried about this? The kid is dead, Theresa,

and all you care about are a group of stupid humans! They aren't moronic enough to come back here again, not when their ring leader was taken out. They already retrieved Kraven's body, and they'll have a white flag in the air by morning. Can you just worry about your son for once?"

The creature encased in metal had been shrieking at her for almost an hour now, but Theresa didn't seem phased. She had cast a preservation spell over Arion's body, and the thick magic was difficult to see through. Other than that, she'd barely batted an eye at the situation.

Kaitlyn felt the complete opposite. She wanted to scream, to bawl, anything that would take her mind away from the pain. Anytime she glanced in the direction of her friend's body, she felt like she was going to be sick. No matter how much magic covered him, she could still see the blood smeared across Arion's face, the ragged hole in his chest.

She pressed her hand to her mouth, forcing herself not to gag. She looked to Theresa, who was pacing in front of the fuming creature. It watched her pointedly, its patience obviously wearing thin.

It was an odd creation, unlike like anything she could even imagine. Still, she could recognize Arion's work from the phoenix that they had used to exchange letters. Most of the creature was made of thin, smooth plates of metal, but Arion had given it more of a flourish than the bird. The shoulders flared out at the sides, and large plates covered the chest, back, and legs like armor covering the body. Most of the metal had grown dull, save for the fresh spot in its chest where Kaitlyn had stabbed it with the spear. Its spine was made of small, thick gears that interlocked in a way that still allowed a wide range of movement.

Chains were welded into the metal to give definition where muscles would be, and Kaitlyn could recognize silver clock hands wrapping around the creature's neck. Large thin scales covered the shoulders, sides, and hips of the creature, as well as the arms. Slick, black glass tipped the beast's fingers and ears, coming to sharp points. Along the length of its back laid a detailed etching of bat wings, folded neatly within the curving metal.

As Kaitlyn studied the creature, she found more designs covering nearly every inch of its body. A shallow etching of fire furled from the creature's nostrils, and smoke billowed to mask the eyes. The stomach had a design of smooth waves that hinted at a storm brewing within. Above the engraved sea rested a distant mountain range she had long gazed at through her window, imagining the grand adventures that took place there. The legs of the creature were the simplest, holding only patterns of spots and swirls. Though there seemed to be no rhyme or reason to the etchings, Kaitlyn found herself getting lost in the mindless drawings.

Gears spun at its temples as it ground its jaws together. It was muttering something, the small pieces of metal of its mouth gliding and lapping over each other like lips. Its purple eyes shined from the dark depths of its face, lighting some of the intricacy within its head. Two beams intersected each other just behind the eyes, and thick wires spiraled out from them to hold each inch of the head in place.

The creature threw its hands up in exasperation and flailed them around. Kaitlyn caught a glimpse of its left hand, a faint lightning bolt carved into the metal on the palm. Kaitlyn gasped. Why would it would have Arion's mark? Arion had told her once that Mage markings were unique and specific to each Mage, passed down only through blood. This was clear in his mother, a faded lightning bolt within her pale white hand. But this was nothing more than a creation. Would Arion have given it his own mark?

But why? she asked herself. She examined the creature, looking past the varying designs. She didn't expect an answer to be found so easily, and she gasped when one came to her.

Just under the cracks in the metal, she could see a faint green glow that pulsed in the emptiness, racing like lightning. Kaitlyn leaned to the side to get another angle at the creature, and she saw more of the same glow at its sides. It looked as though it was rushing through the body, like blood.

Kaitlyn looked down with the realization, her eyes filling with tears. *Whatever this is, Arion gave it his magic for it to live.*

A tear trickled down her cheek, and she sniffed. *If Arion wanted it to live, I can at least call it by its name.*

"Cyllorian," she whispered. She had heard Theresa call it that, though it didn't respond well. She wondered if it disliked its name, or perhaps just the one speaking it. They certainly didn't seem to be getting along very well.

"What was that?" Its voice sounded not far from her, and her head shot up with a start. She held her breath, but not before a startled squeak escaped her lips. She stared into its dark purple eyes, knowing the fear in her own that betrayed her.

"You said my name, didn't you?" It tried again. Its features looked softer than they had a moment ago when addressing Theresa, somehow able to express emotion. The glow from its eyes dimmed. She almost thought that it was sad.

Kaitlyn held her breath and froze under its gaze. She spread her hands out beside her, and tried to scoot away. The creature was more than a foot away from her, but its presence unnerved her. She wanted nothing more than to get away.

To her surprise, the creature's face softened more. It sighed, then held its hand out to her. She stared at it, fear holding her in place. It dropped its hand after a long moment, and squatted down to her eye level.

"You don't trust me. Not that I blame you, we were never properly introduced before. We don't have all the time in the world, so there's not many options for you. You're going to have to trust me, eventually. But if you want to just go home and get away from me, say it now."

She shook her head slowly, her gaze glued to the mechanics of its face as it talked. It was all so intricate. It made her wonder what her muscles would look like moving under her skin.

The creature gave her a small smile, and her breath caught in her throat. *"How about I just tell you what I know, then you can decide if I'm worth trusting. Does that sound good?"*

Its voice was so hopeful, as though her opinion truly did make a difference. When she didn't know what to say, it took it as a sign to continue.

"My name is Cyllorian, but the kid over there always called me Cy. He thought my name was too much of a mouthful." It chuckled at itself, and Kaitlyn could easily hear the sorrow in it. *"I may not look like much, but I'm a demon. Long story short, I've gone through a lot of, let's say 'vessels.' I wound up inside Arion's head, and I was there for quite a few years. I got to know him, and I got to know you.*

"I know that you could take Kraven down if he picked on other kids, but you never cared if he came after you. Unless he gets your books dirty, then he really had it coming. You always have a book with you, but it's usually the same one over and over. The one about the princess in the desert.

"You always wanted to be a heroine, like her. You wanted to be strong, and selfless. This is your chance to save someone's life. More than just one life. You could save a lot of people. The kid may not be 'here,' but he ain't gone for good, I know that. I need to get him back, so I can kick his ass for being so reckless. I may be good, but I'm not good enough to do it alone, and I'm honestly not

sure how much help the old woman is going to be. Will you help me?"

The creature held its hand out to her, and she glanced at it. The bolt etched into the metal was so familiar, so comforting. She looked back at the creature's eyes, full of desperation. Through all the anger, she could tell it was just as lost in this as she was.

She raised her hand, hating how it shook. Carefully, she traced the lightning bolt in the metal, and green sparks flew out from under her fingers. The metal was cool, but it felt good on her skin.

She pressed her palm to its hand. *His,* she corrected herself finally. *He isn't an it.*

He gripped her hand and smiled at her. She looked away from him, her stomach twisting. He pulled her to her feet, legs wobbling beneath her. Cyllorian caught her, and she pressed one hand to the wall to steady herself. She swallowed the lump at her throat, fighting the urge to push him away from her.

"Thank you. Cy," she said through the haze that had settled over her mind.

Too much has happened. Way too much. I need to sleep.

Cy's hands tightened on her arms for a second, but she ignored it. Any minute now, she was sure she'd lose her calm. It was everything she could do just to keep herself sane.

"Who were you calling old?" Theresa asked, coming up behind Cy. He rolled her eyes at her and clenched his jaw, but said nothing. He released one of Kaitlyn's arms, but kept a light grip on the other to keep her upright. Though his touch was awkward and unwanted, she was glad that he didn't let go. She admitted to needing the help right now, even if it was from an odd metal creature.

Cy stepped aside to face Theresa. *"I think it would be best if you showed her to a room. I'll take care of the kid."*

Theresa nodded, and took Kaitlyn's arm from him. Theresa's hand was hot on the cooled spot on her arm, and she jerked under the drastic change. Her eyes flickered sheepishly between the two.

Theresa put her arm around her in a loving motion, but the action seemed alien to her. The woman alternated between rubbing and patting Kaitlyn's back as she led her to the stairs. Theresa settled for simply lying her hand between her shoulder blades, much like she had when she had healed Kaitlyn.

As they ascended the stairs, Kaitlyn glanced over her shoulder at Cyllorian. He was staring at Arion's body, and the look on his face nearly broke her heart.

* * *

Cyllorian

THERESA LED Kaitlyn up the stairs from the dungeon. Cyllorian slumped where he stood, exhausted. He let out a great sigh, though he'd quickly found that he didn't need to breathe in this new body of his. He had a heart, and veins of magic, but that was all. The rest of him was hollow, filled with parts to help him move. He felt empty, emotionless and lost. He barked a bitter laugh at the irony that he had gotten a body that mirrored exactly how he felt.

After a long moment alone, he was sure that Theresa and Kaitlyn had gone far enough into the castle that they wouldn't hear him speak. He walked over to Arion's body and stared at the peaceful expression on his face. It was one he had seen often while the boy slept, but this was clearly different. All the color had gone from his skin. There was no pulse to be seen on the boy's neck, no rising and falling of his chest as he breathed.

There was nothing left of the boy, either. They had both been stripped of everything, and Cy had never felt closer to the boy.

"What happened to us, kid? Things were goin' so well. What did we do wrong?" Cy asked aloud, his strange voice reverberating around the room. He cringed at the sound of, at how different it was. He stared down at the etching in his left hand, where Kaitlyn had traced it. Though it was glowing, he didn't see the magic there. He didn't see the wonder of this body, only the cold metal that reflected back his own grotesque face made of twisted metal.

He forced himself to focus. Cy bent down and scooped Arion into his arms. It sagged in his grip, and he hefted it up higher. Arion's limbs dangled to the side, swinging side to side as Cy walked.

Cy had never realized just how much Arion had meant to him in the end, how much a demon could care for another. He and Arion had been the same, abandoned by their mother. They were bound to each other by magic and fate. They were brothers, regardless of how long it took Cyllorian to accept it.

He trudged up the stairs carefully, as if the boy was sleeping. There was no strain on Cy from the weight of the body, and he carried it easily. But the truth that the corpse carried drug on him, and his feet were heavy as he marched through the castle.

It was a truth that Cy had yet to admit to himself, was too afraid to face. But with the boy's body so lifeless in his arms, with Arion's magic flowing freely throughout his own body, he couldn't hold it back anymore.

Arion's dead, he finally thought to himself. He stopped in his tracks as the words rushed through his mind, over and over. He stood frozen in the middle of the hallway, clutching the body to his chest. He tightened his grip on the boy as guilt flooded him. What could he have done differently? Could he have saved Arion if he had changed one thing? Had he been too selfish, too distant?

Was Arion dead because of him?

Cy dropped his head, his body rattling. He gulped down large bouts of air, but it did nothing to help him. It merely whirled around in his empty chest, whistling as it raced around the steel skeleton. Small sparks of magic shot off of him from gaps in his body, and glided along him until it dripped off of him like sweat. The drops sizzled on the floor, singing the stone.

He held the boy tighter, sure that his grip would have bruised the fragile body if it didn't have the preservation spell over it. He knew this body wouldn't let him cry. That alone made it worse. He couldn't even properly grieve the loss.

Cy stumbled to the side, falling against the wall. He turned so his back hit the wall rather than Arion. He grunted in the discomfort and slid down the wall to the floor. Resting the boy in his lap, Cyllorian stared at the ceiling.

Everything looked different through his own eyes. The cracks in the walls were clearer, the paintings more vibrant. It was as though he was seeing everything for the first time. But at the same time, everything lost its extravagance when he didn't have the amusement of Arion's endless wonder. He stared at everything like it was the most amazing thing in the world, his magic especially.

At least he had, until Cy had tainted him. He knew he was to blame for Arion's change, filling the kid's head with his own anger and hatred until it was too much for either of them. Cy could never find it in himself to look at anything like Arion had. It was all tarnished by anger and pain.

"I'll get you back, kid. Theresa's got a plan. I'd be lying if I said I completely trust her, though. But don't worry, we'll be fighting in no time, you'll see. And if you thought you were going to get rid of me

that easy, then I'm just gonna have to knock some sense into you when you get back." Cy rubbed one hand over his face and sighed.

"I'll get my brother back." With his resolution spoken aloud as a reminder, Cyllorian gathered the body in his arms again. He marched through the castle with his shoulders squared. He fought against the weight that threatened to bury him, determined to rise up despite it.

CHAPTER 2

Kaitlyn

"Why did Arion have to get rid of that candle from before? Now I'm lost," Kaitlyn muttered as she wandered through the dark halls of the castle. She wrapped her arms around her form, uncomfortable in the thin nightgown that Theresa had lent her. She squinted at the paintings she passed in the dark and groaned.

"I swear I've gone through this hallway a dozen times! Where am I? I just wanted to get a drink!" She spun around and looked behind her, but there was nothing familiar to be found. There were a few windows set in the walls, too high to see out of. The moon shone in to show a hallway that looked just like all the others.

"I guess I'll just turn around and try to back track. This place is too big to try to navigate at night." She trudged back the way she came, but the hallways never looked any different. Her head drooped and she drug her feet on the ground. She leaned against the wall sleepily as she walked, closing her eyes in frustration.

"Stupid magic castle," she said, her voice muddled by sleep. "Why can't there be a map? Or a guide?"

The wall fell away underneath her, and she tripped onto the ground. She sprawled out into an intersection, a faint light visible at the end of the adjoining hall. Curiosity taking over her, she got to her feet mindlessly and followed the light.

She ran her hand along the stones as she stalked the illumination. A door was cracked and the light spilled out from it. It was a deep purple, and flickered from inside the room. Kaitlyn poked her head into the small space the door had opened and stared in shock.

Cyllorian stood at the far end of a small room, bare of any decoration. It held a bed that looked unused, and a desk with a candle. A large, purple flame nestled atop the candle, and Cyllorian stood in its glow. He was turned away from her, but she could see the side of his face. He looked sullen and exhausted, his head hanging.

Her curiosity overtook her, leaving her woes far behind. She crept closer, her hand resting upon the door to push it open. Her lips parted to announce herself, but he moved and startled her into silence. With a moment to think, her mind won over her morals. *What if he was lying before? I should see what he does when he's alone, to know if I can actually trust him.*

She shrunk against the door frame, watching the metal demon anxiously.

Cyllorian put his hand into the flame, and the fire lapped at the metal until it turned red from the heat. He removed his hand, and stroked his other arm with his fingers. They left welts in the plating where he touched. His face contorted with the pain, but the hand was steady on his arm.

He dropped his heated hand to his side, staring at his arm.

The metal twisted on itself a moment longer. A wave of green lightning raced over the metal, restoring his arm to its original state on contact. Cyllorian let out a sigh, and dropped his arm. With his left hand, he rubbed his right shoulder.

He doesn't have muscles to ache, so what is he doing? Kaitlyn thought. Kaitlyn stretched herself to get a better view, careful to stay silent and out of sight.

Cy's fingers found a clasp high on his shoulder, then another low one on his side, both hidden under the top layer of metal sheets. Leather straps released, and he swung his chest plate open. He turned to lean one hand on the desk, the other buried in his chest. He gave a small smile at the green light that emanated from within himself, chuckling bitterly.

"You really went all out, didn't you, kid? You probably thought I wouldn't notice it, but I knew you better than you knew yourself. For a while I did, at least. But why give it to me? Did you really give up, after all that fighting you did?"

Cyllorian spoke softly, but Kaitlyn was sure of the sadness she heard in his voice. She lowered her head and began to back away. The guilt of spying was eating away at her, despite the mistrust she felt a few moments before. Just as she turned away, Cyllorian spoke again, and his words stunned her in place.

"I know you didn't want her to get into this, but it's a bit late now. I don't think she'd let us take her home, even if she could go back. I don't know what they'd do with her after she killed their prized pet. They might even have a price on her head now. But I won't let anything happen to her, just like I know you'd want. I'm going to fix everything, Arion. Theresa said your body's dead, but you're not lost. Wherever you are, don't get too comfortable. This is just a break for you, not retirement. Before you know it, everything's gonna be right back to normal. I promise. Normal."

Cyllorian ended his monologue in another sigh. Kaitlyn

watched him close his chest and turn back to the desk. He leaned against it, all the weight of the world seeming to crash down on his shoulders.

Kaitlyn snuck away from his room as quietly as she could, tears stinging her eyes. She swallowed them down and glanced back into the room. Cyllorian was still bent over the desk, running his hand over his head nervously.

Biting her lip, Kaitlyn made her choice. She straightened herself and scrubbed the tears from her eyes, then held her breath to face her fear. Making her steps obviously loud, she walked back to the room. She opened the door with a creak and knocked lightly. "Cyllorian?" she said, faking her surprise at finding him.

He whirled around on the spot, his left hand flying to his chest. She saw his fingers twitch towards the clasps hidden away, and she avoided looking at them. *"Kaitlyn? What are you doing? Why are you wandering around?"* Cy's questions came out in a rush. His eyes darted all around, seemingly afraid to land on hers. Now that she had caught the demon off guard, he was far less intimidating.

She stepped into the room, leaving only a short distance between them. "I woke up, and wanted a drink. I thought I could find the kitchen on my own, but I got lost. I saw your light, and thought it might be a way back." Kaitlyn played with her hands behind her back, pushing her toe against a raised stone in the floor. They spent a few moments staring off in each other's general direction.

"Oh. . ."

"What about you? Shouldn't you be sleeping? Or resting?"

"I don't really sleep in this body. At least, it doesn't feel like it needs it. My magic is my energy, so I'm not sure how limited my supply is. I haven't used much of my magic, and it feels like it recharges slowly while I'm conscious. If I'm careful with how much

energy I spend, I won't have to rest ever again, but I doubt it'll be that easy."

"Oh. . . I'm sorry. I didn't realize," Kaitlyn whispered, embarrassed.

Cyllorian's hands flew up in front of him and he waved them awkwardly. *"No, no it's okay. You didn't know. I don't know the specifics. Arion knew, but he didn't get the chance to tell me. And Tome won't open up to me. It went dormant as soon as. . . Anyway, it won't open, or do anything at all. I'm not sure even Theresa knows anything about this body."* Cy waved his hands out to gesture at himself as a whole.

"This body?" Kaitlyn asked reflexively. She immediately regretted the question, and looked away with guilt. "Sorry. It's not my business, I shouldn't have asked."

"It's fine. You deserve to know, after all. You know I was in Arion's head for a while, but when we got to the castle, we figured out how to get me out. Mostly. I still had to go back to Arion, but I could hop between the statues and sets of armor in the castle. They weren't hard to understand, because nothing really changed between Arion and them. Just that I had to move myself if I wanted something done." Cyllorian laughed at himself, putting one hand behind his head. Kaitlyn couldn't help but laugh a little with him, and this made his small smile grow.

"This body is completely different. I have more energy, and full control. I don't have to share with anyone, and it can do more. The others were just puppets, but this is the real thing. Arion really knew what he was doing. Makes me glad, for once, that he spent so much time making all those birds."

"Birds?" Kaitlyn asked again. She had so many questions with each word that Cyllorian said. There was so much that Arion had never told her. She hadn't realized how much of his world she was missing out on. And now she had the chance to learn it all.

"The phoenix he made to give you letters was the last one he made. He had four others, owls that he had created to look for Theresa. They worked. We found out later, but Theresa had messed with them so we didn't know at the time. But they drew us a map, showing everything in Lontorra. Did you know that there's a giant hole in the middle of the mountains to the north? It goes straight down, and looks endless. Arion called it Plummet Summit, but it never stuck with me."

Kaitlyn laughed at that, and Cyllorian rolled his eyes. Once again, she found her curiosity taking complete control over her. Her weariness had been chased away by her questions, and she wanted nothing more than to listen to Cyllorian's stories. She walked past Cyllorian, and sat on the bed. Looking at him with wide eyes, she asked, "What else did you and Arion do, Cy?"

A wide smile spread on Cyllorian's face. He sat down beside her, putting as much space between them as possible. He turned to her and all of the stories, the missing pieces, spilled out of him. He talked with so much enthusiasm, yet there was an unmistakable undertone of sorrow to his voice. He paused at seemingly random intervals, then would continue with broken pieces of his story.

Kaitlyn listened intently to every word. She was getting more time with Arion through Cy's retellings, and she could tell how grateful he was to talk about him. Even though she'd been selfish in asking, she was glad that it helped the demon. The weight was lifting from his shoulders with each passing minute.

Kaitlyn laid back as Cy began speaking of Centric. He had been there a few times with Theresa, and once with Arion. He described the various creatures he had seen wandering the street, and the displays of magic that were common in the market sectors. He passed along wondrous stories he had heard from others passing through. Many were impossible stories from those that claimed to come from across the sea, but the most incredible were those of Lontorra. A war of great magnitude fought long, long ago; legend of gods and prophets that kept the world in balance; a Mage that swore she was engaged to a dragon. All were stories too complex to be found even within her books.

She closed her eyes, and smiled. His voice was high pitched, but not feminine. It held a certain excitement, rising and lowering with each word. She could hear the mechanisms of his body whirring as though he was breathing, and the magic echoed from his chest like a heartbeat. He sounded human and musical, and it soothed her. The moon shone on her face, and she crossed one arm over her eyes to shield them from the light.

Cy's words became less discernible as Kaitlyn began to slip away, his voice turning into a calming drone. It lulled her to sleep within minutes, feeling as close to peace as she had been in months.

* * *

Cyllorian

CYLLORIAN CLOSED the door slowly as he crept from the room. Kaitlyn laid on her side on his bed, her hands tucked under her head. He had been talking for so long, he had no idea when she had fallen asleep.

He turned away from the room, and jumped at the owl flying silently in his face. Snow hovered in the air easily, though one wing was beating furiously to keep him aloft. Though Arion had permanently damaged the owl, it wasn't impairing his life.

The owl lunged forward suddenly, and Cy ducked. Snow made a large loop in the air and soared down the hall. Remembering Snow's distinct method of communicating from his earliest years with Theresa, he followed the owl obediently.

Snow led Cy to a set of large double doors, pacing in a circle around them as he waited. One door was propped open, and Snow perched atop it when Cy approached. His deed completed, the owl ignored Cy to preen his feathers.

Theresa could be seen inside, holding her arm up. A large silver mass sat on it easily, pecking at her fingers as she reached for it gently. Cy glanced up at Snow, wondering if the real, living owl felt any sort of jealousy towards Arion's creation, but he gave no sign whether he cared or not. Shrugging, Cy proceeded into the room.

"What are you doing with Fletcher?" Cyllorian asked as he entered the grand study in the center of the castle.

Fletcher turned his head toward Cyllorian at his words, the bright eyes of the owl watching him closely. Cy crossed the room to stand a foot away from Theresa, staring the mechanical owl down.

Holding a finger out to it cautiously, he asked, *"You're not gonna freak out and attack me like the damn phoenix, are you?"* He narrowed his eyes in anticipation.

With a surprised hoot, Fletcher took to the air. He circled twice around Cy, the demon flailing below. The owl swooped at him, and Cy dove out of the way. Fletcher lunged for him again, and again, but Cy managed to dodge each attack.

He hadn't been paying attention to his movements, and the owl now had him backed against a wall. With nowhere for Cy to run, the owl dove again. Cy raised his arms to shield himself, bracing himself for the screeching sound of metal talons scratching at his own metal arm.

A soft coo broke through Cy's fear, and he opened one eye

slowly. Fletcher was perched obediently on his arm. Cy lifted his other hand to the bird's head, resting it on the metal. The bird's eyes closed, and it rubbed against Cy's hand.

"It seems that it recognizes Arion's magic within you," Theresa said, watching from afar with little emotion. Cy turned to her, smiling lightly, but her blank expression rose up a bout of irritation within him. He dropped his hand from the bird, who hooted in dissatisfaction. Cy stood in an awkward mix of fear and adoration of the bird, moving cautiously so as to not disturb Fletcher. He closed the space between him and Theresa, the bird hopping on his arm nervously.

"*What were you doing with him?*" Cy asked again. The bird looked from him to Theresa, awaiting the answer along with the demon.

Theresa cocked her head to the side and looked around the room absently. "Where's the girl?" she asked, staring pointedly at Cyllorian.

"Kaitlyn *is still asleep. I thought it best to let her rest, so I left her in my room.*"

Theresa's eyes narrowed at him, and she opened her mouth. She looked as though she would scold him, but he cut her off.

"*She woke up in the middle of the night and found me. She fell asleep, and I didn't want to wake her. Do you have a problem?*" Cy stared Theresa down, challenging her.

Anger swirled in her eyes, but she blinked it away. Her expression blank again, she said, "I simply don't agree with her being here. It's not safe for any of us to have a *human* among us. She needs to go back to where she came from."

"*She's Arion's friend. She doesn't have to go anywhere if she doesn't want to. And since when did you distrust humans so much? I thought you always advocated for things to return to the way they were before the riots?*"

"I was, but I quickly found that humans cannot be trusted, no matter what. Have you forgotten that regardless of her intentions, she's the one that led the murderous group that killed Arion?"

Cy fumed at her words, but could not argue with them. He turned away, fighting the urge to yell at her again. Kaitlyn had been the reason that Kraven had found them, but Cy didn't blame her.

None of the fault could be put on the girl when she hadn't been the one to formulate the plan.

Cy shook his head and turned back to Theresa. Forcing himself to remain calm, he asked again, *"What were you doing with Fletcher?"*

"I was sending a message, if you really must know. We've got a lot to prepare, and it would help to have the owls give us a head start."

"A head start on what?" Cy asked tentatively. He laid a hand on Fletcher's head protectively.

"I've already sent the others to a few colonies and clans I've passed through these last few years, telling them of our plan."

"We have a plan?" Cy cut in, gaining him a glare. *"What's the plan?"*

"I have been studying the cultures of the other races that inhabit Lontorra, and few of them have either myths, legends, or rituals that involve bringing the dead back to life in some way. Though most are farfetched at best, there is some truth to every story. I've contacted the races afore mentioned, and some have accepted my call for help. Unfortunately, only locals of each colony have the true details to each method, so we must have them here for further research and to make any progress. To show our dedication to the cause, they have requested we go to them for the final judgement.

"You will traverse around to these places, to those that

have agreed to help, and gather one representative from each. After you've gathered them all, you'll return here for further instruction."

"So, I'm just picking up a few friends for a play date. Sounds wonderful." Cy rolled his eyes and turned away from Theresa. She didn't say anything, but Cy could feel the disapproving glare he was getting. *"Where is Fletcher going, then?"*

"This one is scheduled to stop at the Pools of Lorile, though I doubt they'll be of much help. Then to the summit of Mount Draken."

"How are Drakens going to help us bring Arion back? They're not healers." Cy turned to address Theresa. She was facing away from him, writing at a nearby desk. She raised her arm and made a clicking sound. Fletcher jumped from Cy's arm and landed on Theresa's.

Attaching a piece of parchment to its leg, she crossed the room. She said something to the bird quietly, and it flew out of the window. It disappeared into the sky within moments, Theresa watching until it was long gone from sight.

She paced to the middle of the room. With a wave of her hand, she was surrounded in smoke that looked like the night sky. It faded quickly, leaving behind a leather bag in its wake, strung over her shoulder.

"Where are you going?" Cy asked, surprised. He watched as Theresa marched through the room, gathering random supplies into her bag.

"There are some colonies that you will be unable to persuade into helping us, but others have demanded my own presence, or they shall not offer any assistance. I'm sure I should return before you do, don't worry, and I will make the necessary accommodations for our guests. You worry about your small list, and I will handle the rest." She paused for a moment. Her outstretched hand shook noticeably, and a shadow had come over her eyes.

"I needn't burden you with this more than absolutely necessary," she said quietly.

Before Cy could ask her what she meant, she was buzzing around the room again. He lifted his hand, wanting to stop her and demand the answers to all of his questions. The frazzled expression she had and the desperation in her eyes stopped him, and he stood frozen in his helplessness.

With her bag full, she made for the door, walking past Cy as though he wasn't there at all. *"Theresa!"* he called after her.

She whirled around, staring at him with wide, confused eyes. It looked as though she had just remembered he was there. *"You're leaving now? You haven't explained anything, what exactly are we doing?"*

"We're gathering allies. I thought I made that clear? Without their physical presence here, we cannot advance our plans."

"And what exactly is our *plan?"*

"Must I really spell it out to you? They will bring their knowledge of unique magics to us, and we will put it to use for our purposes. Are you going to argue with me, Cyllorian, or would you like to do something useful?" she snapped finally, losing her patience. Her gaze on him was steely and cold, and he cringed at her tone.

Cautiously, he pressed further, *"I need to know where I'm going before I can do much of anything."*

"Ah, yes. I nearly forgot. I'm not used to having help, you know." She chuckled lightly, though it didn't seem to help her mood.

"I figured," Cy said bitterly, controlling his reaction.

She marched over to him, digging around in her bag. She pulled a small crystal ball from it, and Cy immediately jumped back. *"Whoa, whoa, whoa! The hell do you think you're doing with that?"*

"Oh, calm down. It's not for you...not in that way, at least. Here."

She dropped it into his hand, and he scrunched his eyes. When it seemed to be safe, he opened his eyes and stared at it as though it would bite him any minute.

"I told you, it doesn't have that purpose. Shake it, and you'll see."

Cy glanced at her for a second, then shook the ball. A white smoke formed in the center, filling the glass. When it cleared, it showed the base of Mount Draken within.

"A map?" Cy asked. He watched the image ripple and fade away, a little disappointed. *"A bit anticlimactic, don't you think?"*

"It will help you reach your destination. That's what's important, not how grandiose it is. Be thankful."

Cy tossed it into the air and caught it. The smoke reformed and showed the mountains again. *"If I have to."*

Theresa turned away from him again, stepping toward the door. "Take the girl back to the village on your way," she said shortly.

Cy nearly dropped the ball, barely catching it before it shattered on the floor. He stared incredulously at Theresa's back, soon replaced with defiance.

"No."

"No?"

"No. She was just as much a part of Arion's life as I was. More than you were, that's for sure. She deserves to be a part of this just as much as us."

Theresa looked at him over her shoulder, sorrow clear in her eyes. He stood his ground, staring her down until she sighed.

"You don't know what you're doing, Cyllorian. Please, just listen to me. Just this once, you have to trust me."

"Trust you? Know what, nevermind, I'm not touching that subject." Cy raised his eyes defensively at Theresa's glare, and continued before she could scold him. *"But I won't force her to leave her friend if she doesn't want to."*

"I just have to hope that she's not as stubborn as you."

Theresa turned and marched out of the room. Cy stood there until she left the grounds, the slamming of the grand doors resonating throughout the entire castle.

CHAPTER 3

Cyllorian

"Where's Theresa?" Kaitlyn asked as she walked into the room. Cy whirled around, the crystal ball still in hand. He looked away, embarrassed when he found her buttoning her shirt, though she had a white blouse beneath it.

Cy glanced at her out of the corner of his eye, stunned at her clothing. He had rarely ever seen her in anything but her favorite blue dress. Now she was dressed in a Mage's attire. It was both shocking and appealing.

She buttoned her navy shirt almost all the way, the lace at the top of her blouse still visible. The sleeves were too long for her, but she remedied that by buttoning the cuffs around her thumb so that they covered most of her hands. Her pants were black, skin tight, and looked to be of a thin material. She wrapped her long hair into a messy bun on top of her head, tying it into place with one of her bright blue ribbons. It fell sloppily to the side, half of it falling out. She tried again, but didn't fare any better. With a groan, she simply tied it all up into a high ponytail, resting on her back in crinkles from their previous braids.

"Well, what do you think?" she asked, spreading her arms wide. She gave a twirl, then stared at Cy expectantly.

"*Uh...I like your shoes,*" he muttered uselessly. He pointed down sheepishly, and she giggled. Her shoes were still the bright blue flats she had always worn, covered in white frills.

"There was a closet full of everything except for shoes, so I'm stuck with mine." She shrugged and shifted her feet. She looked uncomfortable. Cy couldn't tell if it was because of the strange clothes, or simply that she didn't match.

"*I can fix that,*" he said, walking to Theresa's closet. There he found a small pair of black hiking boots. Using his magic, he changed their color to dark blue with white trim. He handed them to Kaitlyn, and she sat on the floor to change.

"So where did Theresa go? You never answered," she said as she struggled with the laces on the boots.

Cy shoved the crystal ball into his pocket. Though he knew he didn't need to cover himself, it felt wrong not to. He had thrown on a simple black long sleeved shirt, and black pants with more pockets than he thought he would ever need.

Cy watched awkwardly as Kaitlyn gave up lacing the tall boots perfectly and simply wrapped the laces around her legs. She tied them into a large knot in the front with a huff. "*She said she had to go gather some comrades, people that can help us get the kid back. She had to meet with some of them, and we get the rest.*"

"We?" Kaitlyn asked. Cy froze as she stared up at him, avoiding her gaze. Unsure of how to answer, Cy held his hand out for her to grab. Kaitlyn hesitated at first, but allowed him to help her up.

After a moment of silence, Cy confessed, "*Theresa said it*

would be best to drop you off back at the village and I go alone. I told her you didn't want to. If I was wrong, I..."

"You weren't wrong," Kaitlyn said abruptly. She squared her shoulders and stared him down in determination. "You didn't think you were going to get all the adventure, did you?"

She smiled at him, but there was something else in her eyes. She looked as though she would cry again, but she blinked and it was gone.

"Not at all. Let's get ready to go. The sooner we leave, the better."

They spent the next few hours gathering their supplies. They stayed together, mostly because Kaitlyn couldn't navigate the castle on her own. After much speculation, they decided to pack enough for a month, agreeing to get more rations when they needed them.

Standing just outside the grand front doors, Kaitlyn asked, "Where to first?"

Cy shifted his pack so that it rested between his shoulder blades. His metal body didn't give under the pressure of the pack, but the bag wasn't giving any either. The weight didn't bother him, but supplies were bulging the material and made the pack uncomfortable to carry.

Cy dug into his pocket and retrieved the crystal ball. He shook it and waited impatiently for the white smoke to settle. He held it up between them, and Kaitlyn stared at it in awe.

"That's where we're going? A mountain?"

"I guess so. And not just any mountain. Mount Draken. That'll be fun."

"Why's that?"

"You don't know what Draken are, do you?"

"Uh, uh," Kaitlyn said, shaking her head.

"Didn't think so. Well, who am I to ruin the surprise?"

Kaitlyn glared at him, but he refused to meet her gaze. "So how do we get there?" she asked irritably.

"*I guess we just start with walking.*" Cy made his way towards the woods, his bag pounding against his back with each step. He paused to adjust it again, and noticed that there were no footsteps behind him. He glanced back at Kaitlyn, who hadn't moved a muscle away from the castle.

"*Are you coming?*" he asked impatiently.

Kaitlyn shook her head slowly, her face twisting up. "Do we really have to go through the woods?"

"*Do you see any other way to leave?*"

"Can't you just use magic to teleport us? Arion could," she grumbled. She walked to Cy's side slowly, dragging her feet.

"*Yeah, well, I'm not Arion. That's the whole point of this, remember?*"

Kaitlyn dropped her head and grabbed onto the back of Cy's sleeve. "Let's just get it over with. You lead, though."

Cy couldn't think of a single thing to say, so he simply nodded. Walking slowly so he wouldn't lose Kaitlyn, they marched into the woods.

* * *

"You got us lost, didn't you, Cy?" Kaitlyn glared at him, but he avoided looking at her.

"*I told you, we're not lost. We're just taking the scenic route.*"

"That means we're lost. Cy!" Kaitlyn whined, falling back against a tree. She slid along it to sit on the ground, groaning. "Can we at least take a rest? We've been walking for hours!"

"*It hasn't been that long. You're exaggerating. You're just not used to this kind of stuff. I'm not tired.*"

"You don't get tired. I'm human, remember? Not a demon in a mechanical body!"

"Oh, yeah. Right. Sorry," he muttered. She closed her eyes and laid her head back against the tree trunk. Her sleeves had been rolled up to her elbows. Her face was beaded with sweat and her cheeks were flushed.

Cy slung the bag from his shoulders and pulled out a canteen of water. He handed it to her and she took it, drinking greedily.

"Calm down there, that's gotta last a while. We've only been at this a couple hours," Cy reminded her. She lowered the canteen and stared at him with sad eyes. She swallowed one last time, closed the canteen, and wiped her mouth. She handed the canteen back to Cy, disappointed, and he returned it to his bag.

He held his hand out to help her up. She grabbed it reluctantly, though she didn't stand. She sat there for a moment just holding his hand, until he gave her a tug. She groaned in protest and pulled away. Cy opened his mouth to urge her on, but a sound from behind made him stop.

He turned around to face the growling, and was met with a pair of bright green eyes in the darkness before him. He heard Kaitlyn scramble to her feet behind him, whimpering. Cy raised his hands as a light gray wolf stalked out from the brush.

Its muzzle was pulled back into a snarl, showing a full row of sharp, stained teeth. The green eyes watched Cy hungrily, and its ears pricked at every sound Cy made. It growled long and low, moving around Cy.

Cy backed away from it slowly, hands still raised. When he got close to Kaitlyn, gripping the tree for her life, he reached out to her. The wolf lunged for his hand, and Cy jumped back. The wolf put itself between Cy and Kaitlyn, glancing back at the girl. Cy watched the wolf carefully, trying to find a way to get around it. Kaitlyn was staring at Cy, desperation clear in her eyes. Cy didn't need any more confirmation of the fear that had been instilled in her by the rogue wolves when she had come looking for Arion.

"Cy," she squeaked. She raised her hand towards him, but jerked it away from the wolf.

Cy stomped towards the wolf. *"You need to back off, mutt!"* he yelled.

The wolf lunged, tackling him to the ground. Cy wrapped his hands in a vice around the wolf's muzzle as it snapped for his throat. He threw the wolf onto its head, stunning it. He climbed on top of the wolf, pinning it down. It squirmed under him and managed to roll on its back. It waved its paws in the air, scratching Cy's arms.

Cy saw a large spot of black fur on the wolf's chest, and his astonishment made his grip loosen. The wolf pushed him off and jumped on top of Cy. The wolf reared back, mouth gaping, and Cy threw his hands up.

"Tuft, wait!" he shrieked, and the wolf halted in mid-attack. He cocked its head, and stared at Cy, his nose twitching madly.

"You smell like Arion. Why do you smell like Arion?" he asked, shoving his nose in the crook of Cy's neck.

"It's a long story. I'm Cyllorian, I was living inside of Arion's head for a while. He made me this body. And this is Kaitlyn. We're friends. I'm not trying to hurt her."

"Friends?" Tuft asked, narrowing his eyes. He looked up at Kaitlyn, who nodded vigorously. He glanced back down at Cy, and climbed off of him. "I've been watching the house for a few days. My pack reported seeing her come into the woods with a group of humans. We saw the humans leave, but not her. I got worried. Where's Arion?"

"Theresa didn't tell you? I was sure she would."

"Tell me what?"

Cy looked away, unable to speak.

"Kraven killed him," Kaitlyn said in a small voice. "Kraven's dead now as well."

"Arion's dead?" Tuft burst, looking from one of them to the other. Kaitlyn's eyes were cast down, and Cy was looking at Kaitlyn in shock. He hadn't the courage to say those words himself, knowing that reality would crash down on him if he did.

Tuft dropped his head and walked over to Kaitlyn. He rubbed his head against her hand, ignoring her petrified state. She shut her eyes, but her hand automatically moved to rub the wolf's ears. Her legs started to shake, and Cy was ready to pull Tuft away for scaring her, but he didn't need to. Kaitlyn dropped to the ground on her knees, hugging the wolf around his neck. She buried her face in his fur, and he placed a paw on her leg.

Cy looked away, giving Kaitlyn her privacy as she cried into Tuft's neck. She finally pulled away, rubbing her eyes. "Thank you."

Tuft nodded once, then turned to Cy as Kaitlyn gathered herself.

"What are you doing out here?" he asked, his voice devoid of his usual joking nature.

"We're on our way to the different colonies in Lontorra, hoping that one of them will have a way to get Arion back."

"Back from the dead? Is that even possible?"

"It better be," Cy said simply, a hint of a threat in his voice.

They sat for a moment, each lost within themselves. Kaitlyn was the first to speak, her voice still thick with tears. "We got a little lost. Can you help us get out of here?" Her voice was barely a whisper.

"I can lead you to the outside world, but that is where my help must end. I cannot leave the woods, not as an Alpha. Not to mention that I can't exactly leave my pups for

Hylot to care for on her own. She'd have my pelt as a rug if I did."

Tuft burst into laughter, his seriousness washed away. He caught his breath, then gave a short howl. He stared into the darkness. Four smalls pups came running from the trees, bumping into and bowling over each other. They rolled in the grass until they ran into Tuft and stared up at him obediently. One was the spitting image of Hylot, with perfect caramel fur, though the ears and tail were tipped gray. One was a muddled brown with light gray around the eyes and paws. The other two looked like two halves of a whole. The first was fully gray with its chest Hylot's caramel, and the second was the reverse caramel with a gray chest.

"They're so adorable," Kaitlyn whispered, a huge smile plastered on her face.

"You think so? Take 'em!" Tuft barked out a laugh, then addressed his pups.

"To attention, little ones. We're going for a walk." The twins yipped in excitement, their tails wagging too fast for the eyes to see.

"I'm glad that you two at least are excited, Baera and Biero," he said, nodding to the twins each in turn. The mostly gray one, Baera, yipped in satisfaction. Biero held his head high.

The other two fell on their backs and whined. The brown pup nipped at the other's tail, and they began chasing each other. "Olligrin, stop chasing your sister! Jayda, watch where you're running. You're going to hit something again!" Tuft called after the two, but they didn't listen.

They weren't paying attention, and ran into Kaitlyn's legs. Olligrin ran to hide behind Tuft, while Jayda looked up at Kaitlyn with a mix of fear and curiosity.

"Hi there, cutie," Kaitlyn said as she bent to pick up the

pup. It nipped at her fingers, yipping at her, but she ignored the pup's attacks. She scooped Jayda up and cradled her in her arms. Kaitlyn ran her fingers through Jayda's fur on her chest, and the pup relaxed. Kaitlyn began scratching her stomach, and the pup kicked out in joy.

It wasn't long before all of the pups were swarmed at Kaitlyn's feet, begging for attention. She squatted down to their level, trying to keep them all sated, but she didn't have enough hands. They tackled her to the ground, rubbing their heads against her sides, tickling her, and licking her face. She rolled on the ground, laughing under them.

"Olligrin, Jayda, Baera and Biero! All of you, get back here!" Tuft barked out, his voice filled with authority. The pups all stopped slowly, and turned toward their father. He raised his muzzle at them, daring them to disobey. They shared a few glances, then walked back to Tuft with their tails between their legs, whimpering.

Tuft let out a sigh, and licked their cheeks lovingly. Tuft began giving out orders, "Alright pups, in formation. Like we practiced. Jayda you're leading today. Baera, Biero, next in line. Olli is in front of me. Straight line now, pay attention to your leader. Biero, leave your sister's tail alone!" Tuft soon devolved into nipping at each pup, doing everything he could to keep them under control.

He threw his head back and howled, and the pups joined in. With their attention now gathered, he addressed them sternly, "Now, you can either all behave, or you can go back to your mother. Who wants to be the one to wake her up and tell her you were bad? Any takers?"

All of the pups stared at the ground. They spared glances for each other, but none made a sound. "Good. Back in formation!"

The pups lined themselves up perfectly, their heads held

high and shoulders regal as they marched. They passed by Cy and Kaitlyn as they led the way out of the woods. Tuft gave them a smirk as he came to them.

"Are you coming or what?" he asked, smugness seeping from his words.

Cy and Kaitlyn shared a glance, then took up the rear, marching in time with the pups' tiny footsteps.

* * *

"THIS IS where we part ways, Cyllorian. We can't leave the woods. There is much here we have to take care of, but I'll be awaiting the day I can be of more assistance to you."

"Since when did you get all formal?" Cy asked, scanning the woods around them. Through the cracks in the trees, he could see Arion's old home. From here, it looked as though it had been untouched. Cy assumed the town would've burnt it down out of fear, and seeing it still standing filled him with curiosity.

"I am an Alpha, after all. I need to start acting my age. My immaturity could cost me in the end. I need to be more cautious." Tuft paused, and a sullen expression fell over him. His voice remained strong, but his stance was strained. "Besides, Arion is my human, bound to me much like Theresa and Goyik are bound. I am loyal to him beyond reason. I only wish I could do more. I didn't realize at the time, but I did Goyik a favor by taking the title of Alpha from him. Now he is free to see to Theresa's wishes without regret."

"It's alright, Tuft. We know you want to help, but you have to stay here with your pups. We can handle it from here, thank you." Kaitlyn scratched behind the wolf's ears. Though the action seemed effortless, Cy could see that her hand shook slightly.

She's braver than Theresa gave her credit for, he thought proudly. He gave a small smile as he watched her.

The pups began to shift anxiously at Tuft's side. The walk through the woods had taken nearly all day to accompany their speed, and it had worn them out. As soon as they had stopped, they had collapsed against their father. After just a few minutes of rest, they were full of energy yet again, and longed to move. It seemed the only thing that kept them by their father's side was their fear of the new area of the woods.

Tuft bowed his head to Kaitlyn. "You can always call on me when you need it. I am at your service, in Arion's name."

Kaitlyn curtseyed in return, and the wolf smiled sadly.

Kaitlyn opened her mouth to question him, but he had already turned to herd his pups. He got them lined up with little difficulty, and set them off into the woods towards their home.

"Bring him back! For me," Tuft called. He paused a few feet away to look back at Cy.

The demon nodded to the wolf. *"I'll bring him back for all of us,"* he said simply. Tuft stared at Cy for a long moment, before flashing a sad smile. He turned on his heels, the weight of an Alpha placed onto his shoulders yet again. With short orders and little patience, he corralled his pups back into the trees.

Since they had stopped walking, the trek of the day seemed to be weighing on Kaitlyn. Cy waved his arm in front of him, towards the house. *"Ladies first?"* he offered, slightly uncomfortable with the phrase.

She smiled tiredly at him and stepped gingerly over the brush, fallen branches, and tangled roots keeping them from a peaceful rest.

They stepped through the back door of the house, and Cy was left breathless by the interior. Nothing had been touched since the day they'd left. Even Kraven's blood stains in the floorboards remained, and Cy cringed. He rummaged through the kitchen cupboards for any food that hadn't spoiled.

When he was successful in his search, he looked for Kaitlyn, but she wasn't in the kitchen. He wandered into the living room, though he hadn't noticed her leave his side.

She was curled up in Arion's huge arm chair in the living room. Her canteen was lying on the floor, the cap off and a small puddle of water around it. Cy picked it up and put it away into her bag. He questioned how anyone could fall asleep so quickly, but accepted that exhaustion had taken ahold of her. He walked silently as he retrieved a blanket from Arion's room, then tucked Kaitlyn in. She gripped the blanket immediately, pulling it over her head to shield her eyes from the setting sun.

There was barely a sliver left of light, and it lit the air around Cy a deep violet. He watched the sun as it was snuffed out by the horizon. The clouds shown with a beautiful violet, and Cy touched his cheek beneath his eye, reminded of his own essence. He turned to look out of the other window. Stars shown brightly, lighting up the night sky just as the sun had.

It's the same sky, but they're so different. They have their own intentions, their own meanings. Cy looked back to the twilight, nearly swallowed up by the spreading darkness. *It sure doesn't last long. Maybe that's the point. Twilight proves that just because something ends, doesn't mean it's a bad thing. But even then, it never lasts for long. So when is it going to go wrong, if this is supposed to be the good part?*

Cy sat on the floor across from Kaitlyn, watching over her. She slept soundly, unlike Arion, who had always tossed throughout the whole night. Kaitlyn barely moved. Cy was tempted to check her breathing, but didn't want to risk waking her for nothing. She muttered a few times, but it was unintelligible.

Cy lifted his arm, admiring the magic that raced within. Arion's green lightning bounced off of the metal walls inside of him, keeping him alive. It was thin, and stuttering on its path, worrying him. *I just have to stop using energy and it should recharge. If I sit here, it should be back to normal by morning,* he told himself. He laid his head back on the wall, and closed his eyes. If he concentrated hard enough, he could feel the energy racing through him, hear the static as it gave him consciousness.

But the static was starting to fade. He forced himself to stop breathing, telling himself that it was wasted energy. Aches had set into his joints, and he wondered if he needed oil, or if the body simply wasn't meant to last. Could it reject him? Could it deny his soul and kill him?

His mind whirred with every negative possibility, and he found himself breathing erratically. Were he human, he would have hyperventilated without even realizing. He clenched his fists at his sides, and stared at the ceiling. *Arion knows what he's doing. He would make sure it would work.*

Though he reassured himself easily, a strong sense of dread had nestled in his chest, clinging to him like a leech.

As the sky grew it's darkest, Cy felt himself slipping. Gripped by panic, he did all he could to hold onto himself, but it only drained his energy more. The magic in him fluttered under his metal skin, and his consciousness faded in and out. He struggled to breath, to move, as the magic giving him life faltered in his chest. *No! Arion wouldn't let me die in this thing! Why isn't it working, why isn't the magic recharging?*

He desperately ripped his chest plate open, and touched the heart within. The magic still hummed vigorously inside of it, sending a wave of calm throughout Cy.

It needs rest, like any other body. I've used too much in a short time, it's shutting down. I'm not dying. Stupid demon, I just need to rest, to recharge the magic. I can't push it, not until we get the kid back.

Cy leaned back against the wall, propping himself up so he wouldn't fall. He hadn't had to rest in this body yet, because he hadn't used it enough. Would it be like sleeping? Would he dream? Or would he just disappear for a while? It scared him that he didn't know, but he accepted there was no other way to find out. And he was far too tired to do anything else.

His sight flickered to darkness, and he no longer could feel himself. Still terrified of losing his new body, and losing Arion forever, he talked to himself as long as he could to force himself to stay awake.

Everything will be better once we get him back. I just have to keep my cool until then. I can do that.

Can't I?

CHAPTER 4

Void

"Hey, you okay? Did they hurt you?" *a small voice said.*

The boy looked up to find the source, but his vision was blurred. All he could make out were a pair of large blue eyes staring at him.

The boy stared at her in disbelief, his jaw slack. She shook his shoulder lightly and giggled. "It's alright, you can tell me. What's your name?"

My name? *He was unable to conceive of such a thing.* Do I have a name? I don't think so. Is that a problem?

The boy opened his mouth, but he had no voice. The girl's eyes tilted, and they swam with worry. "Talk to me, please. Are you okay?"

He was shaken again, and the boy's vision went dark. Now where am I? Anywhere? Nowhere?

A hot pain sprouted from his middle and he stared down at the source. There was no sign of a weapon, but there was a large hole tearing through his pale skin. Thick, white blood poured onto his hands as he tried to hold himself together. It was sickeningly cold. He closed his eyes against the pain, doubling over.

Something sliced across his back. His eyes shot open with a cry.

The boy's vision was filled with a creature he had quickly memorized. Pure black eyes watched him with cruelty, set back in a starved, angled face. It gnashed its razor-like teeth together. Thin arms had inflicted pain with an impossible strength, and black talons tipped the creature's fingers, sharpened to a fine point. Its short, slender tail whipped behind it. It wore a simple beige robe, made of the same material as the boy's own clothing. At first, the boy had thought the creature was sickly, but learned that the pale green skin was natural for this creature.

The boy turned away from the creature, examining his cell to wake him from his groggy state. The dull metal he knelt on had been stained white with his blood in the short time he'd been there. It ran in streaks down the sloped floor, leading to a small grate in the center. The bars of his cell cut through the dim light that inched towards him. A shadow loomed in the pool of light, but the boy could not find its origin. Hanging on the back wall were his shackles and he was relieved that he was not in them again. He was restrained by something much worse.

The creature held the boy by his throat, lifting him from the ground. The boy sat on his knees, his hands clawing at the creature's grip. The boy's own talons, short but sharp, peeled at the creature's skin from its hands, but it barely noticed.

"Look who finally decided to wake up," it spat, its breath hot on the boy's skin.

The boy swung his arms out wildly, connecting with the creature's side. It groaned in pain, and tightened its grip on his throat. The boy gasped desperately for air, but he had no strength within him.

"That's enough, Grite. Give my Void a chance to speak." A man's harsh voice cut through the air, and the boy was released. He watched Grite slink away from him, hissing. The boy watched the creature with disinterest now that the pain had been removed.

"You really are a worthless demon, aren't you?" the man asked, smacking the creature across the face. It was thrown into the wall, and the boy cringed at the shriek it made.

The man stepped forward and grabbed the boy's chin in his thin fingers. Long nails bit into the boy's cheeks, but it was nothing compared to the pain in his stomach and back.

The man studied the boy with merciless eyes, and the boy stared back, no emotion within him. He was not afraid of the man, regardless of his torture, nor could he feel hate for his capture. He couldn't even feel sorry for himself. He simply didn't know how.

The man smiled wickedly at the boy after a moment, his long brown hair falling into his face. His dark green eyes gleamed with malice. It made the boy's stomach flip, but he couldn't tell why. *Is this worry, or fear? Nervousness, anxiety, disgust? What is it?* His face twisted up a moment as he struggled to place the feeling, and the man's face shifted as well.

But the confusion faded from the boy quickly and the man's expression sunk. He dropped the boy, and he fell onto his hands.

I can tell what he feels, most of the time. Can't I just copy that? All I feel is pain, and that's not an emotion.

Thinking of the pain made him remember. He glanced down to his bare stomach, allowing his white hair to fall into his eyes. His dark pants were covered in white blood spilling from a small hole in his middle, with raw, healing skin surrounding it. *He didn't stab me very deeply this time if it's already healing. That's weird for him.*

"Master Crestyss, he was muttering in his sleep again. I heard him, I did, I did," Grite hissed from his place behind the man.

"Was he?" Crestyss asked, drawing nearer to the boy. He smiled again, dragging his nails across the boy's cheek. They dug in slightly, and the boy felt the heat of his skin stitching itself back together. "What were you saying, my little Void?"

The boy thought back to his dream, trying to remember. All that came to mind was his own question. Did he have a name? *He calls me Void. Is that my name? It doesn't sound like a name, but neither does Grite. I guess it's my name. Either way, one less thing to worry about.*

"Void, come back to me," the man snapped, shaking him. "What were you dreaming about? What did you see? What were you saying?"

Void thought again, though he couldn't be bothered to put the effort into it. He closed his eyes and bit the inside of his cheek. *Why am I biting myself? Am I nervous, or bored? I really shouldn't hurt myself, Grite does that enough.*

Void dropped his head onto his shoulder, his mind wandering. *If I can't care, then I can't focus. If I can't focus, then I can't help him, and if I can't do that, I'll never leave. But why do I want to leave? Where did I come from, and why was I brought here? I don't know what they want from me. All I know is this damn cell. What do they expect?*

Void opened his eyes and shook his head at Crestyss, his face blank. His eyes started to droop as what once was a burning pain turned into a vague throbbing in his middle. Crestyss sighed, and Void opened his eyes. He expected to be hit and clenched his fists, but the blow never came.

"You are so perfect," the man crooned, his voice almost loving. Grite hissed again from behind him. "I performed the spell wonderfully, transferring you into the body of a demon. I'm the first to create a Void from a demon, and it went tremendously well! You'll last as long as I need you, with little maintenance. Demons are much more durable creatures, after all.

"It was a disaster the last time, giving me that disgrace of a demon you see behind me. But he is loyal, regardless of anything I might say or do. And soon you will come to love or fear me as he does. You will obey me, do you understand that, Void? You are nothing more than a vessel that I created for my own purposes. You have no desires of your own, no emotions, because you do not need them. You need only to serve me, as Grite does. You will learn, sooner rather than later."

Crestyss began pacing in the small cell, Grite hopping anxiously around his feet. "What method will work best? Grite responded well to burning, but it wasn't quite so. . .unwilling. Stabbing has little effect, and I doubt drowning will do much. . ." Crestyss muttered to himself. Void listened to him rattle off varying tortures.

I should be scared, right? I should be terrified. Come on, Void, panic! Care enough to save yourself! He tried yelling at himself, tried to breathe harder and faster to work himself up, but all to no avail.

"Let me, Master, let me! If I can make him scream, then I can make him talk." Grite tugged on Crestyss' coat, and the man raised his hand to hit the demon away. The creature cringed, but Crestyss paused with his hand raised.

"Perhaps you are right, Grite. Show him what kind of fear he should feel, teach him what it is to be a servant of mine. If you satisfy me now, then I will leave you in charge of his punishment."

Grite pressed its nose to the ground in a bow, then turned on Void. *"A knife, Master, will work best for what I have in mind."*

Grite held its hands up to beg Crestyss. After a moment of thought, the Mage waved his hand, and a thin dagger appeared in the demon's palms from a plume of dark green fire.

Grite cackled as he approached Void. His body recognized the threat in the demon that the man lacked, and responded. He had easily learned to feel fear from the demon's merciless attacks, and Grite was the only thing that could cause such a reaction within him. The boy's eyes went wide and he backed away. His heart pounded in his chest, and his ears were ringing. *I'm afraid. I'm afraid, I'm afraid, I'm afraid already!* He tried to yell aloud, but his thoughts never made it past his lips.

Grite lunged and snatched up his arm. It yanked Void onto his stomach, and his freshly healed wound was agitated as he hit the ground. He felt his skin burst beneath him, and the cold blood pooled on the metal floor and sloshed toward the grate.

Grite stomped its foot down on Void's arm, and the boy screamed at the crunch that sounded in his ears. He tried desperately to get away, even looking to Crestyss for help, but the man only grinned sadistically.

Void looked back to the demon pinning him down, the knife raised high above its head, watching as it came down. It felt as though years were passing in that moment as the blade cut into his flesh and white blood covered the demon's face. He turned away at the last second, his own screams feeling like they would burst his eardrums. His limbs spasmed in pain, and he opened his eyes to inspect the damage.

The tips of his fingers on his left hand had been severed, and they rolled along the floor towards the drain in the center of the room. A cold sweat broke out on his face. He would've been sick had he been fed at all in the time he'd been captured.

Void stared in horror as the dagger came down again, amputating his whole hand at the wrist. Grite rose from pinning the boy, and Void rolled onto his back. He clutched the stub of his arm to his chest, screaming.

"You've only brought this upon yourself!" Crestyss called over Void's yells of agony. "The sooner you give me what I want, what I need to start my war, the sooner this will all end! It's inside of you, you just have to find it! Give it to me, and this all stops!"

Void wanted to believe him, but the look in the eyes of the demon standing nearby told him otherwise.

Grite towered over him, its smile mirroring that of its master's. It bent down and whispered in Void's ear, *"This is for taking everything from me. And I'm only getting started with you. Keep your secrets to yourself as long as you'd like, I don't give a damn. This is my favorite part."*

Grite grabbed his other hand, and wrenched it up into the air. Slowly, it sawed off the tips of Void's fingers, one by one. With each cry of pain that erupted from Void's throat, Grite chuckled under his breath. Its tongue lashed out to clean the blood that splattered onto its face.

Once all of Void's fingers had been removed, Grite paused. Void opened one eye cautiously, half of him wanting to be ready for the next attack, and the other half too terrified to move.

The blade in the demon's hand was now glowing red, and it pressed the flat of the blade to the bleeding ends of the fingers. Void held back a scream, staring Grite down as he cauterized the wounds. *"Don't think I forgot about your talons. You won't be able to grow them back any more. You'll find that magic is quite effective against bodies like ours."*

Grite released Void's hand, and it fell limply onto the ground. Kicking away the severed fingers as it went, Grite retrieved Void's other hand, and burned the bloody ends of them as well.

The demon dropped the hand onto Void's chest, white blood dripping onto the boy's face. He looked away from it in disgust, and into Grite's hate-filled eyes. He snatched Void's attached hand, and sawed it off with slow, long slices to the wrist.

"I'll bleed out!" Void finally yelled between cuts to his wrist. Grite had reached the bone quickly, and was digging into it with surprising ease for the pace. "If you kill me, you'll never get what you want! You need something from me, or else I'd already be dead!"

"*Please. You have a* proper *demon's body. You can't die that easily, even if you wanted to! I can bring you within inches of your life, and you'd heal in the hour, then I can start all over again,*" Grite said happily. It laughed maniacally as it sawed faster with a lapse in its control.

Crestyss stepped beside Grite and placed a hand on its shoulder in warning. Grite froze, Void's hand connected to his arm by only a thin layer of muscle and skin. Void swallowed the bile in his throat and forced himself to look at Crestyss.

"Are you saying that you are ready to tell me what I need?" he asked simply, glaring down at the boy.

Void opened his mouth unsure of what would come out. He remained silent.

Are you okay? a voice said within his head. He stared at the dark ceiling of his cell, then closed his eyes.

Hey, are you okay? the voice asked again, and a pair of bright blue eyes shown in the darkness behind his eyelids.

With the voice clear in his head, Void made his resolve. He opened his eyes and met Crestyss' gaze with all the strength he could muster. The Mage's faded green eyes bore into his own, but he held his ground.

"I have nothing to tell you," he said, wanting his voice to come out stronger than it did. Despite his decision, he couldn't bring himself to put any courage behind it.

As soon as the words were out of his mouth, Crestyss

changed. His eyes darkened and the features of his face looked sharper. The corner of his mouth twitched, and Void watched a shadow come over his features.

"Shame. But you will give in eventually. I've waited this long to get my hands on you, I can wait a little while more for what I need. We'll just have to step things up a notch, try whatever we can think of. Grite, I'll leave this to you."

Crestyss folded his hands behind his back and turned on his heel towards the door. Void shifted his gaze to the demon smiling down at him, and his stomach churned at the murderous intent in his eyes.

"Yes, Master. I won't let you down," it said as Crestyss disappeared through the cell door. The barred door slammed, and the demon's face changed instantly.

With a quick movement, Grite ripped Void's hand from his arm, the thin muscle snapping. Void let out a scream coupled with Grite's malicious laughter.

"I've always been curious how durable my body was. Let's test it, shall we?" the demon hissed to itself as he gathered Void's severed hands. It sounded as though it was singing to itself, an eerie song that stuck in Void's mind.

Void pushed himself onto his knees, the bloody stumps of his hands slipping against the slick metal floor. Grite stepped up to him and kicked his side. Void rolled onto the floor, grunting in pain. He stared up at the demon, but his body had become unresponsive again. The fear faded from him though the threat had not gone. Void guessed it was for his own protection that he felt nothing, but his emptiness did not dull the pain.

A voice sounded within him, separate from his own. It sounded far off, and he couldn't make out any words, but the sound of it was enough to warrant a reaction within him. He pushed himself to his feet, raising his arms in front of him offensively.

Grite only laughed at him, waving Void's hands around carelessly. *"And what do you think you're going to do, fight back? You've got nothing. No strength, no power, not even fists to hit me with. You're not going to do anything, because you don't care enough to do anything. If you really want to help yourself, you'd just give in and help the Master."*

Surprising both Grite and himself, Void charged at the demon. His feet slid on his blood covering the floor, losing his balance. Grite dodged his assault easily, sticking its foot out to trip Void. He stumbled into the wall, and blood dripped from his nose and a cut in his lip. He turned slowly to face Grite, though he was dazed. He spread his feet apart, positioning himself for a kick.

Grite slammed its hand into Void's chest, and the boy was sent flying backwards. His back hit the wall, and he felt the shallow wound from before split open. His back grew cool with the thick blood that stuck to his skin. Instinctively, he bared his teeth at Grite and growled.

He realized what he was doing, and stopped. Grite laughed at him again, throwing its head back. *"You really are pathetic. You don't know how to do anything, or what to do. Why are you still fighting? You have no reason to, nothing to go back to. No one's waiting for you outside of this cell, no one's missing you. You're just hurting yourself, but you're literally unable to care! It's hilarious!"*

"And what about you? You don't care about yourself. You could stand up to Crestyss, but you don't. You have no reason to stay here, yet you do. What's your deal?"

"You really don't know anything. You poor fool. If only you would help us and remember, you wouldn't have to ask such stupid questions. Oh well. If you don't care, why should I?"

Grite descended upon Void. The demon snagged the boy's

arms, and pressed his hands back to the stubs of his arms. The edges of his skin met and knotted together, reattaching his hands. Void held back his screams as his hands rejoined his body, leaving only faint scars on his wrists to remind him.

Grite stepped away to admire its work, and Void glared at the demon. "Now what?" he spat.

"Now I do whatever it takes to make you remember."

Grite lunged for Void, but the boy lashed out at him. He swung his arm to swipe at the demon's face, but his talons were gone and the burned tips of his fingers merely grazed the pale green skin of the creature. It laughed at him, and ripped into Void's cheek with its own claws.

Chunks of Void's flesh fell onto the floor, white blood splattering on the shining metal. Void felt the wound with his fingers, and found that his cheek had been ripped straight through, exposing the inside of his mouth. He licked the edges of the hole in his face, and the growing skin threatened to trap his tongue.

A low growl sounded in Void's throat, making Grite smile wider. He got to his feet and faced the demon. He eyed the dagger that laid forgotten on the ground behind the demon. He dove for the weapon, but Grite kicked him in the stomach, and he fell to the ground.

"Do you really think I'm that stupid? You ought to know better than anyone how smart a demon is. Oh, wait. You don't, do you? I'm sorry, did that bring up any old memories? No? I guess I'll just have to try harder, then," Grite said as it took in the clueless expression on Void's face.

Void went to lunge to his feet, but he froze. The image of Grite coming for him vanished as his vision failed him. All that he could see was a pair of bright blue eyes set in black. His limbs went numb, and he felt himself falling forward.

The eyes blinked at him, and Grite erupted from behind

them, coming within inches of Void's face. The demon's hand clamped around Void's throat, its claws piercing his flesh over his pulse.

White blood filled his vision, blurring the grotesque face before him. The demon's snarling smile remained until the last second, serrated teeth gnashing.

* * *

Void wandered around in shadows, unable to even see his own body. His cell was gone, leaving him in a completely empty space. There were no walls, no ceiling, no light. He wasn't even sure what he was standing on, if anything. He was lost in complete nothingness.

This must be my mind, *he told himself. He looked in all directions.* There's nothing here. Nothing at all. Could it really be what's inside my head?

As he stared into the blackness, he caught a flash of light far off. He took a step towards it, unsure. It flashed again, closer this time. He crept towards it slowly, wandering what he could be walking to.

Is this what they want me to find? If so, should I even go to it? Do I want them to have it? What will they do, once they get what they want. It can't be good, so I should keep it from them. But what is it?

Another flash came, lighting everything up. Before him was a whirlwind of smoke, spinning wildly in front of him. Two glowing, purple eyes shone through the darkness, boring into him.

"What are you?" Void asked, his voice thick as though he were speaking through water. The smoke remained still.

Void flinched at another flash of light from behind the smoke. He stared it down, but it had no effect.

"Can you help me? Or are you just going to stand there?" Void

asked again. He felt a tugging within himself, one that he could only explain as an annoyance.

"Nope. Don't think so. But you could help yourself." *A voice echoed in the air around him. It sounded as though it was comprised of many people. Void couldn't place a single voice among the crowd.*

"What do you mean?" Void asked cautiously. His stomach was churning, and he fought against the urge to retch. Something didn't feel right to him.

"I can't tell you what I know nothing about. But you can find out yourself."

"I've already tried! How am I supposed to do that?" Void yelled. A headache was forming in the back of his mind. A haze fell over his eyes, and his vision blurred. What is this feeling? Why do I feel like I know what's going on? *He placed a hand to his forehead, grunting at the throbbing headache.*

"You don't know where to start, but I do. And I can tell you. All I need is one itty bitty thing from you." *Void could hear the smile in the voices, could feel the malicious intent roiling in the smoke. There was a fire in those purple eyes that could neither be explained nor contained. And it terrified Void that something like this could be inside of himself.*

"And what exactly do you need?" Void removed his hand to stare the smoke straight on. A hand emerged from the smoke, scarily pale with not a vein in sight beneath the fair skin. Red talons inched towards Void, and he stepped back.

The headache pounded, and he fell to his knees. He recognized the words, knew he had heard them before. It haunted him, teased him, but he didn't know why. He stared into the smoke, able to make out a figure trapped inside.

Don't say it, don't say it, please, don't say it, *he begged inwardly.*

"A name," *the voices hissed in Void's ears. The arm lunged from the smoke and snatched his throat, choking him. Cackling filled the air as the darkness was driven away by a blinding light. Void's head felt ready to burst, and his lungs were shriveling from lack of oxygen. He clawed desperately at the hand that choked him, but it was no use. He had no strength here, wherever here was.*

The pain filled his head, stabbing at the inside of his skull. He shut his eyes and screamed as loudly as he could, the last of his air tearing through his throat.

The thing that held Void shook him into silence, the laughter growing louder. His eyes opened despite the brightness, but there was nothing to be seen. Where the smoke had once spun, there was emptiness. There was no arm holding him up, no darkness swallowing him. He was suffocating on his own, and he didn't know how to stop it.

The light invaded his eyes, burning them from their sockets. He longed to scream, or cry, anything to release the searing pain. It was too much for him to handle. He started to lose his grip on himself.

Void collapsed to the floor, his arms sprawling out around him. A weight smothered him, and it was a great feat of its own just to keep his eyes open. His hand fell upon something, and he turned to look. Just in front of him was a small wooden box with a strange glow seeping from the cracks. He inched his fingers toward the circular lock, but he fainted before he could reach it.

* * *

Void was shaken awake, Grite breathing in his face. He scrambled out of the demon's grip, aware of a strange throbbing all over his body. He raised his hand to his face, wiping away blood and tears that had spilled from his eyes.

"Surprise! I hope you like what I've done with the place while you were out. It was tough keeping you under for so long, but I didn't want you to see until I was done. I redecorated a bit, then

realized that you needed a makeover. Has anyone ever told you that you look good in red?" Grite chortled mercilessly.

He stared down at his hands, his stomach churning. He began to gag, but there was nothing for him to lose. Blood spewed from his mouth and dripped from his flesh. As he turned back to glare at the demon, he saw it in the corner.

A pile of pale flesh heaped against the wall, covered in his blood with tufts of white hair sticking out. Repulsed, he dared another look at his arm for confirmation. His arm was pure red, stripped of all of its skin. Veins wriggled from their proper places as the blood rushed through them, and the muscles flexed grotesquely with each tiny movement he made.

Void's lip trembled as he inspected the rest of his body, but it only made him feel worse. Grite had kept him unconscious while he was skinned alive. He thought back to the headache he had in the dream, and put a shaking hand to the back of his head.

Tears stung in his eyes and leaked down his cheek, burning the exposed muscles and tissues. He gingerly felt over the jagged pieces of bone that protruded from his head, inching his fingers around them. In the middle of the wreckage that was his skull, he found the hilt of a blade. Gliding his fingers along the length of it, his burnt fingertips came into contact with something warm and slimy, that squished and pulsated under his touch. His brain.

"I see you noticed my grand plan. Since you were having such a hard time remembering, I thought I'd help you pick your brain. Great idea, right? I really hope it helped, and I didn't have to break open your skull for nothing," Grite taunted sarcastically.

Void was frozen, his hand mere inches from the handle of the blade. He heard Grite walking towards him, but couldn't bring himself to retreat, nor fight back.

He sat helpless as the demon swatted his hand away and

snatched up the dagger. Grite ripped it from Void's brain, gouging out a piece of it. The tip of the blade caught an upturned section of Void's skull and sent it flying across the room.

"Anything? Anything at all? Are you speechless at my generosity, that I would help you? Is that it? Are you impressed?"

"I'm disturbed," Void finally breathed, twitching at the burning over his whole body as the skin grew back. He forced himself to look at the wall in front of him, worried that he might lose himself were he to watch the healing process.

"Disturbed? Not grateful, or enlightened? Just disturbed? You're telling me that you still don't remember a thing?"

Void recalled the glowing eyes from his dream, the conversation that felt all too familiar. He thought of the confusion that had filled him in the dream, that still filled him now. There was no making sense of it, even if he wanted to. There was nothing to be done but to wait.

"Nothing," he breathed.

"Damn. That really is too bad. Especially since after all that, I'm only disturbing. *I guess we'll just have to try again. And again, and again, and again, until we get it right. I have a feeling that it's going to be just you and me for a very, very long time, so we should really make the most of it, don't you think? How about I go for just downright mortifying next time, hmm?"*

Grite wrapped his hand around Void's throat. The demon pulled Void closer. *"One last thing."*

Grite's voice had changed dramatically. It was no longer shrill. It was deeper, more calculating. It froze Void with panic. *"If those* imaginary *friends in your head ever decide to try to save you, I'll slaughter them in front of you."*

Without another word, Grite slammed Void's head into the wall.

CHAPTER 5

Kaitlyn

The rising sun broke through the dusty windows, spilling onto Kaitlyn's face. She woke with a whimper, curling away from the abrasive light. *Who would make a house so that you get the sun rise? It makes for a terrible sleep schedule,* she groaned to herself. She pulled the blanket over herself, burrowing into its warmth.

She hadn't felt the autumn cold the day before. She had been too busy sweating in the humid woods. Now, it was all she could feel this early in the morning. She wrapped the blanket around her, breathing in the scent.

She recognized it immediately as Arion's, and she reached out for him. Her hand found nothing more than emptiness, and the plushness of the chair she had collapsed in. The slight smile fell from her face as her memories flooded back to her. She turned her face into the back of the chair, biting back tears.

I've cried enough! she told herself harshly. *It's not going to help get him back. And even if it did, he wouldn't want me to cry either way.*

She threw the blanket onto the floor with one decisive movement. The cold air sent a shiver down her spine, and she fought against grabbing the blanket again. With a groan, she forced herself from the chair.

She righted her clothing, wrinkled and mussed from being slept in. She looked through her bag for another change of clothes, but only found a few. "A month," she groaned, closing her bag. *We'll be out for a month, and this is all the clothes I packed? I better not get anything too dirty.*

She set the bag aside and took in the house. It was exactly how she'd remembered it, though there wasn't much to remember, especially when compared to the castle.

The walls were bare, the windows small and high against the ceiling. She could see the cracks in the floor where the trap-door was. It had locked itself again as soon as she'd gotten out of it before, and no one had been able to get back in. She knew how the town had talked about coming back to burn the house, but they had all been cowards. Kraven had been the only one brave enough to stand against Arion once they had seen his power. After Arion had nearly killed Kraven in this house, none of them dared to risk their lives going against him.

She hated them all, her father especially. Of course she loved her father as well, but that was unconditional. She chose to hate him, and so she could feel them both strongly, and at the same time. She loved him because he was her father, but she hated him because he was human.

I always forget that I'm human, too, she reminded herself with a sigh. She had argued with herself over this subject more times than she could count, and had never reached a conclusion. She was different. From Kraven, and her father. From everyone. She cared about Arion, always, because he was a little boy that had needed her help. And she had quickly fallen in love with him.

They hated him because they could. It had been easiest to blame Arion for their problems, because he was different. But her father was the worst.

"I'll not allow such treatment of your fellow student. I shall speak with Kraven and his followers, and make sure that they are properly reprimanded. So long as your friend remains a member of this town, he will be treated as such. For you, Kaitlyn, it is a promise," he had told her when she had first befriended Arion years ago.

But it was her father in the end that had asked for his head.

They would have never thought of it if I hadn't offered to take them to Arion, though. They never would have found him. Kraven wouldn't have killed him if...

"Hey, you need to eat," Cy said. He held out a bowl of small berries to her, and she took it gingerly. She averted her eyes from him, terrified that he might read the guilt behind them.

"Thank you, Cyllorian," she said quietly. She popped the berries into her mouth one at a time, eating them slowly but not really tasting them. They were gone before she realized, and her hunger had only grown.

Forcing her guilt-ridden thoughts down her throat, she turned to Cy. "Are there any more?" she asked sheepishly. He nodded emotionlessly, and took the bowl from her. He left to the kitchen, and returned a few moments later. He carried a bigger bowl with a wide assortment of fruits.

"Where did all of this come from? Shouldn't anything that had been here be bad by now?" she asked, inspecting the fruit carefully.

"Theresa delivered it overnight. She left a brief note, just saying that it was for you. Don't worry about it, just eat. You'll need your strength. Today we get to the mountain."

Kaitlyn nearly choked on a grape she had started eating, and swallowed it painfully. "The mountain by the end of the day? How do you expect us to make that much progress?"

"I was looking at a map Arion had left here, and it looks like the fastest way is through the village, then around Centric, hugging the wall of it until we get to an opening in the Kindling Woods. There's only a few safe places to enter, marked on the map. You'll get lost or captured otherwise. They don't call it The Lost Soul Woods for nothing," he ended in a mutter.

"The Lost Soul Woods? Are you kidding?" she asked incredulously. He shook his head, and she let out her breath. "You still think we could get there by nightfall? You might be able to go on forever, but I have to rest, and eat, and..."

"I've thought of all that. I have a solution, but you won't like it."

She narrowed her eyes at him and he looked away. "You're *not* leaving me behind. You got that?" she growled. Cy avoided her gaze, but his shoulders sagged at her words.

"Yeah, 'cause I'm gonna fight you on that just so I can go all by myself? No thanks, I just got this body, and I rather enjoy it." He raised his hands in defeat.

She leaned back against the chair. She relaxed, but her eyes remained narrowed. "What's your plan, then?"

Cy pulled out the map from one of his pockets, and used his magic to levitate it in the air between them. Slowly, he traced the path he had said moments before. *"We follow this path carefully, and we should get to the base of the mountain in no time."*

Kaitlyn leaned away, masking her fear at the unknown trail. She watched as Cy studied the map, seemingly at ease. A thought struck her, and she laughed abruptly. Cy looked up at her in confusion, and she said, "So, you're telling me, that I'm more terrifying to you than the village of ruthless humans, Mages who, most likely, will want to kill us, and the place with the nickname of *The Lost Soul Woods?* Demons make no damn sense!"

"You really ought to watch your language. That's no way for a lady to talk, and you know it." The sarcasm was thick in his voice, but his shock at her words was genuine.

"Fine. *You* make no damn sense. Better?" She cocked an eyebrow at him, challenging him. She popped another grape into her mouth, and smiled at his silence.

He turned away with a grunt, crossing his arms over his chest. *"It's the fastest way. We can get through all of the places if we're careful. We can wait until tonight and go through the village while everyone's sleeping. By the time we get to the woods, there'll be enough light to see by so we don't get lost."*

"I thought you said we would be getting to the mountain by the end of today? How are we going to do that if we don't leave until then?"

"I was speaking with confidence! It won't kill us to have a little, okay? Damn, woman," he ended in a mutter.

"What was that?" Kaitlyn pried, getting to her feet. She stepped up to the demon, squaring her shoulders. She held her head high, though Cy was easily a foot taller than her. She stretched on her toes, trying to meet his eyes and stare him down, but he wasn't budging.

After a moment, Cy chuckled and stepped back from her. He tugged at her ponytail draped over her shoulder and she shoved him away angrily. She turned away from him, her cheeks burning from the way he treated her like a child. She ran her fingers through her tangled hair, and moaned in exasperation. She untied it and busied herself with attempting to tie it up again.

"I'm going to finish going through the house. Take the time to rest up fully. We'll leave just before the sun is gone tonight."

He smiled mischievously as he left the room. She stuck her tongue out at him, muttering, "Stupid demon."

His smile grew, and he winked at her. *"Crazy girl,"* he shot back. He left the room, and she couldn't help but smile as she finished tying her hair up in a loose bun.

* * *

"What does he expect me to do all day? There's nothing left in this house!" Kaitlyn exclaimed. She threw her hand up into the air and paused in her pacing. Cy had descended into the basement hours ago, leaving Kaitlyn alone upstairs. She had explored the house, but there was barely anything to be found. Arion's room still held his furniture, and a few articles of clothing he had left behind. She packed them neatly into her bag, moving slowly to waste time. It took up just under a half hour, and left her more bored than ever when she had finished.

She spent the rest of the early day pacing around downstairs, awaiting Cy's return. She was going crazy with boredom, as though madness itself was seeping from the walls. She banged on the secret door to the basement, yelling through the metal, "Cyllorian! There's nothing to do up here! Can I got outside or something, or do I need your permission?"

She heard his footsteps and backed away from the door. It opened slowly, and Cy poked his head out. *"Why would you need my permission. You're capable of handling yourself, right? Just stay in the back, preferably. We don't want anyone to find us here."*

Kaitlyn nodded, slightly embarrassed. He nodded back, and returned to the basement, dropping the door so it slammed shut.

Kaitlyn sat back in confusion. Why had she felt the need to check with Cyllorian, especially when he didn't seem to care what she did? With a huff, she stood up and marched outside. She kicked at the loose dirt as she tried to make sense of it.

If he doesn't care, then why was he specific about where I could go? Obviously I'm not going to get us caught. I know better than to be reckless. Does he not trust me all of a sudden? And what could he be doing downstairs?

She ignored the questions buzzing in her head and took a deep breath of fresh air. This was all she needed, after feeling suffocated inside the house. Her legs ached from the day before, and she wasn't too eager to be walking around again so soon, but staying cooped up in the house was pointless.

Outside had provided more of a distraction than she had anticipated. There were a few dummies set up, and she allowed herself to take out her rage on the one nearest to the house. She punched it with every wave, every thought, of guilt.

Arion's dead. She punched the dummy in the middle and it bobbed on its perch.

I can't go home. Another punch, this one cracking her knuckles painfully on contact. She shook her hand and continued.

Father took Dragon from me. I have no idea what he did with him. Tears pricked in her eyes. She hadn't had the time to worry about her lost pet, until now. She shut her eyes and swung wildly. She missed the dummy and fell to the ground.

She twisted in the air and caught herself on her hands. The ground was hard and uneven. It cut through her palms and tore her pants as she landed. She scrubbed her eyes clear with the back of her hand, taking deep breaths to control her emotions.

Kaitlyn pushed herself into a sitting position and carefully picked the dirt from the scrapes on her palms. It was hard to discern the dirt in the small amount of blood that pooled around the cut. She dropped her hands to her sides, palms up.

"It's no use. I'm completely helpless, I can't do anything! It's only a matter of time before Cyllorian sends me away, or abandons me. I didn't mean it, I didn't mean for any of this to happen! It's all my fault, and once he finds out that I...I...." she broke off her sentence, unable to say the words aloud.

I told Kraven to kill Arion, she told herself. The accusation in the words crashed over her, and she lost her breath. She struggled for air through her sobs, and she buried her face in her arms.

"No. It wasn't supposed to turn out like this. I meant for Arion to fight back, to scare Kraven away. That's what he told me he would do before, I don't know why he didn't," she gasped, forcing her tears away. "If there's a chance that Arion can get better, then so can I. I can get stronger, and be more helpful. I'll get him back, and then everything will go back to normal."

Kaitlyn stood up, a fierce determination coursing through her veins, boiling under her skin. She swung out at the dummy, again and again until her knuckles were bruised.

"Who are you pretending it is?" Cy's voice behind her made her jump, and she whirled on him, fists still raised. He glanced at her discolored fists and scowled, but said nothing.

She breathed a sigh of relief and dropped her hands. They throbbed and stung, though she hadn't noticed until she had stopped. She coughed into her hand to hide a wince at her pain. *Stronger,* she reminded herself.

Cy looked off into the distance behind her, his hands stuffed carelessly into his pockets. It looked like such a natural pose, despite the unnatural body, and she almost forgot that he was made entirely of metal. Almost.

"Arion used to pretend they were Kraven. He'd spend all day standing back here and trying to hit the one in the back, but he never could. He wasn't even that bad of a shot, for a beginner. Still

not sure why he could never hit it. Probably something stupid, like his lack of self-confidence."

Cy shrugged his shoulder as he finished. There was no sign of the care he had showed the day before, and Kaitlyn stared at him. She searched his features, but the metal was tricky and difficult to read.

Can he really turn off his feelings so easily? Or did he just not care in the first place? Is he actually doing all of this for Arion, or does he have some other motivation to trick me? But why would he want me alone?

Kaitlyn took a step back and readied her fists at her sides. She kept her face frozen, praying that it wouldn't give away her thoughts as she studied the demon's every move.

Theresa doesn't trust him. And there had to have been a reason Arion never told me about him. He's done everything he could to get me here, and now he's acting completely different. Maybe he blames me for Arion's death, and wants to take revenge. He has a temper, but he also seems to have control. His plan was to bring me here so he could kill me, it has to be!

"What do you mean by that?" she asked slowly. She spread her feet apart, and flexed the muscles in her arm.

"He didn't think he could do a lot of things. He never thought he could stand up to Kraven, and no matter how much he practiced when it came to these dummies, he made that one especially for Kraven, and it scared him. Just thinking of him terrified the kid, and he missed every time. I would make him aim at the trees around it, and he got every single one perfectly, so his aim wasn't the problem. He never believed in himself, with anything."

They spent a long moment in silence. Kaitlyn weighed her options carefully. *If I try to hit him, will it even do anything? The spear went straight through his chest and he didn't flinch. I'll probably break my arm if I hit him directly. But if I can just surprise him, I should be able to get away.*

He hadn't noticed the change in her yet. She still had a chance, but there was a part of her that didn't believe her fears. She warred with herself, then said, "Why?"

Cy turned to her. The metal above his eyes opened up, showing his vague interest. *"What?"*

"Why didn't Arion ever tell me about you?"

Cy looked away. *"Honestly, I don't really know,"* he muttered, a bout of anger rising up into his voice. He crossed his arms, tapping his talons against his arm.

He's lying! She didn't give herself any time to change her mind. She lunged for him, swinging her fist towards the side of his head.

He saw her just in time to dodge her attack. He jumped out of the way, but she spun and kicked for his legs. "If Arion really trusted you, then why didn't he tell me?" she yelled angrily. Tears sprang to her eyes again.

"He didn't want to scare you, okay? Just calm down!" Cy burst in return, avoiding her relentless assault.

"That's not good enough! He wouldn't keep anything from me!" she screamed.

Her attacks became even more futile as her emotions raged uncontrollably. She nearly fell on her face, but Cy caught her arm and held her up. She swiped at him, and he released her. She stumbled back and glared at Cy.

"Please. You barely knew anything about him! I was there for everything, but that never mattered! When his house blew up, that was my grand entrance, but I've been backstage ever since. Every time he got his ass kicked by Kraven, every time he nearly gave up on himself, I was there. When he took you to the castle, when he... kissed you... I was there for the whole thing! Hell, I'm the one that pretty much talked him into killing that Mage in Centric!"

Kaitlyn froze at his rant. She had expected his temper, but had assumed he would get violent, not vocal. She took a step back from him, her resolve to attack slipping. Her stomach twisted, and she pressed a shaking hand to her mouth.

"He killed someone?" she whispered. "He wouldn't do that. I know him, I know Arion wouldn't—"

"You knew what he wanted you to. He was the person you expected him to be when you were around, but it wasn't Arion. Not after that, at least. The killing is what changed him. I'm sure you remember how that turned out. Or have you just blocked out the image of Arion tearing Kraven's heart out with his bare hands?"

Kaitlyn shook her head violently. "You're lying. You're just trying to trick me again. It's not true!"

"Believe whatever you want, but you'll see for yourself when he comes back. The Arion you thought you knew has been gone for a long time. Now, are you finished with your tantrum yet?" Cy hissed impatiently. He took a step towards her, and she staggered away from him.

"And what about Theresa, huh? If her son trusted you, then why wouldn't she?" she spat. She put all of her strength into one last punch, aimed straight for Cy's face.

He caught her arm viciously, an irate scowl on his face. He twisted her arm behind her and grabbed her around her waist to restrain her. *"If I knew the answer to that, I'd tell you,"* he growled.

His metal was frigid against her body, and the constantly moving parts ground her skin. Thick steam furled from his nostrils, and she choked on it. *"And for the record, Arion's not her only son."*

Cy released her with a shove and stomped away from her. She stumbled forward and whirled to face him, the fire in her quickly dwindling. "What do you mean he's not her only son?"

"Arion's not an only child. He's not even the oldest. But of course, no one cares, not even Theresa!" Cy threw his hands to his sides. His gears whirred violently, and his metal body rattled.

Kaitlyn watched him puncture his palms with his talons, though he didn't seem to notice.

Kaitlyn was stunned by his words. She knew there could be only one explanation for his reaction, but it couldn't be true. "How could you…"

She was unsure how to finish her question.

Cy understood her perfectly, and his anger dimmed. *"I wasn't born like Arion was. She made me, out of her magic instead of blood. But that never made me any less of her son, not until she got pregnant. Then I became nothing more than a demon, and she locked me inside that damned box."*

Cy cast his gaze to the ground. He took a shaky breath, and it whistled through the metal. He exhaled a bout of thick steam, his temper burnt out. *"I knew from the very start who he was, and I wanted to kill him, so I never told him the truth. He didn't know until the end, when it was already too late. If I would've told him, he might not have gotten as bad as he did."*

There was a long moment of silence before Kaitlyn found the strength to speak again, "Theresa was chained in the cell that night. And that smoke was you, wasn't it?"

Cy nodded without looking up.

"Arion was— the basement was a mess, and there were signs of his magic everywhere. He hurt her, didn't he? He really did get so bad that he would—"

Kaitlyn broke off at Cy's expression. It told her that everything she had been thinking, all of her fears had been real. *If he really had lost it, why did he let Kraven kill him? He should've fought, more than ever! He tortured the town with those storms, attacked his own mother, but he couldn't kill the one person left that was damaging him?*

The new information, and the questions it brought, left a pit in her stomach. *Did I ever actually know him at all?*

Kaitlyn glanced at Cy. His head was still hung and his

shoulders slumped. He was motionless. Kaitlyn wondered if he was resting. She still had one more question

"Do you still want to kill him? How can I be sure that you've changed since then?"

Cy raised his head then. His eyes held all the answers she needed. In the depths of them was the same darkness that had been flooding her own vision. He felt guilty for Arion's death as well.

"It was my anger that drove him to the edge. He had given up on everything, especially himself. Despite all that, he worked to make this body for me every day. I was just a demon to him. He shouldn't have had any reason to do this, but he did.

"The kid was a victim, not the problem. We were both abandoned by Theresa, but I didn't see it like that. I was childish and selfish. I really needed to grow up and start acting my age." Cy ended with a forced laugh.

"How old are you?" Kaitlyn asked sheepishly, her curiosity getting the better of her.

Cy stared at her a moment, before looking away and answering, *"I turned eighteen a couple days ago, on the thirteenth."*

"October thirteenth? That's Arion's birthday, and the day..."

Kaitlyn didn't bother finishing.

Cy nodded at her. He stared at the sky and watched the clouds as they rolled by. Kaitlyn took the opportunity of his distraction to study him again. She had gotten used to the metal body easier than she thought possible, and could now distinguish his emotions. It surprised her how well she could read layers of metal, but she reminded herself that he was more than that. He was a living thing, just as wrought with emotions as she was.

And he was weak. Despite his demeanor, Kaitlyn knew exactly where to find the answers.

His body may not be normal, but his eyes are just as expressive as a human's.

Cy turned away from her and headed back into the house. *"The sun's beginning to set. We should leave within the hour. I suggest using it to rest up one last time. We aren't stopping until we reach Mount Draken."*

He slipped into the house silently. Kaitlyn followed after a moment. She wandered to the arm chair and plopped into it. She hadn't properly appreciated the plushness of the chair the night before, being too exhausted to do anything other than sleep. She sank into the thick cushions of the chair and it formed around her like an embrace. She closed her eyes and rested her cheek against the back of the chair. Though she found great comfort and relief, her mind was far from silent.

Rest? How does he expect me to rest after all of that?

She thought over all she had learned, unable to believe it. Despite her best efforts to deny it, the gnawing feeling in her stomach told her it was true. She had been so worried about Arion for years, but he had always disproved all of her theories.

Arion was good at hiding. He always had been. She knew that, but she never thought he would keep so much from her. She loved him, but if he was never the person she loved, then what did she feel?

She didn't fear him. That could never happen. No matter what he had done, or who he had been, he had never done anything to hurt or scare her. But she couldn't say for sure if she loved him or not anymore. She wouldn't know until he returned, and she learned more about who he really was.

In the silence, she found herself singing the lullaby hidden within Arion's music box. He would often hum it under his breath, and Kaitlyn doubted he realized he was doing it. She had memorized the tune easily. She now hoped it might be able to lull her to sleep.

Footsteps sounded behind her, and she halted her song abruptly. With a sigh, she said, "I know, I know. I'm supposed to be resting up, but I just can't—"

She was grabbed from behind fiercely, and a hand clamped over her mouth.

Chapter 6

Kaitlyn

Kaitlyn struggled under her abductor's grip, but she had been caught off guard and they were too strong for her. She opened her mouth to scream out, and the hand pressed against the corners of her mouth painfully. She couldn't scream, or bite, only choked. She lashed out with her legs, but they made no contact.

"Shh, Kaitlyn. Shh. You have to be quiet, or the monster might come back. Don't worry, we're going home." It was her father, Mayor Benjamin. He didn't loosen his grip. She stopped fighting in utter shock, her body going limp. A wave of fear washed over her, and a few tears spilled from her eyes.

Her father released her slowly when she relaxed. He walked around the chair to stand in front of her, pulling out a kerchief to clean his hand. She watched him closely, studying him.

He looked terrible. There were dark circles under his eyes,

and his once plump face had begun to hollow. Stubble had grown over his chin, and it showed his age. He ran his fingers through his hair, now completely gray. It had been going while she had been there, but there was no color left in it after only a few days. He shook tremendously with every move.

He was a short man that had always carried a lot of weight, but now his clothes hung off of his body. He shifted on his feet and his pants slid down his waist. He hurried to pull them up, but they refused to stay.

"Dad, what are you doing here?" Kaitlyn asked after a moment. Her fear cracked her voice, and she cleared her throat. She looked away from her father guiltily, staring at the hidden basement door. A faint light shined from the cracks, but it wasn't readily obvious.

Her father took a deep breath and said in a rush, "I was so worried about you. When the men came back with Kraven's body, I thought the worst. But they said you were still alive, and a monster was keeping you hostage! There was no one brave enough to go back for you. No matter what I told or promised them, they wouldn't go. But I knew you were smart. I *knew* you'd get away. I figured you'd come here for hiding, so I've been watching, but that damned monster found you. But I'm here. I'll get you home safe, sweetie."

He paused for a moment, and when Kaitlyn didn't speak, he continued, "They told me that the boy is dead. I know he was your friend, and for that, I'm sorry. But it really is for the best, Kaitlyn. You can come home, and everything will go back to normal."

Benjamin reached for her and grabbed her hand. He pulled her to her feet, her brain still trying to process everything. He pulled her toward the door, and she yanked her hand out of his grasp.

"No. I'm not going anywhere."

"Honey, I know you're afraid of that monster, but he can't get you in the village. It'll have to go through everyone else, and most importantly, me. I won't let it get you, I promise. But we have to leave now, before it comes back!"

"No," Kaitlyn said again, more forcefully. "Daddy, you don't understand. Please, just let me explain!"

"There's no explaining necessary. Whatever threat he's told you, he won't be able to follow up on it once we're back in the village!"

He lunged for her arm again, pleading in his eyes. She jumped out of his reach and spun away. He stepped in front of her, grabbing her shoulders. Tears pricked in her eyes, and she tried to hide them.

"Oh, honey. The boy is dead. There's no helping him now. You don't have to put yourself in danger any longer. This is nonsense, now let's leave!"

"You're wrong! He's not gone, not for good. He can't be!"

Her father stepped away from her, but still held her shoulders. He took a breath, and his face darkened. "This is ridiculous. Kaitlyn Rosemary, you are coming home now! That's an order, as your mayor and your father! That boy deserved what he got! I don't care how you felt about him. He was nothing more than a monster, hunted by everyone he ever met. He killed Kraven, your fiancé, and you're still going to stand beside his cold, decaying body?".

Kaitlyn's breath hitched, but her tears halted. She stared her father down as she whispered, "Arion didn't kill Kraven. *I* did. Kraven stabbed Arion in the heart, then came after me. I was the one that ran him through with the spear. How else did you think it could've happened?"

Her father's face paled, and he struggled to find the right

words. She watched his eyes dart around the room. He let go of her and stumbled back.

"There isn't a monster after me. *He's* my friend, Arion's friend. I'm choosing to stay with him, to help him bring Arion back. You aren't taking me anywhere, even if you are my father."

He stumbled back into the armchair, pressing a hand to his head.

"I knew this would happen. That damned boy ruined my precious daughter. I tried to protect you from him, to help you live a *normal* life. I knew better than to let you roam free, knew that that boy would change you. I did everything I could to protect you, mostly from yourself, and where has it gotten me? No daughter, no respect from the village, and no life left in me. It's too late. There's nothing I can do. No way to return things to normal." He rambled on and on, staring at the floor as he talked. Silent tears trailed down his cheeks and onto his lap.

Kaitlyn watched her father's breakdown with guilt. *I'm ruining everyone's lives,* she told herself. Tears leaked from her own eyes, and she scrubbed them away. Unable to stand looking at her father any longer, she turned her head. Her jaw dropped and her heart skipped a beat out of fear as she saw the basement door was ajar.

"*What's so great about normal, anyway? Eh, pops?*" Cyllorian asked. He crept from the shadows, murderous intent clear on his face.

"Cyllorian," Kaitlyn whispered, but he wouldn't look at her. His eyes were trained on her father.

He jumped up from the chair, his legs shaking. He backed against a wall. Sweat beaded his brow, and his eyes were wild.

"M...monster!" he stuttered. His head whirled from side to side as he searched for a way out. His gaze landed on Kaitlyn, desperation clear within them. He was begging for his life.

Cyllorian descended upon the man, his fingers curled, ready to strike. Kaitlyn grabbed his arm, and he stopped. He didn't turn to look at her, and his body moved like a machine underneath her. The magic within him hummed erratically, shooting out of the cracks to singe her hand. He wasn't breathing, and the whirring of his innards working drowned out all other sounds. She could no longer read him, and feared her father had been right about him.

"Don't, Cy. He's been through enough already," she said, tugging on Cy's arm. He took a step back, but he didn't relax.

"Kaitlyn," her father breathed. He looked between her and Cyllorian, understanding dawning on his face. "Is this really what you choose? We still have time to fix this. Please, Kaitlyn, just come home."

"She already told you no! Not like you even care about her, just about your precious village. You'd show more emotion if I went and burned the damn thing to the ground than you would if she died. And you call me the monster! You actually kept her locked up and forced her to marry someone who would've sooner killed her!"

Cy lunged for him, but Kaitlyn stepped in his way. He looked at her for the first time, and it was all she could do not to flinch at the hate in his eyes. She stared him down defiantly until he gave in, looking away from her and stepping back.

Kaitlyn let out her breath, unaware she'd even been holding it. She glanced over her shoulder at her father, who looked like he had nearly fainted. "I think you should leave now. We have to be going soon, and we need to finish getting ready."

He looked at her with a deep sorrow. He swallowed audibly before bolting out of the door. Benjamin spared one last glance for his lost daughter, and Kaitlyn felt a twinge of pain. *Was that a look of relief?*

"He didn't always act like that. He used to be the best dad

in the world, but he's always been protective. Always worried Arion would hurt me, even though Kraven was more likely to. But he didn't have a choice, you know. He had made a deal with Kraven's father before I was born. There wasn't any sign that my father would have an heir to the village, so he'd agreed that the title of mayor would go to the runner up's son when he resigned. He swore that Kraven would become mayor eventually, so when I came along, my father was threatened into arranging our marriage, even when we were babies. He told me this a few years ago, but there was nothing that could be done, not unless I left. Father wouldn't let me, and I had nowhere to go, so I stayed. I thought I could weasel my way out eventually, make Kraven hate me or something."

Cyllorian paused a moment, then walked away. He paced to the wall and punched it, and Kaitlyn flinched. It left a large hole in the wall, and he stared at it.

"He's right. You should've gone home. Kraven's not there to make it a living hell. There's not even a guarantee we can bring the kid back, and that might have been your only chance to go back on good terms. You could've had a normal life, like he said. You don't belong in this mess."

Kaitlyn gave him a small shove. "What's so great about normal, right?"

She smiled at him, and he smiled back. He whipped his head away after a minute, clenching his jaw.

She pretended to punch his arm, but it had no effect.

"I never fit in there, anyway. I'd rather be where the excitement is, like in my books." She gave him a shove again, but he didn't budge.

"You're not chickening out on me, are you?" she taunted. He whirled on her with a glare, and she stifled a laugh.

"Just who do you think you're talking to? I'm a demon, not some bird!"

"Good. Then let's get ready to go. We've got a mountain to get to, right?"

It took them just under an hour to finish getting around. They met the setting sun outside. Kaitlyn raised her hand to shield her eyes from the light, but the glare off of Cy's body was just as bad as the sun itself. She looked at the house instead, surprised by all it had been a part of. Arion's childhood, the death of his father. No matter what, Arion had always kept this house right here. Because the idea of it, of home, couldn't be destroyed. It remained still and strong through all of that, ready to take on what was next.

"This thing better show us the way, or else I don't know how we're getting anywhere," Cy muttered, catching Kaitlyn's attention. She whirled on him, jaw dropped in incredulity.

"What do you mean? You said you knew how to get there!" Kaitlyn shrieked.

Cy cringed at her high pitch, nearly dropping the crystal ball. *"I do, but this damn ball isn't giving us directions! It just shows the mountain over and over."*

"You said there was a map! Why don't we just use that one?"

"It's a bit outdated. The Kindling Woods might have grown since then, and I don't want to take any chances of going in there! If this stupid ball would just show us the way. . ."

He shook the ball for what seemed the millionth time. The white smoke gathered in the center, then parted to show the base of Mount Draken.

With a sigh, Kaitlyn said, "We should just get walking. If the path you saw is closed up by the woods, we'll figure it out from there. We can't waste all of our time here."

She started walking away, expecting Cy to follow her. When she didn't hear his footsteps, she turned, ready to call to him. He was clawing at his head with one hand, cutting open the metal as it healed itself over and over. The other was shaking the crystal ball so violently she thought it might break simply from the pressure.

"Cyllorian!" she yelled, desperately trying to break through his agitation. He looked at her and she met him glare for glare. She pointed to the hand that was still penetrating his scalp. He looked up, and pried it out. He dropped his hand to his side slowly, focusing all of his energy on shaking the ball.

Kaitlyn went to him, putting her hand lightly on his shoulder. He rubbed his forehead with the heel of his hand, letting the crystal ball settle. Kaitlyn watched the ball numbly, but still let out a sigh at the sight of Mount Draken.

"If this damn thing doesn't want to show us how *to get to where we have to go, then what do we still need it for anyway?"* With that, he threw the ball to the ground. It shattered into nothing more than dust, the white smoke that had been inside freed. It swelled around them and engulfed the two. It plunged into Kaitlyn's lungs, and she coughed. It was no use. The smoke was inescapable. It assaulted her throat over and over, and she slowly learned to breathe through it. It swam in front of her eyes, making it impossible to see even Cyllorian. If it wasn't for her hand clutching his shoulder, she wouldn't have thought he was still beside her.

"Kaitlyn, are you okay?" he said frantically. His hand clamped down over hers, and she jumped.

"I...I'm fine, just scared. What's going on? What was in that ball?" With every word, smoke was huffed out of her mouth. It swirled in front of her, getting lost in the storm that surrounded them. She spun her head, searching for any gap in the clouds.

Kaitlyn dropped her head, swatting the clouds out of her eyes. Below her feet, she watched the ground race at incredible speeds. Her stomach lurched, and she shot her head up to look away.

Cy's face appeared an inch from her own, blurred by the smoke. His eyes studied her, and she held back a cough. He backed away after a moment, but his hand still gripped hers.

"I knew I shouldn't have trusted Theresa with that damn ball! They've been nothing but tricks before! Why would now be any different?"

"Why would Theresa want to trick us? We're on the same side!" Kaitlyn cried. The smoke was getting thicker, plugging up her ears. There was a loud buzzing in her head, and her limbs felt hollow.

"She expected you to go home. She probably just wanted to put me back in my cell."

"Your cell? What do you...hey, what's that?" Kaitlyn swung her arm out in front of her through a small hole in the smoke. It swirled around her arm, dispersing. Letting go of Cy, she waved her arms madly. Cy followed her lead, swiping away large chunks of the smoke.

Kaitlyn fell forward into the clean air, coughing out large plumes of the white smoke. She cleared her lungs and pressed her forehead to the cold ground. Her skin was heated, and the ground was refreshing. Winter had already begun to creep up on them, freezing the ground beneath them.

Kaitlyn could hear Cy's voice, but it sounded far off through the haze in her head. She shook herself to clear what smoke had seeped into her head, and the weariness began retreating from her body.

When Cy's voice stopped, she worried. She wanted to get up to look for him, but her limbs wouldn't listen to her pleas for movement. Her hands pressed against the ground as she tried to force herself to move.

"Kaitlyn, you might want to see this," Cy muttered beside her.

His hand came down on her shoulder and around her arm, and he helped her to her feet. She leaned against him while her strength returned, and the breath rushed out of her yet again.

The house was nowhere to be seen, left far behind. Before them stood a great slope, nearly jutting straight into the air. They were completely surrounded by giant spikes of rocks hiding in the shadow of Mount Draken, trapping them.

"A teleporting spell was encased in the glass. That sneaky bitch. She could've just told me it was there. Would've made everything a hell of a lot easier on us. But no, she's gotta be difficult."

"This is Mount Draken?" Kaitlyn asked in awe. She tilted her head back as she took all of it in. the peaks were lost beyond the clouds long before the mountain ended. "How are we supposed to climb this?"

"One ledge at a time. How else?" Cy paced the small area around them. There was nothing to be seen, save for the rocks protruding from the ground. They were surrounded, with no way in or out of the circle. No way other than the mountain.

Cy investigated the spaces between the rocks, at the seams where they overlapped tightly. Miraculously, he found a crack big enough for them to fit through. Cy climbed over first, then held his hand out for Kaitlyn. She stepped between the spikes, grabbing Cy's hand to balance herself. She jumped down from the rocks and promptly released Cy's hand. She leaned against the boulder, glaring at the closest thing to a path up the mountain. There was a thin strip of the mountain less steep than the rest, littered with holes.

"There's our way up. The mountain's said to have hundreds of caves throughout, but the further up you go, the less you'll find. Plenty of places to rest along the way, I'm sure. We'll be climbing for at least a week, though, unfortunately."

Kaitlyn was holding onto the rock for dear life from just the thought of climbing up the mountain. She stared at it in horror, but glanced down when she felt Cy watching her. She forced her hands to release the rock and stepped away from it. Wrapping her arms around herself, she looked in the direction she suspected to be home.

Home? Do I have one now? Theresa obviously doesn't want me at the castle, and I'm not going back to the village. Where do I belong?

Her train of thought was broken as Cy wrapped a thick rope around her waist and secured it tightly. He handed her the remaining length of it, and took she it slowly.

"Tie it from your waist, under your legs. Make a harness, then I'll tie it to myself. You can go up first, so I can catch you if you fall. I'll throw an anchor up to catch us if anything goes wrong. I can use my claws to climb. I won't slip, and I'll be able to pull you back up. I won't let you fall off. I promise."

Kaitly's heart jumped in her chest. After their fight yesterday, she didn't expect any sort of kindness from him. As her cheeks heated, she busied herself with making the harness.

He's so unpredictable, it's making me nervous. Half of what he does is just what I'd expect a demon to be, but the other half . . . is just like Arion. The Arion that I knew, at least. What if this is what he was like when I wasn't around? I don't know what to think or feel around him. It's all so confusing.

She handed the rope to Cy, avoiding touching him just to be safe. She watched as he tied the rope so tightly around his waist that it was biting into the metal. She was shocked that his body didn't snap the rope. He waved his hand over it, strengthening the rope with Arion's magic. The magic raced along the rope to reach her, and her stomach did flips, but she wrote it off as her nervousness.

At the flash of Arion's magic, her memories of the night he died fluttered into her head. She thought of the tortured look on his face, the tears that streamed from enraged eyes. She had been most terrified when he lashed out violently with magic.

A wave of nausea twisted in her gut, emphasizing her fear. Cy turned away from her and changed back into the indifferent demon that didn't seem to care about anything.

I'm risking everything to save Arion, and I'm not even sure if he's more demon or friend.

CHAPTER 7

Kaitlyn

Kaitlyn pulled herself onto the small landing, rolling over to lay on her back, panting. The constant climbing had made her sweat, but the winter mountain air chilled her to her core. She wrapped her arms around herself, wishing for a jacket. She closed her eyes and forced herself not to shiver.

Something came down on top of her, covering her bare arms and neck. Her eyes shot open and looked down at the jacket draped over her. Cy was standing a short ways away, his metal arms now bare. He watched the sun start its descent through the gaps in the peaks.

"How high have we climbed?" Kaitlyn asked, breathless. The slope had only gotten steeper, and her limbs heavier as they climbed, making their progress slow. They were already on their fifth day of climbing, but she still couldn't see the peak.

"We should at least be halfway up. There are less and less caves

this high. It's best if we rest here in one of them. The mountain only gets tougher from here."

Kaitlyn groaned as she sat up, wrapping the jacket around her shoulders. She buried her jaw into the collar. As she warmed up, exhaustion settled over her. Her eyes started to droop, and she shook herself to stay awake.

Snow fell from the sky slowly, gradually picking up its pace. It wouldn't be too long before a blizzard swallowed them up. Kaitlyn watched the snow dancing in the wind around her, drawing her attention to the high walls surrounding the landing.

There were two caves set into the mountain across from them. Cy went to each, peering in, but he turned to her and shook his head. *"It's impossible to see anything without going inside. I heard there's a number of hot springs buried in the mountain, but I don't know if it's true. We just have to pick one and hope we get lucky."*

Kaitlyn nodded. Cy continued to look into each cave, creating a small flame in his hand. Standing, Kaitlyn stretched as she put her arms into the sleeves of the jacket. She walked up to Cy, but still kept her distance.

"This one looks as good as the other, right? Let's just get out of the cold."

"Right," Cy replied, though he didn't sound too sure. *"I'll go first, though. Just in case. Don't mean to brag, but I am a bit more durable than you are."*

He smiled at her smugly, and she opened her mouth to protest. Logic overtook her, and she pulled the collar around her neck and jaw. Glancing into the cave, she nodded.

Cy crept into the cave, the flame in his hand growing. Kaitlyn stuck right behind him, holding onto the back of his shirt. The flame did no good in the cave. It actually made it more difficult to see, casting mysterious shadows over the walls that only frightened Kaitlyn more than the darkness itself.

Cy shook the flame from his hand, plunging them into complete darkness. All that could be seen was a haze of white behind them as a storm raged outside, and the faint glow of Arion's magic within Cy's body. *"Good timing,"* Cy muttered.

They delved deeper into the cave at the slowest pace imaginable, but Kaitlyn felt as though they were moving miles away from the entrance with each step. She clung tightly to Cy's shirt, and he slowed his pace again.

"I don't think there's much of anything in here. Obviously not a hot spring, but at least it's better than staying outside. It should be a little warmer in here for you, even if it's not much. My metal will only make you colder though, so we should..."

Cy was cut off as he was ripped from Kaitlyn's grasp. In her attempt to hold on, she was pulled down to the ground. Her hand fell into a deep pool of boiling hot water, and she ripped it out with a scream. She stared into the water, coming to a decision. Throwing her pack to the side, she reached into the pool. She felt around in the water, biting back a scream, but there was nothing to be found. No edge of the pool, no bottom, and no Cyllorian.

"Cy! Cyllorian!"

She took a deep breath and put her head under the water. The heat was too intense, and she screamed. Ripping her head out, she coughed out what water had infiltrated her lungs. She shook her head and her wet hair fell from its restraint. It flailed wildly around her and stuck to her face. Holding her breath, she dove into the water again. She stretched herself as far into the pool as she could without falling in herself, grabbing at empty water.

She lost her breath and retreated. She rubbed at the numbness from her face, and gasped at the sight of her hand. Her sight had become clearer, more accustomed to the darkness, but it was still difficult to see accurately.

She carefully pushed her sleeve up to her elbow. It stuck to her skin, and came apart with difficulty. As her arm was revealed, she lost her breath. It had turned blue and purple, with patches of raw skin visible either from her jacket melting to skin or from the extreme heat.

"My arm. It's burnt, or bruised. I can't keep doing this, but I can't let Cy drown."

Her eyes pricked with tears as she plunged into the water yet again. She put both hands in, balancing on her legs as she searched as much of the pool as she could. The water was darker than the cave, though she didn't know there could even be something darker. She couldn't see a thing, and the intense heat was gnawing at her. It was impossible. She would never find him.

Don't give up now! she yelled at herself. She pushed herself, leaning more and more into the pool. By the time she realized she was slipping, it was too late.

She fell into the pool, and the heat tore at her victoriously. It stabbed into her like knives, and she screamed. Water tore through her throat and filled her lungs, burning her from the inside out. She flailed wildly, trying to find the surface, but it was too dark. She was being drug down to the bottom, drowning slowly. She begged for air, and opened her mouth without thinking. Water plunged into her chest, and she choked. Her body convulsed into itself. Her head was throbbing, blood pounding wildly beneath her scorched flesh. She floated motionless in the murky pond. She had given up fighting.

Her eyes searched for any escape, whether it be death or air. She didn't care, she just wanted to be free of the pain.

Just as her mind had decided on her fate, a vivid light

engulfed her, and she panicked. Reality had taken hold of her, reminding her what must be done. She pleaded with her limbs to move, to take her away from the light. *No, I can't die. Cy's still somewhere, and Arion's waiting for us to bring him back! I can't die now, not this soon!*

She tried to yell at the light to leave her alone, but it resulted in more torture. She closed her eyes, willing the light to just let her be. It grew brighter, blinding her even through her eyelids. She tried to whimper, but bubbles formed thick in her throat.

She was seized up and pulled toward the light, restrained by something powerful. She tried to fight against her binds, assuming them to be the clutches of a monster, but they held tight. She wasn't getting free. Her burnt skin was agitated as she was dragged through the water.

Cold air hit her face, causing more pain than the heat had. She collapsed onto the ground, unable to hold herself up. Whatever had saved her from the water kept her above the ground, gripping her waist enough to keep her steady, but not enough to hurt her further.

She screamed, spitting and coughing up water. Her throat was ripped to shreds as it poured out of her, gagging with the effort to drain her lungs. She struggled to stay conscious, and she would've slipped under if she wasn't being held up.

Something slapped against her back, and she yelped. It caused another coughing fit, and more water was forced out of her, mixed with her blood. The haze was slowly clearing from her vision, and all she could see was her arms. They were covered in burns and bruises, swollen and flaking in places. Seeing the damage only made the pain worse, and tears streamed down her cheeks. The salt in them stung her face, but the pain only made her cry harder.

The pressure holding her up vanished suddenly, and she

fell to the ground. She tried to pick herself up, but she was far too weak. It was all she could do to keep herself awake. Above anything else, her heart ached for home. She longed for the simple days of harmless stories and made up monsters. She missed her home, her father. She missed Arion, and the countless days she spent with him, even if they had been false.

Kaitlyn had made her choice, and cursed at herself for letting go of that so easily. This wasn't a fairy tale, and her problems wouldn't float away on the wind if she wished it. Only she could fix herself, and telling herself that she was strong would only last for so long. She had to act, and soon.

Small luminous crystals shone a faint light in the cramped cave, just barely bright enough to see by. "Were these here before we fell in? There wasn't any light before. Did I end up in a different cave?" she wondered aloud, her woozy gaze gliding over the scarce gems. A glint of light caught on the disturbed water behind her.

"Cy. . . Cyllorian. . ." she mumbled, reminding herself. She crawled with renewed strength to the water's edge as bubbles surfaced. "Cyllorian!" she yelled. It hurt her throat to exert herself, and she coughed uncontrollably. Blood fell to the ground, splattering on her face. She needed to go back in for him, but she couldn't bring herself to get near the water. The threat of drowning, of burning froze her in place.

"Damnit! What am I even good for?" she cursed at herself, slamming her hand down. It stung her arm as the force of the blow radiated through it, but she didn't care. She reached for the water again.

A hand shot out of the water, tainted the same colors as her own. It caught her shoulder with precision and shoved her away. A figure surfaced from the water afterwards, climbing gracefully from the depths with one hand, and dragging a familiar body with the other.

Cy's body lie motionless before her. The only sign of life was a spot of magic pulsing within his chest, and it was flickering with the effort to stay alight. She lunged for him, her own pain and weariness forgotten. The heated metal singed her skin, and she clenched her jaw against the new burns. Though he had been submerged far longer than she, he was already beginning to cool off as the magic of his body worked for his benefit. She shook his shoulders and head, pounded on his chest, but he wouldn't wake.

"It's been filled with water. The magic inside of it is drowning, even though the body cannot die," the person said, now perched beside her.

She glanced at them in the faint light coming from crystals hanging from the ceiling, shocked by their appearance. The voice had been neither male or female, and all Kaitlyn could see of the person in the darkness was a slight frame. Despite the human-like features, she didn't have a single idea as to what kind of creature her savior might be.

The person had a thin stomach and relatively flat chest, covered by a skin-tight top that left its middle exposed, as well as its shoulders and arms. Its shorts were made of the same slick material, hugging its thighs. The figure was not muscular, but it wasn't out of shape either. It was well defined in shape, but there were no gender-specific features that Kaitlyn could find at a glance. Even her savior's face was neutral, with big crystal marine eyes, thin lips, and high cheekbones. It had no hair, and small holes where the ears should be. Its hands were webbed between the fingers, and its feet were long and thin, like flippers, with skin that was naturally a dark blue hue.

Kaitlyn shook her head, forcing her attention back to Cy. Her hands fluttered over his body, racking her brain for anything she could do to save him. Her mind flashed back to when she had found him in his room, his chest plate open.

She shoved her fingers under his shoulder blade, the metal biting into her skin. She felt for the leather and opened the clasp. Sliding her hand along his side, she found the second clasp and opened it. She pried his chest open, and water spilled out of it.

"There's holes in his body. How did it stay inside?" she mused aloud. Though the water was draining, a bubble of water was left suspended around Arion's magic that had been keeping him alive. It was thick over a heart that nestled inside. The heart was golden, adorned with metal roses in full bloom. Through Arion's green light, a deep purple glow could be seen. The light in his chest pulsed lightly, smothered by the pressure of the water. It was growing faint, and a sense of urgency filled Kaitlyn.

"It's magic, right? It's not supposed to let anything in, which also means nothing can get out," her savior said, a bit disinterested. "Besides, these waters are magic in themselves, made to protect my people. It's only doing its job."

Kaitlyn ignored the person and tried to scoop the water out with her own hands. "Come on, Cy, you can't leave now! You can't die this early into the quest. We still have to get him back, remember? So you can kick his ass! You told me you have to get him back so you can kick his ass! You can't leave me alone, not now!" Tears were filling her eyes again, and she scrubbed them from her vision.

Nothing was working to help Cy. Kaitlyn sat back. Her hands were shaking in her lap, and her anger was replaced with sadness. In a last futile attempt, she touched the heart within his chest. She was both desperate and entranced. It was the most beautiful thing she had ever seen, and it held the last bit of Arion's magic that he had left with Cy.

The metal was hot against her skin, though the rest of his body had cooled. A sudden flash of green burst out from the heart, dissolving the water as it expanded from Cy's chest. The light returned to the heart, and shot out in thin wisps throughout all of Cy's body.

"I never did like swimming," Cy's pained voice said. Kaitlyn's gaze shot up to meet his purple eyes, and she lunged at him. Wrapping her arms around his neck, she hugged him. He held himself up with one hand, and put the other on her back slowly.

After a moment, Cy said, *"Um, Kaitlyn? Can I breathe now? I know I don't need to, but I want to."*

Kaitlyn released him, her cheeks burning. He laid down and breathed deeply, Kaitlyn watching the magic swell in his chest in silence. Her mysterious stranger was silent though all of it, sitting beside her with its legs tucked under it.

"He made it for you, you know," Cy whispered.

"What?" Kaitlyn asked, caught off guard.

"This heart. Arion made it for you, but never was brave enough to give it to you. When I found it in my chest I realized how bad he really got, in the end. If he gave it to me, then he actually did give up. But I know he would still want you to have it."

Cy reached into his chest and pushed against the sides of the heart. With a click, it split in half and flew open. From it, Cy pulled out a small silver ring that gleamed in the light of his magic. He held it up to Kaitlyn, and she took it gingerly. Running her finger over the smooth metal, she found engravings of stars all along the band. It fit perfectly on the ring finger of her right hand, as though it was made for her.

"He was always trying to talk himself into giving it to you, but you know how he was. I called him a coward, but I was right there in his head. I knew how hard it was for him. Maybe he knew that if he gave it to me that I could give it to you, eventually."

"Cy..." Kaitlyn started. "We can fix him, once we get him back. It might not be easy, but there's nothing left to hurt him.

We'll make sure he knows that, and he'll be safe. We can help him. I know we can."

She paused. Cy was staring at her with sad eyes. She tried to smile at him. His expression hardened and he turned away from her.

Kaitlyn dropped her head and tried again. The words came out thick and slow, sending her heart into a frenzy as she spoke. "Together, we can make it all right. If we can get him back together, then why can't we make him better, too? He won't be depressed or scared, because we'll all be together. It'll be the three of us, right? Like it was before, except for real this time."

Her words ended at his silence. She slumped at her helplessness.

"Kaitlyn, it's not going to be that easy. Nothing is. Not getting him back from the dead, and not getting him back to... normal, whatever that might be for him. It's not his emotions that did this to him." Cy said the words gently, though his bitterness cut through his soft tone.

"What do you mean? What did it then? What changed him?"

The stranger cut him off before he could answer. Kaitlyn felt a twinge of anger towards him, but it was quickly chased away by guilt. She made her resolve to continue their conversation in private.

"So, you're a demon then. And you are...?" it broke off, looking at Kaitlyn.

"I'm a human. Kaitlyn," she answered sheepishly. She felt awkward under its scrutinizing gaze.

"A human? Alright, then, if you say so."

"Just what is that supposed to..."

"What are you doing wandering around the pools? Don't you know how dangerous it is for outsiders?"

"We were just trying to get out of the storm, calm down. We don't care about you, we just want to get to the Drakens," Cy mumbled. He pushed himself into a sitting position and closed up his chest. He glared at the stranger as he did, noticing how it studied him. Though Kaitlyn was struggling to make out the features of the stranger in the minimal light, neither it nor Cy seemed to be having any problems.

"Drakens. What do you want to see them for?" For the first time, the stranger's tone was not indifferent. It held an immense pain, and even a bit of betrayal. Its façade was slipping away, and Cy knew that as well.

Cy opened his mouth, and Kaitlyn feared how he would answer, so she spoke before he could.

"We're looking for ways to bring someone back from the dead, and our. . .*friend* said that the Drakens might be able to help. We have to go meet with them and find someone who will come back with us."

"Back from the dead? I don't know much about that, but if you want healing, then you should go to the Droll. Drakens are nothing short of barbarians. They only care about fighting."

"What are Droll?"

"Me. I'm a Droll. We're water based creatures, and we live under the mountain. We do well in heat, so this mountain is perfect for us. Or it would be, if we didn't have to deal with those damn Drakens." The Droll cast his eyes to the ceiling of the cave, a sneer on his face.

"So a Droll could bring the dead back to life? Could you?" Kaitlyn asked enthusiastically, grabbing the Droll's arm.

The Droll looked at her curiously for a long moment, much longer than Kaitlyn felt comfortable, its gaze boring into her in the dim lighting. She shifted under their stare and pulled away, but its eyes never left her.

"I don't know," it said finally. "If it is possible, the Court will know. You would have to bring your questions to them."

"Can you take us there, or is this conversation pointless?" Cy asked bitterly.

The Droll smiled mischievously. "I could. But you would have to swim, and you can't. You'll simply drown, and after all the trouble I went to get you out. To be completely honest, I don't really know why I *did* save you in the first place. Must be habit, I guess." The Droll squirmed noisily. It was already replacing its farce, but it was clear there was something worthy of being hidden now.

"Is there any way to get him there? Anything you can do? Please. . .um, we still don't know your name. . ."

Kaitlyn trailed off. She inspected the Droll's body again as her mind became clearer, trying again to find any hint at its identity. *Are they a he, or a she? I can't tell, and I don't want to be rude.*

The Droll gave Kaitlyn a crooked smile, and patted its hand on its chest. "I'm Gil."

"Gil? Really? Quite original, if I must say," Cy said bitterly, obviously examining the Droll as well.

So much for the name telling me. Maybe Cy will be able to figure it out, Kaitlyn thought. She shook her head, reminding herself that it wasn't her business, and even if it was, it didn't really matter. From the way Gil was taunting Cy, and the strength with which it had saved them both, Kaitlyn took a guess that the Droll was male, but would wait to address him as such aloud until she knew for sure.

"So can you help us, Gil? Please?" Kaitlyn clapped her hands together and widened her eyes as she stared at the Droll.

Gil rubbed the back of its head, looking away from her. "If I bring in outsiders, it could turn out really bad. But the Court has been saying something about getting more involved in the world, so maybe this could be the first step. At any rate, they could just as easily kill you once there, I doubt the two of you have much power between you."

Gil glanced at Cy and winked at him. Cy sat up quickly, lunging for the Droll, but he missed. Cy was still recovering from his near death encounter, and he doubled over in the pain from exerting himself.

"There is the matter of getting the demon down there, though. You'd have no problem swimming through the tunnels, Kaitlyn, with a little help and encouragement. That I'm sure, but the other one. I doubt it will be easy to get it to Lorile. If I have to carry it, it could take a while, even if it works at all. Oh, that's right!" The Droll reached behind him, into a small pouch tied around his waist. From it, Gil retrieved a small, white pearl, no bigger than his fingertip.

"You've got a compartment inside, right? Just put this there, and the water won't harm you. It'll still get inside, but it won't drown you. Here, Kaitlyn, I'll give you one as well, though I doubt you need it. As long as you have it, you'll survive Lorile."

Kaitlyn held her hand out, and Gil dropped another pearl into her palm. It was surprisingly cool to the touch, and she could feel the power within it. It hummed a low tone that resonated within her, calming her very core. She rolled it around her palm, and it left a glowing trail behind it along her skin. It faded quickly, dissolved into her skin to leave her feeling exhilarated.

She had only ever been a witness to magic, never a wielder, and a great deal of possibilities flooded into her mind. Her imagination got away from her at the thought of having her own magic, of being on a level equal with Arion and Cy. Her reveries were making her drunk with fantasies, and she clenched her fist around the pearl to ground herself back to reality. Magic was clearly just as much of a burden as it was a blessing, something she had never considered before it was her own fate that was entangled in the dealings of the world unknown to her.

She pulled her ribbon from her hair and wrapped it around the pearl multiple times to ensure it was completely encased. She then tied the loose ends around a loop on her pants and stuffed the makeshift pouch into her pocket.

"That's all fine and dandy, but what about our supplies? Mine are already soaked and ruined, but how are we to keep the rest dry if we take them with us?"

"Easy. You don't have to worry about them because they've already been left behind. The currents in the underground rivers can be pretty fierce. When I found you, I brought you to the nearest exit, but this one doesn't show any signs of you having been here before. It doesn't matter, though. As long as you're accepted in Lorile, everything will be provided for you. You can restock before leaving again, and take special water-proof packs with you. Either that, or sacrifice the rest of your stuff just so you don't have to leave it behind. Take your pick, but make it fast. The wind outside is starting to dry me out, and I need to get back."

"Cy, we have to go. We have no idea how many people Theresa was able to gather. If they can help us, we have to take the chance."

"How are we supposed to know if we can trust this guy?" Cy said slowly, watching Gil. Kaitlyn caught the question in his voice, and dared a glance at Gil as well. The Droll's eyes narrowed a miniscule amount in response, but showed no other signs that it had even been paying attention. Disappointed, Kaitlyn focused on convincing Cy.

"What if no one else can do it? What if they have a secret,

and this is our only chance? If we try to come back, we'll just drown. Gil won't be here to save us again."

"Did you just gloss over the part where he said they could kill us? I'm pretty sure I heard you say something about it being too soon to die, right? How do we know we'll make it back out of this?"

"We don't know we'll make it past any of the others we have to go to, either. Did Theresa ever tell you it would be as simple as saying, 'Hi, we're here to pick up someone that can resurrect a Mage. Any takers?' Someone is bound to be suspicious of us. We have to go through such hardships just to get to them before we even know if they want to help. That doesn't seem like a sign of good faith to me. Did you think of that?"

Cy turned away from her, pouting. His eyes darted back and forth, and the resolve fell from his face. *"Fine. But if you try anything against us, buddy, I'll kill you."*

"Yeah, yeah, sure. You might be a demon, and I don't trust you for that, I guess, but you aren't all that scary. Especially after I just saved your ass."

Gil stood and returned to the edge of the pool. Kaitlyn and Cy followed suit, Cy hurriedly locking the pearl away inside of his heart. They stepped up beside Gil, and the Droll grabbed onto their arms. Kaitlyn tensed at his grasp, her terror creeping up on her again.

If I go back in there, I'll die. I'll drown, or burn to death. Doesn't he know that? Can't he tell I can't go back in? I can't swim. A pearl can't make me able to swim just like that. I'm going to die. I'm dead, I'm dead! She thought in a panic. Her breathing was labored and thin, her head felt lighter than air. She had never known she was afraid of the water, and now it was too late to make a difference. There was nothing else to do but to trust Gil.

"No going back now," Gil whispered, and he shoved Cy and Kaitlyn into the burning pools of Lorile.

CHAPTER 8

Cyllorian

Cyllorian fought to keep his balance as Gil shoved him and Kaitlyn into the pool. He whirled to slash at the Droll, but he was already sinking into the water. He reached out and caught Kaitlyn's arm. With the help of his magic, he lit up the depths of the pool, and saw that Kaitlyn was struggling.

She held onto her neck, her head swinging back and forth wildly. Her face was twisted up in terror, though she was holding her breath fine. She flinched away when Cy grabbed her, then relaxed momentarily. But Cy was dragging her to the bottom because of his metal, and he couldn't risk Kaitlyn's life on Gil's word. He released her and continued to sink, and she reached out to him. He had to let himself fall to the bottom alone, or Kaitlyn would drown.

Gil dove into the water between them and snatched Cy's arm. With strain clear on the Droll's face, it kept Cy from sinking, and Cy didn't resist. They swam back up to meet Kaitlyn, who was headed to the surface.

Gil grabbed her leg with its free hand, and yanked her back down to them. She clutched at her throat, saying she was out of air. Gil ignored her, and simply motioned for her to breath. Cy opened his mouth to scream at the Droll, but he couldn't make a sound underwater.

Kaitlyn shook her head, looking back up to the surface. "The pearl. You have the pearl, you'll be fine. I know you're scared, but you won't die here." Gil's voice came through clearly, though a bit muddled in the water.

Kaitlyn pulled back in shock, her lips parted. "Droll have adapted to being most efficient in the water, so of course we would need to communicate as well. You, though, will not be able to speak."

Kaitlyn shut her mouth, then closed her eyes. She parted her lips to breathe slowly, but instantly began coughing. Gil reached out to her, wrapping its hand around her neck. Cy pulled on its arm, but he was swatted away. The Droll continued caressing Kaitlyn's neck while she ran short on air, until her expression turned to surprise and her chest expanded and deflated as she breathed.

Gil let go of her, and waited. She ran her own fingers over her neck, tracing an outline of gills. They opened and closed with each breath, her eyes wide with realization.

She turned to Gil, looking for an answer, but the Droll merely smiled at her. Without a word, Gil was swimming toward a large opening near the bottom of the pool, pulling Cy along.

Cy went to grab Kaitlyn's hand, fearing she would be left behind, but she was gone. He scanned the waters behind them frantically, but there was no sign of her. Gil tugged on his arm, urging him to help swim for himself. Cy whirled to yell at the Droll, to attack, but was stunned.

Kaitlyn was swimming circles around them, a smile clear on her face. She waved to Cy as she passed in front of them, and bubbles escaped her mouth as she laughed. Her hands had gained webbing between her fingers, and she moved with a natural grace through the water. Cy turned to Gil, who had an annoyed expression, though still smug.

Cy resolved to interrogate the Droll as soon as they came to land, and did his best to swim.

They swam through a series of winding tunnels that eventually connected to one large tunnel where the current was stronger. Kaitlyn lost track of where she was going, still swimming ahead of Gil and Cy, and was swept up into the current.

Gil let go of Cy and went ahead to help her as she spun through the water uncontrollably. Cy sunk to the floor of the tunnel and walked through the heavy water as fast as he could. Even still he could only watch as she was thrown around by the vicious current, limp as a doll.

Gil caught her and steadied her in the water. She shook in the Droll's grip, staring at Cy. He could tell by the look in her eyes that her fear of the water had returned. Gil returned her to Cy's side, and she clutched onto his arm.

Cy looked at Kaitlyn, but she didn't seem to be harmed. She was shaken up and her clothes disheveled. The ribbon that she had tied the pearl into was hanging out of her pocket, but still attached to her pants. Cy pointed it out to her and she hurriedly stuffed it back into place.

"From here, we'll go as one unit. It will be safer," Gil said, bubbles wriggling from its mouth.

Kaitlyn and Cy nodded. Cy grabbed the Droll's hand, and Kaitlyn held onto Cy's arm as they swam. The strong current in the tunnel helped them a great deal, leading them to their destination without much work from the three.

The tunnel ended in a shallow pool illuminated from above. The three surfaced, Kaitlyn gasping for breath, though she had been able to breathe underwater. She closed her eyes in relief, still clinging to Cy.

Gil pulled himself from the two of them, wrenching their attention to the world they had entered. They were in a large cave system, the ceiling domed and copious amounts of the glowing crystals hanging from above. They lit the entire room perfectly, like Lorile's own sun, and their water world gleamed beautifully.

The buildings were placed in the center of the room, and walkways shot out to the outer walls of the cave. The cave beneath was at least as large as the mountain itself, as they couldn't see the other end of it. Most of it was flooded, with grand buildings resting half in and half out of the water, nearly reaching to the ceiling. Every building came to a point at the top, clearly made from hollowed out stalagmites. Glowing vines sprouted from the center of the ceiling and sprung out to crawl down the walls. They covered the tops of the buildings as well, lighting the whole place comfortably, though it was dim.

The structures were all crafted from dark stone and opaque crystals that reflected the simple light they had for themselves. It bounced between the buildings, and the center of the room was alight brilliantly. Though they were all jagged in shape, Cy felt no threat from this peaceful world hidden under the mountain. It was calming, the sounds of the water lapping against the natural city. It looked completely untouched by the outside world, holding a magic that was unique in its simplicity.

Droll filled the space around them, populating the vast

colony under the mountain. They could all be seen swimming gracefully within the clear waters, mingling with each other atop the rough walkways. The scales that covered them complimented the shining crystals, almost absorbing the light to make themselves luminous. They were all dressed similar to Gil, wearing skin tight leather created specifically for their life underwater. Eyes like rare gemstones cast them suspicious glances, but they quickly avoided them as they spotted Gil.

"This is beautiful," Kaitlyn whispered, her eyes alight in the majesty of it all. Cy glanced at her from the corner of his eye, enjoying the wonder in her eyes.

"Yes, but if you're done gawking, I have to take you to the Court now. This way," Gil said from a walkway. The two of them waded through the shallow waters and climbed onto the solid land. He walked forward a few steps, then halted abruptly and turned to them.

"Pearls," he chirped, holding his hand out. Cy glanced around them, then quickly retrieved the pearl he had locked away in his heart. Kaitlyn pulled the wad of soaked ribbon stuffed into her pocket. It had loosened when she was thrown about in the current, but she still found it difficult to untie.

The pearl was gone. Her knots had appeared to have held during her struggle underwater. "I don't have it," she whispered in shock.

"You don't?" Gil asked, though its voice lacked surprise.

Kaitlyn shook her head slowly. She shoved her fingers back into her pocket and stretched them into every corner. It was nowhere to be found. Her breathing turned shallow. Cy could see her mind turning, working through the information.

"If I lost it in the water, how was I able to keep breathing? Her hand shot up to her neck, but the gills were already gone. Her fingers traced faint creases in her skin where they had been, scars that proved it had all been real.

She looked between Cy and Gil, looking for answers. They shared a glance, a hint of a smile on Gil's face. His eyes never leaving the Droll, Cy said, *"We were lucky the after effect lasted long enough."*

Kaitlyn nodded her head. She looked worried regardless of her response. Cy had to be careful of this Droll. Gil played dumb and careless, but he was far more dangerous than Cy had originally given him credit for.

"Will we get in trouble for losing one? Will they know?" she asked nervously.

"No," Gil replied calmly. "They're everywhere on the floor in the waters. We don't keep a record of them. They'll just go get more if we need it."

With that, Gil tucked the single pearl into his pack, and spun on his heels.

Gil led them through the great city of Lorile at a fast pace, giving them no time to stop and process anything. They ended at a small building that looked like a human cathedral Kaitlyn had seen depicted in her books from the past with its grandiose nature, but it seemed so much more than that. It had a dome roof with three large spikes jutting toward the ceiling. The vines hung low and wrapped around the points as though they were holding the building up. The walls were made of a light blue crystal, though it couldn't be seen through.

"You two wait here, and don't move a muscle. I'll go talk to the council," Gil said, pointing at the ground.

"We should go with you, so we can explain our story," Kaitlyn offered.

"No, you stay here. I have to go alone."

"And why is that? So you can plot how to kill us?"

"No, because it's underwater! If they find out that I willingly gave you the pearls in the first place, let alone if I give them back so you can get in here, they'll have my head. I'll tell them what I know, and if they decide they want to know more, they'll send someone back with me to find out the details. If it goes that bad, I can always say you snuck in, and save my own skin. Just don't. Go. Anywhere. I mean it."

With that, Gil crept into the Court building, closing the door quietly.

"Do we just wait?" Kaitlyn asked sheepishly.

"That sounds terrible. I say we investigate this place. I'm sure it's got its share of juicy secrets." Cy's smile was full of mischief, and he glanced over his surroundings hungrily.

"We should stay here. If we're caught anywhere else, we'll probably get in trouble. Gil already said they might want to kill us, so let's not give them a reason to," Kaitlyn pleaded.

Cy rolled his eyes with a groan, and leaned back against the building. *"Fine,"* he mumbled, irritated. He tapped a claw against the glass to the beat of his old lullaby, scanning over Lorile.

It was amazing that this whole place was underneath a mountain. It made him wonder what other secrets could easily be hidden in this world. What else might they find on their journey?

The Droll traversing the paths and waters of Lorile stared at Cyllorian with suspicion, and he met each with a sneer. He unsheathed all of his talons for show, letting them glint in the dim lighting. A small group of younger Droll passed them by, walking as far away from him as they could. His smile was devilish with satisfaction.

"Cyllorian, behave," Kaitlyn scolded him. She batted at his hand, and he retracted his claws for her own safety. He stared at the ground, ignoring the whispers around him as best as he could.

From the corner of his eye, he watched Kaitlyn sit on the ground beside him and close her eyes. Her mouth moved slowly, but there was no sound. She smiled often during her mumbling, growing careless. She began to speak the words aloud, and Cy easily recognized them as her favorite book from home.

"You really do have that thing memorized, don't you?" he asked.

Her head shot up, her cheeks bright red with embarrassment. She stared at him, momentarily stunned. He shot her a cocky smile, and she instantly turned away from him.

"I'm nervous. Everything's so different here, so much has happened so fast. It was the first thing I could think of from... before. Something to calm my nerves. Anything else would make me remember what's going on, when I don't want to," she confessed. Guilt was clearly eating at her, and she picked at the hems of her shirt.

"I thought you wanted to have your own adventure?" The bitterness came through his voice, and he cringed. He cursed at himself and turned away.

"I did, but I never thought it would be like this. Everything was always so easy for the people in my books. It feels like I can't do anything, like I don't belong here. I wasn't made for exploring, just for listening. . ." she trailed off, staring into space. She pulled her knees up to her chest and wrapped her arms around herself, reciting the book faster, but it was no longer calming her.

Cy clenched his fists and pushed away from the building. Ignoring Kaitlyn's worried look, he paced around the building. Once out of her sight, he unsheathed his talons again, and dug them into his biceps. Pain shot throughout his arm, and he watched the magic within him turn red at the initial wound, then back to green. He pulled his talons from his arms slowly, and watched as the metal reformed into its proper place. He continued around the back of the Court building, digging his claws into the metal again, deeper this time.

He rounded the building to the front, his talons still out. Gil was standing beside Kaitlyn, and the Droll's eyes instantly found Cy's. They flicked to his arms, to the slight holes still healing, and then to his talons. Cy sheathed them with a flick of the wrists, staring down the Droll.

"What's the verdict?" he asked coarsely, stepping up to the Droll.

Gil opened his mouth, but another Droll stepped out from the building, this one clearly male, and an authority figure as well. Instead of the slick wetsuits every other Droll was wearing, he wore a thin black shirt and long slacks. Tied around his neck with thin strings was an emblem of a horse with fins sprouting from the back of its head. With a calm, clipped voice, he answered Cy's question. "The Court has decided to evaluate your behavior before coming to a decision. You will be kept company by a member of the Court at all times, and after a week, we should have our answer."

"So do we have to stay with tough guy here, or are you gonna do the honors?" Cy jutted his thumb toward Gil, who fumed at the remark.

The second Droll raised his hand, and Gil calmed obediently. "The task will be assigned to a few different members, so that we can get varying opinions on the matter, though we will not restrict who you can and cannot talk to. So long as the people of Lorile wish to speak to you, you may speak to them. But you may not ask for information that you do not need. We will intercede the first time you overstep your boundaries, but if you insist on crossing them, that will be your own mistake."

"Right. Makes perfect sense. So, what's first, Mr. Boss?"

"My name is Kolry, if you would be so kind, *Mr. Demon,*" Kolry hissed. Gil busted into laughter, covering its mouth to avoid being rude. It seemed now that the role of responsibility had been handed over to Kolry, Gil was nothing more than an immature teenager.

"So this guy ain't the only one with a sharp tongue, huh?"

Kaitlyn stepped between Cy and Kolry, raising her hands. "How about we just start over, okay? We want you to trust us, but we have to trust you, too, just a little. I'm Kaitlyn, and I'm a human, so I don't really know what this is all about. All I know is that we need your help, and my friend *promises* to be on his best behavior. Right, Cyllorian?" Kaitlyn glared at him, daring him to oppose her. Her gaze was firm as she held his, and he sighed.

"Yep. Cross my heart, and hope to get sucked into a tiny crystal ball for all eternity," Cy said sarcastically, raising his hand as he drew an X on his chest. Kolry raised an eye at him, disbelief clear on his face. *"I'm gonna guess you've never had that happen to you, have you? Believe me, it's worse than death."*

"Fair enough. Your actions will speak for your intentions soon enough either way. Let's just begin with a tour, shall we? I'll tell you where you may and may not go."

"Sounds delightful. I was worried I'd have to go this whole time without getting to know that information."

"Cyllorian," Kaitlyn hissed, jabbing him with her elbow. He bent away from her, worried she would hurt herself on his resilient metal. She seemed to take it as a sign that she had made her point, and raised her chin.

Gil chuckled, then clapped Kolry on the shoulder. "Good luck with this one, Kolry. You're gonna need it." Gil jogged off without another word.

Kolry sighed and motioned for Kaitlyn and Cy to follow him. "I'll make it clear now that I won't stand for any disrespect from you two during your visit with us. You are nothing but guests here, and I expect you to be on your best behavior.

Rules are what keep us in order, and I won't stand for chaos. No matter what that Gil might tell you is acceptable, I assure you, it. Is. Not. Understand?"

Kolry glanced back at them. Kaitlyn nodded her head dutifully, an angelic smile on her face. Cy studied his talons in a show of disinterest. *"Whatever you say, Mr. Boss,"* Cy said lightly.

He looked up and caught the glare from Kolry, and feigned an offended expression. *"Don't you trust me? I'm just a sweet, innocent demon."* Cy smiled wide, displaying his pointed teeth.

Kolry grunted, but turned to start the tour. Cy grinned mischievously at Kaitlyn, but she shot a glare at him as well. Defeated, Cy fell into step beside her, silent.

Despite his resentment at the Droll, Cy found their architecture and design amazing. Buildings like this weren't possible on the surface, most of them being made from stalagmites jutted up from under the water. A few even hung from the ceiling, and Cy was impressed with how well the Droll could climb.

"And this is where you'll be staying, though it is not the end of the tour. Guards will be stationed outside every exit of the building, though we have decided to respect your privacy inside of it. You'll be greeted every morning by your attendee for the day and..."

Cy groaned as Kolry droned on and on, describing their life in observation in great detail. Kaitlyn was engrossed in Kolry's lecture, though, and it peaked interest in Cy.

"Though we can breathe and survive for extended periods of time underwater, it is not indefinite. Hence why most buildings have an above and below to them. We are most comfortable in the water, so the intense humidity found under this blistering mountain provides the perfect shelter for us. Quite hospitable, though I'll admit that I had not seen our previous location." Kolry waved his hands in the air as though he were depicting the most interesting story. For the life of him, Cy couldn't make sense of the story, but the Droll was having a blast.

"We Droll used to be more agreeable with other races in the world, but the war we fought and inevitably lost left a deep wound in our culture and our hearts, though there isn't a Droll left alive that was witness to the tragedies. Our world has not been the same for quite a while now."

Kolry paused in his speech as they passed a statue of a small army, equipped with intricate crossbows and spears taller than the soldiers. He tilted his head toward it, and Kaitlyn copied the move. A silver plaque in the ground glistened, but Cy couldn't read the names etched into it. Kolry didn't pick up his monologue again until they were yards away from the statue.

"In this era, we entertain ourselves with mundane rituals that keep us from the outside world. Many Droll are skilled in hunting, and prey that is not needed is shipped to other parts of the world, as well as our unique clothing materials, jewelry, crystal statues, and even weapons. Travelers from nomad tribes loyal to us come often to pick up the goods and sell them throughout Lontorra, and then bring equivalent wares and currency back to us. It may not be an exciting lifestyle that we live, nor an extravagant one, but it is safe and peaceful. Something the Droll before us desperately gave their lives for."

"What about the Draken? Don't they live on the mountain as well?" Kaitlyn asked, her voice full of wonder. Her worry and hopelessness had been driven away by her curiosity.

Kolry stopped his walking. His voice became subtly distraught, but spoke with the indignation of an instructor, "From the day Droll arrived at this mountain seeking refuge, the Draken have been kind and welcoming. It was difficult at first for us to trust them, and for some that hate still courses through their veins. We owe them much, and it is a great disappointment that we are not on better terms with them currently. The Drakens would like to speak and renegotiate our peace treaty, but the court won't have it. We may not be strong, but the council are convinced the Draken haven't the numbers to force us out, so they do not fear retaliation."

Kolry shook himself, and his tone turned to one of exhilaration. He abandoned talk of their neighbors in favor of their dietary habits. Cy rolled his eyes and groaned, staring mindlessly at the buildings they passed.

He wanted to explore, to run throughout and cause some innocent mayhem. He leaned to the side to whisper to Kaitlyn, but when he glanced over, she was gone.

"Hey, Mr. Boss?"

"What did I tell you about interrupting me? This is important information that you must commit to memory. And if I hear you call me that one more time, Cyllorian, I swear I'll..."

"Yeah, yeah, that's all real interesting, Mr. Boss. But Kaitlyn's not here, and she's the one that's going to care about this, not me."

Kolry whirled around, his usual calm expression twisted in outrage. "Gone? How can the young lady just be gone?"

Cy shrugged.

Kolry huffed at him, then spun in circles looking for Kaitlyn. "She must've taken a wrong turn, or was distracted by something that we passed. She can't be too far off. Surely we'll find her."

Cy leaned against the closest building, shoving his hands into his pockets. He watched Kolry scramble about in his search, a smug grin plastered to his face. *"And you thought I was the one you had to worry about. How's that discrimination working for you, now, Mr. Boss?"*

Kolry glared at Cy, but didn't say a word. He called out her name, gaining himself a few odd glances from Droll that walked by. Kolry questioned each as they passed, but none could help, until he found one that he clung to like a life line. Cy tilted his head, trying to get a glimpse of the person, and groaned.

Kolry had Gil by the arm, dragging the young Droll back towards Cy. Kolry nearly threw Gil at the demon, and he side-stepped out of the way. Gil stumbled into the building, glaring at Cy.

"Looks like you've lost something there, Kolry. Where'd she go?"

"That's what I'm trying to figure out! Gil, you stay with Cyllorian while I retrace the tour to find her. You search everywhere else. She could have wandered off, or gotten lost. Hurry, they cannot go unsupervised!" Kolry ran off back the way they came without giving Gil another option. Gil moved to chase after Kolry, but stopped.

"*Bye bye, Mr. Boss!*" Cy called after Kolry, waving his hand in a large arc over his head. He heard the Droll yell something unintelligible back, and laughed.

Cy cringed away as Gil turned to him. Gil's eyes were narrow and filled with pure suspicion. "You don't really seem to care," Gil said, watching Cy closely.

Cy's face twitched, wanting nothing more than to punch Gil square in the face. He clenched his fist, then thought of Kaitlyn.

"*Who said I didn't?*" he asked simply. Gil's eyes narrowed further, and Cy wasn't sure if the Droll could even still see him.

"Do you wanna know where she is?"

Cy's eyes widened and he jumped from the wall. Grabbing Gil's arm automatically, he demanded, "*You know where she is?*"

Gil smiled slowly and patted Cy on the shoulder. With two

fingers, Gil pried Cy's metal hand away and dropped it. Embarrassed, Cy stepped back.

"If you know, we better go get her. Who knows how much trouble she'll be in if Mr. Boss finds her first. Which way?"

Gil's smile was smug, and it made Cy's insides twist up. *What the hell is this guy's angle?*

The Droll turned away from Cy, towards the outskirts of Lorile. "Some of the others around here were talking about a weird looking blonde girl walking around by herself. I guess she found our greatest secret, from what I heard."

Greatest secret? Shit, now we're really in trouble.

Gil walked with confidence, head high and shoulders back. Cy noticed that Gil got a few looks from other young Droll they passed. Upon closer inspection, Cy found that he couldn't tell any of their genders.

"All right, I give. What are you? Guy, girl, mythical flying unicorn? I don't care if it's rude or whatever, but Kaitlyn's not here to yell at me. So there, I asked."

"Yes, you asked. Doesn't mean I have to answer. And I'm pretty sure a flying unicorn is just called a Pegasus," Gil retorted.

"Oh, come on, just answer me! I know it pisses you off when I call you guy or anything, and I'm sure you've figured out I'm just doing it to get under your skin! I'll make you a deal. You tell me what you are, or what you want to be, and I'll follow it, okay? It's seriously too confusing to figure out, and I've got enough on my plate as is."

"Are you saying you'll be nice to me?"

"Yeah, whatever. Don't get sappy on me, though. I don't do sappy. It's just a lot of work being this bitter, you know."

Gil glanced back at him. Cy avoided his gaze. He didn't even know why it bothered him so much, but not knowing was just so *annoying*. Gil stopped walking and burst into laughter.

"Man, you are one weird demon, I'll give you that. Sure, deal. I'll tell you, and you be nice. I'm neither."

"Wait, you're what?!"

"Neither. I'm not male, and I'm not female."

"I'm sorry, how old are you? Have your mommy and daddy not had the talk with you yet? You can't be neither."

"Droll can. Until we reach a certain age, we're genderless. We have until we're seventeen to find ourselves. At that time, we get a gender, can change our names if we want, and find a mate. I'm only sixteen, but honestly, I'm leaning more towards male. I've definitely got the body to impress the ladies. So, you can call me a guy until I change my mind."

"Uh, huh. And how does all that work? I mean, in real life."

"There are a lot of sea creatures that change their gender over the course of their lives. We work like that, sort of. Instead of changing gender halfway through, we don't have one until maturity."

"Word of advice, puberty is gonna suck if it all happens at once. And if it's anything like humans, let me tell you, it gets messy."

Gil shifted away from Cy with a disgusted look. "How would you know that?"

"I had front row seats. You know the kid we're trying to bring back? I was in his head before I had this body, since he was thirteen. So many emotions and tantrums, but at least he didn't have to worry about acne too much. Boy, that kid was a handful."

Cy hung his head and let his arms go limp as he followed Gil.

At the long silence, Gil added quietly. "You can drop the tough guy act with me. I don't give a damn that you're a demon. I've never been outside the walls of the caves, so I don't really know what a demon is supposed to be. All I can tell is that you're lashing out."

"What the hell would make you think that? You don't know me.

I could be an ass just because I want to, and you wouldn't know the difference,"

"You're not like this around Kaitlyn, which means she doesn't like it and you don't want to upset her. And your friend that you're trying to get back? She refuses to look at me when he's mentioned, but you don't. But what I bet you don't notice is that your magic glows brighter when you talk about him, and I'm guessing that's the equivalent of your pulse racing. That's his magic, isn't it? And the purple wisp-like magic, the one that was inside your heart, that's yours. *His* magic protected it, kept the water from drowning your soul."

"You seem to know a lot about magic for someone who's never left home," Cy said suspiciously.

Gil was silent a moment before responding. "There used to be a Mage that would visit once a month. She would teach us about the outside world so we weren't completely left in the dark. I haven't seen her in years, though."

"Sounds familiar," Cy grumbled, but he gained no response on the subject.

"So, about that kid you're looking for. He must be really important, even though you act like you don't care."

"What are you talking about?" Cy growled.

"Everytime he's mentioned, you go stiff. And not because you're sad he's dead. You look angry, almost like you hated him."

"What the hell is that? You don't get anything, do you? And he's not dead until we give up." Cy chose his words carefully.

"There it is. That love-hate relationship. But you can drop the act with me."

"What act?"

"The tough guy act. Don't' worry. I didn't figure it out because it's so obvious. You're doing a pretty good job of hiding it, really. I know what's going on because I know what signs to look for."

"Signs of what?" Cy finally asked, his voice coming back to him.

"Guilt. You're drowning in it, but you don't want out. You're tearing yourself up over this, maybe even hurting yourself. But you won't let Kaitlyn see it, because you know it will just make it worse for her, and you only want to punish yourself, not everyone around you."

Gil took a breath. "I know, because I went through the same thing when my little sibling died."

Cy choked on his words. Gil was silent while Cy thought of something to say. They had stopped walking just out of the busiest section of Lorile, but it didn't stop the glances they were getting. Gil didn't seem inclined to continue talking, and Cy was in no hurry to talk about his own feelings, let alone someone else's.

Giving a mock smile of encouragement, Cy punched Gil lightly on the shoulder, pushing him out of his guilt. *"Don't worry, you're not alone in this sinking ship to hell. I'll go down with you."*

Gil turned to Cy, and nodded. He shook himself out, then set to walking again, his cockiness back in his stride. *Tougher than I thought,* Cy remarked to himself.

"How old are you, anyway, Cyllorian? Do you know, or have you lost count of the years? Though, I doubt you'd even tell me," Gil said, sounding as though he was mainly talking to himself.

Cy paused, counting through the years again. Age had never mattered to him. Skill had. He added up the years, even those he spent in the ball after his first body. With a shrug, he thought to himself, *Why not?*

"Eighteen," he said after a long moment, shocking himself as much as Gil.

"Eighteen? You're a demon, and you're really only eighteen? Oh, I get it. You mean eighteen hundred, or thousand right? Which is it?"

"Eighteen years. That's it. I was created eighteen years ago. My 'birthday' was just last week."

"Did you do anything for your birthday?" Gil asked cautiously. There was a hint of a smile in his voice, and Cy guessed he was waiting to make a joke, regardless of the answer.

Cy lowered his head, his steps coming heavier now. He clenched his fists as the memory flooded into his mind, berating him after he had avoided it this long. The magic inside of him was sluggish, and he stopped in his tracks. His talons cut into the metal of his palm. The words came out like knives stabbing into his chest, constricting him.

"I let my only brother die."

Cyllorian

Gil stopped at the edge of Lorile and leaned against the wall of the cave. It was excessively overgrown with dark vines climbing over each other. They curled toward Gil as he touched them, and small buds opened to reveal light pink flowers. They stuck out gaudily against the dark greens and blues of Lorile. The vines covered every inch of the wall making it impossible to see what might be behind. Gil crossed his arms over his chest and watched in satisfaction at Cy's confusion.

"The hell is this? She's not here. Was this just some trick to get me to spill my guts or something?" Cy burst, spinning in place as he scanned the area around them. *"Or were you trying to get us in trouble so we'd be executed? Which is it?"*

Gil shook his head, then reached a hand out to the vines behind them. With what looked like great effort, he pulled a section of hanging vines away to reveal a small hole. The walls inside were lit better than Lorile itself, with large formations of the glowing blue crystals.

"You really don't think very highly of me, do you, Cy? Even after I saved your life. Besides, I might have been stretching the truth a bit when I said they'd kill you. Droll are peaceful, the most the court would do is kick you out into the cold after wiping your memory. A little detour like this never hurt anybody."

Cy glared pointedly at Gil. Ignoring his knack for lying, Cy inquired further on the subject at hand, *"How could she have found this on her own?"*

"She didn't," Gil said, a hint of humor in his voice. "I told her where it was. The magic is more concentrated here. There's a spring inside that's significantly cooler than the water everywhere else, and it's cold to us. To her, it would be the perfect temperature for a hot spring, and it has healing capabilities. I figured it would help to heal her burns."

"And the manly bonding was just a plus, right?" Cy asked sarcastically.

"I used it as a test. You genuinely cared where she was, so you passed. Even if the Court decided to kick you out, you're okay in my book."

"Thanks. That's really...comforting."

Cy stepped around the vines, bending awkwardly to fit into the hole. After adjusting to what little light Lorile had, the intensity of the crystals in the small space was blinding. He shielded his eyes from the harsh light and crept through the cave carefully, avoiding the jagged edges that reached towards his metal.

He heard a *swish* and turned to find the vines back in place. *"Aren't you coming?"* Cy yelled back, fearful that this was a trap.

"Nah. I think I'll let you handle this one on your own. Good luck." Cy detected a strange hint to his voice, but couldn't place it. Suspicious, he inched further into the cave, his talons at the ready.

All at once, the cave opened into a large room in the shape of a perfect dome. The crystals were scarce inside the room, and they cast odd shadows off the hanging vines. Bright pink flowers sprouted from every surface, filling the room.

In his awe, Cy nearly didn't see her. Kaitlyn was submerged in the pool, her back to him. Her blonde hair flared out around her in the water. Her clothes were strewn about at the edge of the pool. She sat up in the water, and Cy was relieved to find her shoulders and back free of any burn. Her skin reflected the soft light like scales, though Cy knew it was impossible.

Cy felt his magic stop within him, then stutter to a start again and whirl away. He felt as though he couldn't breathe, and his magic was stuttering. It whirred through the gears and springs, making high pitched whines.

He took a calming breath, then knocked against the wall of the cave. Kaitlyn gave a yelp, and water was splashed about.

"Cyllorian," she asked breathlessly, embarrassed. "What are you doing in here? Get out!"

Cy cringed. He avoided her glare and turned away from her, embarrassed. *"Gil told me where you were. Kolry's been freaking out, and is looking for you. We should get back before the poor guy has a heart attack. Gil wasn't kidding when he said he takes the rules seriously."*

"Why would we get in trouble? Gil's the one that told me about this place."

"Kolry is the one we have to worry about, and he specifically said not to listen to Gil, remember? So just get out of there and get dressed."

"What do you mean, 'get out?' You need to leave first, Cy! Why would Gil bring you here anyway?"

Cy tilted his head back to argue with her, to tell her it was his plan to test him. Before he even got a glimpse of the water out of the corner of his eye, he was struck in the head.

He spun around, rubbing his injury out of habit rather than pain. His face cleared and his mouth dropped when he saw Kaitlyn, leaning out of the water and clutching her top to her chest. Her eyes were daggers pointed at him, and she held her shoe in her free hand. Cy glanced down to see her other shoe at his feet.

She lifted the shoe to throw it again, but Cy tossed his hands up. He turned on his heels and marched out of the room. *"I'm going, I'm going! Just don't take too long."*

He made his way through the tunnels, trying to settle himself. His magic was racing throughout his body, and he couldn't get a grip on any of the emotions going wild in his head. His breath came sparingly until he parted the vines and stepped into the heat of Lorile.

Gil looked at him with a cocky smile. *"The hell are you smiling at?"* Cy spat, his voice cracking. He turned away from Gil in frustration, resisting the urge to hit him. Cy leaned against the wall on the opposite side of the entrance as Gil examined his talons absentmindedly.

Kaitlyn emerged a few moments later. Her hair was still wet, and it dampened her shoulders. Her cheeks were flushed, and she gasped at the dramatic temperature change. She looked from Gil's cocky smile to Cy's clear expression. He refused to look at her, and she glanced away from him after a moment, her cheeks redder than when she had come out of the spring.

She turned her back to Cy, and he took the opportunity. He glanced over her arms and neck between locks of hair. There was no sign of the burns she had just an hour earlier. Cy sighed in relief, glad that Gil had a semblance of good intention to his mischief.

"There's somewhere we're supposed to be?" she asked pointedly, glaring at Gil. He laughed under his breath, and lurched away from the wall. He began the long walk back towards the populated section of Lorile. Kaitlyn marching behind him and Cy lagging behind.

Cy stared at the ground as they walked, avoiding the glances they were getting from the Droll. When he did chance to look up at Kaitlyn ahead of him, he saw the same glint on her neck that looked to be scales.

Gil took them straight to the Court building, where they found Kolry bent over himself with his hands on his knees. His face was pale, and his wide eyes were wild.

"Kolry, I found them!" Gil called.

Kolry rushed to meet them, his eyes taking in everything. He noticed Kaitlyn's wet hair and Gil's mischievous smile, and his face went dark. He grabbed Gil by the shoulders and shook him, yelling at the Droll. "You little pond scum! What have I told you about interfering with Court affairs! Do you know what kind of calamity could have ensued from this reckless behavior of yours? You never think of the consequences of your actions, Gil! You should know better by now."

Cy saw Gil's face twitch at Kolry's last statement, but Gil simply shrugged it off. He pushed Kolry away and waved a hand in the air dismissively.

Kolry whirled on Cy and Kaitlyn next, "And you two. I deliberately told you *not* to listen to Gil, not to run off with him! This is not an ideal way to show your *pure intentions* on your first day as our guests. Should you get another chance, I hope you will not squander it."

"You worry too much, Kolry. I had everything under control. Nothing bad happened, and they didn't go destroying the city. That means they can be trusted, right? If they were here under other orders, they would have taken the first chance they got and killed us all, but they didn't." Gil patted Kolry on the shoulder, bursting into laughter. "Everything's fine. Actually, how about you let me watch over them from here? You're a bit too stuck up for them, I can tell."

"But, Master Gil..." Kolry started, defeat clear on his face.

"What could go wrong? I am their appointed guardian, remember?"

"Wait, you are? What about Mr. Boss over here?" Cy asked.

"Kolry's the attendant of the Court, like a butler. I told him to take over for today, because I don't do tours."

"You're on the Court?" Kaitlyn asked carefully.

"I'm the representative for my age group. Mostly because my dad's on the Court. He put a good word in for me. Not like I get much of a say in anything. Nothing important, at least. This is the first real assignment I've been given. Everything else has just been kid stuff."

Cy glared at Gil, and the Droll stared sassily back at him. *"Anything else you might have forgotten to mention?"*

Gil tapped a finger to his chin. "Let's see...my name...my profession...my whole life's story...I feel like there's something I'm forgetting. Oh, that's right! I'll be living with you for the next week while you're here!"

Gil clapped his hands together, erupting into maniacal laughter. Cy's jaw dropped, and Kaitlyn let out a small moan. Cy dared a glance at Kaitlyn in exasperation, and she mirrored him. All signs of their awkward encounter gone, they glanced at each other hopelessly. Cy lost control of himself and began chasing Gil around in a circle, while the Droll laughed to himself. Kolry narrowly avoided the two, mumbling to himself about the difficulty of teenagers.

* * *

"Why are you being especially bitter today?" Kaitlyn asked Cy, splashing water at him. She was swimming in one of the shallow pools near the entrances to Lorile, using a Droll wetsuit Gil had lent her. He explained that only the tunnels outside of Lorile were scalding, to prevent intruders, but inside was a more comfortable temperature. Though the Droll thought it was a cool temperature, it was still near burning. Kaitlyn ignored the heat now, and Cy didn't question it as long as she wasn't in danger. She had gotten much better with practice, and now was almost as good as the Droll.

"You're looking good, Kaitie! You'll be an official Droll in no time!" Gil called out from Cy's side. Cy glared at him, but Gil ignored as per usual.

Kaitlyn blushed and dove backwards, under the water.

"You shouldn't call her that. It's not her name," Cy grumbled. His arms were crossed tightly over his chest and he drummed his talons on his arms. He lost control of his strength a few times, puncturing the metal, but it healed easily. Gil watched in suspicion as he hurt and healed himself. Cy didn't care, just let him watch.

"It's just a nickname. She doesn't call you by your full name. Why do you?"

Cy looked at the ground without answering. He clenched his fist, aware that Gil was watching his every move.

"She has a point, you know. You are being extremely bitter today. What's up?"

"It's been a week. We need to know the Court's decision. We can't stay here. We have other places to be. The longer we're away, the harder it might be to bring Arion back."

"Relax," Gil said, bumping into his shoulder. Cy scowled at him, but it didn't break through Gil's carefree nature. "Think of this as a vacation! Or prep time, whatever. Just chill out. You'll know when I know, and I'll know when the Court tells me. Easy as that."

Cy's worried expression didn't falter, and Gil groaned. They watched Kaitlyn play with the Droll children in silence. She waved at them, and her arm looked almost blue.

"She's been in there a while. Maybe we should make her get out."

"Why? She's having fun."

"She's turning blue again. It's not good."

"Are you really so sure about that? She doesn't look like she's in pain, does she? Maybe she's tougher than you thought." Gil was just as carefree as ever and Cy glared at him.

Cy looked at Kaitlyn more closely. When she rose out of the water, he could see the same shine to her skin as that first day in Lorile.

"Is there anything in the water? Fish, or rocks, or sand? Anything that would stick to the skin?"

"What are you talking about?"

Cy thought for a moment, debating whether or not to say what had been on his mind for days. He took a deep breath, and said in a rush, *"There's something wrong with Kaitlyn. Her skin's not just bruised or burned, there's something else. It looks like she has scales all over, and I don't think she's even been paying attention. Is there something in the water doing it, or is it my imagination? I want to know what's going on, and if there's anything you're not telling me."*

He looked to Gil, but the Droll just stared straight ahead with a small smile. "So you noticed, too," he muttered.

Cy turned to Gil in anger, wanting to demand he tell him everything. Kolry's hand came down on his shoulder, stopping him. He froze in place, and Gil came to stand in front of them.

"Hey, Kolry. What's up?"

"Masters Gil and Cyllorian. Where is the young lady?"

"She's swimming. Don't worry, I'm keeping an eye on her, too. This is the one I really have to look out for." Gil jutted a thumb towards Cy, a lopsided smile on his face. His eyes were clear and calm, but Cy caught how his hand shook slightly, how his smile was forced.

Kolry made an irritated noise, and stepped away from Cy.

"What's eating you, Mr. Boss?" Cy said, though he didn't take his eyes off of Gil. After spending a week straight with the Droll, there had been some interesting secrets he had found. Gil slept terribly, and couldn't always keep his carefree facade when they were together. He saw the pain inside of him, and could now tell when he was faking his smiles. Something haunted him, and he did everything he could to keep it inside.

Around others, Gil was active and vocal, but when he could get away with it, he preferred to stay on the sidelines. This caused Cy and Gil to spend a lot of time together, though it wasn't of much quality. Cy would often catch Gil staring at the exit tunnels, a deep longing on his face, but he would always deny what was written clearly on his face.

As he watched the two Droll talk, Cy found his mind running away from him. He thought of all the times he had wanted to run away with Arion, wanted to get him away from everything else. Cy had always forgotten that he was just a child, and he pushed him further than he should have.

Gil was the same age as Arion, still just a kid. He held such responsibility for himself that it was hard to remember his age, even when he was joking. And now he was getting dragged into this mess, too, if even just for a short time.

He felt the guilt creeping up on him, but Gil shook him and it fled. "Cy, did you hear that? Hello, anybody in there? The Court has made their decision!" Gil yelled in his face. The smile he wore was genuine, but a spark of sorrow could be seen in his eyes.

Cy pushed him away automatically as his mind processed his words. *"Seriously? They're done? We can leave now?"*

"I don't know what they decided yet. We have to go see. Let's get Kaitlyn." Gil ran into the water and swam out to meet her. Cy watched him wave his hands wildly as he spoke. Kaitlyn's face lit up as he talked, and she jumped into Gil's arms to hug him.

"I haven't seen that in a while," Kolry said quietly.

Cy looked at him inquisitively. *"What? Him swimming? I know. It's weird that he doesn't like the water much, for a Droll."*

"Not that, though I have noticed his aversion to the water as well. It's been a long while since I've seen a true smile on that boy's face. A very long while."

Cy watched Gil and Kaitlyn return in silence. A new kind of guilt washed over him. *And here I thought I wouldn't have a heart any more without Arion,* Cy thought. *I'm still not sure if it's better to have one.*

Kolry led the way to the Court building. Kaitlyn and Gil chatted excitedly, and Cy followed behind them, wringing his hands nervously. Kaitlyn glanced backwards, and grabbed his hands. She pulled him between her and Gil, and the three of them kept pace.

Gil and Kolry went through the doorway while Cy and Kaitlyn held back. Gil turned to them, and waved a hand in summoning. "What are you waiting for? Come on!" he called. Cy and Kaitlyn shared a glance, then entered the building.

It was even more beautiful on the inside. The whole of the building was one gigantic room, complete with a large bell hanging from the ceiling filled with multiple clappers. The bell's exterior was covered in stained glass of varying shades of blue.

The windows of the building could only be viewed from the inside, and they showed an array of scenes depicting Drolls, both in mundane life and in combat, fighting alongside large seahorses. Colored lights shone through, and the shafts of light looked tangible in front of them.

A large statue of a half horse, half sea creature reared up in the center of the room. Its head was twisted to the side, mouth open. Hoofs jutted out in front of it, as though it were ready for battle against an unseen enemy. Though there was nothing for the horse to fight, it was guarding a wide set of stairs descending to the ground.

"What's that?" Kaitlyn asked, pointing at the statue. Her mouth was agape as her eyes darted upon it.

"It's a kelpie. They used to be our companions, like the dragons are for the Drakens, but we were separated from them during the riots. When the humans revolted against the Mages and we were forced to relocate, the kelpies could not follow. I think they still exist, but there isn't a Droll alive that has seen one. Not that I know of, at least," Gil said as he walked leisurely towards the stairs.

Kaitlyn jogged to catch up with Gil, but Cy proceeded cautiously. Both of them were excited for the news, but realization had sunk in for Cy. When they had met, Gil had made it very clear that they could die here by the choice of the Court, even if he had been exaggerating. The war-crazed look on the statue's face made it clear to Cy just how much of a reality their deaths could become.

They descended the stairs for what felt like forever to Cyllorian. More and more, it felt as though he was walking into his own grave, and he was the only one that seemed to care. Kolry had no connection to them, so it made no difference to him if they lived or died. Gil wasn't risking his life, either.

He knew Kaitlyn only saw the best in people. It was what

he was banking their entire relationship on. He admitted that he didn't want her to see the world for what it truly was, selfishly needing her to stay blind to his own evils, but he worried that her trusting nature would get her hurt. She had trusted Arion, and that trust had claimed her family, her home, and ultimately the only friend she had.

What am I making her lose by asking her to follow me? I have nothing left to care about, but Kaitlyn has given up her life twice now.

The stairs finally ended and they came upon a small, circular room. There was a large dais where many Droll were seated that curved with the wall. They sat in tall, regal chairs against the wall, their hands clasped on the counter in front of them.

Kolry bowed and stood close to the doorway. Gil took a seat at the edge of the counter and placed his hands atop it like the others. His face cleared and set with a steely resolve. He was no longer the carefree child. He was the burdened Droll, given the tasks of an adult.

"Step forward," the eldest Droll said. He wore an ornate black robe adorned with yellow jewels, a surprise compared to the Droll's interest in blue. A black veil with a navy-blue underside draped from his head to his shoulders. Aside from Gil, each member wore the same robes and headpiece, but only the leader carried the symbol of the Droll. A large talisman hung on his chest, the head of a kelpie with a red gem between its teeth.

He raised his hand and gestured to the center of the room, where the tile floor depicted a seven-pointed star made of clear glass. The water of Lorile flowed pristinely beneath the Courthouse, carrying with it a school of bright orange fish with wing-like fins.

Slowly, Cy and Kaitlyn did as commanded.

"For record purposes, state your names and your reasons for asking for our aid."

"I am Kaitlyn Rosemary, a human," Kaitlyn said clearly, throwing her shoulders back. She met the eyes of every Droll in the room. Gil flashed her a smile, small enough that it would not be noticed by the others.

"I am Cyllorian, a demon. I come in the name of Theresa Luna to ask for your help in retrieving the life of a lost companion. Will you help us?" Cy spoke clearly, and with more confidence than he felt. His nerves ate away at him.

"Over the week you have been kept under close observation, as per the agreement. While some remained suspicious of your presence here, many have found you to be harmless—"

The leader was cut off by a middle aged Droll woman sitting at the opposite end as Gil.

"Harmless?" she shrieked, her voice sounding like a siren's. "The girl may be nothing special, but we cannot overlook that a *demon* has found its way into our territory! They are no better than Drakens. If Theresa truly intended peace for our race, she would have come herself! You know this to be true, Jo-nye!"

At the mention of Theresa, Cy was instantly on guard. *What do they know about her? Was it actually her that Gil was talking about, the Mage that came to teach them? What have they been discussing this whole week?*

Jo-nye raised his voice to be heard over Hedra's hysterics, "Calm yourself, Hedra. This is no time to lose your temper. We have heard your objections for the past week, and came to a decision, have we not? They gave her name as proof of their association with her, and that is enough! Not only have we seen their nature for ourselves, but Theresa sent them herself. All we can do is trust them."

Jo-nye's words were final, and Hedra settled herself in her

chair. Her jaw was stiff as she glared at Cy, but he felt no threat from the woman. She feared him, that much was certain. *Just what exactly did they know about demons to make them so quick to judge? We aren't exactly common.*

Jo-nye collected himself with a deep breath and returned to his professional manner.

"We, the Court of Lorile, have observed your actions and behaviors, and we have come to a consensus. We shall send one of our own to help with your endeavors, with one condition. No matter what shall happen to you, you must die with the knowledge of our whereabouts locked behind your lips. I will not sacrifice my people so carelessly. We shall not go to war for the humans, nor for the Mages. We will remain here, waiting to take back the world we once had from the rubble after the dust settles on this world."

War? What the hell is this guy talking about? Cy thought. *We're not asking for an army, we want a healer! Just what is Theresa getting us into?*

"Pardon me, sir, but what are you talking about?" Kaitlyn said, raising her hand as though she were in school. "We don't want a war. We just want our friend back."

"War is waged, not desired, child," Jo-nye's voice was solemn, and it gave away his age and experience. "The humans and Mages have been at each other's throats for the past century, waiting for the perfect chance to strike. With Crestyss at the head of the Magicern, we fear it is far too close. This is why we shall remain as though we never were. If the fighters cannot find us, they cannot recruit nor slaughter us. We shall send what help we can for your companion, but that is all. You shall not be permitted to return to Lorile once you have gone."

Kaitlyn opened her mouth. Cy saw the questions on her face before she asked them. Knowing it would be best not to push their luck, he cut her off. *"Who have you selected to accompany us?"*

There was a moment where the Droll paused. They looked between each other, nodding hesitantly. "From what information we have gathered through observation and questioning, we have made a difficult decision. The youngest among the Court, Gil, shall aid you in your quest for the lost life."

Gil's face went blank at the news, and he paled. His hands shook on the counter, but he pulled them into his lap to hide them. His eyes swam with a mixture of fear, shock, and joy. Though Cy had easily been able to tell he wanted to leave, it was clear now from his reaction that he had never actually given the idea any thought.

"You'll find your lost pack in the home you were using, retrieved for you with minimal damage. You are free to take whatever supplies you might need, but you have only until nightfall. When it is time for you to leave, Kolry shall escort you out. Gil has told us of your difficulties in the current, so you are permitted to leave through the dry exit. It will take you to the back of the mountain, but you will have to be capable from there. Court meeting adjourned."

The Droll stood abruptly and left the room, and all but Gil followed suit. Cy and Kaitlyn went to his side, and Kaitlyn put her hand on his back.

"I'm leaving. I'm actually leaving," he muttered.

Kolry came up behind them and cleared his throat. "If I may, Master Gil, you have nothing here that you wish to stay for. It's best for you to go. I know how you've longed to leave the guilt-ridden walls of this place for the past few months. We all have noticed, and that is why you were chosen. You will do more good to help these two than you will to stay locked up in these walls with your own sadness."

Gil stared at Kolry for a long moment, and the resolve came on his face clearly. He nodded to Kolry once, a stiff movement, and Kolry smiled at him.

"Come now, you three. We must get you ready to embark into the harsh world."

CHAPTER 10

Cyllorian

"What do you still want to go to the Drakens for? They'd sooner eat you alive than help you! I knew you were insane, Cyllorian, but not suicidal?" Gil whined. They had spent a full day trekking in the tunnels on their way out of Lorile, and Gil was only getting more and more anxious with every step they took.

Before leaving, Gil had changed from his wetsuit into skintight, dark blue pants, and a black, sleeveless top. A thick black jacket was draped over his shoulders, and his bag was slung on one arm. A glowing crystal from Lorile hung around his neck on a black cord, imbued with magic that would allow him to survive outside of Lorile. Though he had the protection, he still had to be cautious, and stay hydrated more than anything.

Cy rolled his eyes, and Kaitlyn answered, "Theresa told us we need to go there. We haven't gotten any other instructions, so it's all we've got. Besides, they might be able to help us."

"I highly doubt that. Drakens are nothing but brutes. All they know how to do is fight, and breathe fire. None of them will be able to heal your friend. Trust me on this one, I beg you!"

Gil fell to his knees, his hands clasped. He was scarily pale, and he shook.

Cy stepped up to him and Gil flinched at his scowl. *"What do you have against the Draken anyway? They don't cause you any problems, other than both of you being selfish over the mountain. I was always taught that Droll and Draken rely on each other. They prove their loyalty by entrusting the burial ceremonies for the dead to the other species. You send your dead to them for cremation, and you get theirs for a burial at sea. That was the agreement made by the those that settled here as a sign of peace. 'If we can trust our dead to you, then we can trust our living to you as well,' was the intention. Or was I mistaken?"*

Gil lowered his eyes and slumped his shoulders. "You're not wrong," he muttered, anger and defeat mingling with his words.

"Well? What's your problem with them then?"

"We've had that agreement for as long as I can remember. But it's changed recently. Rumor is that they joined with Crestyss years ago. They stopped accepting our dead. My sister was the first one that they rejected."

Cy was caught off guard. *"I'm sorry. But we still need to go there. We're nearly out of the tunnel, right? There's bound to be more caves and water outside. You can stay there. It'll probably be better for you anyway. That necklace won't be able to protect you from freezing in the cold, or drying up in the Drakens' territory."*

"Please, Cy. I can't work with one of them. I just can't."

"You're gonna have to. We need all the help we can get, and this will give you the chance to find out what's really going on. Take a swing at them, if you really need to, I don't care as long as you don't

start a war. Besides, if you can buddy up with a demon, a Draken should be no problem, right?"

Gil thought for a moment, rubbing his face. He groaned under his breath, pulling at his skin. "Fine. But I don't have to get along with them. Not like there's a good chance of them helping you anyway."

Cy clapped Gil on the back, knocking the Droll off balance. Gil fell to the ground, then whirled around to glare at Cy. Without a word, Gil stood and dusted himself off. He marched towards the end of the cave, ahead of Cy and Kaitlyn.

"See, you'll do fine. Nothing can be more of a handful than me, after all."

"That's funny. Just you wait till you get up there. I doubt you've ever seen a..."

"Dragon!" Kaitlyn yelped, freezing on the spot. Gil shrieked and jumped into the air, on the verge of fainting.

Cy looked to Kaitlyn. She was staring at the mouth of the cave, her whole body shaking uncontrollably. Her hands were pressed to her mouth and tears glimmered in the corners of her eyes. Just as Cy was about to jump in front of her and face whatever danger had come, she lowered her hands. The smile she wore was clearly that of pure joy and relief.

Kaitlyn broke out into a run, bolting for the open air outside the cave. She dove to the ground, skidding along the frozen mountain. She sat up and turned back towards the boys, her hands clasped in front of her. She looked to Cy, her eyes shining with tears.

She held her hands out to Cy as he approached, Gil left behind in his stupor. Cy lowered his face to her hands, only inches away from her enclosed fingers. He opened his mouth to question her actions, but a head popped out from between her fingers and startled him.

Cy stumbled back with a small yell. The pet lizard that

Kaitlyn had had years ago stared Cyllorian down, his eyes menacing. It raised its hood and hissed at Cy, making Kaitlyn giggle. She brought the lizard up to her face and nuzzled it against her cheek. It gripped onto her fingers tightly with its limbs and tail, rubbing the top of its head against her.

"I can't believe we found him! How could he have gotten all the way up here? Did you follow me, Dragon? That's so sweet. I've missed you so much!"

"Did she seriously name that thing Dragon?" Gil asked as he sauntered up beside Cy. His voice was shaking, and he was smacking his hands against the sides of face to calm himself.

"Yeah. She told me it was because he looks like one. She had it as a kid, but her dad took it away a while ago. I didn't know lizards lived this long."

Kaitlyn ran around them, Dragon bouncing around in her hands. "Look, Cy! He missed me, and he came to find me! Isn't that incredible?"

"More like impossible. You sure that thing's just a lizard?"

"What else would it be?" Kaitlyn asked, examining her pet. "Maybe he's magic, like Tuft! He's my companion!" Kaitlyn burst into ecstatic giggles.

It seemed she had completely forgotten that they were on a mountain, and that there could be no way for Dragon to have found them. But Cy let it slide, seeing how happy it made her.

"It is pretty miraculous, huh?" he said, humoring her. She beamed at him, placing Dragon on her shoulder.

"I'm never going to lose you again. I promise." Kaitlyn rubbed the top of the lizard's head, and it nestled into the crook of her neck, where it quickly fell asleep.

Gil sneezed, startling Cy and Kaitlyn. "Oh, so you judge me for being afraid of dragons, but you jump at a sneeze? Pathetic."

"Who said we were judging?" Kaitlyn asked, full of innocence.

Cy raised his hand, fighting against the urge to laugh. Gil turned on him, screaming profanities, and Cy lost control. He burst into laughter, falling back into the thin layer of snow on the ground. Gil tried to kick him, but only hurt himself on the hard metal. *"You know, you'll probably get along with the kid. Neither of you can appreciate my sense of humor!"* Cy said as his laughter ended.

"Whatever, I'm going back into the caves. It's too cold for me out here." He retreated further into the cave, slipping his arms into his jacket and hugging himself for warmth.

"You really gonna let a bunch of Drakens scare you away?" Cy taunted.

"I'm not scared! You said it yourself, I'll dry up or freeze before we even get close. I have to stay in these caves. I'll get as close as I can to their land, and you can find me later. If you make it out alive, that is. You guys just go to the Drakens, up that way about an hour or so." Gil waved his hand towards a rocky wall of the mountain, ideal for climbing. He stomped off into an adjoining cave, muttering to himself the whole way.

"Thank you!" Kaitlyn called after him. He waved a hand above his head dismissively, but his steps became lighter after her gratitude.

"So that's where we have to go now?" Cy said. He got to his feet and stepped beside Kaitlyn, staring towards the path.

Kaitlyn put her arm against his, and he froze. He slowly looked to her out of the corner of his eye. Her face was calm, showing no signs of thoughts or emotions.

He ignored the questions that fluttered through his mind, and distracted himself. *"Gil's really got a lot of baggage, doesn't he? He's got some growing up to do, that's for sure. Really, what could be so bad about Drakens? He's such a drama queen, isn't he?"* Cy joked.

But Kaitlyn didn't laugh. She shoved him with all of her weight, catching him off guard. Cy went sprawling to the ground, staring up at Kaitlyn in shock.

"You really need to be nicer to people! We're lucky Gil tolerates us, but you can't scare off anyone else who might be willing to help. We're going to go up to the Drakens, and you *will* be on your best behavior, you got that? Too much is at stake for you to make a joke out of everything."

Cy watched incredulously as Kaitlyn reprimanded him. When she finished, her face was bright red and her hands were balled into fists at her side. Dragon had woken up to glare at Cy as well, emphasizing Kaitlyn's threat.

Cy cracked a smile, letting a short laugh slip through his lips. Kaitlyn's eyes narrowed further, and Cy burst into full chortles. *"I'm sorry, I'm sorry,"* he gasped. *"You're scary, really! Terrifying even. It's just too much that you're yelling at me like you're my mom!"*

Kaitlyn let out a sigh, and Cyllorian struggled to get control of himself. It seemed too much for her, and she broke into giggles as well.

After a moment, she nudged Cy's foot. "Come on, we better get going. If they've been expecting us, we've already kept them waiting long enough."

Cy pushed himself onto his feet, still recovering from his laughing fit. *"Yes, ma'am,"* he muttered, following her to the path. She glared at him over her shoulder, but a small smile tugged at the corners of her mouth. Cy coughed to cover his laughter as they climbed the mountain to face the mysterious Drakens.

* * *

"He said it would only take an hour, right?" Kaitlyn called a few strides ahead of Cy. She paused a moment, catching her breath, and clung to the rope tied around her waist. She turned her head to look down, but thought better of the idea and faced forward. "How long have we been climbing anyway?"

"I don't think it's been that long. But I think we've passed the cloud line. One day in that cave system made more progress than a week trying to climb! It can't be much further. Just keep going, we can rest when we get there," Cy called back.

Kaitlyn groaned, but pressed on. There was no energy left in her, though Cy had no idea where it all could have gone to. He was sure Arion had had more energy than this, but he had more experience exerting himself. Kaitlyn spent her childhood reading, not exercising.

He watched intently at every slip of her hand, at the shaking of her legs with each step up. It was slow going, but he didn't dare ask her to go faster.

He looked down below them. The air was thinner up here. A fog had settled around them, and he couldn't see the peak of the mountains anymore. It was impossible to tell just how high up the mountain they really were. He couldn't even see the landing where they had parted ways with Gil.

Kaitlyn let out a small scream, and Cy whirled around. He had been climbing without thinking and had nearly caught up to Kaitlyn. While he had been climbing absentmindedly, they had reached their destination. And they had been greeted with a spear resting on Kaitlyn's collarbone.

Her face had gone pale and her lip trembled, but her gaze burned as she stared into the bright red eyes of the Draken threatening her.

The Draken was the complete opposite of the Droll. He had very defined muscles, and his skin was an ashy gray. His hair was white at the roots, darkening to look charred at the tips.

Instead of freckles, the Draken's face was splotched with shiny black specks that could have either been burnt skin or scales. The only color to the Draken was in the fire of his eyes, and the vibrant white armor that covered him.

"Up," he growled in a rough voice from deep in his throat. He inched the spear away, and Kaitlyn pulled herself onto the ledge slowly. Cy followed, and was met with another spear prodding at the side of his neck when he came close to the edge. He hesitated for a split second before ascending the rest of the way. He raised his hands into the air, watching the Draken that held the spear from the corner of his eye. Now on level ground, they were surrounded by half a dozen Draken, each wearing a different color of polished armor.

The first Draken severed the rope that bound Cy and Kaitlyn, and he heard Kaitlyn whimper. The Draken turned back to her, and she raised her hands as well.

"Walk," the second Draken said, jabbing the spear in Cy's back. It was clear this one was female by the curves in the armor that hugged the shape of her body, and large, colorful feathers sprung from the helmet that covered her face, setting her apart from the men. Cy felt the spear pierce the metal, a small prick in his armor. He grinned evilly at the gasp that came from the Draken. She stabbed at him again, and he walked forward.

Kaitlyn was already following the first Draken, and he hurried to catch up with her. As quietly as he could, Cy whispered to her, *"Whatever you do, don't let Gil know he was right."*

Kaitlyn snorted and covered her laughter up with a cough. It seemed she couldn't stop coughing after forcing the first one, and she stopped walking to finish her fit. Cy moved to go to her, but the female raised her spear to him, and he backed off. In his confinement, he tried to gather his bearings of where they were.

From what he could see, they had arrived at a plateau atop the mountains, completely devoid of snow. They had reached the flattened peak that marked the Drakens' territory. A thin layer of smoke covered everything around them, and visible heat waves rose from the ground. The fog at their feet made it impossible to tell just how large this area was. In the distance, small buttes and mesas rose from the fog to surround them. Cy could almost make out what looked to be statues on a few of them before he was herded forward again. They were completely left in the open atop the mountain, and it made Cy worry.

Kaitlyn had recovered from her coughing fit, but Cy could tell that her breathing was labored now. Sweat beaded her flushed face, and she was doing her best to remain calm.

Cy readied himself to yell at the Drakens, but they stopped in place and turned on Cy and Kaitlyn. They pointed their spears at them, backing the two against each other.

A wild roar rang throughout the air and Kaitlyn clapped her hands over her ears. Cy stared in horror as a swarm of shadows engulfed them from above, covering the mountain peak.

Drakens jumped out from every direction, twelve of them now surrounding them with thick, curved blades and long spears. The smoke thickened around them, creating a small pocket of barely breathable air. Countless dragons slithered out of the smoke.

The smallest of the dragons, barely larger than the Drakens, shared the same umber tone as the mountain, their scales dulled by the smoke. They crawled on four legs, their large, leathery wings outstretched to make them seem larger. Black, forked tongues shot out between pointed teeth, tasting the tension in the air. These dragons stayed on the outskirts of the plateau, while the larger dragons rested just behind the Drakens.

It was easy to see now. Each Draken had their own dragon, and their armor was made from the scales of their companion. The Draken in charge, in the white armor, had a long, slender dragon. It stood on its hind legs, raising itself to nearly four times the height of the Draken. Feathered wings rested neatly at its side, the dragon being too thin to fit them on its back.

One dragon was only as tall as its master, looking more like an insect than a dragon, with its translucent wings that stuck out from under a hard shell. It had six thin legs and it held itself close to the ground. Four red eyes shown against the dark brown skin that covered it, watching Cy and Kaitlyn hungrily.

The female Draken from before lunged her spear toward Cyllorian, her two-limbed dragon snapping forward with its long neck. It was a dark yellow color, with red markings along its back and face. It moved gracefully at her side, curling around the Draken's body protectively. As Cy stared on, the dragon shrunk, changing into a large python that slithered along its master's arm. It crawled up her weapon to get as close at Cy as it could. It opened its jaws at him, as though it thought it could eat him whole.

Cy looked around him at the other Drakens. Half of them were missing dragons, but instead had small creatures perched on them. *These dragons aren't normal. They can change into smaller creatures to stay with their Draken. Why didn't Theresa ever tell me about this?*

Two twin Drakens had large birds with red and yellow feathers, with small beaks that curved into a sharp point, and silver claws that matched the armor they rested on. Another had a creature much like a ferret, but it had tan scales instead of fur. It had large, black eyes, and two pairs of thin wings that laid along its back.

Cyllorian turned to look behind them, wanting to see what other creatures they might be up against, but the white armored Draken shoved his spear into Cy's throat and prevented any movement.

"Are there more of you?" the Draken demanded, using his weapon to draw Cy's attention from the dragons that were huffing thick black smoke from their nostrils.

"No, it's just us. We come to..."

"Silence!" the Draken yelled, and the angelic dragon curled around him roared as well. Its hot breath swelled around Cy and he fought against the urge to cough himself. "Outsiders are not welcome here. You will be exterminated."

"No, wait!" Cy yelled, leaning forward. As one, every Draken reared back to strike. They lunged forward, leaving no way to escape. Cy spun on his heels and grabbed Kaitlyn, trying to shield her from the attacks. Her pet lizard that rested in her pocket woke, and squirmed violently. It stopped moving almost instantly, as though it had disappeared completely. Cy was almost worried he'd killed the thing, but he had to save Kaitlyn first. As the blades rushed towards them, Kaitlyn screamed.

A manic screech tore through Cy's ears, leaving a painful ringing in his head. He clung to Kaitlyn, awaiting the onslaught of slashes to his body. The ground quaked beneath him with the footsteps of something terrifying, the air growing thicker than he would have thought possible. Something brushed up against him, surrounding him, and he thought of the python. *Are they letting their dragons have the first dibs?*

Readying himself for whatever reaction he might need, Cy opened his eyes. In front of them was a giant blue dragon, easily twice as large as any that belonged to the Draken here, its tail curling around his and Kaitlyn's feet. A double arrow of what looked like metal tipped the tail, and the claws that dug at the mountain looked to be made of the same. Though it was hunched down on all fours, it was clear that the dragon had wide paws with apposable thumbs, making them look more like hands. It waved its head all around them, hissing at the Draken with a purple forked tongue dripping venom. Its horned head was backed by a menacingly red hood. One bat-like wing was draped over Cy and Kaitlyn, blocking them from sight. Large sapphire eyes with thin pupils met Cy's, and he gasped.

Murmurs were rising up from the Draken, and they slowly lowered their weapons. The dragon guarding them held its ground, eyeing the strangers with suspicion. Kaitlyn wriggled in Cy's grip, breaking free of his arms. She glanced up at Cy. There was something curious in her eyes that Cy couldn't place as she turned slowly to face their savior.

She froze in fear at the creature in close proximity, stepping back into Cy's grip. She was shaking violently, and she reached behind her to grab Cy's hand. The dragon glanced back at them for just a second, his sharp gaze turned soft, before continuing to stare down their captors. It let out a low rumble in its throat, though it wasn't a menacing sound like the shriek it had let lose before.

Through the small gap under the dragon's wing, he watched the Draken shift about uncomfortably. Nearly all the dragons were hiding or in their smaller forms. The angelic dragon had even shrunk itself, now in the form of a thin gecko atop its Draken's head.

Cy felt his magic surge at the realization, and he squeezed Kaitlyn's hand reassuringly before releasing it. She flailed frantically to grab him again, but he avoided her grasp. He placed his hands on her shoulders and bent down to speak to her.

"Look closer," Cy whispered, pushing her toward the drag-

on's head. She stared back at him in disbelief, but he simply nodded toward the creature.

She stepped forward slowly, raising her hand to lift the leather of its wing from her head. Her legs were shaking, but her shoulders were set as she approached. Her mouth moved for a moment without sound before she finally found her voice. "Dragon?"

The dragon turned to her, its eyes trying to communicate. A smile pulled at her mouth, and she laughed. Cy smiled at the relief in Kaitlyn's voice.

"I think we can all tell it's a dragon, Kaitlyn, but thanks anyway," Cy said in an attempt to break the tension, though his heart wasn't in the comment. He couldn't look away from the dragon, but it seemed to have forgotten everything except for Kaitlyn. *How can this happen?*

She shoved her hands into her pockets, and her smile got wider. "That's not what I meant, Cy. I mean that *this* is Dragon. *My* Dragon." Kaitlyn whirled to show Cy her pockets, but he only nodded.

Why is there so much happening right now? What is going on? He felt suspicious of the situation. Kaitlyn had had that lizard as long as he could remember. What would be the odds that it's a dragon? What would it be doing with a human?

Dragon stepped toward her, wrapping one hand around her waist carefully. Very slowly, it brought its head to Kaitlyn's and rubbed against her cheek. She laid her hand against its face, giggling as though there was nothing else going on at the moment.

The Draken's words cut through to Cyllorian then, and they approached them. "The girl has a dragon protector. We must take her to the Chieftain. He will know what to do with her."

A Draken reached toward Kaitlyn through the small

opening under Dragon's wing, and Dragon reacted instantly, snapping for the Draken's hand. The Draken yanked his hand away, stumbling backwards as Dragon raised its head as high as its long neck would allow.

"I am Vyekrin, and any that attempt to harm my girl shall perish, along with those lives around them. I dare any challengers to step up now, so that I may smite you sooner rather than later!" the dragon said, his voice deep and majestic. It broke through the crowd easily, silencing all around them.

"Vyekrin," Kaitlyn whispered, staring up at her dragon in amazement. The dragon looked down at the sound of his name. His tail swished at her feet, thumping softly on the ground. She stepped closer to the dragon, resting a hand on his back.

After a long moment, a Draken stepped forward, then fell to his knees in a bow. It was the Draken that had first attacked them, and now he was stealing terrified glances at Vyekrin. Confused, Cy looked to all the other dragons around them, and realized that not a single one of them was Vyekrin's size. He was easily thirty feet tall in total, and his neck alone was five feet long. The other dragons were lucky if they topped at seventeen feet. They bowed low to the ground. Cy couldn't tell if it was out of respect for the superior dragon, or fear.

"My sincerest apologies. We did not know that you had a dragon among you. If you will allow, let me take you to our Chieftain so that we can right the wrong we have done to you. Please, miss...?"

Kaitlyn stepped forward, throwing her head back and forcing a commanding glare. "I am Kaitlyn, and my companion is Cyllorian. We are here to speak with your Chieftain, so yes, you may take us to him. But I expect complete honesty from you, and no tricks."

The Draken glanced fearfully at Vyekrin, who returned the

glance with a murderous fire in his eyes. "No, my lady. We do not dare to oppose your guardian, Vyekrin. Whatever reason you have come to us for, the Chieftain will see to it. This I swear."

"Good. Then lead the way for me and my company." Kaitlyn waited expectantly, but the Draken did not stand. He glanced awkwardly at Cy, then back at Kaitlyn. "Is there a problem?" she demanded when he turned his attention back to her.

The Draken looked to his comrades around him for help, but they gave him nothing. With a sigh, the Draken answered, "No, my lady. This way to our Chieftain. He will see you at once."

"Why the hell do they need a week? We don't have that much time! They said the Chieftain would see us right away, but he's not even here right now? What is up with that!" Cy growled as he paced the small house they had been ushered to after their meeting. It was a small dome made of packed mud and brick from the mountain. The hard furniture was made of similar stone, though it had been polished so it gleamed like marble. Where the Droll lived in comfort, the Draken didn't seem to care. Even the cushions and bedding were made of tough leaves from the foliage that grew on the mountain. The only soft thing to be found was, ironically, a dark blue blanket from the Droll.

"And what were they saying about a stupid war? They don't make any sense, damn it. What kind of meeting could be so important for the Chieftain to just be gone like this?"

"The Droll said something about a war, too. Do you think there's something else going on here?" Kaitlyn asked, twisting her ribbon up in her hands. Cy could feel her gaze on him as he paced, but he couldn't stop. He was tired of waiting around and getting nothing done.

"Hell if I know. They're all just cowards, thinking anything they do will set the humans off into another riot. Or maybe it's just an excuse not to help us. Whatever it is, it shouldn't take a week to answer a yes or no question. This is ridiculous!" Cy kicked a large jar that decorated the room, and it wobbled on its side.

"Better now?" Kaitlyn asked as Cy stood over the pot, breathing heavily.

He glanced at her, and the worried expression softened him a bit. *"A little,"* he muttered. He let out a deep breath and his shoulders slumped. Feeling utterly useless, he went to the small couch and sat beside Kaitlyn. He fell onto the seat heavily, making Kaitlyn jump. She slowly moved away from Cy, and he leaned away from her reluctantly when he noticed.

"I just wish there was something to do. We're doing absolutely nothing up here while Arion's getting farther away, and Gil's freezing his ass off." Cy collapsed against the back of the couch, his arms sprawling over the back of it. He stared at the ceiling, admiring the patterns in the stonework from fire exposure.

"Didn't they say we could go outside? Maybe if we show them we can be cooperative, it'll help the time go by faster," Kaitlyn suggested. She looked to the entrance of the house they were using. There was no door, just a large archway carved into the stone of the home. Two guards were stationed outside, motionless. "It's better than nothing."

Cy jumped up from the couch, stretching. *"Yeah, fine whatever. Let's go mingle with the locals."*

They exited the house and the guards immediately responded, crossing their spears to keep Kaitlyn and Cy from wandering. With a polite tone that sounded forced, Kaitlyn said, "We just want to take a walk around. Get to know the

Drakens a little better. It's only fair, right? Since we're asking for help, we should know more about you."

The guards looked at each other, slowly lowering their spears. "I suppose that should be fine, so long as we accompany you."

"I'd like that," Kaitlyn said, holding her arm out to stop Cy when he stepped towards the guards. They gave her a quizzical glance, but she either didn't notice, or simply ignored it. "If we have any questions, you'll be right there to answer them. Besides, we don't want to get lost, right?"

Kaitlyn cocked her head to the side, and Cy knew that her eyes were shining. Though her words sounded scripted, there was no denying that she was thrilled by the chance to learn more about the Draken. The guards moved the spears slightly, and Kaitlyn ducked under them and out of the house. Cy followed, smacking the weapons out of his face with a sneer.

A high-pitched roar broke through the hesitant silence of the guards, and Cy clamped his hands over his head. The sound reverberated inside of him painfully, and he groaned. The ground started to shake beneath him, and his eyes shot open to see that he was the only one affected. The guards and Kaitlyn were keeping their balance, while Cy's metal was buzzing with the sound wave. Kaitlyn looked around them wildly, but the guards were as unphased as before. Just as Cy was beginning to think he was going insane, Vyekrin came charging toward the guards.

They dropped their weapons to the ground and backed away from Kaitlyn just as Vyekrin's head came within inches of their faces, teeth bared in a threat. Though the guards lived with dragons, the terror they felt for Vyekrin was clear in their eyes.

"Vyekrin!" Kaitlyn chirped and she skipped over to him. Vyekrin turned to her, pure joy on his face as she stood on her toes to rub the top of his head. He closed his eyes and made a low rumbling sound in his throat, like a purr. Kaitlyn giggled, and said, "Where did you go off to? I lost you after the meeting."

"He came willingly to answer a few questions, and for an inspection. We wanted to be sure he was a true dragon, and not just a shape shifter under false pretenses. The fact that he has returned proves that all went well, so there is nothing to worry about," one of the guards answered. He stepped towards Kaitlyn as he explained, and Vyekrin glared at him.

"It's alright, Vyekrin. They're just doing their job," Kaitlyn soothed him, and the dragon complied.

"Not that I'm not moved by this touching reunion, but can we go on that walk or not? I'm bored to death over here," Cy grumbled from his place in the doorway of the house. All eyes turned to him, and he shrugged. *"I'm a demon trapped in a metal body. A big dragon isn't all too surprising. Definitely not enough to get worked up about."*

Cy watched the guards closely during his last statement, but they had no reaction. *So they already knew what I am. This should be interesting, then. Does everything in this world have a freaking demon detector in their brain or something?*

The second guard said, "Yes, we can take you through our colonies. We weren't told that we can't take you, at least."

"Great! So what are your names?" Kaitlyn asked, looking between the two guards.

The first guard bowed low to Kaitlyn, crossing both arms over his chest. "I am Lane, at your service." He was clad in orange armor with large red scales on his shoulders, elbows, and knees. He had thin, yellow eyes, and short spiky hair that quickly turned from white to pitch black.

The second guard bowed as well, though it seemed an uncomfortable motion for him. "Orthros. I am but a new recruit, but I am sworn to my cause." He was a young man, shorter than Cy, with pure white hair cropped close to his head. His armor was light green, with teal accents. His cheeks and neck were covered in the small black scales.

Kaitlyn curtsied back to the guards. They bent to pick up their weapons, and Vyekrin hissed at them. Kaitlyn gave the dragon a stern look, and he lowered his head to rest it on the ground.

"Where to first?" Kaitlyn asked, stepping in front of Vyekrin. Cy pushed away from the wall to join her.

"If you want to learn the most about us Draken, there is only one place to take you," Lane said, a wide smile spreading across his face.

Orthros bounced on his feet, a devious gleam in his eyes. "The Arena."

Kaitlyn and Cy looked at each other, and he could tell they were thinking the same thing. *Do they really only care about fighting?*

They followed the guards throughout the colony, Vyekrin close behind them. Most buildings were the same brick huts that Kaitlyn and Cy had been given, but there were a few that were made from hollowed peaks that hadn't been leveled. Dragons, both wild and tame, soared overhead, circling the mountain. Cy watched as one flew straight into the mountain, but it emerged a moment later on the other side.

"The dragons live under us, in the catacombs they dug out for themselves," Lane said when he noticed Cy's confusion. "We have holes that we dug so we can get down to them, too. Most don't like living directly with us, but they don't mind us visiting. Not even the wild ones."

Sure enough, they passed a small hole dug out at an angle, set with a steep staircase descending into the mountain. Thin wisps of smoke trailed up from the hole, accompanied by a chorus of roars and rumbles from the dragons.

Vyekrin stared at every Draken that they passed, as though he wanted to fight, but none ever took the challenge. His long tail swished back and forth, forcing the Draken to keep their distance from the small group.

The Arena was a large stadium that jutted out over the cliff's edge, and was ten times as tall as Vyekrin. Instead of walls, there were pillars around the building, holding up a ring that acted as the roof. The pillars were four feet wide each, with small gaps in-between. There was a small area between two layers of pillars that was shaded, and Drakens filled the walkway on their way into the heart of the Arena. It was held up over the edge by statues of two dragons tangled in each other in a duel.

Roars and yells sounded from the open top of the Arena, making it difficult to hear anything else once they had gotten near. Vyekrin huddled closer to Kaitlyn and Cy as they stopped before the stadium, curling tightly around the two and pressing them together.

The guards went ahead towards the large opening into the Arena, but Kaitlyn had frozen to the spot. She clutched at the spikes on Vyekrin's neck, staring at the open space below the stadium. Cy put his hand on her shoulder, ready to comfort her, but her gasp stopped him. Her hand lunged out, pointing to the edge of the cliff.

Someone was falling, tumbling over themselves into the thickness of clouds below the stadium. Everyone watched as the Draken plummeted, screaming desperately.

"Kaliyah's fighting again," Orthros said without concern.

Lane let out a bark of a laugh, and replied, "When isn't she? She sure likes to toss them out, doesn't she?"

"Aren't you guys going to help?" Kaitlyn shrieked, her face

going pale.

"Why? Jayr can handle himself. Besides, he's got Wayonn with him, no doubt," Orthros said with a wave of his hand. "He should know by now that he's never going to beat Kaliyah, anyway. It's his own damn fault for continuously challenging her."

"*Wayonn?*" Cy asked, unable to look away from the Draken being swallowed up by the white fog below. A deep, primal roar sounded close by, and a dragon sprung out of the stadium and dove after the Draken. They both disappeared into the clouds and emerged seconds later, the Draken now on the dragon's back.

"That's Wayonn," Lane said with a smirk. He stepped up to the largest opening in the pillars and ushered them in. Cy walked absentmindedly, focused on the dragon and rider that landed inside of the stadium. Kaitlyn grabbed his arm and followed close behind, despite Vyekrin's objections.

As they passed through the shadows into the Arena, Vyekrin leapt into the sky, over the wall. He landed just inside the stadium, blocking them all from sight.

They crept in around Vyekrin, who curled around Kaitlyn and Cy once more, shoving Orthros and Lane out of the way. The dragon pulled his lips back in a snarl at the vast amount of Draken that hugged the wall. They had all stopped their cheering at his appearance, but those fighting in the center were too focused on each other to notice the new arrivals.

There wasn't any sort of seating, but the outer most ring of the Arena was slanted so that the standing viewers could see over each other. There was nothing separating the competitors from the spectators other than a thick black circle that marked the fighting ring. Lane and Orthros ran ahead until their toes were nearly over the line, and Cy and Kaitlyn ran after them. Vyekrin barreled through the crowd mercilessly to follow.

A fierce battle was taking place in the very center, the combatants wrestling on ground level. Even the two dragons were grounded rather than fighting in the air.

One of the fighters was the man that had fallen from the Arena, Jayr. He was of an average build, but he was fast and light on his feet, jumping from one position to another easily. He added flare to each attack with flips and spins, with a seemingly endless amount of energy. His hair was long and mostly gray, though his features said that he couldn't be much older than Cy himself. Though his armor was polished and shined in the light, it was dull in color compared to the rainbow of armor among the other Draken. The scales he wore were a mixture of beige and light brown, matching that of the dragon fighting behind him.

Wayonn, his dragon, had large, leathery wings, and slitted eyes. Four horns donned the back of the dragon's head, one pair rising upward and the other curling along his jawline. He had a short snout equipped with two rows of thin, dagger like teeth. He had a square body that sat low to the ground and six legs. A long tail with a bulbous tip lashed forward with great speed and force towards his opponent, but the stinger never met its mark. His main weapons seemed to be the long pincers that snapped forward with grace, the edges looking sharper than a blade.

The second fighter seemed to be a girl, though she moved too fast to be seen well. She was a blur of purple and rich brown. Where Jayr fought with a thick, curved weapon, the girl fought with her bare hands, and she was winning.

The dragon beside her, a small, thin creature, moved perfectly in sync with each of her master's attacks. She was covered in large purple scales with a black underbelly. All of the dragon's features were long, from her limbs, to her two tails, and her neck and head. Frilly fins lined the sides of her neck, and small horns split her face down the middle, ending with a large horn on her nose.

Four wings spread from her back as she reared up on her hind legs. She swiped forward with black claws as her master did, and they each caught their target. Jayr and Wayonn fell to the ground, their faces bleeding. They stood together as one, refusing to let themselves be beaten. The fight resumed, though Jayr and Wayonn were clearly damaged. The girl and her dragon didn't let up on their assault.

"Shouldn't we stop this? He's getting mauled out there!" Cy yelled at Lane, shocking himself.

The Draken was shaken out of his enjoyment, and he called back. "You can't! Once a challenge has been accepted, the only way to end it is to surrender or get knocked out. It goes against our pride for someone else to interfere, not to mention the punishment is so severe. You could get locked up, or even killed since you're an outsider."

"Killed?" Cy asked in shock. Lane had lost himself in the fight again, chanting mindlessly along with the crowd.

Cy turned back to the fight in a stupor. Jayr looked like he was barely still standing, half of his face covered in blood. Wayonn had curled in on himself beside Jayr, lashing out help-lessly with his stinger.

In one sharp movement, female master and dragon charged Jayr and Wayonn, sending them flying to the edge of the fighting ring. They skidded to a halt just in front of Cy and Kaitlyn, and Vyekrin tightened his hold on them.

The victors stalked the defeated, standing over them as the crowd went wild. Cy looked around wildly, hoping that he and Kaitlyn weren't the only ones not swept up in watching them fight for no clear reason. Lane and Orthros had gotten caught up in the action, discarding their weapons to pound their fists in the air as they cheered.

Through the gaps in Vyekrin's body as the dragon tried to hide the two from sight, Cy studied the victor. She was as far from a Draken as Cy was from a human. He wasn't quite sure what she was. Now that she had stopped fighting and had slowed down, her features were clear. She was very small with a slight build, but her muscles showed easily. She had brown skin and long, purple hair that was messed and wild around her thin face. Her triumphant smile showed a row of sharpened teeth, and her golden eyes shone with pride.

She wore little to nothing. Scraps of black fabric and armor barely covered her. The purple that Cy had seen had been her own scales that covered most of her body, including her arms, legs, back and stomach, as well as the edges of her face. Her hands were tipped with black claws, as were her feet. A short tail swished happily behind her, and two wings were folded against her back, too small for use. She looked more like her own dragon than anything.

Noticing Cy's stare, Orthros said, "That's Kaliyah. Her dragon is Polae. She's not a Draken, but you can't deny that she belongs here. Not only does she have the strongest bond with her dragon of anyone here, but she can turn into a dragon herself, for the most part. She came to us a few years ago. No one knows much about her. Only the Chieftain knows her past. What everyone does know is that she's the strongest person in Deidrich. She's completely undefeated. She can even take down a full-sized dragon by herself!"

As Orthros had been giving his explanation, Kaitlyn had become interested. She struggled against Vyekrin's grip, though the dragon didn't notice. She got free, standing just outside of Vyekrin's grasp, staring at Kaliyah without a shred of fear. Cy worried she had forgotten she wasn't simply in one of her fairy tales.

Kaliyah scanned the crowd, and her eyes met Kaitlyn's.

They turned dark. Cy saw the reaction in the other girl, and moved to grab Kaitlyn, but Kaliyah was too fast. With a voice as loud as a dragon's, Kaliyah yelled out, "Who will be my next challenger?"

The crowd swelled as they pushed and shoved, either to get out of the way or to be the first to approach her. Cy fought against the raging crowd, but he was no match. As he lunged for Kaitlyn, he tripped and pushed into her. She stumbled into the fighting ring, landing on her hands and feet just in front of Kaliyah.

Cy stared in horror as the girl's smile became twisted. Cy crawled forward, inching for Kaitlyn. Ignoring Cy altogether, Kaliyah said, "Just who I was hoping for. So, you're not a Draken, but you got a dragon, too, huh? That's no fair. You can't just come in here and steal my fame. But I'll show them just how worthless you are."

She bent down and grabbed Kaitlyn by the back of her shirt, yanking her to her feet. Kaitlyn yelped as she writhed in the girl's grasp, gaining Vyekrin's attention. The dragon sprang into action, using his tail to knock Kaliyah's feet from under her. She dropped Kaitlyn, and Vyekrin scooped her up and set her down on the back of his neck. She clung to his small, curved horns as the dragon reared back and hissed at the girl.

Polae tackled Vyekrin, and they rolled over each other on the hard ground. Kaitlyn was flung from the dragon's back, sprawling toward the center of the Arena. Cy lunged to his feet and tried to chase after her, but he was held back by every Draken that could reach him. He clawed at them with his talons, but he couldn't break through their armor. He tried cursing and pleading, but they wouldn't release him. Cy could do nothing but watch as Kaitlyn was forced into a fight against Kaliyah.

Kaitlyn

Kaitlyn felt Vyekrin tense under her, but it was too late. He fell to the ground, and Kaitlyn lost her grip on the dragon's horns. She was thrown onto the hard ground and skidded further and further into the fighting ring.

Kaitlyn! Vyekrin's voice screamed in her mind, and she cringed at the sudden intrusion. *Please speak to me! Run, Kaitlyn, run from here and do not stop until you are safe!*

We can speak through our thoughts? Kaitlyn asked herself automatically. She shook her head at the thought, sure that she was imagining things, but she did as Vyekrin said. She felt her limbs, but they were all stiff and sore. *I can't move,* she thought in response, her words slow and slurred even in her mind.

You must, do whatever you can to get away. Once I remove this threat, I will come to you. I swear. But you have to save yourself!

Vyekrin called back, confirming her curiosity. *We have a strong connection, you and I. and I refuse to lose you again!*

At his words, she could feel a strange tugging in her chest, pulling her towards the dragon. It felt as though there was a leash binding them together, a tangible force that held the dragon to her side. Even this short distance felt like too much now that she knew of the bond.

Vyekrin's pleading was enough to motivate her. Echoing his desires, she wanted nothing more than to eliminate the space between them.

She gathered all of her strength and pushed herself onto her knees. Her arms throbbed and stung, scraped from the fall and covered in a coarse red dust. She tried to wipe them off, but found that the red color was from her blood, staining the pale ground.

Roaring close by caught her attention, and she turned to see the two dragons lashing at each other. Polae coiled her neck and sprung like a snake, but Vyekrin caught her easily in his large hands, pinning the dragon to the ground. Polae had the advantage with her flexibility, and smacked Vyekrin with her two tails, stunning him. She jumped and grabbed Vyekrin, wrestling him to the ground.

Behind the thrashing dragons, Kaitlyn could see Cy's horrified face. His metal features were mangled by pain and rage as he struggled against a hoard of Draken that held him back. Their two guards were lost in the crowd, and Kaitlyn wondered if they would've helped if they were able.

Kaliyah appeared before Kaitlyn, her twisted smile showing off her pointed teeth. With one swift movement, the other girl pulled back her leg and kicked Kaitlyn in the side. She was flung a foot away, landing on her side hard enough to bruise. She groaned as she rolled onto her back, head ringing. She stared up at the sky, unable to hear anything around her.

Sadistic laughter in tune with the bells in Kaitlyn's ears rung as Kaliyah stepped up to her. She said something, but the words were unintelligible. When Kaitlyn didn't react, Kaliyah scowled. With a shrug, she raised her foot above Kaitlyn's head, an evil gleam caught in her eye.

Kaliyah slammed her foot down, missing Kaitlyn's face by less than an inch. Kaitlyn's breath caught in her throat, Kaliyah's scream piercing her ears as it echoed Polae's. Rolling away, Kaitlyn covered her ears from the harsh sound. Daring a glance up, she saw that Vyekrin had Polae's throat in his teeth, black blood dripping down her scales. He had wrapped her up in her own wings, and her struggling only made her wounds worse.

Vyekrin was not unscathed, though. One eye was closed as black blood spilled from a hole in his forehead, and one wing hung limply onto the ground.

Kaitlyn found her gaze wandering back to the crowd, where Cy hung limp in the arms of the Draken. Even from this far away, she could see that he was shaking uncontrollably, his talons unsheathed.

Kaliyah stopped screaming, and Kaitlyn snapped back to attention. "You bitch! How dare you hurt my Polae! You're nothing!" Kaliyah screamed, stomping over to Kaitlyn.

Acting on instinct, Kaitlyn flipped herself onto her back, and kicked her legs out wildly. Kaitlyn winced when she connected with Kaliyah's ankles. The other girl fell to the side, her head cracking against the ground. Blood spurted from the wound, and the girl held herself up on wobbly arms.

Kaitlyn forced herself to stand, stunned at what she'd done. She backed away from Kaliyah, wanting nothing more than to flee. But even in her damaged state, Kaliyah still had an angry fire in her eyes. She glared at Kaitlyn, getting to her feet.

The girls stood facing each other. Kaliyah looked relaxed,

but Kaitlyn could see how tense her muscles were, ready to spring into action at any second. Not knowing what else to do, Kaitlyn raised her fists in front of her face, watching the girl from behind her knuckles. They stood there for a long moment, waiting for each other to move. She thought back to when she had punched Cy, and her hope fled her.

Polae screamed again, fighting against Vyekrin and making him bite down harder on her neck. Kaliyah screamed as well, bolting towards Kaitlyn. Closing her eyes, Kaitlyn swung her arm wildly, praying that it would work.

Her arm flew through the air without hitting anything, and she lost her balance. She stumbled forward, catching her fall with her hands. She pushed herself forward, stumbling into a standing position. She looked around her, expecting a sneak attack from Kaliyah, but the girl could not be seen. When Kaitlyn realized she had been engulfed in shadow, she dared to look up.

A great golden dragon hovered above her, each flap of its great wings silent as though the beast weren't there at all. It was the simplest of all the dragons, looking as though it had come straight from the oldest story, but also the most stunning. It was larger than Vyekrin and carried an air of royalty on its wings. Regal blue eyes watched Kaitlyn curiously before turning to the other two dragons. They halted at once under the great dragon's gaze, and Vyekrin dropped Polae. Moving as one, the two dragons bowed low to the ground, both forgetting their injuries.

The golden dragon had scooped Kaliyah up in its hind paw. She hung limply in its grasp, glaring at Kaitlyn with pure hatred in her eyes, ignoring the blood that should have blurred her vision. Kaitlyn sat on the ground with incredulity, awaiting the dragon's next move. Kaitlyn leaned to the side, hoping to get a view of its rider, but all that could be seen was a silhouette holding itself regally on the dragon's neck.

After a moment, the dragon left the Arena with Kaliyah. Polae followed close behind, her head hung both from shame and her wounds.

No sooner was Kaliyah taken away than Vyekrin was upon Kaitlyn. He picked her up in his paws and drew her close to his face to inspect her. She rubbed his snout weakly, feeling as though she would be sick.

Safe. You are safe now, Vyekrin whispered in her mind over and over. Though his voice was soothing, she knew he was speaking more for his own comfort.

Cy was at the dragon's side next, yelling for Kaitlyn. Vyekrin lowered her slowly, and Cy checked over her wounds as well, but she paid him no mind. Her vision was failing her and it was all she could do to stay awake. She felt hollow inside.

Cy's hand begun to glow green, and he touched the light to her arms gently. She winced at the initial touch, but the magic was warm and familiar, comforting. She smiled at Cy and he returned the gesture, though it was clear it wasn't genuine. Kaitlyn gathered herself to reassure him, but she was cut off as Lane and Orthros ran up to them excitedly.

"I can't believe you held your own against Kaliyah! She must have been going easy on you, since you're new," Lane said. His face was still red from all the excitement, and his smile was glowing. Orthros nodded his head energetically, though he didn't speak.

"I don't think she was going easy," Kaitlyn muttered, finding her voice.

"Hell no, she didn't go easy. Do you see the wounds she's got? What kind of guards do you think you are, letting her get dragged into something like this!" Cy rounded on the two Draken. His

fists were shaking at his side, green sparks escaping from the metal.

"We told you, no one can interfere with a duel once it's begun. Especially not against Kaliyah, she's brutal!" Orthros raised his hands to ward Cy off.

"I noticed! Screw Theresa's orders, I don't want anything to do with you Draken anymore. We're leaving as soon as Kaitlyn's better, with or without your help."

"Cy, it's fine. I don't feel that bad, just scraped up a little. We need all the help we can get, and you know that," Kaitlyn said.

Cy shot her a worried glance. His eyes skimmed over her again, and she put her hands over the worst wounds on her arms. He turned away with a huff. *"We're leaving as soon as we can. I'm not staying here as long as you're in danger."*

Kaitlyn reached for Cy, wanting to argue with him, but the golden dragon had returned. She retracted her hand, a lump forming in her throat. Kaliyah was nowhere to be found.

Lane and Orthros dropped to their knees. "Chieftain Kyros," Lane said in awe.

It landed just in front of Vyekrin, and the dragon bowed again. The golden dragon laid on its stomach, and revealed its rider to be the Chieftain, Kyros. Cy stepped up to him as he dismounted his dragon, but Kaitlyn couldn't hear their conversation.

She studied the Chieftain instead, overwhelmed by him. Kyros wasn't young, but he wasn't old. His features were sharp and defined, the definition of royalty. He held his head high and his shoulders perfectly square as he talked. Long white hair was gathered into a large bun on the back of his head, and a short beard covered his chin. Golden armor made from his dragon's scales covered him from head to toe, but Kaitlyn doubted he had a hard time moving in the weight. In the gaps in the armor, it was easy to see the vast amount of muscles he had. A light blue cape danced in the wind behind him, matching his crystal eyes.

He was the only Draken she had seen with a normal color eye, and it puzzled her. Her curiosity tugged at her, but she hadn't the strength to ask him now. She worried she wouldn't get another chance, and her heart sank.

As Kaitlyn was lost in her mind studying Kyros, he approached her. Taking her hand, he spoke to her, though she could not hear the words. He grazed his fingers along the outline of her face, then down her arms, gentler than she would have thought possible for a Draken. He took in all of her wounds with guilt clear on his handsome face.

He turned back to Cy, and they nodded at each other. Kyros mounted his dragon yet again, and took to the skies. Vyekrin shifted Kaitlyn in his paws so that he could pick Cy up and put him onto his back. Holding Kaitlyn as tight as he could without hurting her further, Vyekrin straightened out his wings, whimpering through the pain as his dislocated wing popped back into place. He launched into the sky, and Kaitlyn fainted.

* * *

Kaitlyn woke to the sound of hushed voices all around her. She rolled onto her side and pulled the blankets over her head, groaning. Her ribs were bruised and her arms throbbed when she moved them. At her movement, all noise stopped.

Removing the blanket from her face, she peeked into the room. It was different than the small house she and Cy had been given for their stay. It was made of a lighter stone, and multiple candles lit the room. It was mostly empty but for a few other beds all in a row.

Sitting around her bed were Cy and Kyros, Vyekrin perched

on her pillow in his lizard form. His face was only an inch from her own, and he stuck his tongue out to lick her nose. With a smile, she moved her hand out from under the blanket, and stroked the top of his head with her fingers.

"What happened?" she asked. She remembered Kaliyah had made her fight, and Vyekrin dueled with Polae. What she didn't understand was why.

"I must apologize deeply for Kaliyah's actions. She's not very sociable, picking fights with anyone that meets her eye. I did not think she would go so far as to attack our guests, but my guess would be it was out of jealousy. She felt threatened," Kyros started. He leaned forward in his chair, clasping his hands on his knees.

"That's not an excuse. She could have killed Kaitlyn! She's only human, and Kaliyah dragged her into a death ring," Cy grumbled, clearly holding back his anger.

"Cy, I told you, it's fine," Kaitlyn protested, feeling guilty at Kyros' calm demeanor.

"No, it's not fine. We came here on an errand for Theresa, and she said we would be welcomed, not attacked. For all we know, this was some sort of sabotage. We were told you were absent, Kyros, but you showed up pretty quick to play hero," Cy snapped.

"Cyllorian! That's no way to speak to someone, especially not their leader," Kaitlyn hissed, before flashing Kyros an apologetic smile. "I'm so sorry he's being difficult, Chieftain."

"No. He's not in the wrong. They sent a messenger to me informing me of your arrival, but when I returned, you had already been taken to the Arena. Orthros and Lane have both been reprimanded for their behaviors toward you as our guests."

"He gets my anger," Cy muttered triumphantly, leaning back in his seat. He crossed his arms over his chest, clearly still not appeased.

Kaitlyn weighed her options a moment, then spoke her mind. Kyros seemed to be level headed, so she felt confident taking a risk with him. "You said she was jealous of me. Why?"

Kyros sighed, letting his shoulders slump. "It is not my story to tell, and I do not feel comfortable sharing the lives of my people so easily."

"Either way, we deserve an explanation. If I tried to kill you for no reason, you'd want to know, right? And you said you'd like us to stay on good terms," Cy pressed.

Kyros nodded slowly. The wear of his title of Chieftain could be seen in his sunken expression. Without meeting their gaze, he began quietly, "You see, she has had a difficult past. I must ask you to leave this secret with you when you depart from here, and not speak of it again. Kaliyah was deserted by her family and home. She came to Deidrich from across the sea, from a land unknown to us, but seems to possess great similarities to our own."

"Across the sea?" Kaitlyn asked, her intrigue taking over her better judgement. "I'm sorry, I didn't mean to interrupt, but... I've never heard of any lands other than Lontorra."

"I haven't heard much of them either, to be honest. Kaliyah has never felt comfortable talking about her place of origin, but I trust that what she says must be true. She flew to our land looking for refuge with Polae, after being chased out when she gained her power to transform into a dragon. None of us here truly understand her gift, but we are accepting of it. Despite this, I doubt she fully trusts us, even after these two years she has resided with us.

"I believe she thought herself to be special to have gained a dragon companion, though she is not a Draken. To have met you, to learn that she is not the only one, threatened her. All of the attention has shifted from her to you, given that you are even more of a curious case."

Kaitlyn sat up and thought for a moment, hanging her head. "I didn't want to mess things up for her. I'm just trying to get things back to normal. I'm sorry."

"It is not your fault. Kaliyah has overreacted, and she will be reprimanded for her actions towards you. You are our guests, and I will not have my people treat you poorly. I wish for Drakens to be accepted into the whole of Lontorra, not feared."

"Maybe Gil doesn't give you guys enough credit, after all," Cy muttered, balancing his chair on its back two legs. He held a calm expression on his face, but it was clear to Kaitlyn how worried he actually was. His fists were clenched, and his eyes never left her face. She squirmed under his gaze, feeling her cheeks go hot as she avoided looking at him.

"Gil?" Kyros asked, his curiosity genuine.

"He's a Droll that's agreed to help us. He doesn't like the Draken very much," Kaitlyn explained. As an afterthought, she added, "Sorry."

Kyros' eyes twitched at the mention of the Droll, but he waved his hand dismissively. "No, you're alright. Draken and Droll have never had the best relations, though not for a lack of trying. Perhaps we should send you with aid ourselves just to prove our kindness. It could be just the spark we need to relieve the tension between our kinds. If two individuals of our kinds can work together for a cause, why can't our colonies as a whole?"

Kyros lost himself in thought, stroking his thin beard. Cy was silent in his chair, balancing himself on one leg. Kaitlyn looked over herself, examining the damage that had been done.

"My wounds are healed perfectly. I was actually under the impression that you didn't have a healer," Kaitlyn confessed as she noticed most of the wounds faded or completely gone.

Kyros and Cy shared a glance before Kyros said sheepishly, "I'm afraid our healers didn't get to you in time. You had already recovered before they could assess your condition."

"Did you do it then, Cy? I remember you healing my arms before."

"That's all I did. Maybe Kaliyah isn't such a hard hitter after all, or she was holding back for some reason. What matters is that you're fine now, right?"

Cy was avoiding the situation, but asking the questions on her mind wouldn't get her any answers, not now. Kyros glared suspiciously at Cy, which only confirmed Kaitlyn's need for answers. There was something they weren't telling her, though it seemed Kyros wanted to.

Kyros sighed heavily, then stood. Making his way to the door, he said, "At any rate, you need to get as much rest as you can. I shall meet with my advisers in light of the recent incident. Cyllorian, you've expressed your desire for a swift departure. I'll do what I can to find a suitable volunteer for your quest by this evening. We will keep Kaliyah under surveillance, but I still ask that you remain here for the rest of the day. We'll have you ready to leave by morning, so long as you'll be patient enough to wait. I'll take my leave now. I hope for your swift recovery, Kaitlyn."

He opened the door to leave, but paused. Quietly, almost threateningly, he added, "Cyllorian, watch her well."

Cy's face was serious as he turned and bowed to the Chieftain. He exited, and his dragon's roar was heard moments later.

"Well, you heard the Chief, you better get some rest. No good staying awake and worrying anyway."

"I don't like sleeping this much, but I am still tired. I definitely don't want to go outside again. Goodnight, Cy."

"Goodnight," he said, trying one last time to perfect his balance on the chair. He moved too sharply and fell to the floor

with a loud BANG. Vyekrin jumped at Kaitlyn's side, hissing. Kaitlyn giggled as Cy began arguing with the lizard, falling back to sleep with a smile.

* * *

"What's going on?" Kaitlyn mumbled, unable to open her eyes. She was being pulled somewhere, her legs unable to work. Her head was throbbing, and she waved her arms with little energy, trying to untangle her hair from whatever had a hold on it.

"We're finishing what we started," a familiar voice hissed in her ear. "Just the two of us. No one to interfere this time."

Kaitlyn was yanked forward, and she tripped over her feet. Her hands shot out to catch her, one of her palms scraping against a rough edge. Her one hand fell forward, and she hurried to catch herself with her other hand. Her eyes shot open, staring into the darkness that pooled below her, surrounding the mountain.

Kaliyah cackled behind her, and Kaitlyn whirled around. The other girl was standing above her, though it was hard to tell it was the same girl. She looked perfectly normal with smooth, darkened skin and straight purple hair. She lacked the claws, wings, and tail of her dragon form, but she didn't look any less threatening.

"Did you really think those stupid guards could hold me?" Kaliyah snapped. "I'm stronger than any Draken here. There's no way they could've held me against my will. You should have known I'd be coming back for you. And with you out of the picture, things will go right back to normal around here. I'll go back to being the center of attention, and Vyekrin will hightail it out of here, hopefully taking that. . .*thing*. . .with him. It'll be like you were never even here at all."

Kaliyah lunged forward and Kaitlyn tried to dive out of the way, but her body was not ready for a fight. Kaliyah caught her by the hair again, and Kaitlyn screamed in pain as she was held over the edge. Tears stung her eyes as she stared into her death.

Kaliyah changed, turning into her dragon form. Her wings beat quietly, and her tail whipped into Kaitlyn's sides. She could feel the claws of the other girl cutting through her hair, piercing into her scalp. She reached her hands around her to grab onto Kaliyah's arm, hoisting herself up. The scales poked into Kaitlyn's palms, and she bit her lip to keep from panicking.

All at once, the fear fell away from Kaitlyn. The pain faded, numbed by the adrenaline that raced through her veins. She tightened her grip on Kaliyah's wrist, unsure of what her plan was. Everything slowed and Kaitlyn's vision dulled as her body moved on its own.

She twisted on the spot, flinging one arm out. It hit Kaliyah in the side, and Kaitlyn felt a rib break under the pressure. Kaliyah buckled. She gasped in shock, stumbling backwards. Kaitlyn got to her feet, taking a fighting stance.

She spread her feet and her fingers curled like talons. Her muscles were stiff with tension, and her skin felt taut over her arms and legs. She blamed her odd feeling on the adrenaline. Though her vision was still blurred by stress and darkness hung in the air like a fog, she could see a shape she expected to be Kaliyah, and she watched it closely.

The two girls circled each other, Kaitlyn defensive and Kaliyah more hostile than ever. Kaliyah jumped for Kaitlyn, but she grabbed the other girl's shoulders and used her leg to propel Kaliyah overhead, rolling onto her back. She heard the girl's claws scraping against the stone, and turned to see her hanging off the edge. Kaitlyn inched closer. She debated whether or not to kick Kaliyah's hand and make the girl lose her grip, but she didn't get the time to make a decision.

Kaliyah hoisted herself onto the ledge, her wings beating furiously. Kaitlyn's vision was beginning to clear, and she could see the strain on Kaliyah's face.

Catching a glance of her own arms, Kaitlyn was shocked at the shine on her skin from the moonlight. It nearly blinded her, and she did her best to ignore it. *I'm sweating so much. Is it fear or the fight?* she thought absentmindedly. Her attention was focused on the girl in front of her, drowning out her thoughts.

Kaliyah ran at her, yelling in rage. Her scream gave Kaitlyn just enough time to react, and she sidestepped the girl at the last second. Her foot caught Kaliyah's, and both girls tumbled to the ground. Kaitlyn hit the side of her head on the ground, stunning herself.

Kaliyah was on top of her in an instant, her knees pinning Kaitlyn's arms. Kaitlyn squirmed under the other girl, and though Kaliyah was small and lightweight, she was all muscle, and was holding Kaitlyn down with sheer strength.

Kaliyah's hands came down on Kaitlyn's throat, strangling her. Claws dug into Kaitlyn's flesh, and her blood was hot against her already flushed skin. Kaitlyn bucked desperately, doing anything she could to get free of Kaliyah. With a last burst of energy as her vision started to fade again, she kneed Kaliyah in the back. A sickening crack resounded in the air.

It caught the girl in her spine, and she arched in pain. Her hands fell limp around Kaitlyn's neck. While Kaliyah gasped, Kaitlyn used all of her weight to throw the other girl off. She rolled away from her, chugging air into her lungs at a rate that burned her throat.

Kaliyah was on the ground, holding herself up with one shaky arm. The other was wrapped around herself, feeling her back. Her mouth was agape and her eyes wide as her hand moved from her back to her legs. She rubbed them at first, then began pounding them with all her might, screaming manically. She slashed at her legs with her claws. Blood pooled around the gashes, staining the shorts that she wore. Tears glistened on her cheeks, and sobs hitched in her throat

The adrenaline rushed out of Kaitlyn as quickly as it had come, and she fell to her knees. "Kaliyah..." she gasped, coming into herself. She couldn't believe what was happening. She reached out toward the girl, wanting nothing more than to help the person that had tried to kill her.

Kaliyah's head shot up, and she glared at Kaitlyn. Despite her pain and anguish, a fire roiled within her eyes. With another scream of insanity that pierced Kaitlyn's ears, she used her arms to fling herself on Kaitlyn.

Though Kaliyah didn't have the control she had before, Kaitlyn no longer had the fighting spirit. She threw her arms up to shield her face from the flurry of swipes. Kaitlyn cringed with each hit Kaliyah landed, but the pain she had expected wasn't there. There was a ringing in Kaitlyn's ears that she couldn't place, and she put her questions to the back of her mind.

Footsteps could be heard in the distance, though just barely. Kaitlyn's arms finally gave out, and Kaliyah leaned over her in triumph, raising a hand to strike.

Kaliyah's arms swiped within an inch of Kaitlyn's face. With a desperate yell of her own, Kaitlyn lashed out and slapped the girl. Kaliyah was thrown off of her, and curled up on her side. She clutched her face, cursing and whining to herself.

Kaitlyn crawled over to the girl and saw blood between her fingers. Long gashes ran across Kaliyah's entire face, bleeding profusely. Doing the only thing she knew how, Kaitlyn screamed for help, pressing her hands to Kaliyah's face to stop the bleeding. Despite Kaliyah's threats and protests, she didn't fight Kaitlyn any further.

Within seconds, a group descended upon them. Strong arms tore Kaitlyn from Kaliyah and held her tight. Vyekrin appeared between them, pacing in the small space. His tail twitched in agitation, a continuous hiss streaming from his mouth.

"Kaitlyn. Kaitlyn! Are you okay? What the hell happened? I was gone for five minutes! How could this happen. Oh shit, your arms. What the hell is up with your arms?!"

Cy turned Kaitlyn to face him, but she couldn't see him. The moonlight was reflecting off of his chest, showing every detail of Arion's craftsmanship. She found herself getting lost in each line, in every overlapping piece of metal.

"My arm…?" she asked in disbelief. Cy lifted her arm to his face, studying it. "I don't care about my arm, we have to help her, I don't know what happened. What I did…" Kaitlyn lost her words as she glanced at the other girl. She was curled up on the ground, her arms wrapped tightly around herself.

Cy put his hands on her shoulder to steady her, and she gazed into his eyes. He looked afraid and angry. *"I couldn't give a damn about her! There's something wrong with you!"*

"Wrong? Because I care about someone other than myself? I'm not in pain, I can't even feel anything. Happy now?" Kaitlyn burst, losing her temper.

"Not that, Kaitlyn. They're covered in scales! And you have claws. What exactly happened out here?"

Kaitlyn stared down at her arms in shock. What she had thought was sweat glistening before were tiny blue scales covering her arm from her fingers to just past her elbow. She grazed her fingers, now tipped with thin white claws, over them, relishing in the smoothness. They began again at her shoulder, and she couldn't find where they ended on her back.

Lifting her fingers to her face, she found more scales splotched across her cheeks, forehead, chin, and around her eyes. They covered her hairline, leaving very little skin left on her face.

Kaitlyn dropped her hand to her side, where it shook wildly. She looked behind her, at Kaliyah now restrained and unconscious on the ground. Vyekrin was pressing her down with one large paw, and her face was bleeding freely now. Kyros stood over her, his face solemn as he watched her. Without her dragon form, she looked like nothing more than an injured little girl.

She turned back to Cy, her eyes brimming with tears. "What have I done?"

CHAPTER 12

Kaitlyn

The cave was dark, the opening facing away from the rising sun. The rock wall was cold on Kaitlyn's back, even through the jacket she wore. Her mind was racing and nerves were eating at her insides.

Kyros had found a Draken to join them, but the preparations would take a little longer. They had sent her away, to wait with Gil while Cy and Kyros finalized their plans. She had so many questions she had wanted to ask Cy, but he wouldn't answer any of them. He told her to wait until they had left the Drakens.

"They sure are taking a long time," Kaitlyn whispered. She glanced up at Gil, leaning against the wall across from her. Gil's arms were wrapped around his body, keeping himself warm from the incoming wind. He was as far from the entrance to the cave as they could be while watching for Cy and their Draken.

Kaitlyn squirmed closer to the entrance as another gust of

wind blew past. She tightened her grip on her chest, the thick coat awkward over her arms. The scales from the night before hadn't faded, nor had they been a dream. Cy had made her promise to keep them a secret from Gil until he joined them.

Vyekrin was curled up in the darkness of the cave, but his blue eyes shone brightly. She hadn't seen him with his eyes closed since they had found her last night. He hadn't even blinked, and it scared her. She could read the fear and guilt in his eyes, but nothing she had said or done would calm him.

Kaitlyn thought back to their fight, to the primal rage in Kaliyah's eyes, then to the sorrow of her defeat. The way she had been curled up after Kaitlyn kneed her, the fact that she had dragged herself by her arms, gave Kaitlyn a bad feeling in her stomach. *Did I paralyze her? Did I do something permanent?*

The questions whirled through her head, and she felt dizzy. She stepped outside of the cave, scratching at her scaled wrist.

"If you're too hot, why don't you take off that coat? It looks too big for you, anyway. It would fit me better," Gil said, coming close to Kaitlyn. He reached out to grab the sleeve of the coat, and a breeze caught his hand. He jumped back with a yelp, examining his skin.

The cold could be deadly to him, Kaitlyn knew, but Cy had been strict when he told her to keep herself covered until they figured things out. They hoped that Kyros would know more, but Kaitlyn was sure there was more to the situation than Cy was telling her.

She glanced at Gil, scarily pale in the bitter cold. She was extremely hot under the coat, as the scales gave her an extra layer of protection. Even her insides seemed to be warmer. She was sweating. Biting her lip, she shrugged off the coat and tossed it to Gil.

He caught it easily and put it on as fast as possible, burying his chin in it. He held it to himself, sighing in content. "So warm," he muttered. His eyes fluttered open as he started to thank Kaitlyn, but he stopped short. His eyes went wide and his jaw fell slack. His mouth moved slowly as he worked out the pieces in his head, and finally said, "What happened to you?"

Kaitlyn looked away, unsure how to feel about the situation. It had scared her at first, but in all honesty, it didn't feel too out-of-place to her. It felt like it was how she was supposed to be. She raised her arm, the blue scales glinting in the light. She stared at Vyekrin. Her scales matched his perfectly, like Kaliyah's had matched Polae's. Maybe she was like Kaliyah.

"It's a long story," Kaitlyn said slowly. "I got attacked by a girl. She wasn't a Draken. She was mad that I had a dragon and was taking all the attention, so she tried to kill me. Twice. The second time, I guess I just transformed to defend myself. I was tired, and it was dark, so I didn't realize what was going on until after it was all done. They haven't gone away, but it just happened last night."

"One of them attacked you, and you stayed long enough for there to be a second attack?"

"They had her locked up, but she's the best fighter they have, so obviously she got away. It's not like they had intended for her to attack me. They tried to keep us safe. They're not all that bad, Gil. Maybe you should try to work something out with the Draken that comes with us."

"I don't want anything to do with them. They stay away from me, and we won't have any problems."

Kaitlyn sighed as Gil stomped his foot in determination. Though he was much thinner than the Drakens, Kaitlyn was sure he was agile and fast enough to hold his own in a fight. *With all the testosterone in the group, he might have to.*

"Kaitlyn, I thought I told you to keep the coat on?" Cy said as he jogged up to her. Ice crystals were forming on his shoulders.

She pulled him under the shelter of the cave. He shook the snow from his body, but seemed otherwise unphased.

"Gil was cold, and I wasn't. So I gave it to him. He was going to find out eventually, and we trust him, right?" Kaitlyn looked at the ground, ashamed that she was making him worry about her again. She knew he wasn't being warry of Gil, just concerned. She wished she would have just listened to Cy, but it was too late now

He glanced towards Gil, retreating into the cave to lean against Vyekrin. The dragon's tail twitched nervously, though he didn't seem to mind.

"Right," Cy said with resolve.

"Are we going to just stand around, or are we going to get moving?" a voice said from outside the cave. A Draken with long gray hair and solid features stood holding the straps of his pack. Steam rose from his body between the creases of his light brown armor. Wayonn remained just outside the cave, and through the heavy snowfall, Kaitlyn almost thought the dragon was playing.

"Jayr?" Kaitlyn asked, remembering the Draken that had fought against Kaliyah. "It was you that volunteered? But we don't even know you."

"No, but I know you. I feel as though I have a debt to repay, for Kaliyah's mistreatment towards you."

"Why would you feel responsible for her? Didn't she kick your ass the other day, and every other day, from what we were told?" Cy asked scathingly.

"That she did. Regardless, I would like to pay my respects to you in hopes to make up for her poor behavior."

"Seriously what's going on here? You got some ulterior motive, don't you? You have to," Cy insisted.

Jayr sighed. "If you must know, I take responsibility for Kaliyah's actions because she is my betrothed. I am the strongest male in Deidrich, second only to her. It only fitting that we wed."

"So it's an arranged marriage?" Kaitlyn asked. She felt sorry for Jayr. Not only for who he was engaged to, but that it might not even be his own choice.

"It is. It is our custom."

"Your custom? Ha! Why don't you just break it like you do all your other customs?" Gil remarked from the depths of the cave. Vyekrin jumped at his sudden outburst, growling at the Droll.

"I assume that voice is that of the Droll within our party. Keep your words to yourself, Droll. And I shall keep my blades to myself," Jayr said.

"Ah, yes. Greet me with a threat, just like I knew you would. You're so predictable, though I wouldn't expect much more from the likes of you." Gil stomped to the mouth of the cave, fists at the ready.

Jayr took a step forward, his hand resting on the handle of his blade.

Gil puffed at the clear threat in Jayr's actions. "Give me a crossbow and you won't even have a chance to draw your swords. That's a promise," Gil hissed.

"Enough!" Kaitlyn yelled, stepping between them. "We don't have time to fight like this. You have a problem, you take it up with me, which *really* means that Vyekrin will squash you. We've got more important things to discuss right now."

Vyekrin was at her side at the sound of his name, glaring at Jayr and Gil. Jayr backed down first, returning to a relaxed position. Gil forced himself to calm, though his jaw remained clenched.

"Cyllorian," Kaitlyn said pointedly, turning to Cy. He looked away from her, and the gears on the sides of his head spun fiercely. "What did you find out?"

All eyes were on Cy, but he refused to meet a single one. *"Do we have to do this now? I thought we were in a hurry?"*

Gil looked between Kaitlyn and Cy, understanding in his expression. "You still didn't tell her?"

"Tell me what? Gil, do you know something?" Kaitlyn whirled on Gil, and he looked away from her gaze.

"Cy wouldn't let me say anything," he answered, glancing at Cy.

Kaitlyn turned to him again, but he didn't look too willing to talk. "What aren't you telling me?" Kaitlyn tried forcing herself to remain calm. Cy tilted his head back, staring at the ceiling with a vacant expression. "I thought you trusted me, that you wouldn't keep any more secrets from me? Have I just been following you around blindly for no reason? Does it have to do with this?"

Her questions all came out at once. She lifted her arm, taking a step towards Cy.

He took an unsteady step away from her. The plates that made up his jaw were shifting continuously. His glowing eyes were darting toward Kaitlyn. She stared him down, her breath looking more like smoke in the cold air. Cy's hands were shaking at his sides. His eyes went dark for a moment, then his voice boomed throughout the cave behind her.

"You're not human, Kaitlyn! I don't know what you are, but magic has a strong effect on you. I didn't want to tell you, because I didn't want to ruin the possibility of you being able to go back to normal once this is over." Cy confessed this all in a rush. He finally met her gaze, his eyes dull.

"I'm not... human? How is that possible? I've always been human. Maybe I'm just sick, or cursed. I can't be..." Kaitlyn's gaze fell. Horror was set on her round features, and shock had left her frozen.

Kaitlyn's words faded as she stared at her hands. The blue

scales shimmered over her skin, and the white claws were undeniable.

Gil stepped up to her and put a hand on her shoulder. His touch was cool against her skin, burning from the scales.

Everyone was silent for a long moment before Gil broke the silence, "What do we do now?"

"The next step is getting off this damn mountain. That means we start climbing," Cy said as he marched toward the mouth of the cave. The storm that had been so violent just moments before was already fading, large clumps of snow drifting slowly to the ground.

"Not necessarily. I have a better option," Jayr said. "We've got two dragons, right? Each dragon can carry two, and we'll get to Kindling Woods in no time."

"Kindling Woods. You have got to be kidding me," Cy snapped. *"What makes you think we'd ever go there?"*

Kaitlyn looked to each face, taking in the terror rooted in their features. "What's wrong with the Kindling Woods? I don't know what you all are so scared of. They're just fairies and pixies, right?"

Cy didn't answer, and he refused to meet her gaze. He was too preoccupied with Jayr.

Jayr spoke next, never breaking eye contact with Cy. "They have a strong affinity with life. They're the most likely ones to have a way to help your cause. Theresa told me when I made my decision to join your cause."

Cy's eyes narrowed. *"When was that?"*

Jayr hesitated. "Last night. I was with Kaliyah, and I told her. I'm afraid my decision had set her off and caused the second attack on your life, Kaitlyn. That is why I am more determined than ever to help you in any way that I can."

Cy's face contorted so suddenly that the metal bent under pressure. The smooth edges of the individual plates twisted into each other, forming sharp edges. He balled his hands into fists so tight that his fingers tore through his palms like paper. *"Theresa was here* last night! *And she didn't bother to check up on us, or tell us herself what to do next? That bitch! I swear I'm gonna..."* Cy stomped his foot with enough force to buckle the metal at his knee. Kaitlyn was sure that the only thing keeping him from going into a full rampage was his body crumpling with each move.

"Cyllorian," Kaitlyn said, cutting him off. She glared at him, though she could feel the hint of fear that shone through her strict demeanor. Cy took a deep breath, then shut his mouth tight. Whatever else it was he had planned to say, he locked away in his mind. He set himself to prying his hands apart, his metal groaning in protest at his abuse.

"It doesn't matter now, does it? We have a destination. Vyekrin will carry Kaitlyn and the Droll, and the demon and I will ride on Wayonn," Jayr said. He turned on his heel to mount Wayonn.

"Don't you think I should ride with Kaitlyn?" Cy asked. He glared at Jayr, but the Draken paid him no notice.

"You really expect me to ride with *him?*" Gil retorted, disgusted. He had draped his arms protectively around Kaitlyn's shoulders and was resting his chin against her head. Vyekrin was laying obediently on the ground behind them.

Kaitlyn felt guilty at the relief that ran through her knowing she didn't have to ride with Cy. She couldn't bear to be with him right after finding out he had kept something so drastic from her. How could he just decide on his own to hide that from her, let alone force everyone else to stay silent? Even if he said it was for her own protection, how could she believe him now?

"I'll be fine with Gil, Cy. Besides, we don't want them to fight." Kaitlyn wiggled out of Gil's grasp. Without waiting for

Cy's response, she climbed onto Vyekrin's neck, taking his horns into her hands, and Gil sat behind her. She did her best to stop her shaking, knowing it would only worry Gil.

"You don't even know how to fly! What if you can't hold on?" Cy argued.

"I don't need to know. Vyekrin can do it on his own. He won't let anything happen to me. It'll be alright, Cy, I promise. We need to get moving, don't we?" Kaitlyn argued. Vyekrin raised himself. Kaitlyn could almost touch the ceiling.

"Now or never, demon. Get on," Jayr snapped. Wayonn had snuck beside Cy, his scales scraping against Cy's metal.

With a groan, Cy hoisted himself onto the scorpion dragon, putting a few inches between him and Jayr. He crossed his arms over his chest defiantly, but the magic in him was stuttering. The metal plates chattered together as though he were shaking.

Before Kaitlyn could ask if he would be okay, Wayonn took to the exit of the cave. Vyekrin darted after him, and Kaitlyn let out a sharp yelp at the sudden movement. She held her body close to Vyekrin's, closing her eyes as the two dragons began to scale the side of the mountain. Gil clung to her tight enough to restrict her breathing.

Vyekrin jumped off the cliff side, and Kaitlyn's eyes shot open. The dragons dived toward the ground, leaning this way and that. They pulled up suddenly and rolled midair until they righted themselves, gliding effortlessly through the sky. They climbed higher with large beats of their wings until they were level with the mountain being left behind them.

It was easier now that Kaitlyn couldn't tell how high they were, but she didn't dare look down. Wayonn was ahead of them, and she watched the way the odd dragon moved.

He had his six legs curled under him, and his arms bent over him to hold Cy and Jayr in place on his wide back.

Wayonn's four wings were long and thin, like a dragonfly's, and they reflected the light into a rainbow of colors around him. His tail was coiled carefully behind him, clearly ready to strike if necessary.

Gil loosened his grip as well, though Kaitlyn could still feel his face buried in her shoulder. She shakily let go of Vyekrin with one hand to pat his head, and Gil hugged her tighter. "Cy's gonna kill me," she heard him grumble.

Kaitlyn wanted to ask what he meant, but she couldn't find her voice at the elevation. The air was nearly too thin to breathe, and she wanted Vyekrin to fly lower, but they couldn't lose the others no matter what.

Kaitlyn sat silently as Vyekrin flew, watching Lontorra appear around the mountain. She could see so much of the land, but it never seemed to end. And beyond Lontorra was the sea, sparkling under the sun. *Kaliyah came from across the sea. I want to know what's there. I want to go for myself!*

Kaitlyn's excitement replaced her fear. With Vyekrin, she could go wherever she pleased, making her own adventures and learning about the world. *I don't even know everything about this land, though. Not even close.*

Finding it easier to breathe, Kaitlyn turned to Gil. "What are Kindling?" she asked over the rushing wind in her ears.

Gil shook his head against her back. "The best way to explain it is they're nature's advocates. They care for the natural world, and hate those that disturb it. They have a lot of influence and magic, including special healing rituals. If we can get their help, great, but if not...I just hope we can make it out. They don't take too kindly to strangers."

"Cyllorian called it the Lost Soul Woods before. Is it really that bad?"

"Once you enter, you can't leave without the help of a Kindling. The magic of the forest won't allow it. Many people have died in there just because they wandered in without realizing, or they were lured in. The Kindling can be cruel when they want to be."

"Why would Theresa send us there without being sure they would help? It has to be safe, right?" Kaitlyn's stomach was doing flips after hearing Gil's words. He didn't answer, and she felt him slump against her in defeat.

She wanted to yell out to Wayonn, to stop Jayr. If it was so dangerous, they didn't need to go. With the dragons, it would be all too easy to find their way back to the castle. She glanced below her, hoping to catch sight of it.

Her chest felt as though a vice had caught her, and she lost her voice again. The ground was so far away, and she knew that a drop from this height would kill her instantly. Her breathing was labored, and she tried screaming. She didn't want to fly anymore. She just wanted to land, to get out of the air.

Almost as though Vyekrin had heard her thoughts, the dragon turned his nose towards the ground. It came at them with great speed, and Kaitlyn felt her hands slipping from Vyekrin's horns. She dug her heels into his sides desperately, knowing that if she were to fall, Gil would die as well. In a last attempt, Kaitlyn released the horns altogether and flung herself onto Vyekrin's neck. She winced as her claws chipped his scales, but she couldn't let go. She held on with all of her strength until Vyekrin jolted underneath her, and came to a halt.

Gil was off Vyekrin instantly, collapsing onto the ground and gasping. Kaitlyn pried her claws from Vyekrin's neck guiltily and slid off his neck. Her legs felt hollow, and she fell to her knees. Cy was already at her side, and he caught her shoulder, keeping her upright. She grabbed onto his arm for support. She felt her claws pierce into his metal, and she loosened her grip, though Cy didn't seem to notice.

Vyekrin wrapped his tail around Kaitlyn and Gil, pulling the four of them into a huddle. His warmth was comforting, and Kaitlyn found herself soothing easily. She reached out to Gil. He was breathing deeply through his mouth, and his shaking had stopped. She rubbed his back with her shaking hands. He reached behind him to squeeze her hands, letting out one final, rattling breath before he calmed completely.

Kaitlyn pulled herself up onto Vyekrin, examining the area around them. The trees were twice Vyekrin's size and stretched to the horizon in either direction. There was no way around them. Their bark was dark in color, with prickly spines on the branches instead of leaves. Vibrant yellow-green moss was scattered along the ground, climbing up the trunks of the trees to overrun them.

On the other side of the woods, the great walls of Centric could be seen. They seemed so close, as though there was no distance between the group and the Mages. It seemed impossible for there to be enough woods for a civilization to reside in.

"We have more to get done today, don't we?" Jayr scoffed from Wayonn's side.

"Does it look like they can keep going? They never flew before, give them a minute!" Cy yelled, stepping out from the circle of Vyekrin's tail.

"Fine, but we can't just lay here in the open forever."

"We should make camp," Gil said sheepishly.

Kaitlyn shook her head at him, but found that no one else objected. "We just started for the day. We'll be fine without rest until later." She didn't want to give herself the chance to think, didn't want to guess at what was next. She didn't want to worry about Arion, or about how she was changing. She just wanted to fix the problem as quickly as possible.

"We don't have a plan, Kaitlyn. No one knows how big these woods really are, or where to even begin looking for the Kindlings. Our best bet is to camp and set up a plan while we can still see."

Jayr and Gil nodded in unison, but stopped in a hurry when they noticed they were moving in sync. Gil let out an annoyed huff and turned away from Jayr while he smirked at the Droll.

"Vyekrin?" Kaitlyn turned to her dragon, desperate for support.

"I will not fit within those woods. The trees have grown too close to each other. The longer I can remain in my true form, the happier I will be." The great dragon lowered his head to the ground, guilty at betraying his master. His large eyes begged her for forgiveness, and she was reminded of a puppy.

Kaitlyn's shoulders slumped, as she was outnumbered. She sat on the ground, near enough to the trees to be shaded. Her scales were still present, and it was unbearably hot compared to the cruel snow storms of the mountain. While she had accepted being magical at first, she had secretly hoped she would go back to normal once they had left the Draken. She didn't know how to fit into this world, and she feared it was too late to learn.

"Fine. We make camp. We leave as soon as the sun rises," she grumbled finally, her internal irritation slipping into her voice.

She fell backwards slowly, and Vyekrin slid behind her for her to rest on. Though it was still early, she had yet to recover from the events of the night before.

The others bickered around her, and she waved her hand to shut them up. "Wake me when it's time to go. You magical people can figure out how to find the fairies."

Magical people? I'm like them, now, aren't I? Kaitlyn pulled her legs to her chest, forcing her mind to go blank.

Vyekrin used his wing as a blanket to cover her, and the darkness made her fall asleep instantly.

She slept fitfully, dreams of wandering throughout the Kindling Woods filling her mind. In her dreams, he was lost and alone, caught under the malicious gaze of unknown threats.

Kaitlyn jolted awake. Gil was leaning over her, his face scarily pale in the shadows that surrounded them. She sat up and looked around, willing the grogginess from her mind.

She was no longer laying on Vyekrin. She felt his small tail wrapped around her neck, and a light weight on her shoulders that told her he was in his lizard form. The trees around them were clustered close together, giving them barely any room to breathe, let alone stay together. Jayr stood a foot away, standing over Cy who was laying on the ground. Jayr was yelling and kicking at him. Kaitlyn looked back to Gil, a question in her gaze, and the fear that contorted his face had Kaitlyn alert in an instant. She shot herself from the ground and bolted for Cy, her suspicions from just a few hours earlier entirely forgotten.

"Cy. Cy, wake up!" Kaitlyn screamed as she shook Cy. The light in his eyes was gone, though a faint spark of magic could still be seen in his chest. The others were standing around her, though none were inclined to help.

Jayr was glaring at Cy's body, looking like he was ready to kick it again. "Damn demon! I knew we shouldn't have trusted him."

Gil was concerned, though he looked helpless in the situation. He was more worried that they had been swallowed by the Kindling Woods while they had slept.

Vyekrin was pacing across Kaitlyn's shoulders. They were

all so on edge, yet she couldn't grasp the situation. They were in the Kindling Woods? Why, and how did they all get in here. She looked to Gil first for answers, but it seemed he had been stunned into silence.

Jayr was roiling at her side. "It's all your fault we're in this mess, demon. Get up and take responsibility!" he burst, fists ready at his sides.

"Enough!" Kaitlyn snapped. She whirled on him and abruptly shoved his legs. He stumbled away from Cy, falling to the ground as he was caught off guard. His wide eyes shot to Kaitlyn, and it took everything she had not to sneer at him. *A few hours isn't long enough to judge him*, she reminded herself.

Shaking her head at the others, Kaitlyn quickly opened the clasp on Cy's chest. The metal heart inside was just as stunning as ever, filled with the glow of Arion's magic. Wary of the silver claw that still tipped her finger, she tapped the heart. Sliding her talon along the clasp, the heart fell open, and the magic burst from within. It filled Cy's body, and he came to life with a start.

"Glad you finally decided to wake up," Jayr snorted, spitting in Cy's direction. Though he was as snide as before, he had put as much distance between him and Kaitlyn as he could in the cramped space. Cy put a hand to his head and stared at the Draken curiously.

Kaitlyn glared at him, a short hiss escaping her lips. "I told you that's enough, Jayr. This isn't anyone's fault, so just shut up."

"He was supposed to be keeping watch over us last night, and he went and fell asleep. Now look where we are."

Kaitlyn resolved to staring the Draken down, but she couldn't argue. She had fallen asleep long before them, and had no idea what had taken place after. Whatever it was, it had stewed up resentment in Jayr.

Cy looked around them, not breathing. Kaitlyn looked with him, wondering what he could be thinking. *"We've been invited inside,"* he breathed, pure terror in his voice. *"I figured they would be expecting us, but I never thought they'd be so eager."*

Cy had found something menacing about the forest, but Kaitlyn only saw beauty here. Even though it was the middle of the night, the leaves around were glowing. The ground barely held any grass, most of it covered with bright flowers, weeds, and berry bushes. The trees were amazingly tall, and smelled wonderful. There was a chorus of animals in the forest surrounding them, playing a song in perfect harmony with one another.

Cy stood abruptly and turned to face away from the group, closing up his chest. He took a long, ragged breath that shook his frame. The rattling of the air through his body rang throughout the trees, quieting the creatures that chattered around them. His arms fell to his sides, knocking against something in his pocket, searching through them and gathering the interest of everyone. He pulled out another crystal ball, this one filled with a dim pink light. He shook it angrily, but the image never changed.

"Was Theresa here?" Jayr asked dutifully.

"Hell if I know. You think she actually ever tells me anything?"

"Would she have done something like this? Thrown us in here if we didn't want to go?" Gil asked, stepping forward. He was wringing his hands nervously, avoiding looking at the light within the ball.

"I wouldn't put it past her, honestly. She's probably pissed we've taken this long already. I swear, she's gone as soon as we get back. She's been nothing but trouble."

"How can you say that?" Jayr hissed. He stepped forward, a fire alight within him. "She is a great Mage, and teacher."

"How? You really *wanna know how? Maybe because she never*

cared about me, or anyone for that matter. She was supposedly dead for sixteen years, until she shows up on my doorstep and ruins every-thing! What I want to know is how you can be so damn loyal to her?" Cy burst, his hands curling into fists. He sneered at Jayr, clearly fighting to keep himself in control.

Wayonn had appeared on Jayr's shoulder as Cy yelled. His smaller form was that of a scorpion with gnarled wings, its stinger more bulbous than should be possible.

"I am loyal because of her devotion to us. She has spent many nights with us, healing our injured and teaching us of the rest of the world. She is a welcomed member of Deidrich, and a great ally to a cause we share," Jayr argued.

"Theresa taught us, too. We're not very good, but she taught us how to fight without relying on ranged weapons," Gil said quietly. "But is that really important right now? We've got bigger problems, our bags-" Gil started, but Cy cut him off with his ranting.

"She spent more time with you guys than she did with us. Unbe-lievable. Just great." Cy stepped back, losing his will to fight. Though he'd calmed, Kaitlyn could see it was just the begin-ning. Anything would set him off now.

"Cy," she said softly, taking a step toward him. He raised a hand to ward her off, and she saw how badly he was shaking. Vyekrin was stiff on her shoulder, feeling the tension in the air.

"Why would someone like Theresa ever care about some-thing like you? As if a *demon* could ever be worth her time," Jayr spat, a triumphant grin on his face.

At the remark, Cy completely froze, not even the gears scat-tered over his body dared to spin. With a savage yell, he lunged for Jayr. He smacked the dragon from the boy's shoulder and tackled him into a tree. Cy lifted him a foot from the ground, his talons digging into Jayr's throat. Jayr's eyes were wide as he searched the ground for his dragon, but Wayonn was stunned from hitting a tree.

No one so much as breathed in that moment. Kaitlyn watched in fear at Cy's rage. Gil was taken aback, looking at Cy as though it was the first time he had seen him. Jayr was sweating profusely in Cy's grip, reaching towards his blade slowly. Cy caught the advance, and moved so fast that Kaitlyn couldn't even see what he had done. He was now holding Jayr with the opposite hand, twisting his arm to the side. His blade spun through the air, landing a few inches in front of Kaitlyn. It was buried up to the hilt into the hard ground, wobbling.

Cy was smiling viciously at Jayr, his pointed teeth nearly grazing his skin. *"That's right. I am a demon. That means I don't give a damn about anyone but myself, especially you!"* Cy released Jayr's arm and raised his hand to strike.

Vyekrin hissed on Kaitlyn's shoulder and sprang. He turned into a dragon midair, crushing five trees before he had no more room to move. He snatched Cy, and threw him across the clearing. He flew into Gil, knocking both of them over. Cy was on his feet in an instant, growling at Vyekrin, but stopped short.

Jayr was pinned underneath one of Vyekrin's large paws. His face was turning red with the struggle for air, his hands clawing at the ground for escape. He spotted Wayonn, now conscious, and begged him for help with his eyes. The scorpion looked away, too frightened to go up against Vyekrin and too ashamed to look at his master.

Vyekrin drew his face within inches of Jayr's. The Draken froze when Vyekrin spoke. *"You will do well to not speak of things of which you have no knowledge. If you do not agree with our choices, or the makeup of this group, then by all means, get out of this forest alive by yourself."*

Vyekrin released Jayr and the boy rolled onto his side, gasping for breath. The dragon then looked to Cy, and they shared a long, meaningful glance. Cy was the first to look away, with a gleam in his eye that Kaitlyn thought could have been tears if Cy could cry in this body.

Kaitlyn observed the exchange in confusion. Vyekrin had been with her all along. He knew all about Arion's childhood. She had no idea how old he was, or what he had done when he wasn't with her. Vyekrin had worked alongside Cy to protect her, so they would have enough in common. What could they have talked about when she had been asleep or unconscious?

Cy rubbed his face with his hands, his claws creating a high-pitched whining to split the air. Gil grabbed his hands and yanked them away. The fear was gone from Gil, replaced by irritation.

"Can we just get out of here already? And besides, I thought you promised me first go at the Draken?"

"I said you'd have your chance. I didn't say you get first pick," Cy grumbled, stepping away.

"How are we supposed to get out? We don't even know where we are," Kaitlyn said, wanting to distract them from the fight.

"What if we use the dragons to go over the trees and look for the edge?" Gil bent backward dramatically, his hands on his hips. He twisted this way and that, trying to catch a glimpse of the sky through the treetops.

Vyekrin was the first to speak, his voice regal and solemn. *"That will not work. This form of mine is too large to fit through the canopy, nor do I have the strength to level enough trees. The same goes for Wayonn. In our smaller forms, we might get out, but it would take quite a long time to climb the trees and there is no guarantee of a decent view once we reach the top. These woods are made for one creature, and one creature only...Kindling. Anything else, save for small animals, will perish in these woods."*

"What are we supposed to do now?" Kaitlyn asked, wrapping her arms around her. Vyekrin shrunk himself slowly, detangled his limbs from the crushed trees. He climbed onto Kaitlyn's lap, and she rested her hand on his back instinctively.

"I don't know about you, but I sure ain't just rolling over and dying in here. I've got shit to do," Cy grumbled.

"You got any bright ideas?" Gil asked. He watched the Draken closely as he retrieved his sword, but Kaitlyn was more distracted by Gil. Where he normally looked careless and simple, the expression he wore now was much more mature, calculating.

Jayr crouched to pry the sword from the ground, but halted suddenly. He sat still for a long moment before Gil took a step towards him.

"Hey, hothead, I'm talking to you!" Gil said as he came within inches of Jayr's back. With a grunt, he pushed Jayr with his foot. Jayr caught himself easily on the hilt of his blade. His grip was tight on the handle, and Gil backed away slowly.

Kaitlyn watched in silence. She couldn't believe what she was seeing. She dared a glance at Cy, but he seemed entirely uninterested, kicking at the ground and muttering to himself.

What is this place doing to us? They're all so hostile towards each other now. What could have happened while I was asleep? Kaitlyn's attention wandered. Across from her, she thought she saw a pair of small blue eyes, but they faded before she could be certain they had even existed at all. A shiver ran down her spine and she hugged herself tightly. Suddenly, this place was no longer beautiful to her. It was deadly.

Are we being toyed with? The thought flitted through her mind without her consent. A nasty feeling was settling in the pit of her stomach and she bit her tongue to chase away the nausea.

"What about this?" Jayr said, diverting Kaitlyn's attention away from her worrying thoughts. Turning to face them, Jayr held up his hands to show a bright pink ball of light nestled in the palm of his hand.

He held the ball up and it danced in his hands, swaying in the wind. It dove toward the trees, but bounced back, waiting for him.

Cy scrambled to bring the crystal ball from his pocket. The light inside matched the wisp that Jayr had found. Cy glared at the Draken over the crystal ball. *"Where did you get that?"*

"It just showed up. Maybe it heard us. We weren't exactly being careful or quiet, you know."

"It's probably a trap. It's the only thing that makes sense. Either way, we don't have any better ideas. Best case scenario, it takes us to the Kindling and they kill us."

"Don't you mean 'worst case?'" Kaitlyn said slowly. She picked Vyekrin from her lap and coaxed him onto her shoulder. He curled up against her, wrapping his tail around her neck to anchor himself.

"Nope. The only way out of here is to be a Kindling, or to be with a Kindling. We can follow this thing and come up with a plan along the way. When they try to attack us, we ambush them instead, then make them take us out of here."

Everyone was silent as Cy waited for praise. When none came, he grunted and kicked a rock at his feet.

"It's not a very good plan," Jayr started, playing with the pink wisp. "But it's still a plan. And the only one we've got. I say we do it."

Kaitlyn was relieved when Jayr's last sentence shut Cy up, grateful that they at least knew what they were doing.

Gil was looking between Cy and Jayr, mortified. "Wait, are we actually going to try kidnapping a Kindling? Are you insane?"

Kaitlyn put a hand on Gil's shoulder to calm him down. "It's just fairies and pixies, right? What could go wrong?" She was doing her best to calm them, but even she no longer believed her words.

"Would you rather we leave you here?" Cy asked impatiently.

"No..." Gil muttered, defeated. "But how far do you honestly expect us to get without our supplies? I tried to say something earlier, but you seemed to think arguing over Theresa was more important."

Kaitlyn's eyes went wide as she spun around frantically. There was nothing in the small space other than themselves. They lost their only chance of survival when they had been forced into this forest.

Jayr was letting loose a stream of words Kaitlyn couldn't understand, and she was momentarily grateful. Cy on the other hand, was so still that it scared her more than their situation.

"This is their game," he whispered, and the small sound silenced the others. *"They brought us in here to be the pieces. They're playing with us."*

His words sobered them all up, the tension scattering from the air. Kaitlyn put a hand to her chest, hoping to calm her heart. Jayr was watching the wisp circle around him slowly, and Gil was gripping his elbows hard enough to blanch his knuckles.

Kaitlyn looked desperately between them. No matter how she looked at it, this was worse. She wanted them, any of them, to get angry, to scream or curse. She wanted to see any sort of reaction to dispel the fear that they had given up. Just as she was getting ready to yell at them herself, Gil broke the silence.

"Anybody know what plants are edible in these woods?" Gil eyed a plump fruit with rough, purple skin that hung from a tree. He poked at it, unsure what to do. The others turned to him, then came to life as they surveyed the small area they had been dropped in.

Jayr picked a few bright red berries from a bush. He inspected it closely, while Cy crept up behind him. Jayr lifted it above his head, ready to drop it in his mouth, but Cy smacked his hand and the berry went flying.

"The hell are you doing?" Jayr snapped, rounding on Cy. "Do you want to fight again already? Let's go, demon." Though he glared furiously at Cy, Jayr's voice held no bite or threat.

"Those berries are poisonous, as well as that tree fruit, Gil," Cy said, glancing back at Gil. The Droll was just about to pierce the tough skin of the fruit with his teeth, but dropped it to the ground instead.

"How do you know that? You can't even eat." Jayr rounded on Cy, tossing the berries to the side. They splattered against a tree, and Jayr ignored the steam that rose from the bright orange goop.

"Because Theresa taught me as well. I learned about all the creatures, including you. I learned how to survive. It's relatively bright in this area, especially compared to the rest of the woods. The safe fruit grows in the darkness. If we start following that wisp, it should take us deeper into the woods. We'll find something to eat as we go."

Cy passed Jayr, ignoring the stunned expression. The wisp was dancing and twirling at the edge of the light that broke through the trees. It did loops in the air, beckoning them. Cy approached and it dove into the shadows, nearly disappearing altogether.

Kaitlyn was the first to follow Cy, Gil close on her heels. Jayr was hesitant, but took up the back of the line. Once they had plunged into the depths of the woods, it was impossible to see where they were going. They followed the dim pink light in the distance blindly. Gil quickly grabbed Kaitlyn's hand. He was shaking in her grasp, and she gave him a comforting squeeze. Following suit, she reached ahead and entwined her fingers with Cy's. His steps faltered when she grabbed him, but he clasped his fingers around her hand. She felt the metal lock into place.

Gil yelped behind her, and Kaitlyn turned to investigate. Gil had a hand over his chest as he gasped for air. Jayr was as far behind as he could be, nearly lost in the dark. His hand was resting lightly on Gil's shoulder, and neither looked happy about it. Kaitlyn turned back to face forward, stifling her giggles.

There was no way to tell how long they had been walking, or if they had even made any progress. No one even dared to ask about food again, the fright of the woods chasing away any hunger they had. After what felt like hours but could have been minutes, Jayr called to the front, "So how's that great plan coming, demon?"

"Working on it," Cy mumbled under his breath. He then stopped suddenly. The woods had only gotten darker, and Kaitlyn came closer to his light.

"Cy, what's wro-" she started, but the knife at her throat made her stop. She heard the groans of Gil and Jayr behind them, and knew they were surrounded.

"What about now?" Jayr asked, desperately and sarcastically.

"If you've got any suggestions, I'm all ears," Cy snapped back bitterly.

Kaitlyn was snatched up by two sets of hands. She whimpered in pain as she was tied up, then pushed forward through the woods, the light of Cy's magic snuffed out.

CHAPTER 13

Cyllorian

Cy growled as he felt a strange buzzing beneath his feet. The Kindling led him quickly through the woods. He could hear Kaitlyn and Gil yelping as they were rushed over the rough terrain. Cy was the only one of them that could see in the dark, though he wouldn't consider himself lucky.

The trees on either side of them were sprouting long thorns that oozed a sickeningly thick poison. The creatures that were clicking and squeaking watched them with hungry eyes. Worst of all were the Kindling that made it look as though the forest itself was dragging them to their tombs.

They stopped suddenly, and the four of them crashed into each other. Cy was only barely able to keep them from tumbling to the ground until the Kindlings pulled them apart.

A Kindling pricked himself on a nearby thorn, and the rest copied. Then, one by one, they pressed their bleeding fingers to small bulbs that had nestled in with the thorns. At the taste of the blood, the flowers bloomed and released large bursts of luminous pollen that floated in the air.

"What are you doing here?" an old man asked as two dozen more Kindling emerged from the trees. Cy was forced onto his knees in a bowing position, and he glanced up warily. The sight of the man sent him into shock, and his mouth hung open, useless.

The man was obviously older than should be possible, but he still had so much life within his eyes. They were pure brown with no whites to them, and dark green pupils that were barely noticeable. His long hair and beard were made of wrinkled, brown leaves, a crown of bright blue flowers sprouting from his head. His skin was rough and as red as the trees around them. He wore a robe of dull, dried flowers held together by crude stones instead of buttons. He looked more plant than human.

"What are you doing here?" he asked again.

Cy looked at him incredulously. He cleared his throat to answer the man, but stopped when he noticed the man's gaze shift. His eyes hardened, and Cy angled his head sneakily to catch what the man was looking at.

Behind them was a girl that looked scarily similar to the man, though her hair was long and made of gorgeous ivy, with bright green eyes and yellow pupils. She was thin, and the bark that was her skin looked smooth, moss growing across her shoulders. Her dress was made of braided blades of grass, and it barely covered her. She stared at the man defiantly, and he groaned.

"Are you going to answer my question, demon?" the man spat, drawing Cy's attention again.

Cy stared the Kindling down with more courage than he felt. *"Oh, I'm sorry. Were you talking to me? Didn't really seem like it."*

A murmur spread through the crowd at his defiance, and he smirked. The old man's eyes flashed, and Cy swallowed nervously. He already knew an unnatural creature like him was despised, and his bad attitude would only make it worse. Even still, he knew he had to push them.

The man pressed his hand to a tree, and the ground below Cy rumbled. Weeds broke through the ground and began wrapping themselves around his legs, crushing the metal. His body instantly tried to heal itself, but it was too confined by the plants. The magic inside pushed back against their grip, and Cy locked his jaw against the suffocating feeling. The man didn't need to ask his question again.

"Wouldn't it be better to ask your people? They're the ones that dragged us into these woods in the first place," Cy groaned. He sighed in relief as the vines loosened the smallest bit, though they didn't release him.

"It was not *my* people that brought you here, but that crazed woman, Theresa, with her impossible requests," the man said. His gaze slipped to meet that of the Kindling girl behind them, and Cy smirked at the anticipated response.

"If you know, then why did you ask?" Kaitlyn's soft voice sounded from Cy's side. She had crawled forward on her knees, and was pleading with her eyes. Her tone was polite, but Cy could hear the slightest bit of annoyance in her voice. He spared himself a brief second to wonder if he was being a bad influence on her.

"You dare question me? Girl, do you have any idea with whom you are speaking?"

"My guess is that you're one of the elusive Kindling that everyone's so afraid of," Kaitlyn mused. "I don't know why. These three act like you're nothing but killing machines, but if that were true, you would have already killed us. If you know everything, like you said, then you'd have no need for us. And if you don't care at all, there's no reason to keep us alive."

The Kindling stared at Kaitlyn with incredulity and fear. Cy's face contorted, his metal scraping against itself noisily. Just once, he wished that she was more afraid. She ignored them, lifting her chin and staring down the Kindling.

"You are quite the clever little thing, aren't you?" The Kindling king stepped forward and brushed his hand along Kaitlyn's jawline. The rough bark of his hand cut into her skin, but she stayed perfectly still as the blood dripped onto the ground. She held her breath as the scratch healed, replaced by a thick layer of bark that mirrored that of the Kindling's.

"So interesting. I would have loved nothing more than to play with you just a bit longer," the king crooned, stepping away from them. The bark continued to spread across her cheek, and her eye changed color slowly to a deep blue with a bright yellow pupil.

"We did not come to play. We came for your aid," Kaitlyn said in a commanding voice. It sent a chill throughout Cy's body as he watched this Kaitlyn he didn't know. Though she had shown surprising strength the past few weeks, this was entirely out of character for her. He worried that the spell of the woods was still affecting her.

The king chuckled to himself, and it was the sound of leaves caught in a breeze. "I know of the boy you seek to retrieve, and of the Mage Theresa, who has sent you to us. What you ask is an impossible feat, yet you still dare to ask it. I'm sorry to say that your impressive display of bravery is all for not: we will not help you." The king ended his statement with a dark tone and a click of his tongue. It sounded like a twig snapping, and it echoed in the still air.

"Not that you can't, but you won't?" Kaitlyn asked, her anger burning through her demeanor. "Why not?"

"The woman has caused a great amount of despair and destruction, and we cannot forgive this. Even the creature beside her is evidence enough of what little respect she has for the natural world. We cannot condone nor forgive her actions. But for the debt we owe her, we shall spare you. Be warned that if you dare to return, or if she foolishly sends any others to us, we will not hesitate to kill. As short as they are, I wish you good luck on what remains of your lives, demon and company."

The man turned and left with a great flourish. In an instant, his simple brown cloak turned to bright colors, adorned with oddly cut rocks that reflected the little light around them in a rainbow.

With a wave of the king's hand, the restraints holding Cy vanished, slithering off of his body. Cy tried to get to his feet, but a Kindling at his side grabbed him by the back of his neck. Cy froze at the grip that had him, but stared angrily after the old man. He faded into the darkness, a swarm of Kindling following close behind him. Once he was completely gone from sight, Cy whirled on the Kindling that was holding him.

Before he could even get his legs out from under him, Cy's vision was stolen from him. The Kindling dropped him to the ground. He pressed his hands to the back of his neck and was shocked to find a small puncture wound that refused to heal. Cy had always believed that the Kindlings only had influence over the natural world, and it terrified him that they could over power him in such a way.

Nearby, he heard Gil's whimpers and Kaitlyn's strained breathing. He wasn't the only one that had been blinded.

A soft pink light was the first thing to break through the darkness. His vision returned slowly, but he blinked and the light was gone.

"What the hell was that?" Cy asked as he shook the lingering feeling of the Kindling's magic from his shoulders.

Cy stood up, ignoring the stiffness in his neck. The rest of them were lying on the ground, in varying states of regaining their senses. Kaitlyn was the first to have recovered, and she sat on the ground, sulking. Her skin was clear of any sign of changing into a Kindling. Vyekrin was in her lap, still in his lizard form, and the concentration in her eyes said that they were speaking within their minds.

Next was Jayr, being brought back to his senses by a sting from Wayonn. Jayr shot up with a start and rubbed a red spot on his arm, glaring at the scorpion.

Gil was curled up on himself, hugging his knees to his chest. Cy was unsure when he had regained his sight, but he was staring at the luminous pollen that still hung in the air. His face was still twisted in fear. Though he had never said it, it was clear to see Gil was terrified of the dark, and Cy couldn't blame him.

"What do we do now that they won't help us?" Kaitlyn asked quietly. "They were our best shot, no offense."

"We go along with the plan just like before. We just have to hope these two are enough, and head home."

"How exactly do you expect us to get home from here? There's no escape from these woods," Jayr snapped, waving his arm toward the trees that still towered over them.

"The ball..." Cy started, but Kaitlyn stopped him by holding it up. There was no smoke to be found in it, only the same pink light as before.

"We need a Kindling, Cy, or else we're not getting out of here. The ball even says so." Kaitlyn dropped the ball and it rolled along the ground. It came to rest in the middle of the group, and everyone stared at it in confusion.

Cy crawled forward and scooped up the glass ball. He

shook it violently, growling, *"We don't need them! We need to leave. Stupid thing, take us back! We don't need a Kindling."*

"Are you sure?" a small voice asked. Cy's head shot up, and a small pink light hovered in front of him for a moment before buzzing around him back towards the darkness. He turned quickly, afraid of losing the light. It stopped just inside of the cover of the trees.

A girl emerged from the shadows, and the pink light landed on her shoulder in the form of a small, human-like creature, with pale pink skin and large, pitch black eyes. She wore leaves as a makeshift dress, which barely covered her body. Wings made of soft yellow petals fluttered on her back. She couldn't be more than six inches tall. A pixie.

The Kindling girl stepped out from the shadows, revealing herself to be the one the king had been glaring at. She looked at the ground shyly, and brushed a lock of hair from her face. Cy thought he caught a glimpse of bright blue bulbs buried within the mess of vines atop her head.

"I saw you before," Cy said as an accusation. The girl nodded her head, but didn't speak. When Cy went to speak again, the pixie stepped off from the girl's shoulder and flew into Cy's face, her wings beating furiously.

"You will treat my lady with respect, *demon,*" she hissed, but her small form made it very difficult to find her intimidating.

Cy leaned back and tried to swat the creature away. Kaitlyn came up behind him and snatched his hand out of the air. "Be nice!" she hushed. She turned to the pixie, whose face was flushed a darker pink in frustration. "I'm sorry. He doesn't get along well with others. What's your name?"

Kaitlyn looked to the Kindling girl, but she looked away from Kaitlyn's gaze. The pixie spoke for her. "This is my Lady Adoette, princess and daughter to the King. I am her faithful servant, Noma. My Lady does not speak, so I am her voice. If you wish to have any dealings with her, you will go through me." The pixie put her hands on her hips as she hovered in the air.

"Why are you here?" Jayr finally spoke up, and his voice was even ruder than Cy's had been. Kaitlyn shot him a steely look, and he shrunk away from her.

"My Lady has decided to help you, despite my begging and protests," Noma stated. "She does not agree with the King's ruling, and has chosen to betray him. My Lady believes that he is the selfish one, for being so worried about his own kingdom that he is so unwilling to help others. He foolishly believes that the war will leave him be if he acts as though it does not exist. Were he to turn his back on the rest of the world, he shall receive no aid in return when he needs it most. My Lady does not wish to see her people abandoned, so she is doing what she can to gain allies. She was determined to help you even if I had not come along, but I am bound to her and will follow her into hell if I must. Even if it gets us banished, or worse."

"*Banished?*" Cy said, still processing all of the information.

"Yes. Once the King has discovered our treachery, we will surely be banished. As long as he does not send a party for our heads, that is."

"Would he really kill his own daughter?" Kaitlyn asked.

Noma looked back at Adoette questioningly, and the Kindling nodded once to her. "The King is a cruel man that hates all others, barely sparing his own kind from his hatred. He deems them impure, and claims that they do nothing but taint the land. Kindling are creatures of nature, and we are tasked with protecting it. The King lies in wait for the day that the rest of the world is destroyed so that he might salvage the ruins for himself, all in the excuse of preserving nature."

"He sounds pretty harsh. How can we be sure you're on our side?" Cy asked.

Adoette stepped out from the trees, the bright light accenting every crack in the bark that was her skin. Her eyes grew wide and the corners of her mouth dropped in a deep frown. Bright blue tears rolled slowly along the rough bark.

Noma flew closer and smacked Cy in the middle of his forehead, but he didn't feel a thing. "My Lady is the one that brought you into these woods! Ever since your entrance into our land, she has been begging the king to join you. How dare you accuse her of malicious intent!"

"That's even more of a reason to be suspicious. We didn't ask to be brought into the woods, we would have come when we were ready," Jayr said, standing up.

Adoette was looking desperately between the four of them while Noma buzzed annoyingly close to Cy's face. He blew a puff of purple smoke at her, and the pixie backed away, coughing. While Noma recovered, Adoette ran to Kaitlyn. She grasped the other girl's hands and pulled Kaitlyn to her feet. They stood frozen for a moment before Adoette slowly placed Kaitlyn's hand on her cheek.

At Kaitlyn's touch, the bark began chipping and falling from Adoette's face, revealing perfectly smooth, red skin.

"My Lady is willing to forsake her entire being as a Kindling in order to gain your trust. She is borrowing your friend's ability to make the transformation, without even knowing if she will be able to change back," Noma explained, now standing on Cy's shoulder without care or concern. There was a deep sadness in the pixie's voice that complimented the pain on Adoette's face as she changed.

Cy stood abruptly, causing Noma to stumble from her perch. He marched over to the two girls, and snatched Kaitlyn's hand from Adoette's face. The Kindling turned to him with a questioning gaze. More than half of her face and her neck had been stripped bare of bark, her right eye now normal with a green iris. Her lips were thin and her hair had changed to thick locks of knotted green hair.

"There's no need to go that far," Cy said softly. He released Kaitlyn's hand, and continued, *"As long as you can get us out of here, I'll trust you. Can you change her back, Kaitlyn?"*

Kaitlyn raised her hand to touch Adoette's cheek again, but the girl backed away, shaking her head furiously. She held her hand out for Noma, and the pixie landed dutifully in her palm.

"Until My Lady is certain that she has gained all your complete trust, she wishes to stay this way. She hopes you will understand."

Cy looked among the other members. Gil and Kaitlyn nodded. Jayr stayed silent, which was better than protesting. *"We do. My name is Cyllorian, and this is Kaitlyn."* Cy began the introductions, clasping a hand on Kaitlyn's shoulder. He ignored the way she jumped at his touch, writing it off as nervousness around the Kindling. *"The Droll is Gil, and the Draken is Jayr. We have two dragons with us, Vyekrin for Kaitlyn, and Wayonn for Jayr."*

Gil and Jayr gave short, awkward waves. Kaitlyn held up Vyekrin in her hands, and the dragon posed with pride. Wayonn scuttled forward on his six legs, clipping his pincers together in greeting. Adoette waved in return. Noma flew to each dragon in turn, and curtseyed to them midair, then returned to Adoette's shoulder.

"Shall we?" Cy asked, inviting Adoette to lead the way out of the woods. She smiled widely and skipped away from them. She waved them on after her, and they delved into the depths of the Kindling woods.

As they walked, Adoette brushed her hands along the trees, and they lit up under her touch. With a Kindling as an escort,

Cy could understand how the woods were beautiful and alluring. Everything danced in Adoette's presence, and many small creatures skittered out from their hiding places. Flowers bloomed before their very eyes, and a breeze followed them, creating a symphony out of every leaf and branch.

Though they had wandered on their own for hours before, Adoette led them to the edge of the woods within minutes. They stepped into the open air of night, but their relief was short lived. Just outside of the Kindling Woods, the walls of Centric were waiting.

Adoette turned happily and swung a small bag made of thick leaves out from behind her. She pulled a scroll made from a pale leaf and unfurled it excitedly to show a small purple house with a heart shaped window in the door.

"Where is that?" Jayr snapped, pushing his way from the back of the group to look at the scroll. Adoette pointed at the wall, and they all turned in dismay.

"*Centric. How the hell do we get in there?*" Cy asked, crossing his arms over his chest.

Adoette grabbed his hand and pulled him to the wall. She pressed her palm to the stone and closed her eyes. Cy stared at her a moment, and she opened one eye to watch him. Noma fluttered between them, and she sighed dramatically.

"She would like you to help her with your magic."

Cy looked down at the etching of the lightning bolt in his left palm. He'd never been left handed before, but ever since Arion, he felt compelled to do things as Arion had. He would've blamed it on muscle memory, if he had any muscles of his own.

"*My magic?*" he finally said aloud, flexing his fingers.

"You are a Mage, aren't you?" Noma asked, baiting him with the question.

Reluctantly, Cy answered, "*I'm a demon. Everyone knows that.*"

"But you have magic."

"Technically. It's borrowed."

"Good enough for me. Put your hand over Lady Adoette's, but only as long as necessary. Don't try anything, demon."

Adoette looked at Noma, scolding her with her eyes, but Noma acted as though she didn't see. Cy shrugged and place his hand over Adoette's. She closed her eyes, and he did the same.

Door.

The word ran through his head, and his eyes shot open. He looked at Adoette in astonishment, but she was otherwise unphased. As he stared at her, a bright light erupted from the wall. The stones crumbled to pieces in the center, and pulled away at the edges, forming a doorway. Beyond was the calm, empty streets of Centric, completely unaware that it was about to get a band of uninvited guests.

Once there was nothing left under their hands, Cy and Adoette pulled away. She smiled at him and he looked away, slightly embarrassed.

Adoette stepped into the doorway, but Jayr cut her off. "Don't you think we should make some sort of plan? You said this was Centric, right? We can't afford to be caught. I say we should split up and meet at the house at different times."

"No way. We're not splitting up now. What if something happens? We have no way to communicate if we don't stick together," Cy said.

"It'll look too suspicious for this big and diverse group to just be wandering around Centric, given that none of our races really get along, and you know it. We don't have another choice. I'll go with Kaitlyn and Gil. You can go with Adoette and Noma, since they seem to like you more."

"No way in hell am I separating from Kaitlyn. You should know

that. Besides, why would you of all people want to go with Gil? You're not making any sense, Draken," Cy spat.

While they were arguing, Adoette grabbed Kaitlyn's hand and pulled her into Centric, giggling. Cy dove in after them, Gil and Jayr on their heels. They chased the girls until they reached a small house that looked old and rotting. Cy couldn't believe a place like it actually existed in Centric.

Though Adoette had been waiting for them to catch up, as soon as they were in sight, she pulled Kaitlyn into the house. Cy followed immediately, nearly ripping the door from its hinges as he went.

The house was full of items filling up every possible inch of space. Clothing hung from the ceiling with maps and magic scrolls covered the walls. Rugs were stacked on top of each other, making the floor uneven. Charms and jewels spilled from a large ornate chest in the corner, glittering in the multi colored lights that flickered from varying sizes of candles. The most abundant item, though, were packs and bags overflowing with spoiled rations and unnamed treasures.

Adoette hopped to the side of the room and held up two bags made of water proof material from the Droll, one of which had Kaitlyn's blue ribbon tied to the strap. "All belongings taken by the Kindling from foolish travelers are teleported here upon entry to the woods. Since you are lucky enough to have escaped our grasp, you may have them returned to you," Noma explained.

Adoette passed their bags back to them, and Cy checked the contents. Everything was accounted for, and he let out a deep sigh. While he was lost in relief, Adoette shoved a large black cloak into his hands. He looked up to find her wearing a similar robe with a large brimmed hat. She winked at him and pulled the hat further down on her head.

"Late night wanderers aren't uncommon in Centric. So as

long as no one can tell what we are, we don't have to split up. These will shield us from unwanted attention." Noma spoke for Adoette, and she glanced at Jayr. He reluctantly put on the cloak that he was handed, and pulled the hood to cover his scowl.

Cy glared at the Draken, waiting for him to object. Though he had been so adamant before, he didn't dare speak up now. He wandered sullenly out of the house. Gil and Kaitlyn followed shortly after, Gil talking in hushed tones as he described what he knew of Centric to Kaitlyn.

Cy watched them through the door, Jayr's previous attitude worrying him. He quickly threw on his cloak and smoothed it out over his rough frame. He turned to follow the others outside, but Noma was flitting an inch from his face, blocking his path.

"What the hell is your problem, bug?" he yelled.

She stomped her foot in the air and headbutted his cheek. She hurt herself more with her attack, and fell through the air. Adoette caught her easily, and held the pixie up to her face.

Noma jumped up suddenly, clutching Adoette's fingers. Her voice became painfully high pitched when she spoke. "I am not a bug, you hear me! Not!"

"Maybe not, but I could squash you like one," Cy hissed, bringing his face closer to the pixie. She gasped, and Adoette pulled Noma away from him quickly.

The terror on her face filled him with guilt, and he took a step back. *"Sorry. How about we just go into Centric now? I don't want to give Jayr the opportunity to run off on his own."*

Adoette ran out to join Gil and Kaitlyn who were running from streetlamp to streetlamp, bathing themselves in the varying colors that bled into the streets. Owls and bats filled the night sky. They moved elegantly and with a purpose. Cy stepped into the doorway to watch them.

Adoette was pulling the two by the wrists to look at each house along the street. Each was built completely different from its neighbors. From stained glass windows to no windows at all, and large, sloped roofs to flat or dome topped houses. Their sizes and even building material varied between wood, stone and metal. The three of them seemed to have endless interest in the magical city at the heart of Lontorra.

Not Cy. He ignored it all, hating the memories he had of Centric. This was where he had lost Arion: where he had first lost himself. He wanted to just go straight through, towards home, but it was impossible now. He couldn't even be sure if he had a home to return to anymore.

CHAPTER 14

Cyllorian

"*For the last time, we are not lost!*" Cy growled.

"Then why are we wandering around? I can tell that you're stalling because you don't know where we're going," Noma said again, buzzing annoyingly close to Cy's face. He waved his hand through the air, deliberately missing her. Noma didn't see it that way and went straight back to Adoette. "My Lady, he's becoming violent! Please, we must return home before it's too late for us."

Cy glanced behind him to see Adoette's reaction. Without hesitating, she shook her head, caught Noma from the air, and sat the pixie down on her shoulder. She pat the pixie on her head with a finger. Noma crossed her arms and resolved to pouting.

Cy's attention strayed to Kaitlyn, who was smiling peacefully as she chatted with Gil. The Droll had his arms wrapped around himself. He walked as close to Kaitlyn as possible, and they were nearly tripping over each other. Their conversation was hushed, and Cy couldn't hear them. His magic hummed loudly in irritation as he watched Kaitlyn grasp Gil's hand firmly. She smiled sweetly at the Droll, and he relaxed.

Jayr brought up the rear of the group. He watched the shadows intently. The Draken was on edge, though Wayonn was sleeping soundly on his shoulder, curled up tightly as though he were a pet.

With a few skips, Adoette caught up to Cy and looked at him apologetically. He let out a sigh, and the air whistled throughout his metal body. Adoette covered her mouth and giggled. She nudged him playfully with her arm. She stared him down with a wide smile on her face until he forced a grin to appear in the metal plates.

Noma was hovering in front of him in an instant. She stomped her foot in the air as her wings flitted. She opened her mouth to complain, but Adoette scooped her from the air first. Noma lost her balance, and fell back into Adoette's hands.

Noma glanced at Adoette, then rolled her eyes. "My Lady would like to have a pleasant conversation," she said in an agonized voice. Cy turned to Adoette nervously, and she nodded her head excitedly.

"Pleasant conversation? With a demon? Like I even know what to talk about," he grumbled, picking up his pace.

Adoette kept up with him easily, Noma hovering around her like always. "I know. Why don't you tell us why you're collecting different species from all over Lontorra? That sounds like a good topic to start with," Noma said, a smug look on her face.

"Collecting? Why do you make it sound like I have some sick fetish? They all chose to come with me, you two included. Either you didn't need a reason to come along, or you already know. So which is it?" Cy rounded back on Noma, who paused in a fluster.

She giggled mischievously instead of answering, and

turned the conversation back onto Cy. "You're just avoiding the question. I want to hear it from you, why you need all of us. Because let's face it, you do *need* us for whatever reason. So what is it?"

"My reasons are my own. All you need to know is that I'm following Theresa's orders," Cy growled.

Noma was silenced for the moment. Cy held his breath, waiting for the onslaught of questions he was sure the pixie was preparing. He closed his eyes to enjoy the peace.

The voice he heard next wasn't the one he expected. "Who are you strangers? Why are you in the streets so late at night?" a deep voice called. Standing a few feet away from them was a man donned in shining armor. His shoulder was branded with the mark of Talgrin Tower: a book laying open with fire resting on its pages.

They all froze in terror, and Cy pulled the hood of his cloak further over his face. He felt Kaitlyn grab the back of his cloak. He clenched his fists in anger. This wasn't supposed to happen. He hadn't a single idea on how to get out of this.

To his surprise, Gil stepped forward. He pulled Jayr with him by his arm. "We have both been asked to help sell wares in the market district starting tomorrow. We were called on such short notice, and were provided with escorts for the night's trip."

He motioned behind him to Kaitlyn. Cy could feel her press closer to him, shaking her head against his back. Gil held his hand out to her, and whispered, "You can do it."

Kaitlyn took a deep breath, then pulled herself away from Cy. She stepped up to the man with her right hand outstretched. Cy moved to stop her. Gil grabbed Cy's arm tightly, surprising him. Gil's face was set in determination, though his hand was shaking.

The man grabbed Kaitlyn's hand and turned it over. The

outline of a rose was clearly visible on her palm, and it seemed almost to glow in the flickering lamplight.

The man stared at the mark for a long time. No one breathed as they waited for his response.

"Make sure you reach your lodging safely and swiftly. Master Crestyss has enforced a curfew for all of Centric."

Cy flinched at the name, but kept himself in control. He knew very little of Crestyss, but none of it was good. Adoette squeaked beside him, her gentle face twisted in fear. She gained the man's attention, and he approached.

Adoette tried to back away, but the man grabbed the hood of her cloak and threw it back. Adoette threw her hands up to shield her, but it was too late. There was no hiding the bark that still covered half of her face and the ivy that tangled within her hair.

"A Kindling," the man breathed in anger. He reached for a sword that hung on his hip.

Noma jumped from Adoette's back and slammed into the man's face. He shook off the blow as if it were nothing and smacked the pixie out of the air. She fell against Cy's chest, stunned. He scrambled to catch her.

Adoette was no longer afraid. She was furious. She lunged for the man and wrapped her hands around his neck. She pushed until he tumbled into a bush on the side of the road. She squeezed the air from him as vines slowly covered him.

Carefully holding the unconscious Noma in one hand, Cy dove after Adoette. He grabbed her shoulder, and the bark cracked under his grip.

Adoette whirled on him. Her face softened as she caught sight of Noma. She looked back to the man and released him quickly. He struggled to breathe, though he remained unconscious.

Adoette stood and backed away from the guard. She turned

to Cy, though she refused to meet his eyes for the first time. She held out her shaking hands, and Cy set Noma down gently. She pressed the pixie to her cheek. Her mouth moved slowly, though she made no noise.

"We need to get out of here as soon as possible. Kaitlyn, I want you stay close to me, okay?" Cy said monotonously.

There was no answer. *"Kaitlyn?"*

He spun around, but the road was completely empty. They were gone.

* * *

Kaitlyn

"Jayr, why are we running? Where's Cy and Adoette?" Kaitlyn yelled at the Draken that had a tight grip on her wrist. Gil was being dragged behind her. She was shocked either of them could keep up with Jayr as he wound his way through a maze of streets.

She tried to wrench her hand away, but it was no good. "Jayr!" she screamed. It was no use as she gasped for air.

"No matter what, we can't get caught. They'll figure it out, just keep running!" Jayr called back. He wasn't out of breath in the slightest, but Gil seemed like he would collapse at any moment.

With all the strength she had, Kaitlyn pulled Jayr to a stop. Gil fell to his knees on the cobblestone, clutching his chest.

Jayr whirled on her, angry. "Why are you stopping? We have to keep going!"

"Not without Cy," she said defiantly. She stared Jayr down, unwavering.

"Damn that demon! He couldn't even lead us to the destination safely! And *you.*" He turned on Gil. "What was with the pathetic excuse, huh? I didn't think I would ever meet someone dumber than you, but I guess that guard must have been, since he fell for it."

"Just shut up, Draken. You talk so big, but I didn't see you trying anything! You just ran away like a coward, and you're supposed to be a warrior. Do you even know where we are anymore, because I sure don't. Have you even ever been to Centric?" Gil snapped. It was the first time Kaitlyn had seen him lose his temper.

"At least I'm not as bad as you. You're too afraid to even set foot outside your caves, Droll. You've been nothing but useless this entire time. What are you doing here, anyway?"

"That's enough!" Kaitlyn screamed. She turned away from the boys and started to retrace their steps.

"Where are you going?" Jayr called. He caught her arm and stopped her.

Biting back a growl, she spun out of his grip. She caught his arm with her claws, smirking as she chipped off scales from his armor. He narrowed his eyes at her, but didn't go for her again.

"I'm going back to find them. You can't just leave your friends."

Jayr groaned, but she ignored him. She stared down the unfamiliar road, defeated. She hadn't paid attention to anything once Jayr had dragged her away. It was all she could do to hold onto Gil so they wouldn't get separated.

"Kaitlyn, I hate to agree with him, but I actually don't think that's a good idea," Gil spoke from the ground.

"Not you, too! I thought you got along with Cy?" Kaitlyn moaned in exasperation.

"I do, but that's not the point. We're already here."

Kaitlyn turned around to look where Gil was pointing. In front of them stood a small purple house squished between two gray buildings. It looked exactly like it did on the scroll. Jayr was already walking up to the door.

Gil stood with a sigh and held his hand out to Kaitlyn. She grabbed it tightly. He led her after Jayr, and it took all her energy to keep herself calm. She wasn't sure if she wanted to scream or cry, but she couldn't do either.

They came up behind Jayr as he knocked on the door. It burst open and a tall woman with seductive curves opened the door. Purple silk hung loosely on her clothes, draping down from her hips and billowing out around her arms, leaving her stomach bare. The fabric was connected to fingerless gloves. A heart shaped mark could be seen on her palm. Narrow, purple eyes shone with anger in her rounded face, and big, shiny black hair flowed down her back.

Jayr was the first to speak. "I am Jayr, a Draken."

"And I can assume you have a dragon with you? You can't hide anything from me. Introduce him," she said, snapping her fingers in the air. She was glaring openly at the Draken, though Kaitlyn wasn't sure how this woman could already dislike him.

Jayr groaned, but pulled the scorpion out of a pocket in his armor and held him up. "Wayonn."

The scorpion looked at the woman for a long moment before bowing to her, surprising Jayr. The woman smiled and rubbed Wayonn's head with a finger. As she pulled away, her hand brushed against Jayr's and her eyes shot back to his own.

She turned to Gil next, and his whole body stiffened. "I'm a Droll, ma'am. My name's Gil."

He was very abrupt with his words, shaking nervously. The woman smiled to him as well, and patted him on the shoulder. He let out his breath and collapsed against a wall.

She glanced at Kaitlyn before snapping at the boys, "You two, start a fire in the main room. I have a feeling we have a long night ahead of us."

Gil and Jayr exchanged glances, unwilling to work together.

"And I don't want any more fighting from you two, or there'll be hell to pay."

"Who says we fight?" Jayr asked innocently.

The woman glared at him in annoyance. "You *do* realize you were just screaming at each other right outside my house. Now get to it," she snapped.

The boys nodded, then made their way awkwardly into the house. Kaitlyn dropped her head as she waited for the woman to turn on her.

"Come on now. It's cold outside, come right in," the woman said, her voice now soft and kind. Kaitlyn stepped nervously into the woman's house, but was too scared to take more than few steps inside.

Kaitlyn looked at the ground nervously. Following suit of her companions, she spoke, "My name is Kaitlyn. I'm a..." Kaitlyn's voice trailed off as she wondered how to continue. She swallowed the lump in her throat, and finished uneasily. "I'm human."

"You may call me Jemmina," the woman said. She extended a hand in greeting. Kaitlyn forced a smile and took her hand.

Jemmina's face fell, and a deep sorrow set in her eyes. Without a word or a sign of why, she enveloped Kaitlyn in a hug. Kaitlyn stood still in her embrace, at a loss for what to do.

"You poor thing. You've been so strong through everything, no matter how badly you've wanted to break. You're safe now. No one will think less of you. Remember, there is strength in showing weakness."

The woman rubbed her back, and Kaitlyn felt an over-whelming flood of dread and sorrow. Everything flashed through her mind at once...Arion's death, the loss of her home and family, her own near-death experiences. She grabbed onto the woman for dear life and cried more than she ever thought she could. The woman held her through her sobs and settled her shaking.

A long time passed with Kaitlyn wrapped in the woman's arms, and by the time her tears had run dry, she felt better than ever. The grief was slowly replaced with hope, and she pulled away from the woman.

Kaitlyn wiped her face clean of tears. "How did you know?" she asked quietly. She was too embarrassed to meet Jemmina's eyes. Her sudden shift in demeanor shocked her, but Kaitlyn felt relieved.

"In simplest terms, I am a fortune teller. I have the ability to see into someone's soul." Jemmina spoke softly, slowly.

Kaitlyn raised her head to ask further, but a crash from the other room cut her off. Anger flashed across Jemmina's face. She whirled and stormed through the door. "I thought I told you two to get along?" she yelled.

Kaitlyn could hear Jayr and Gil talking at the same time, trying to defend themselves.

"Enough!" Jemmina silenced them. "You, just leave."

Gil was shoved out of the door. He was pale and sweating. He moved silently to stand beside Kaitlyn. He watched the door cautiously.

Jemmina and Jayr had picked up conversation, but their voices were indistinct.

"What happened?" Kaitlyn asked, praying that her voice didn't give away that she had just been crying.

Gil looked at the floor sullenly. "Jayr just said something stupid. Don't worry about it."

Kaitlyn sat down against the wall. She pulled her legs to her chest and wrapped her arms around herself. Most of the scales had fallen off, remaining only on her upper arm. She opened her hand and willed the mark to appear again. She winced as her skin gave way, and the rose stood out bright pink.

"I knew you could control it," Gil said. His carefree tone was forced. Kaitlyn looked up at him, but he wasn't paying attention to her. His gaze was fixed on the front door.

"Hurry up and get here, Cy," he muttered.

"Come sit by the fire," Jemmina called from the room. Gil took Kaitlyn's hand and helped her to her feet. She kept her head down as they joined Jayr and Jemmina. Her chest ached as she silently echoed Gil's wish.

CHAPTER 15

Cyllorian

Adoette followed Cy easily as he ran through the streets of Centric. *"I'll kill that Draken,"* he grumbled under his breath. *"Please be there. Please be there."*

The purple house came into view quickly, and he ran to the door. A faint light could be seen through the heart shaped window, and he took a nervous breath. Adoette was very near to him on the small porch, and he shifted his weight to lean away from her. Holding his breath, he knocked on the door with three sharp raps.

There was a moment where everything was still, and Cy could sense the panic that came from within the house. Hoping Kaitlyn was inside, he wanted nothing more than to break through the door, but he couldn't give them any more reasons against him, so he waited.

Locks turned in the tumblers, three altogether. The door opened slowly, and a familiar woman stood blocking the entrance.

"Jemmina?" he whispered in shock, recognizing the fortune teller that Arion and he had met during their trip to Centric. Her eyes flashed at her name, but she acted as though he had never spoken.

"Can I help you? Are you lost?" she asked, irritated. Her eyes were narrowed in suspicion.

Cy raised his chin, and spoke clearly, *"Theresa sent us."*

Her eyes thinned further, and her fingers twitched where they held the door. Cy heard a gasp from within the house, and scuffling. He leaned to the side, trying his best to see around the door, but the woman mirrored his movements to block his sight.

She raised a hand to his face, and he froze. In one swift movement, she flicked the hood of his cloak from his face.

"I'm terribly sorry, but you've missed your window of opportunity. I'm currently not taking any in who claim to know Theresa. You could always try again later, but I doubt I'll forget a face like yours."

She started to close the door, and Cy panicked. *What the hell is going on? What did they tell her? I've got to get in there. Think, you stupid demon. Think!*

Cy searched his head for anything he could say to convince her, anything Theresa might have told him, but there was nothing. In a last spur of hope, he though back to Arion, hoping he could use him as an excuse for her help.

At the thought of Arion, a realization hit him. He slammed his foot between the door and the frame, and flashed a smug smile at the woman. She glared at him intently, waiting his next words.

"Holten sent us, Jemmina."

She smiled back at him, and threw the door open with a wide gesture. Cy crossed the threshold into the room, his pulse racing within him.

"My apologies for the demeanor. I had a theory I wished to test, though I'm sorry I had to be right. For you to be here means that things have finally gone south. If you'd please?"

She held out her hand, and Cy placed it in hers. She closed her eyes for a moment, and her face twitched. "You better get ahold of that temper of yours. It'll be the death of you, demon."

"What was your theory, exactly?" Cy asked as he pulled his hand away. He examined it closely, worried her magic might have damaged the metal.

"The last person Holten had ever sent to me had been the boy. Theresa had given me orders to stray anyone that came looking for her, either by feigning my ignorance of her, or convincing others that she was dead. I did only as I was ordered. I cannot set someone's fortune off of their set path. I tried once. I was bedridden with a deathly illness for a month, and without powers for two. Though that seems harsh, I know it was only a warning."

"That's all well and good, but what does that have to do with testing me?" Cy said, impatient with the backstory. Jemmina was perched in front of another door. It was obvious she was blocking him from going any further.

"It was difficult to read the boy, very difficult. At first, I thought it was some sort of protection that had been put on him, but it was different than any protection I had seen before. It was a big, confusing mess inside of him, and when I focused hard enough, I could have sworn I heard two voices. When Theresa came to me a few nights ago and told me to expect a group of hers led by someone close to her, though it would not be her son, that's when I knew. You were with him, after all."

Not her son. So now I know how Theresa sees me, even if I wasn't sure before, Cy thought bitterly, turning away from Jemmina. She had moved on to Adoette and Noma, who needed no explanation and held their hands out to Jemmina.

As she finished explaining, Jayr burst out from behind a door. "Why did you let him in after I deliberately told you not to?"

He stormed straight up to Jemmina, and Cy thought he would have to step up to protect her. Though she was very slight in comparison to Jayr, she stood her ground until the Draken backed down.

"Given that you were eavesdropping on my conversation, I can only assume that you heard it all. Theresa and I are close friends, and she informed me of everything. She told me there would be six, and that you had to remain together no matter what. From now on, you better watch your tongue around me, Draken, or the group will dwindle down to five." Jemmina raised her palm. It glowed with a menacing purple light that lashed out and wrapped around her arms like serpents.

Jayr stepped back to press himself against the wall. With a final glare, Jemmina turned back to read Adoette and Noma, making a wide variety of faces with both of them.

Cy's eyes never left Jayr. The Draken was to blame for everything. It was all some plot to get rid of Cy, to take Kaitlyn away from the last thing she had in her life before all hell broke loose. He was working up the nerve to slam Jayr's face into the ground when Kaitlyn came running through the door and bolted right up to Cy. Gil was jogging behind her, his expression flustered.

Her cheeks were flushed and her eyes were glossed over. Faint trails ran down her cheeks where tears had run down her face. She smiled at Cy.

"*You told her not to let me in?*" Cy asked slowly.

Jayr turned away. Kaitlyn looked between the two of them, shock overcoming her features. "You did what?" she whispered.

Jayr sneered. "It had to be done."

In a furious rage, Cy stormed over to Jayr and grabbed him by the front of his armor. He growled at Jayr as he slammed him into the wall, baring his teeth. *"You want to tell me what's been going on here? I made you a promise, remember? Time to make good on that."*

Cy pulled his hand back, talons at the ready. Kaitlyn was begging him to stop, trying to reason with him, but he couldn't hear her over his rage. Jayr's eyes were full of fear, the edges of his armor biting into his neck.

Jemmina was on Cy in an instant, launching him backwards. Though she wasn't as strong as he was, she had caught him by surprise and he fell to the floor. Jayr collapsed in front of him, gasping for breath.

"What did I tell you about watching your temper, *demon?*" Jemmina flared, looming over him. Her hands were on her hips, but the snake-like tendrils of magic were reaching for him.

Cy got to his feet quickly, ushering Kaitlyn behind him. He clenched his fists at his sides, forcing the talons back into their sheaths. *"I have a name,* temptress," he hissed, containing his anger as directed.

"Congratulations, Cyllorian. But you will have to do much better in the future if you wish to succeed in your endeavors. And I must say, you are showing impressive control over your borrowed magic," Jemmina said with another wicked smile.

Does everything have to be a test with this woman? I swear, it's driving me freaking nuts! Cy thought until her choice of words hit him. *"You said my magic was borrowed. Do you know anything? Can you help us?"*

"I'm sorry. I am doing all I can for you. I know less about the situation than you do. I am entwined with your fates no further than giving you shelter."

Cy cursed under his breath and paced in a circle. Noticing

all eyes staring at him, he made his way to the far edge of the room. He felt the eyes boring into his back like knives, all of them watching and waiting for his next move.

"On that note, we are all here. You must rest. You'll not get another chance like this for quite some time, I can assure you. Here you are perfectly safe and welcomed, with no responsibilities other than those to your own bodies. All of you, off to a room to rest. Kaitlyn, Gil, Jayr, I've showed you where to go. Adoette and Noma, I can show you to your room. Cyllorian, would you be so kind to watch things down here? You don't need to sleep, do you?"

Jemmina turned to him, and he whirled to yell a sarcastic remark. The look in her eyes caught him off guard, and he stood there, speechless. There was a deep sorrow when she looked at him, with no one else to see. Even without touching him, it seemed she could read him perfectly. She knew how he would like to be alone.

He looked away. He nodded awkwardly, and turned back to the wall. He rested his fist against it and leaned his forehead on his hand for support. He listened as Jemmina herded the rest up a set of stairs, and sighed. Though he'd wanted to be left alone, he didn't know just how lonely the sudden silence would be.

* * *

"THIS IS SUCH A MESS!" Cy growled, burying his face in his hands. The outside air was brisk as it entwined with the magic in his body, and he was jealous of the others' body heat. The stone bench he sat on gave him no solace from the cold, but he ignored it.

Jemmina had a beautiful garden behind her house. There were small red flowers poking out from under the purple rose bushes and large blue sunflowers that were too tall to support themselves. In the farthest corner, leaning against the wall for support, there was a tall green flower with a teal stalk. Its petals were thin and pointed, turning violet at the ends.

Cy tilted his head back to stare at the sky. The light of the towers located further into Centric drowned out the stars, and clouds rolled eerily across the empty sky. *"None of this would be happening if I had just been left in that damned box."*

He heard someone walk up behind him, but didn't bother to see who it was. After a moment, they laid a hand on his shoulder, and a familiar soft voice flitted into his mind. *Join?*

Cy leaned forward to rest his arms on his knees. *"Who am I to tell you what you can and can't do? That's Noma's job."*

Adoette sat down quietly next to him, resting her hand on his gently. *Lonely?* she asked.

"I'm used to it," Cy said simply, staring at the ground.

Why?

Cy could feel her saddened gaze on him, and he shifted under it. *"Because no one ever wants to be around a demon."*

You want to be alone. It wasn't a question, but he nodded reluctantly anyway. He spared a sideways glance at her. She was a lot like Kaitlyn. Overly trusting. Curious. Gentle. And most importantly, innocent.

"Why are you so determined to give up your life to help me? I need to know," Cy asked. He never had the courage to ask Kaitlyn, so asking Adoette was the next best thing. Her answer didn't matter to him, so there was no risk in the question.

You have good intentions, she said simply. She looked up and smiled, Cy following her gaze. Since she had come outside, the stars were shining more brightly, their light dwarfing even the moon.

After a long moment, Adoette said, *Your anger is genuine, but it is not at the others. You wear the target for your hatred and guilt. You are missing something, that I can tell, and you do not know how to function without it.*

Cy looked down at his hands, and the engraving of Arion's lightning bolt stood out in the darkness. His magic flared with his guilt as he warred with himself. *What does it matter if she knows? I have to tell someone, and there's no one else. I just have to get it over with.*

He took a deep breath, then said, *"Would you believe me if I said I had a brother?"*

Family? She said enthusiastically. Her smiled beamed, but faded shortly.

"You could say that. I had a brother, but I hated him. I wanted him dead more than anything, because I blamed everything on him. But that was before I met him. I was forced to spend a lot of time with him, and he grew on me. But I was still so angry, and there was no one else to take it out on, so he got the short end of the stick. I was selfish, and my actions got him killed. That's who we want to bring back, my little brother. The worst part of it is that he never even knew we were technically related."

It all came out in a rush, and once it was gone, he felt like he would collapse. He was fueled solely by his regret, and now that it was out in the open, it was like he had nothing else.

Adoette was silent for a long moment, and pulled her hand away from his. He snuck a quick glance at her, expecting fear in her eyes. He was taken aback to find tears flowing down her cheeks.

He cleared his throat and continued, more for his own benefit. *"Theresa's our mother. She created me first, but it's not like I'm her flesh and blood. But for those first two years, I was her son. Then out of nowhere, Arion came along, her real son, and I was just a burden. She locked me up for years, and when I was let out, it was by Arion, of all people. How ironic that the one person I hated more than anything was the one to set me free, and the one I'd end up bound to for the next few years. Hell, he's dead and gone and I'm still bound to him. Pathetic, right?"*

Cy scoffed at himself, and buried his face again. Adoette's breathing hitched on a sob, and Cy sat up. She was wiping her face on her arm, a strict determination set in her face. Her eyes darted around the garden and her mouth hung open.

"I...I trust you, Cyllorian. I will help you get your brother back," Adoette said aloud. Her voice was barely more than a whisper, hoarse from lack of use. Even so, it was a musical sound that brought the garden to life around them.

The drooping blue flowers lifted themselves to bathe in the moonlight, dropping pollen that glowed when it touched the ground. More and more red flowers sprang out from under the weight of the purple roses, and the two plants fought to occupy the small space. The trees at the edge of Jemmina's yard swayed without a breeze. The shadows they cast danced over the grass that was thriving despite fall setting in. Owls chimed into a chorus all around them, mimicking her voice. It was as if everything had been given life when she spoke.

She smiled at Cy, blushing brightly. He smiled back and nodded to her. Adoette yawned, and though she fought against it, it overtook her. She stood and bowed sheepishly, holding her long dress out to her sides. She retreated back into the house, leaving Cy to await the sunrise on his own.

CHAPTER 16

Kaitlyn

"What makes you think I started it?" Jayr's voice could be heard clearly throughout the entire house. It was far from a pleasant way to be woken up.

"Maybe because you are *always* the one who starts it!" Gil yelled back.

With a groan, Kaitlyn forced herself out of bed. Her body was just starting to feel the wear of their adventures, and everything was sore. She pulled her hair into a tight ponytail while Vyekrin wriggled out of the blankets. He climbed onto her shoulder.

Kaitlyn groggily followed the sounds of the argument, not bothering to pay attention to what was said. She came down to the living room to find the boys sitting around each other. They were separated by thick lines of black fire on the floor.

Jemmina was slumped over in a chair. Her face was scarily pale, and she held onto her stomach. "If any of you dare to cross those lines, I'll kill you," she muttered, though her threat lacked spirit.

Kaitlyn padded to Jemmina's side, refusing to look at the others. Almost on instinct, she rubbed small circles on Jemmina's back. She felt the Mage relax under her touch, and she grinned.

"What could you three have possible found to fight over this early in the day?" Kaitlyn asked. She turned to the others, but no one answered. Gil stared down at his lap. He looked guilty, but determined. Jayr had his arms crossed over his chest, his jaw clenched tightly. Cy was lying on his stomach and playing with the fire in front of him.

Kaitlyn looked between the three of them, but they refused to answer. She sighed heavily. "Jayr, stop antagonizing Gil. And Gil, stop reacting to him every time. He just wants your attention. This isn't the time for a lover's quarrel."

Cy burst out laughing. Jayr and Gil talked over each other, neither one able to make a complete sentence to deny her claim. Jayr's face had turned bright red while Gil's had drained of all color. The smirk on Jemmina's face was clear as day.

"That's exactly what I said. Were you listening in?" Cy asked when he settled down. Kaitlyn shook her head. Cy dropped his head onto his arms, chuckling under his breath. The fire around them died out, but no one moved. Jayr and Gil avoided eye contact at all costs.

"This house hasn't been this lively in so long. It's nice," a new voice sounded. All attention turned to the doorway to the entrance. A large, dark-skinned man stood just inside the room. He wore a loose shirt over plain slacks, and metal bracers on his wrists. His smile was radiant, reaching all the way to his ice blue eyes

"Welcome, Holten," Jemmina said without raising her head. Holten's smile softened, and he moved to stand behind

Jemmina. All eyes were drawn to him, and they watched his every move. Only Cy remained unaffected as he lay perfectly still on the floor. Holten's presence had been so engaging that no one had noticed the guest he had brought with him.

Theresa leaned against the doorframe, gaze locked on Jemmina. The tension in the air at Theresa's appearance was smothering. Kaitlyn looked to Cy for help, but he was as lost for words as she was. His fists were clenched tightly, and there were small holes in the floor in front of him.

Adoette ran into the room, her arms full of bright colored flowers. Noma flitted behind her slowly, carrying a large orange orchid. She stepped before Jemmina first, ignoring her stress. She placed a crown made of yellow tulips and pink daisies on her head. Adoette moved onto Kaitlyn next, quickly tucking bright blue peonies into her hair. Finally, she approached Theresa easily and presented Noma's orchid with the biggest smile possible.

Theresa took it carefully and rested it on her ear. Adoette twirled once, then dropped onto the floor in the middle of the boys.

"What is a Kindling doing here?" she asked quietly.

Adoette didn't react to the harsh question, but Noma was clearly agitated as she paced across her shoulders.

"*What do you mean? You told us to go get one, right?*" Cy retorted immediately.

"I don't know what you're talking about. My instructions were to follow a path around the woods in order to reach Centric."

Cy glared at Jayr. He shrugged his shoulders, and responded, "I guess I misunderstood her orders." His words sounded forced and his expression was clear of any confusion. Kaitlyn couldn't deny that he was acting suspiciously, but she knew better than to call him on it now.

"You all made it here alive. What's done is done. Shall we, Jemmina?"

At the sound of her name, Jemmina stood obediently. Theresa led Jemmina and Holten to a room at the back of the house. As they left, it felt as though the air had finally returned to the room. Gil relaxed and let out a long breath, and Cy stretched along the floor. Jayr stood abruptly and entered the back half of the house behind the adults.

Kaitlyn made up her mind and followed him as he exited the house into the garden. "It's amazing that Theresa met us here. Don't you think so?" she asked as soon as they were alone.

Jayr whirled around in shock. "Yes. It'll be much easier to move forward from here."

"I've been wanting to ask her a few things, so this is the perfect opportunity. A lot has happened in the past couple weeks, and I was hoping she could make sense of it," Kaitlyn said, feigning innocence.

"Now isn't the time to explore your simple curiosity, Kaitlyn. You shouldn't waste her time."

Kaitlyn walked closer to him. She focused intently and controlled the change in her body, as well as her tone. "You're right. Maybe you could answer my questions, instead. I'm sure that would be better than her finding out how you were trying to get rid of Cyllorian this entire time."

She was only a few inches from him. She held her shoulders straight and her head high as she stared him down.

"I don't know what you're talking about," Jayr said quickly. He shifted his weight uncomfortably.

"You've taken every opportunity to try to cut him off. Suggesting we split up in Centric, then dragging me away by force. Lying about Theresa, telling us to go into the Kindling Woods rather than around. Even back in Deidrich, you tried leading me away from where he and Gil were waiting. Or am I wrong?" Kaitlyn took a small step forward, and Jayr began to retreat.

"You seriously don't understand anything, do you? You've said it yourself: you're a human, you don't belong in this world. You don't know anything," Jayr snapped defensively.

Kaitlyn smirked at him. "Do I still look human to you? No. I need to start getting used to this world, and I already know more than you realize. You think Cy can't be trusted because he's a demon. Theresa sent him specifically to get you, when she clearly could have gone herself, right? You told us she showed up to talk to you, so why didn't she just take you back with her then? Why send you along with someone she doesn't trust—"

"Shut up! I already told you, you wouldn't understand even if I spelled it out to you. So be a good little girl and be silent!" Jayr snapped. His fists were trembling at his side, and he was sweating.

Kaitlyn held her ground. "I understand all I need to. But by all means, if I'm wrong, then prove it. Go tell Theresa right now, before I do. Let's see how well she takes it."

"I don't need to prove anything to you," he scoffed.

Kaitlyn lost her resolve. As quickly as she could, she hooked one foot behind Jayr's ankle and grabbed the collar of his shirt. She pulled his leg out from under him and tackled him to the ground. "I don't give a damn what your selfish reasons are, whether it's jealousy or prejudice. If you get in the way of what we're trying to do, or go against Cy again, I'll take you down one way or another. You're nothing more than a bully, and I've spent my whole life dealing with them. You don't scare me."

Kaitlyn shoved him as she stood. Without looking back, she returned to the house. She shook her head to calm herself down.

The house was already in another uproar when Kaitlyn returned. Gil was holding Cy back as he screamed at Theresa. *"What are you saying? Of course we have to go, this is our best chance!"*

Theresa stood tall, a small white owl perched on her shoulder. A torn letter was clenched in her fist. "My orders are final," Theresa said simply.

"This isn't a trap, Theresa. You know the information comes from an ally," Holten pressed.

"You never said anything about having informants inside Talgrin. I can't risk it, not when we're this close."

"Close? What the hell do you mean? You just said that your research was useless, that nothing we have can bring him back! Crestyss has what we need, and you're trying to stop me!"

"Cy, just calm down," Gil hushed nervously. Cy tried to shake him off, and his talons cut through Gil's arms. Blood dripped on the floor, and Cy stilled.

"What's going on?" Kaitlyn asked. She stepped into the room and all eyes shifted to her.

"We got a note saying Crestyss has a way to bring Arion back, but Theresa won't let me go," Cy growled.

"I don't blame her. I won't let you go either," Kaitlyn said strictly.

"Kaitlyn—"

"Not alone, at least," she finished. "We're all going with you. Right, Jayr?" Kaitlyn turned her head to catch Jayr's gaze as he tried to sneak around her. He glared at her, and she flashed a threatening smile.

Jayr groaned. "Of course. That's what we were gathered for in the first place, right?"

"I forbid it!" Theresa's usually cool voice was a knife that cut the air. Her cheeks were bright red. The owl had moved from her shoulder onto Holten's.

"We have time, Theresa." Jemmina spoke for the first time. Her words held a strange weight that smothered Theresa, and the Mage finally stood down.

Theresa held her arm for the owl, and he obediently jumped onto it. She leaned against the wall, her shoulders slumping.

Holten turned to Cy, who had finally calmed down. Adoette had suddenly appeared and wrapped dark green seaweed around Gil's injury. Kaitlyn took Cy's side opposite Gil. Jayr stepped closer reluctantly, though his attention was fixed solely on Theresa.

"Let's not waste any time then," Holten said. He led the group out of the house swiftly.

"Watch them," Jemmina called after them.

Holten quickly ducked into a nearby rotten building, pulling the others in one by one. An inch of water covered the floor and the swollen wood was groaning under the weight. A corner of the floor was broken, showing a bubbling pool of water. "Heavy rain flooded the water system that runs beneath Centric. These tunnels can lead us straight into Talgrin. Gil, Kaitlyn, Adoette, and I can breathe underwater. Cy will be fine if I put a barrier around his body, and the dragons and Noma can stay in his chest. That just leaves you, Jayr."

"I'll make my way to Talgrin on land. You'll need someone on the outside when this is all through. Getting out is never as easy as getting in," Jayr answered with a huff.

"We're counting on you, then," Holten said just before Jayr left the building. He paused a moment, then disappeared without a word.

Cy tried to go after him, but Holten grabbed his shoulder. Noma and Vyekrin were standing in his hand. "Can we entrust them to you?"

Cy nodded and opened the plate over his chest. Noma sat

crossed-legged on top of his heart while Vyekrin climbed into the metal frame that was his ribcage. Holten's blue magic covered Cy as soon as his chest was sealed shut.

Gil tapped on Kaitlyn's shoulder. "You have to get ready, too."

Kaitlyn nodded and shut her eyes to focus. She remembered the scalding waters of Lorile and the blue scales that had protected her. She flexed her fingers as thin webbing grew between them. Stretching her neck, she could feel multiple slits open on the sides, and she took a slow breath through her gills.

Though the change was complete, she couldn't help but feel nervous. *What if I lose control while we're under, and drown. What if I forgot something important and don't even last a minute in the water. What if...*

Gil's hand in her own stopped her panic. "You can do this. It's who you are, right?" He gave her a warm smile, and the fear drained out of her.

"Right."

Adoette was the first in the water, waiting eagerly for the rest to join. Holten popped something into his mouth, grabbed Cy's arm, and dropped in next. Gil and Kaitlyn hopped in together, but Gil separated to lead the others.

Thick vines grabbed at them as they swam, wrapping around their limbs. Kaitlyn let out a yelp as her hair was yanked free of its restraint. Holten was being held against the wall while Gil was moving frantically, to evade the vines. The violent roots were even trying to pry Cy open, but he tore them to shreds with his talons.

Adoette spun through the water gracefully. She caressed the plants as she passed them, and they slowly curled in on themselves. She swam ahead of the others, shielding them from the threat.

The water became shallow and the floor sloped upward. Before the group could break the surface, hands reached into the water and snatched them out. Holten's magic broke and he gasped for air. Cy was ripped from his grip and thrown into the hall. His shoulder collided with the stone, breaking his chest open. Noma and Vyekrin tumbled out and scrambled on the ground so they wouldn't get squashed under the feet of the guards that had caught them.

Kaitlyn squirmed free of the guard that held her, thankful that Droll skin was slick. She spun quickly and grabbed the guard's head. Sweeping his feet from under him, she dragged them both to the ground and slammed his head into the ground with enough force to dent his helmet.

Holten had already regained his bearings and frozen the legs of four guards that had tried to subdue him. Cyllorian had two guards pinned under his weight while they failed to pierce his metal with daggers. Gil looked as though he were dancing with the guards, avoiding their advances and using their own momentum to throw them into the water. Adoette was controlling the vines from the water like whips, entangling the incapacitated soldiers.

Footsteps and yells sounded from behind them. Reinforcements were coming.

"Go ahead, I'll hold them off!" Holten yelled above the noise. Kaitlyn wanted to argue, but Cy grabbed her wrist and pulled her along. She looked over her shoulder to check on Holten, and was surprised to find the entire floor frozen with a thick sheet of ice. The guards slid along the ground, piling into each other and falling into the water.

Cy led them along a trough of shallow water until they found the center room with five different hallways to choose from. They stopped in the middle, breathing heavily. Noma flitted to the entrance of each hall, but gave no sign of finding which to take. When she approached the last, she let out a shrill scream and fell a foot in the air. She recovered quickly and retreated to Adoette.

"You got here a lot faster than I expected," a whining voice sounded from the darkness. A pale green creature with a lizard's tail emerged from the tunnel, a sickening smile splitting its face in half. *"That informant sure was easy to crack once I got my hands on him."*

Gil stepped up beside Kaitlyn, his frame rigid. "Another demon," he breathed.

Kaitlyn's view of the creature was blocked and Cy stood protectively in front of her. *"We don't have time for a cheesy 'end of the line' speech here. Don't make us waste our time with you,"* Cy snapped.

Kaitlyn peered around Cy to catch a glimpse of the thing in their way. She immediately wished she hadn't. It looked like a giant lizard, with sickly green sick and a long, thin tail. It was equipped with sharp nails and teeth. Something about it was familiar, and Kaitlyn suppressed a shudder. Her instincts were screaming at her that this thing was a demon.

"Fine, then. I'll end you quickly," the thing hissed. It moved faster than Kaitlyn had thought possible and aimed straight for Cyllorian. It pulled a glowing dagger from its sleeve at the last second, and slashed it across Cy's face.

Cy stumbled backward with a yell. He pushed Kaitlyn as far from the other demon as possible. She caught herself on the ground, and saw the deep cut that ran through Cy's left eye.

The other demon was standing over him. *"I wonder how much you'll scream."* It raised the dagger over its head and paused. Its eyes flicked to Kaitlyn, and winked at her. A chill ran down her spine.

Adoette jumped on the demon's back. Vyekrin sank his teeth into the demon's ankle and it lost its balance. It fell on its stomach as Adoette wrapped her arms around its neck. Her rough skin bit into the demon's neck, and it cackled.

"You aren't part of the plan," it growled. It thrashed its legs wildly until Vyekrin was thrown against the wall. Noma flew to the lizard's aide. The demon grabbed Adoette by her hair and pulled her off its back.

Adoette yelped. She rolled in its grip and grabbed its arm. Her hair moved on its own, wrapping around the demon.

"You little! Let—"

"Let go, Adoette!" Gil yelled as he grabbed the demon around the chest. Adoette released the demon and Gil dragged it away.

"Hurry and go find what you need, we can take care of him." Gil reached the edge of the platform and fell back into the water, pulling the cursing demon with him. Vyekrin had awoken easily and jumped into the water after them. Adoette used the vines to make a cage on the water's surface.

Cy pulled Kaitlyn to her feet. The wound in his face didn't seem to be healing on its own. They ducked into the hall that the demon had been guarding.

It was then Kaitlyn realized that she didn't even know what they were looking for or where to find it. All she could do was follow Cy with blind faith.

CHAPTER 17

Void

What are those voices? *They said they were done for the day. Have I slept that long already?* Void rolled on the floor, shutting his eyes tightly. *If they think I'm asleep, they might leave me alone. They'll think I've remembered something.*

Void curled into himself, hoping he would go unnoticed. The voices grew closer and clearer, coupled by hurried footsteps. Cautiously, he opened his eye and peered into the darkness of his cell. The bars that faced the hallway were nothing but dark blurs against the open air. A faint ghost of light could be seen from the end of the hallway, but never reached him. He listened with a vague interest that surprised him, waiting for his sight to adjust to the dark.

His cell was no different than the day before with its slanted floor and white stained walls. The hall on the other side was much the same, though it was cleaner. Uneven stones made the walls and floor, and he could see a torch just across that he had never seen used.

"I can't believe we haven't found a damn thing! It's not even confusing down here. There's just nothing!" the first voice said. It was a lot like Grite's voice, but didn't have the hissing tone to it. It was more intelligent, but there was that underlying hint of malice that gave away it was a demon's voice.

"If we stopped to check more places, maybe we would find it! I keep telling you there *has* to be some sort of secret in here," a female voice sounded. Where the demon's voice had been steady and clear, this one was strained. The voices bounced off the walls, and they only drew closer to Void.

I don't know those voices. They aren't Crestyss or Grite, obviously, but that doesn't mean they're any better. They won't even see me in here, I'm sure. They're looking for something specific. It can't be me.

Void wriggled away from the direction of the voices, pressing himself up against the wall. He still had yet to adjust to the lack of light. As the people grew nearer, he could distinguish the two. The girl was soft on her feet, only making noise because of hard sole shoes. The demon, on the other hand, barreled through the stone halls loudly. With every step, there was the clang of metal that rumbled the ground. It even sounded as though the demon was crashing into the walls.

"If we just keep running like this we're going to get lost. We have to figure out a plan from here, because going in blind isn't doing any good," the girl called, slowing down.

The demon halted as well, stopping just before the bars of Void's cell. A green light inched around the corner, stretching towards the boy curled against the wall.

They have a light! They can see me! His thoughts worked into a panic, but the body he was trapped in had no reaction. *Just go away! Leave me alone.*

"What else are we supposed to do? We don't have much time left down here and we've been pretty much everywhere!" the demon shouted, his voice reverberating along the corridors. Void cringed at the volume of it, but quickly regretted his action.

"We haven't been here. Look," the girl said slowly. The curiosity in her voice set another bout of panic through his mind, and he was finally able to make his body move. He twitched in the darkness, jerking his head around to get a glance, but he could see nothing.

The demon came into view, bringing with him the strange green light. It outlined his whole body, showing what could only be plates of armor. Nearly lost within the green were two gleaming purple eyes, staring straight at Void.

"It's a prisoner. This is a dungeon, what did you expect?" the demon asked, and Void relaxed at the uncaring tone.

Go away, now! Void wanted to yell, but he couldn't move. He didn't care that they had seen him, or what they thought of him.

But then...why did he feel so strange every time they spoke? He could only explain it as dread, though he couldn't recall ever feeling it before. Fear had been the only thing that had properly been extracted during the torture, and that had passed as the pain became more regular. He had already forgotten the sting of the whip as it peeled flesh from his spine, how Grite cracked his ribs only a few hours ago when Crestyss had been called away suddenly.

"Should we help him?" the girl asked. She waited a long time for an answer from the demon, and Void waited impatiently. He held his breath, wanting nothing more than to get away from the people just outside his cell. The bars had always kept him in, but now he was grateful that they kept the intruders out.

"We don't have the time," the demon said finally, a hint of

pity in his voice. *"We've got our own list of people to save. How about we get what we came for, work things out, beat Crestyss' ass, then we can rescue him. Deal?"*

The demon started to leave, his armor clanking with each heavy step he took. But the girl didn't follow. She grabbed onto the door and shook it violently, then there was a terrible scraping. Void jumped up and stared at her, his eyes going wide. The light from the demon glinted off the black, curved talons on the girl's hands.

"We don't have time! Do you want to get him back, or would you rather have whatever's in there?" he said sharply. He grabbed the girl's arm and she glared at him. The glow from the demon's body caught her face, and the bright blue eyes from Void's dream came to light.

"Leave me alone!" Void yelled, backing away from the girl.

She whirled to him, just now realizing that he was awake. She reached her hand through the bars towards him, and he shook his head. Fear had overtaken him again, though there was no threat of pain to entice it.

"Look, he doesn't want help, Kaitlyn. We need to go!" The demon eyed Void suspiciously. He reached for the girl again, but she ducked out of his grip.

"You're awake! Are you okay? What's your name? Why are you in here?" She launched question after question at him. Void slapped his hands over his ears, trying to shut out the words that haunted his sleep.

"You have to leave now! There's no reason to save me!" Void pleaded with her. His back had hit the wall, and he slid down it. An immense pain split the inside of his head, and he frantically ran his hands through his hair, terrified of what damage would be done.

Grite's threat rang in his ears: *If those* imaginary *friends in your head ever decide to try to save you, I'll slaughter them in front of you.*

Though he hadn't cared when he had first heard them, the words now made him feel sick to his stomach. He couldn't explain why, but he knew that he couldn't let Grite near them.

"Shh, shh. It's okay, we can get you out. Come on, Cy, help me!" She yanked on the door again and then lashed at it with her claws, ignoring Void's cries.

"It's not worth it! I'm nothing! Just leave!" Void urged, on his knees. Tears stung his eyes, though he couldn't place the cause. Why did he care now, of all times? What had him so scared that he couldn't even think?

"Listen to the...thing...in the cell. We have a mission here. We can't afford to blow it! This is our last chance, and you know it."

"Then help me get him out of here quickly so we can continue." The girl's voice was strong and determined.

The demon sighed, then pressed his hand to the lock. Void watched mortified as it was blown to pieces by a blinding green light, and the door swung open.

The girl ran to Void's side, and he flinched away from her outstretched hand. "Whatever you're here for, I'm not worth it. I have nothing, I am nothing. Just get out of here, don't care about me!" Void yelled.

The demon was standing in front of him in an instant, and Void froze. This close, he could see that the demon wasn't wearing armor. He was made of it. There was nothing but pure magic underneath the metal.

"Great, we got another martyr. Look, kid, there ain't no way in hell I'm dealing with that shit again, so get a move on." The demon grabbed Void's arm and yanked him to his feet. He pulled Void out of the cell, the girl close behind. As much as Void tried fighting, it only proved how weak the starvation had made him.

Void walked weakly beside the demon as they wandered through the dungeon with no clear objective. "Do you know if Crestyss keeps anything down here? Anything special?" the girl asked, smiling widely at Void. He shook his head frantically, shrinking away from her. He bumped into the demon and froze, expecting retaliation. The demon gave him a quizzical look, so he just continued walking.

Void stared at the ground in front of them while the other two looked at everything they passed. *"We're never going to find it at this rate. The others can't buy us time forever. Hey, kid, if you know anything, you better start talking."*

The demon shook Void gently, and he cringed under the movement. "I don't know anything, I swear. Nothing at all." He tangled his fingers in his hair, threatening to rip it out.

The girl placed her hand on his arm, and he glanced at her. "It's okay. He's just stressed. We understand you were probably locked in there a while. We're looking for a book, or scroll, we think. Something with secret knowledge in it. Do you know anything about that?"

"Nothing. My mind is empty," Void replied, emotionless. His sudden loss of tone made the two stare at him oddly. While they paused in their questioning, Void heard a high pitched chime and distant yells.

The two looked at each other, then broke out into a sprint. The demon drug Void behind him, who was barely able to keep up.

"The prisoner's escaped! The intruders must have gotten to him! Find them at all costs! Kill them if you must!" A loud voice boomed through the halls, its origin unclear.

"I knew you should have left me. We're all going to die! Well, you are at least, and I'm going to get it. You should've listened to me!" Void screamed, falling behind.

The demon launched Void ahead of him and yelled, *"Well,*

too late now! Get us to the exit, kid! You have to have gone through it at least once!"

Void shook his head, fear rushing through him again. His legs grew heavy, unmovable. He collapsed against a wall, tears blurring his vision.

The girl grabbed his arm, pulling him forward. "I know you're scared, but that's fine! Use it to get out of here, then you'll be free! You won't have to be scared anymore!"

He stared into her eyes, wanting to tell her that she was what was making him so terrified. The light in her eyes struck him, and he thought about all of his dreams that had turned into nightmares. They had always ended with those same eyes, watching his torment and doing nothing.

But it was Grite who ruined the dream, had engraved fear into his mind. The dreams had once been an escape, but now, they were just another torture to dwindle his sanity, if he even had any to begin with. If he got out, there would be no Grite to carve into him, to twist everything he had.

He shook the tears from his eyes and abandoned all thoughts and emotions. He thought to the one time they had shown him the castle, attempting to bribe him into remembering. They hadn't cared if he knew how to get out, sure that he wouldn't have the spirit or courage to try to leave.

He took off in the direction, his mind working without a trace of fear or emotion. He acted impulsively, doing whatever instinct dictated. He didn't have to look behind him to know that the others were close behind. He could feel them, as though all of their emotions were tangible forces around them. Without emotions of his own, he seemed to cling to those around him, feeding off of them. And the two people behind him were swarming with determination.

They found the stairs to the surface, and Void launched himself up them two at a time. They burst into a brightly lit hallway and Void crashed into a wall, blinded. The demon grabbed him by the wrist, leading him through the halls.

They were heading towards the sounds of a fight, and the fear began to creep up on Void again. "Shouldn't we be going away from the people?" he yelled, his lungs on fire with the effort to keep up.

"They caught our friends, I can hear them up ahead. We have to regroup and get out of here together," the demon called back.

They rounded a corner into a grand main hall, filled with a hoard of guards. They were surrounding someone, blue flashes coming from the middle.

The demon pushed Void against the wall. *"You wait here, and don't get caught."*

Before Void could protest, the demon was charging the guards. He dove straight into the thick of the crowd, and green lightning shot into the air. Void turned to the girl for guidance, but she wasn't paying attention to him. She stared at the crowd with confidence, shaking her limbs out. As she did, they were covered in light blue scales. The black claws on her hands grew longer, and sharpened teeth protruded from her mouth. She smiled evilly, and pounced onto the back of a guard. She climbed over them towards the middle, felling many with shallow cuts from her claws.

Void watched the outbreak in confusion, unsure of what to focus on. All he could see was a writhing mass of bodies. He watched as the floor became littered with bodies and the crowd was thinned. Through a wall of guards, he could pick out the demon and the girl, as well as a Mage and a teen in brown armor who were fighting the guards as well.

A pair of guards broke away from the crowd and noticed Void. They started for him, and he raised his hands to defend himself before he remembered that his only weapons had been cut from his hands.

"There it is! Grab it, quick, before it takes off. Crestyss will have our heads if we let this thing get away from us!" one of the guards said, drawing a dagger from his belt. The second followed the lead, pulling out his own blade.

Void scanned the room around him. He wanted to fight back, wanted to run away, but he didn't know how. He caught a glimpse of the demon tackling a few men at the edge of the circle.

"Hey, hey! You have to help me! Hey!" Void yelled, waving his arms. The guards were watching him, closing in quickly. Void was backed into a wall, and the men cornering him laughed sadistically.

"I heard you could cut this thing into a million pieces and it still wouldn't die," the second guard said, slashing his dagger through the air.

"I heard they burned it alive for five hours straight, and it healed itself up in just a few minutes!"

"I don't believe it. I say we test it out for ourselves."

"Agreed. We have to make sure this is the prisoner, right? No use saving something so worthless. I mean, look at it! It looks ready to piss its pants!" the first guard barked. He planted his foot on the ground and darted forward. The blade was aimed straight for Void's heart.

Void glanced to the demon again, praying that he was coming to help. He was preoccupied by a hoard of guards that had surrounded him. They grabbed his arms and forced the demon to his knees. His head dropped, and Void's hopes sunk with him.

With speed that seemed impossible, the demon swung his legs around him, knocking the guards to the ground. He kicked straight up into the air as he jumped, and his foot connected with one guard's jaw. He ducked under another running for him, and flipped him onto his back.

The demon finally caught sight of Void, paralyzed as the guard charged for him. He had gotten used to Grite coming after him, knew what Grite would do and how he would attack. It was an all-new experience to be the target of someone else.

The demon bolted, but Void knew he wouldn't reach them in time. He turned to face his attackers, and something clicked in his mind at the last second. He ducked under the man's arm and stepped around the man. Shifting his weight, he spun back toward the guard and raised his leg into the air. His heel hit the man's cheek, driving his head into the ground. He landed facing the second guard, wasting no time. He crouched low to the ground and pounced, grabbing the man around the waist. They fell to the floor and Void slammed the man's head into the ground, knocking him unconscious.

He stared at the man lying underneath him with disinterest, though his thoughts were screaming incoherently at him, begging him to react in some way. Before he could grasp what he had just done, the demon was at his side. He snatched Void by the arm and yanked him to his feet. Void was dragged through the thresh of the fighting, where they met up with the girl and two other fighters.

"We need to get out of here," the Mage said. He attacked only from a distance with magic that looked like shards of ice. The teen held off any guards with his bare hands, having a fair amount of brute strength on his side. The girl was darting from the center to the edge and back again, dispatching one or two guards at a time that were getting too close.

The demon shoved Void behind him. He bumped against the teen and froze. He stared down at Void with pure hatred and disgust, not unlike Grite. Void held his gaze until the teen looked away uncomfortably.

"Good, you got him. Now we can get out of here!" the girl

said, returning to the group. She stood on her toes to look over the demon's shoulder and waved at Void. He waved back awkwardly. Her cheerful smile was in great contrast with the blood that covered her black talons. Void found himself wondering if this group really was a better alternative to the cell he was accustomed to.

"Holten, lead the way," the demon said, grabbing onto Void again. The demon glanced at the girl as she filed behind Void. There was an apology in her eyes.

The man wasted no time before barreling through the guards that stood in their path. The teen drew a sword to keep the guards at bay, and the girl was able to pick off any that strayed in behind them. The demon was the only one not fighting the guards. His only concern seemed to be with Void, holding him as close as he could while they ran.

I'm not what they came here for. They don't even care about me. Why is he being so protective? Void thought, staring at the demon ahead of him. *Did I miss something?*

He was doing his best to keep up, thankful that his body had listened to the logic of his mind for once and sent adrenaline rushing through his veins for aid. It was the only thing keeping him going, he knew. It burned in his arms and legs, swelled in his chest to the point that it was difficult to breathe, but he kept pushing forward. If they were risking so much for him, the least he could do was not make it difficult.

They came upon the front doors quickly, and they burst out into the open air. The sunlight was harsh to Void's eyes, never having seen more than the pitch blackness of the dungeons. The rest of the tower had been painful enough, but the outside world had him on his knees instantly, covering his entire face.

"Get him up! We can't stop now!" the man yelled. The demon was pulling on his arm again, cursing and yelling. Void shoved him off, crying out in pain as he moved his hand away from his face.

"Get off! I can't go any more, just leave me here! Please, just leave me alone already! Don't get killed for something like me. Just go!" he screamed frantically, shaking his head wildly.

He was lifted from the ground by solid arms that cradled him awkwardly. *"You know, kid, you're really not as heavy as you look,"* the demon grunted. *"I already told you, I'm not dealing with the martyr shit anymore."* The demon's last statement was hushed, as though it was only intended for Void to hear.

"Give him to me! We won't get far with you bearing his weight," the man said. Void was lurched around in the demon's arms.

"You need your hands more than I do. Just get us out of here, fast, and we don't have to worry about who carries the big baby!"

"I'm not a baby," Void muttered reflexively, though he knew he had no room to argue given the position he was in.

"Could've fooled me."

The demon's arms tightened around him, and Void stopped squirming. He turned his face into the demon's chest, raising his arm to shield his eyes from the light. Void grabbed onto the demon's shoulder when he started running and held on as tight as he could.

With only his hearing to tell the situation, Void didn't think it was good. They were surrounded by yells of anger and fear, and footsteps followed as they ran. He felt smothered by the excess emotions around him. Something grazed his arm, and he flinched from the shock. He dared a glance behind the demon and saw a crude arrow sticking out of a wall, separating them and a guard that was on their heels.

"Why didn't you tell me you were an archer?" the demon yelled above the chaos.

"I'm only good underwater!" a new voice replied.

"What happened to the other one?" The demon's voice was frantic.

"I lost him in the tunnels, I don't know where he went. Now just get going." Another arrow struck the wall and broke in half just in front of the guard's face. Void careened his neck to find the source, but the demon rounded a corner and everything was lost.

While the screaming faded, the sound of a chase was endless. They came to an abrupt halt, and Void nearly fell from the demon's grasp.

"Holten, what do we—"

The demon stumbled backward, squeezing Void painfully tight. He heard the girl's soft yelp beside him. Something heavy was dropped into his lap.

"Exit through the east and follow the wall until you find a path to lead you home." The man's voice boomed with force. A loud rumbling sound erupted just inches away.

The demon dropped Void to the ground suddenly. He looked up to see the demon clawing at a stone wall that was rising from the ground. Void felt the item given to him, and found a mottled pile of cloth.

Void sat motionless. Everything had drained from his body, and he was left a husk again. Any hint of emotion, any semblance of a person inside the body, was gone. He lost his grip on what he wanted to be, but the pure nature of what he was prevented him from caring at all. The events that had just unfolded had drained everything from him.

The demon held his hand out to Void, offering him help to his feet. Void ignored him and stood on his own, brushing the dust from his legs absentmindedly. The clothing had dropped to the ground, but no one cared. He was aware of the blue eyes glued to him, but it had no effect on him.

"You mean we have to go through the Wastelands? Why don't

you just take me to a junkyard? At least they'll treat me better!" the demon shouted. His anxiety was apparent. Void wondered what that felt like. It must be different for the demon, being in a body that didn't react to emotion the same way a person's would, but it seemed close enough to what Void expected. The demon was playing with his hands nervously, and his voice came out at a higher pitch than normal. He tried to mimic the demon's reactions, thinking he could instill the emotion on himself. The demon glared at him from the corner of his eye, and Void ceased.

"Don't worry, Kaitlyn will protect you. At least this was a success." The man's voice was barely audible over the wall forming between them.

"Success? We didn't get anything done in there except get in Crestyss' sights!"

"You never know what treasures you hold, you ought to know that by now. You did the right thing, in any case."

"The right thing, ha! He wasn't the one we're supposed to save!" the demon screamed. He flared his arm out toward Void, and he flinched automatically. The only response were the sounds of fighting.

"Stop scaring him!" the girl hissed, pushing the demon's arm down.

"Now you're on his side? What about Arion? Don't you even still care about him?"

"Of course, I care! We searched that whole dungeon, Cy, and there was nothing there for us! We might not be able to get Arion back this way, but at least we could save this boy! I just want to help someone for once, rather than leaving them to die!"

The girl stomped away, tears springing to her eyes. The demon dropped his head. He angled his body away, but not before Void saw his talons pierce the metal in his arm. The demon snatched the clothing from the ground and shook it out to reveal three large cloaks. He threw one around his shoulders and clenched the other two in his fists.

The girl was beside Void again. The smile on her face was forced, as well as her cheerful tone when she asked, "Now that we're safe, why don't you tell us your name?"

The boy shrugged. "I don't have one. I'm just Void."

Chapter 18

Cyllorian

"I can't believe we're stuck walking home because you wouldn't let us leave this guy behind! I should've just listened to him and left him in the cell. Not too late to ditch him, you know," Cy groaned, walking ahead of Kaitlyn and Void. She was walking next to the boy on purpose, keeping an eye on him.

The Wastelands were very open, scarcely dotted with trees to provide relief from the harsh winds. The shadow of Centric's wall stretched far, and blocked them from the heat of the sun. Though winter was only beginning, it was showing signs of being merciless. The frigid air had formed frost where the metal overlapped, making his movements stiff. Even his magic felt sharp like ice.

Void was extremely slow, and Cy had to keep stopping so he could catch up. Each time, he glared at Void. The boy stared right back, with no sign of life in his eyes. It sent chills throughout the veins of magic that rushed through him, and he looked away.

Every so often, Void would meet him glare for glare, but it seemed like he was only copying him rather than expressing himself.

"We're not abandoning him, Cy! It wouldn't be right to just leave him on his own, and you know it!" Kaitlyn yelled back. Cy glanced over his shoulder at them. Kaitlyn was walking far too close to Void for his comfort.

"I say he can't be trusted! What if this is some kind of trap, and we're leading him straight to Theresa? What if he kills us in our sleep tonight? They knew we were coming, Kaitlyn, so how do you know we can trust him?"

"I could say the same about you. This could be a trap set up by Crestyss to make me trust *you*, then tell him whatever he wants from me," Void retorted, his tone perfectly matching Cy's. It was a complete change from the weak, miserable kid he had been just a few hours before. It put Cy off seeing emotion in him, knowing what he was.

"Yeah, sure. That's what you want us to think, so we can agree that we don't trust each other and that we're all just being stupid. I've got my eye on you, kid. You so much as wipe your snot away when you start crying, and I'll take you down."

"I'm not too eager to betray the first people I've known that haven't greeted me with a sharp object of some sort. So you can relax. Besides, you really think I'm in any shape to be a threat to you?" Void stopped and lifted the side of his shirt. Ribs protruded from his sides, nearly breaking the skin that was stretched over them. His filthy pants kept falling from his waist, and bone thin legs could be seen through tears in the fabric. His thin white hair was grimy, stuck together with hardened globs of some white substance. Dark shadows on his face created a great contrast with his piercing white eyes.

"We need to help him, Cy," Kaitlyn started. "He needs food,

and water. New clothes, too. We have extras, just give him a pair of..."

"No. He isn't getting anything of his. Not while I'm still alive." Cy cut her off, glaring with the most malicious intent at Void, but the boy was as emotionless as ever. Cy tightened his grip on the bag that had been delivered to them at the edge of Centric. Snow had brought them one of their packs from the journey, and it came with a letter of anger from Theresa that practically screamed at them itself.

Kaitlyn stared Cy down. "Cy, we're helping him. Give me the bag, and I'll find something for him." She held her hand out. With a growl, Cy flung the bag to her.

Cy looked away, his arms crossed over his chest, as Kaitlyn searched through the bag. She handed Void a small pile of clothes. Cy peered over his shoulder to see Void stripping with no shame, and Kaitlyn blushing as he did, and she awkwardly averted her gaze.

Cy shook his head and turned away again. *Is she going to dress him, too, like the brat that he is?* Cy thought snidely.

Kaitlyn's scream shook him out of his anger, and he turned and bolted for them in one movement.

He tackled Void to the ground on his stomach, twisting one arm behind the boy. Kaitlyn was staring at Void's back with her hands covering her mouth, her face gone completely pale. Once Cy had confirmed that she was safe, he was able to see why she had screamed.

Void's back was covered with an immeasurable number of scars. There were thick scars that looked like they were from whipping, and thin slash marks from knives. The tops of his shoulders were mangled and twisted from burns, and a strange pattern like stitching overlapped his spine.

"What...what happened to you?" Kaitlyn finally breathed.

"Crestyss and his demon, Grite," Void said simply, seemingly uninjured under Cy's weight.

"They did this to you? I...I can't even tell what some of this is from." Kaitlyn stepped forward and ran her fingers over the scars on his spine. He shivered under her touch, but remained expressionless.

"That's from when they put my...actually, it's best if you don't know," Void said, watching Kaitlyn's tortured expression.

"You want us to trust us, then you speak. The more you hide from us, the more suspicious you look," Cy said, shaking Void once.

Void glared at him, then back at Kaitlyn. With a sigh, he said, "From when they put my skin back on my body."

"What?" Kaitlyn gasped, stepping away. Tears leaked down her cheeks, but she made no noise.

Void continued. "Do you want to know what else they've done? They did something to me so I can't die, but I can't remember anything. They used to hang me for days, my neck healing and breaking over and over again. Dismemberment and reattachment, that was Grite's favorite. He would drown me in my own blood afterwards."

"Enough!" Cy said, slamming his face into the dirt. Kaitlyn was sobbing now, her hands clamped over her ears. Cy leaned down and said in Void's ear so Kaitlyn wouldn't hear, *"You make her cry or scream again, and I'll make sure you die. They wanted you for something, but I've got no reason to keep you around any longer."*

For a second, Void looked fearful, but it slipped from him just as Cy saw it in his eyes. With another shove, Cy stood and went to comfort Kaitlyn. Void changed his clothes. It disgusted Cy to see him dressed like Arion, but after what Void had put Kaitlyn through, he wasn't about to argue with her now.

"Don't kill him," Kaitlyn breathed, calm now that Void's

scars were out of sight. She watched as the boy struggled to button up the shirt she had given him, and gave up halfway, leaving most of his chest bare. His hands were shaking. They looked scarred, but Cy didn't dare ask.

"Look at him, Cy. You saw what they did to him, and that's just what shows. We can't let him get taken back by them. We just can't," Kaitlyn begged. "Please, be nice. I know you're angry that we missed this chance to save Arion because of me, but we'll figure something else out. Just please, try to get along."

Cy let out his breath and nodded, and Kaitlyn smiled at him. She traced the wound on his face lightly. "This still hasn't healed," she said quietly.

"The blade was heated with magic. I'll have to cut off the burnt bits before it'll heal, but it can wait till later." Cy peered over Kaitlyn's shoulder to see Void watching them intently. He held Cy's gaze long enough to catch Kaitlyn's attention as well.

Kaitlyn left Cy to help Void with the rest of his buttons, and fixed his collar. Void watched her fix his clothing. He looked lost in the new clothes, and it reminded Cy of how Arion looked the last time he had seen him.

Void

Kaitlyn had fallen asleep quickly. He only had to wait until Cy slept. He wasn't sure if the demon ever would, but his magic dimmed eventually, and the demon became unresponsive.

Cy had the bag through most of the day, and kept it with him late into the night. Void held his breath and pulled the bag from Cy's side, and began to rummage through it. *They have to have a knife in here somewhere. Cut off the burnt pieces, that's what he said.*

In a hidden pouch at the back of the bag, he found a small hunting knife tucked away. He pulled it out and examined it in the moonlight. *This will work.*

He glanced at Cy and wondered how easily the blade would cut through the metal body, if at all. He shook his head with disappointment, and turned to Kaitlyn. She looked so peaceful in her sleep. Void found himself wondering if he ever looked like that. He could never feel peace. Only a dull, numbing sensation throughout his entire body. It was strongest in his chest, as though there was a physical barrier inside of him that kept his heart from working the way it was supposed to. He knew how he was meant to feel and react, but it was literally impossible for him, though the amount of emotion slipping through his cracks recently had been surprising him.

He crawled away from the two, the knife held firmly in his hand. He found a large rock and hovered over it, placing his right hand in a beam of moonlight. He angled the knife perfectly over his fingers, aiming just below the scarred flesh covering the tips of his fingers. He sliced through the flesh slowly at first, sawing away at the muscle and bone. White blood splattered onto the rock, and Void bit the inside of his cheek to keep himself silent. *I've been put through worse by Grite, so why does this hurt so damn much?*

Cutting through the bone with only the knife was slow going, so he dropped the knife to the rock and lifted his hand to his mouth. He placed the exposed bone of his finger on his molars, his bitter blood sliding down his throat. He closed his eyes, then bit through the bone, groaning through the pain. It broke off in jagged edges that punctured his gums and stuck there. He yanked his hand from his mouth, ripping out a chunk of flesh from his gums. He spat the severed fingertip onto the rock, and swallowed the blood and bone chips in his mouth.

Nine more to go, he told himself, and set to work on the other fingers on his right hand. The pain only got worse as the minutes passed. He could feel the flesh growing over splinters of bone that had gotten wedged under his teeth. Tears leaked down his cheeks, but his right hand was done and already healing.

He shifted the knife over to his right hand awkwardly, it shaking with the pain. Blood covered his palm, and he struggled to hold the blade steady. He made several incisions on his left hand, none of them hitting the mark he was aiming for. With a short yell, and brought the knife down with all of his force on his fingers. He was able to cut through the bone with one swipe, though he had taken off more than he had intended. The fingers hung by strands of muscle, and they flailed wildly as his hand shook. He lowered the mostly detached fingers into his mouth, and ripped them off with one sharp jerk of his head.

The pain had become too much for him at the end, and he screamed in pain. Kaitlyn stirred awake, and she caught sight of him. She got to her feet woozily and made her way to him with a sleepy smile on her face. He stood and threw his hands behind his back, hiding the bleeding stubs along with the knife. He could only hope that she wouldn't notice the mess on the rock behind him, or the blood that dribbled down his chin.

"Wha' are you still doin' awake, silly? You need to get your rest," she said, her words garbled by sleep. She grabbed his arm and slid her hand down to his wrist. Before he could pull away or stop her, she reached his hand and intertwined her fingers with his. She stopped short and pulled their hands into view. Her eyes shown with concern and fear, all hints of sleep chased away.

When she got a glimpse of his hand, she screamed and shoved him. He fell over the rock behind him, the dagger falling to the ground. He turned to catch it, the remaining stubs from his fingers spilling from his mouth. He hit the ground and the dagger pierced straight into his hand as he fell, sticking into the bone.

He twisted over himself to look back at Kaitlyn to explain, but Cy was standing in her place. She was hiding behind him, latched onto his shoulders. Void raised his right hand protectively. Small black claws growing from his fingers shone in the light.

"What did I tell you about making her scream again? What the hell are you even doing, you little shit?" Cy lunged for him and pulled Void to his feet. Kaitlyn backed away as Void drew nearer to her.

Cy grabbed the hilt of the blade that was driven through Void's hand, and ripped it out. He threw it behind him, and it buried itself into a tree far from them. He pulled Void's hand into the light.

"What the hell would you want to cut off your own fingers for?" Cy hissed, disgust clear in his voice.

"The first thing they did was cut off my claws, and make it so they wouldn't grow back. He burned them the same way as your face, and you said this was the way to fix it," Void snapped. He wrenched his hand from Cy's grip and stepped away from him.

"You sick little freak. I really ought to just kill you now. What else would you need your claws for other than to kill us in our sleep? I bet that was the next thing on your to-do list, wasn't it?"

"If you're so determined to kill me, then do it. I encourage you, no, I *beg* you. Kill me!" Void yelled. "Just get it over with, and end me already! You think you scare me with your empty threats, but I *want* you to do it! After all I've been through, I should be dead at least twenty times over by now. I'm not still alive because they needed me alive, but because they couldn't kill me. So please, if you've got some magic knowledge about how I can finally end myself, then share it with me. You'll be doing both of us a favor! And until you figure out how to actually get it done, just shut up!"

Void's face was burning, but Cy could only stare at him. Kaitlyn had fresh tears in her eyes, but she held them back.

"I thought you were a Void? So what the hell was that all about?"

"The hell if I know! Maybe you're just rubbing off on me, damn demon!" Void yelled. Cy was silent as he studied Void, and the boy writhed under the demon's gaze.

Seeing no end to his temper, Void sat on the rock next to him, ignoring the blood that covered it. He examined the claws that were fully grown, and the faint scar on his palm from the blade. Using his claws, he dug into his gums to relieve himself of the bone shards.

"The hell are you doing now?" Cy asked, disturbed. Kaitlyn had left to stand by a tree far off, refusing to look their way.

"Picking out the chunks of bone that were lodged in my teeth. You wanna see?" Void held up a piece of bone that he had successfully recovered. His thick blood covered his new claws.

Cy made a noise of disgust and turned away. He walked off into the distance, and the three of them spent the rest of the night separated. Despite the immense amount of pain he had put himself through, and the new experience of rage, Void smiled. He had been victorious in this night, against Grite and against Cyllorian.

* * *

Kaitlyn

"I DON'T KNOW what you're so worried about, I fought back in Centric!" Kaitlyn argued, chasing Cy around the small group of trees they had stopped in. It was as though the three of them had gone into their own world, safe from reality that demanded so much from them.

"That wasn't supposed to happen. Why can't you just stay as far away from that thing as possible instead? In fact, let's just leave him here and get back home!" Cy responded as he paced.

Kaitlyn glanced at Void, finally asleep against a tree. Cy had tied his hands together after Void had cut his fingers off, and they lay in his lap. He looked so peaceful in sleep that it was difficult for Kaitlyn to believe how twisted he had been during the night.

Kaitlyn shook her head and turned back to Cy. "How many times do I have to tell you that we aren't leaving him behind?" she snapped.

Cy ceased his pacing. *"How many times do I have to say that I don't trust him? And last night just proves which one of us is right. He got into our stuff while we were asleep and could have killed us at any time."*

"But he didn't. I don't think he ever wanted to."

"How do you know? Because he told you he didn't? He's lying! Of course, he's gonna say he doesn't want to kill us. He's insane, not stupid."

"He's just a little lost. That's why we have to get him back to Theresa. If anyone can help him, she can."

"How's this then. We tie him to a tree somewhere, then tell Theresa all about him when we get back. Then she can decide for herself if he's worth the trouble."

"You don't make any sense, Cyllorian. You trust me enough to give me a dagger, but not enough to give him a chance?"

"Because you aren't going to use that dagger. Ever. The main

reason you have it is so he doesn't. Besides, a weapon for self-defense can't betray you."

"Self-defense. You sound like Arion. That was his excuse for everything," Kaitlyn scoffed. She wrapped her hand around the hilt of the dagger, uncomfortable with how it felt in her hand.

They stood in silence for a long moment, Cy looking uneasy. *"This isn't an ideal situation, Kaitlyn. You know that. We're lost, exhausted, and without any semblance of a plan. We just can't keep him."*

Cy walked away and leaned his forehead against a small tree, balancing against it. He looked like he might fall asleep, but the light of his magic never dimmed.

Kaitlyn stood with her hands on her hips. She couldn't argue with him. She threw her hands into the air with a frustrated groan. Her hand hit the dagger at her side, and she ripped it from her belt angrily.

She curled her fingers around the hilt and threw the sheath to the ground. Cy had cleaned the blade and it shined in her hand. It was heavy. It fit uncomfortably in her hand, and she compared it to the feeling of her claws on her left hand. They were natural for her now, and she could barely remember what normal felt like. This change had been forced upon her, but she didn't regret it.

And she didn't regret her decisions either. She cleared her mind. Crouching low to the ground, she brandished the dagger at her side. With a burst of energy, she charged at Cyllorian.

He must have heard her moving, because he turned around at the last second. He jumped away from her and she dove under his flailing arms. Twisting in midair, she swiped at his face with her claws. The tips dug into his cheek, piercing into his face. Her back hit the tree and Cy reared away from her, utter shock clear on his face.

"Kaitlyn, what are you doing?!" he shrieked, placing a hand to his cheek.

"If I can beat you, if I prove that I'm stronger now, then we keep him," she hissed. She lunged at him again, pushing off the tree for more momentum. Cy caught the knife just before it struck his chest and flung it from Kaitlyn's hands. She abandoned the knife, trading it for the ease of hand-to-hand combat with her claws.

Her speed surprised even her, but Cy's reaction time was better. She scraped against his metal a few times, but never did any damage to him. With her claws failing her, she dropped to the ground and swung her leg out at Cy. He tried to jump over it, but was just a second too late, and he tripped over her leg. She caught him on her back as he fell, and used the force to flip him onto his back. She jumped on top of him, and put her claws to his throat.

"I win," she gasped, catching her breath. A smile formed on her face, triumphant and in awe of herself.

Cy stared up at her in disbelief, a hint of fear sparking in the back of his eyes. He wasn't breathing, but he was shaking. *"You only won because I didn't fight back. You were slow and didn't have any idea what you were doing. If that had been a real fight, you would have been killed within seconds."*

Kaitlyn climbed off him, and he got to his feet easily. He brushed the dirt from himself, examining all the places Kaitlyn scratched him with her claws.

"You just don't want to admit you lost to a girl," Kaitlyn teased, smiling playfully. She stepped away to retrieve the dagger from the ground, aware of Cy watching her cautiously.

Cy shot her a lopsided grin. *"Rematch,"* he breathed. He walked toward a denser section of the trees waving her after him.

Kaitlyn followed, sparing a look at Void where he slept. He

hadn't shifted his position, but as Kaitlyn turned to him, she thought she saw his eyes flutter shut. *Did we wake him?* she wondered, but she let it go.

Cy stopped in a section with small saplings a little taller than himself. He motioned for Kaitlyn to stand across from him. She lowered herself in preparation, but Cy didn't move. She ran at him, aiming for his stomach with the knife.

He grabbed her wrist and spun her around. One arm wrapped around her waist, pulling her against his cold body. She tensed and curled up on herself, her heart beating wildly at his touch. Her cheeks burned despite the chilly night. She willed herself to calm down.

He pressed her elbows to her sides. He used his foot to spread her feet shoulder-length apart, and she felt her weight spread evenly.

"Make sure you keep your arms close to your body for protection. If they get close, you want to be able to put as much force into your punches as you can," he whispered in her ear. He jabbed forward with her hands, short sharp movements that strained her muscles. *"Your instincts are pretty good at telling you when and how to move, so you should be good with that. You made a good choice to trip me with your leg, so you're like Arion there. He was better with kicks, too."*

Cy stepped back from her, and the air came back into her lungs. She tensed her muscles to keep her stance, though her body had relied on Cy's support until then.

Kaitlyn spun around quickly, lifting her leg to kick him in the side. He swatted her foot out of the air, and she fell forward. He caught her effortlessly, holding her at the small of her back. She blushed again and rolled out of his grip. He laughed at her while she scrambled away from him.

Focus, she told herself. while she desperately sought a plan of attack, Cy approached. His body was too noisy to attempt a sneak attack, and he charged for her head on. She twisted out of his path at the last second. She threw her arm up to shield herself as he slashed at her. His talons caught on her scales, and she shoved him away. Cy tumbled backwards, and Kaitlyn laughed when he hit the ground.

She couldn't remember the last time she had laughed so lightly, the last time she had felt so carefree. She began grabbing the rocks at her feet and tossing them at Cy, laughing all the while.

A coy grin formed on his face. *"So, now you think this is funny?"*

He dodged the flying bark and ran at Kaitlyn. Forgetting about the point behind the match, she fled behind a tree. She ran from Cy while he chased her in circles.

Kaitlyn turned to taunt him, running backwards. She tripped over the pieces of bark littering on the ground, her ankles folding painfully as she tried to right herself. Cy dove for her. His arms wrapped around her, encasing her in a thick shield just before they hit the ground.

Kaitlyn twisted in his grip to look at him, to thank him, but found her voice caught in her throat.

Cy was looking at her with a great torment in his eyes. It looked as though he was warring with himself, his gaze burning. Because of how they had landed, they were very close together, and neither one of them could breathe. Her heart raced in her chest, and her skin burned more than could be attributed to the scales.

"Cy," she started, but he had closed his eyes. It seemed he had made his decision, for he was leaning closer to her ever so slowly. Unable to think, unsure of how to react, Kaitlyn waited.

Kaitlyn was thrown from Cy's grasp when Void tackled Cy to the ground. He was sitting on Cy's chest and was shaking him, screaming incoherently. Void reared his hand back and put all of his weight into a punch to Cy's face. He hit hard enough to dent his cheek, though Void's hand looked far worse for wear. The metal had bit into his knuckles, and the fingers were bent at odd angles.

Void readied himself for another punch. He had gone silent, his lips trembling too much to get a single word out. He was frozen in place, his claws ready to strike, hands shaking violently.

Kaitlyn jumped up and ran to Void. She grabbed onto his shoulders, her claws digging into his flesh, and tried her best to pull him off. "Void, stop! What are you doing, get off of him!" she begged, tugging at his shoulders.

Her grip kept slipping from him, and her claws were tearing his flesh to ribbons, but she didn't have time to change. She had to separate them before it got any worse.

"I said *get off!*" she screamed. She latched her hand over his face and dug her heels into the ground. She pulled Void off of Cy, her claws cutting through half of his face.

He fell back onto the ground, clutching his face and growling low in his throat. Kaitlyn rushed to help Cy up. He was stunned, but the damage Void had done with his punch had already healed. Still, he didn't move.

Void was well before Cy was, and he sat up. Kaitlyn crouched in front of Cy, ready to stop another fight before it happened. "Stop it, Void. Just stop fighting, and talk to me. What were you doing?"

At Kaitlyn's voice, the rage vanished from Void's face, replaced by immense confusion. He stared down at his hands, the cuts still in the healing process. "I don't know. . . he was. . . I thought he was going to. . . what *was* he doing to you? I had to stop it, no matter what it was, but I don't know why. I. . . I just don't know what happened to me."

"This is what I was warning you about. He's too past the deep

end to pull him out. He attacked, who's to say he won't do it again? We get rid of him now, Kaitlyn!" Cy hissed, pushing himself into a sitting position. He had recovered so suddenly that Kaitlyn jumped at his voice. He looked far angrier than he ought to be from a single punch. Could he have made sense of Void's screams when Kaitlyn couldn't?

"No, there has to be a reason, a good one. He wouldn't just attack us for no reason, I know it! We just have to figure out..."

"There's nothing left to figure out, Kaitlyn. He just proved that he would *attack us out of nowhere. I know you feel responsible for him because you think it's your fault Arion is dead, but that's all bullshit! You didn't do anything wrong, but you're putting us in danger because you think you're the one at fault!"*

"What are you talking about? Of course I did! If I hadn't taken Kraven directly to Arion, he would still be here! I know he told me to, but I didn't know how bad he had gotten. I shouldn't have listened to him, I should have..." Kaitlyn trailed off, fighting against the images that flooded her mind.

"It's not Arion's fault either! It's mine, alright? I'm the one that was writing to you, going behind Arion's back. I told you to bring that son of a bitch to us, not him!" Cy burst, unable to hold onto the guilt any longer. *"The only letter he ever saw was the last one you sent, and he lost it after that! I couldn't tell you, couldn't warn you because he destroyed the damn bird. The only one to blame for this situation is me! So please, Kaitlyn, just stop!"*

He collapsed forward onto his hands and knees, his body shaking with tearless sobs. *"Stop hating yourself. Stop justifying keeping this thing around because you feel guilty. Hate me, blame me, because I do. I thought I wanted him gone, but I'm nothing without him. Just a pathetic mess. A god damned selfish demon!"*

Kaitlyn stared at Cy as he broke down. His metal frame shook violently, rattling eerily as he sobbed tearlessly. She had been so overwhelmed with emotions that it felt like she had shut down. Rage, sorrow, defeat, betrayal. All of it flashed within her for a split second before it was too much for her to handle.

She dropped to her knees beside him, her legs unwilling to hold her any longer. "You... Cyllorian, you can't..."

Kaitlyn started, but she couldn't tie her scrambled thoughts into a sentence. "Is there... anything else?" she inquired, finally looking at Cy.

She waited a long time for him to stop crying. Her anger burned hotter within her every moment that passed without an answer. She thought back to the letters she had received, and put the pieces together to match them to Cy.

Once Cy had calmed down, he looked up into Kaitlyn's burning eyes, and flinched away. He put his head to the ground, going limp with defeat. "*You,*" he breathed heavily. "*I did it all because I wanted you, Kaitlyn. I thought I just didn't want him to have you, but I was wrong. I want you for myself. I don't know what this is, and I'm too scared to find out. All I know is that even though I know I don't deserve anything, I still want you.*"

Kaitlyn's heart jumped in her chest, and her throat closed up. She couldn't believe it, it couldn't be true. Everything in her mind scrambled, and when it settled, only one thought remained.

"Are you sure you wanted me?" she whispered, remembering how much Cy had hated Arion before. "Or did you just not want him to have me?"

Cyllorian didn't move or speak. The demon remained as still as a statue.

Without another word, Kaitlyn grabbed Void's wrist and led him back to their camp to bandage his wounds. Cy didn't follow.

CHAPTER 19

Void

Void stared at his hands, bound together by magic-infused rope as the three of them walked in silence. Cy was leading the way a few feet ahead, and Kaitlyn was walking beside Void reluctantly. She watched the ground as they walked, her expression as empty as Void expected his own to be.

"We're nearly to the Junkyard, now. We'll keep going through the night, and hopefully we won't be noticed. The Loren Woods should be just on the other side, but it won't be as thick as it is at home. We'll still have a ways to go before we're in the clear," Cy called back. Emotionlessly.

Void stared at the demon peculiarly. Since he and Kaitlyn had gotten in their fight a few days prior, the whole group had been set in a silent depression. Void could sense the anger from Cy boiling just under the surface, though it no longer seemed to be directed at Void.

The Junkyard came upon them quickly and suddenly, piles

of trash straddling a worn and uneven path. In the distance looked like mountains, though they didn't look natural. The ground was dry and flat, and cracks were visible underneath the garbage. Large insects gathered in the shadows while bright colored snakes and lizards were tangled together on top of metal pieces that still gave off traces of heat. Though the sun was still emitting heat, the walled path created a stream of strong winds that whipped around them, carrying with it the promise of a freezing night ahead. There were very few plants to be seen, and those that somehow survived in this barren land were rotting with trash infused into them as they grew through the piles.

"This is all the waste from the riots a hundred years ago. Machines, transportation, inventions. Everything associated with the Mages that didn't get locked in Centric ended up here, including some Mages and outcasts from both worlds. Anyone that wasn't useful to the Mages were sent to live here. Not that they mind, from what I've heard. They got all the spare parts they could ever ask for here," Cy explained when he noticed Void's curious glances at everything.

There were pieces he recognized in the heaps of scrap parts, though he had no idea where he had seen them before. Large muzzles from cars, and wings from planes jutted out into the path, rusted and discolored. He spotted various curved pieces crumpled on top of each other. It reminded Void of the plating to Cy's body.

Something shiny gleamed in the moonlight, half-buried in the scraps, and Void paused to look at it. He dug it out from the pile with difficulty, and held it in his hands. It was heavier than it looked, but the weight was comforting. He rubbed the dirt from the face, revealing large eyes and the beak of an owl. Its wings were missing, and its body dented, though an hourglass pattern of dots could still be seen etched into the metal of the stomach. Void ran his fingers over the pattern, and looked to the sky when he realized what the dots were. "Orion," he whispered when he found the constellation.

"Void, come on. We have to hurry," Kaitlyn called to him impatiently. Void spared another glance for the broken owl before dropping it on the ground and jogging to catch up with Kaitlyn. She stared at the owl he had been holding until he came to her side. She turned and followed Cyllorian without another word.

"There's a lot of lights here," Void mused aloud. Kaitlyn looked at the various colors shining around them. Cy pulled his cloak tighter around his body and quickened his pace.

"This isn't a place for tourists," a voice called out from behind them. Void turned on the spot, but Kaitlyn backed up until she was nearly touching Cy.

A man jumped out of the shadows, a lantern with a white flame inside swinging from a tall cane. He swung it towards Void, and he retreated from the light.

"What are you doing here?" the man asked, coming closer. He twisted his hand on the cane and a spear tip sprung out from the top. He jabbed it at Void, pushing him further back. He bumped into Kaitlyn, sending her into Cy. Void went to apologize, but froze when he saw numerous shadowy figures climbing over the mounds of scraps and trash. They were surrounded

"Please, our friend is very ill. We must get him to the Loren Woods. We heard there is a powerful Mage hiding there that can help us," Kaitlyn lied, putting a stiff arm around Cy. He retreated further into his cloak and faked a cough, though it sounded wrong from his metal body. Another man lunged a faint orange light towards Cy, and he turned away.

"Why don't you have him in a cart? If he's so gravely ill that you trespass through our lands, then he shouldn't be walking on his own. Show your face, stranger!" The man lunged for Cy, but he dodged easily. Void caught sight of Cy's hand as he lashed out and shoved the man away.

"You got quite the strength for being sickly," the first man said skeptically. He stabbed at Void again, and he jumped out of the way. But the man didn't stop there. His spear continued past Void, and snagged on Cy's cloak.

There was a stunned silence as the cloak was torn from Cy's body in pieces, exposing the gleaming metal to the moonlight. Cy's luminous purple eyes were filled with panic as he studied the men around him. His claws unsheathed themselves, slowly so they wouldn't draw attention to them, but it was too late.

The group surrounding them swarmed around Cy, shoving Kaitlyn and Void out of the way. Their voices had turned into an uproar with unintelligible words. Kaitlyn was pounding on their backs, shrieking wildly. She clawed at them, but they swatted her away with canes and spears.

Void looked everywhere, his brain searching for any clues for what he should do. He could run, none of them were paying any attention to him. Kaitlyn would most likely be spared, but Void had no doubt that the people would disassemble Cy until he no longer existed. All Void had to do was walk the other way, and he would be free of his newest source of torment.

He watched Kaitlyn charge at the group without caution, her arms and sides bleeding from where they had slashed her with their spears. Her face was covered in sweat and tears, and her voice had already begun to go from screaming.

Void could see Cy lying in the middle of everything. He was fending the crowd off with a domed shield made of a bright green light. The people struck at it over and over, cracking the shield. Cy was immobilized by fear, barely able to keep what was left of the shield over him. A chunk broke off from the edge, and a spear pierced into his leg. The scream that he let out was filled with pure terror. For once, Void felt like he could truly relate to someone, knowing the look on Cy's face all too well.

Void scrambled to his feet and dove for the nearest junk pile. *A weapon, a sharp object, there has to be something here!* he thought as his eyes grazed over everything in sight. Anything could be a weapon, if only he had his strength back. He was in no condition to fight, but he knew he would need something threatening if he were to stand a chance against a hoard of crazed lunatics.

His hand came across something small, and he nearly threw it aside because of its size, but he hesitated with it. It was bent at a ninety-degree angle, with a leather handle and a thick, hollow tube attached. A trigger stuck out from the inner curve, and Void studied it with a sense of dread forming in his stomach. Grite had told him about this once before, he was sure. He had called it a gun.

But it wasn't exactly like Grite had described. There were no holes or openings to put bullets into, and from what Void knew, it wouldn't work without them. But maybe he was the only one that knew that. He could still scare the others with just the sight of it. He didn't want to shoot anyone anyway.

Void got to his feet, holding the gun with both hands. They trembled immensely as he pointed it at the crowd as a whole. "HEY!" he yelled, but he went unnoticed. "Look at me!" he tried again, though he had lost his volume, along with his confidence.

I can't do anything. Nothing. He's going to die, he thought. The dread in his gut turned to panic, and he pointed the gun to the sky without thinking. He pulled the trigger without hesitation, and a white flash lit up the air.

The sound that came from the gun was deafening, and a thin trail of smoke reached towards the heavens. *It fired?!*

The crowd paused in their assault and dropped to the ground. Kaitlyn jumped over them to get to Cy, and helped him stand. Both of his legs had been punctured multiple times, and putting weight on them made the healing process stutter.

Void lowered the gun to the crowd, and they cowered away from it. "Let them get out," Void demanded. His hand was steady now as he glared at the helpless people. *This is power,* he told himself. *This is how it feels to instill fear into the lives of others. This is how Grite felt, and now it's my turn!*

Void followed each person with the gun as they crawled out of Kaitlyn and Cy's way. Void gestured for them to go ahead, and they broke into a run once they were past Void.

"You pathetic things are going to stay right here with your junk, and we're leaving. I won't hesitate to kill any who follow," he hissed before whirling around and running after the others with as much speed as he could conjure.

The three of them ran until the Junkyard was far from sight and trees were the only thing to be seen. They ran long past the point of exhaustion, until there was no energy left in them to keep them going. They collapsed into a huddle against a large tree. Even Cy was gasping desperately for air.

"Why'd you do that?" Cy asked once they had stopped running. He looked up at Void, his eyes wide and unreadable.

"Do what?" Void responded. He could no longer feel his legs, and his fingers had stiffened around the handle of the gun.

"Save me."

Void looked down at the gun in his hand. He still had no idea how it had worked, but he figured it was better not to question it. He also didn't want to think too much about why he had acted the way he did.

"I don't know," he said honestly.

"It's because he's not bad, Cy." Kaitlyn paused between words to catch her breath. They shared a glance that seemed to last forever, and Kaitlyn rested her head on Cy's shoulder. "It was...all of us. We got into this...together, and that's how we'll fix it," she whispered to him, being the first to gain control of her breathing.

"Agreed," Cy said.

"We're in the Loren Woods now, right? How much further?" Void asked, breaking the awkward silence between them.

"It's going to be hard to navigate in here. We have to find a guide first, but odds are that they'll find us first."

Void only nodded, though he didn't understand. He didn't have the energy to ask. All he wanted to do was sleep. He closed his eyes and fell onto his side.

"What is that, Void?" Kaitlyn asked, a twinge of fear in her question.

Void opened his eyes slowly. She was pointing at the gun in his hand. "It's a gun. Grite told me about them, that they were made for one purpose...to kill. It worked at intimidation just fine though."

A strange feeling twisted in his gut as he stared at the gun in the darkness. Everything about this night had made him feel uneasy, but he had no explanation for it. He shut his eyes to the uncertainty, longing for the night to be finished.

The thought of Grite sent chills running down Void's spine. The demon's twisted smile was set into the darkness behind his closed eyes. Void could even remember its scent. Damp and musty, like rotting wood and tainted earth. The smell grew stronger and Void threw his hands over his mouth and nose. He sat up slowly, stifling the urge to vomit.

The memory of the demon was so vivid that he could even hear its voice whispered on the wind.

"Aww, I'm touched you still remember me! I thought you would have forgotten all about poor Grite, what with your new friends and all," Void imagined it saying. He shook the words from his head, and rested against a tree.

Silence. He was sure Kaitlyn and Cyllorian had just been speaking, but they had gone quiet. Only Grite's voice could be heard, *"Don't tell me you forgot about the promise I made to you. I'm here to make good on that."*

Void's eyes opened slowly, hoping to end the waking nightmare. He took in the fresh air, the trees clustered close together, and reminded himself that he was safe. He was safe, he was free. He was—

"You've always been so boring. At least these two are giving me the response I want. Who should I break first, Void? The oversized lantern, or the puzzle of creature parts?" Grite mocked as it stepped from the shadows. Its voice was deeper than before, more confident, but it still sent chills down Void's spine. The half of its face that remained was twisted into a triumphant sneer as it gazed hungrily at Void.

Void sat up and pointed the gun, but his hands shook yet again, and he couldn't aim properly. He glanced over at Cy and Kaitlyn, fearful that it had been a trap all along. Cy was in front of Kaitlyn protectively, pressing her to a tree. They looked just as terrified as Void.

"Master misses you," Grite continued, envy clear in his tone. *"He wants you back, no matter the cost. As if you ever cooperate with us."* Grite cackled joyfully as he descended upon Void.

Cy tackled the other demon to the ground, tearing his clothes to shreds with his claws, exposing a large hole in Grite's chest with pitch black, burnt edges. Cy was able to slash through Grite's flesh at the edge of the hole, but it had no effect on the demon.

Though Void had just saved Cy's life, he never would have thought that he would do the same. Cy was still healing, and lacking most of his energy. Grite chuckled at Cy's attempt, and grabbed him by the head. It threw Cy off easily and got back to its feet.

"You're a pathetic excuse for a demon, Cyllorian. Always have been. You would have been so much better off in Master Crestyss' care than with that bitch, Theresa. I have no idea what Master ever saw in her," Grite said, gaining a curious look from Cy.

"What do you even want with me, Grite? Just tell me what it is, and I'll give it to you. Just leave me alone, please! I'll do anything!" Void begged. In the presence of Grite, seeing his torturer in a new environment, he could do nothing but cower at the thought of the pain that would soon befall him.

"What do I want? It's about time you asked. I want my body back, you thief!" Grite shouted. *"If it wasn't for you, everything would be as it should! Master wouldn't be angry at me all the time, I would still have my proper body, rather than be forced into this shitty human's body. It doesn't heal like that one does, and I have to look like that son of a bitch for the rest of my life! All these damn scars that you gave me, and I can't even get you back for them properly because you have no idea what I'm talking about! But I can't have any of that, so I'll just have to settle for your life, you half breed freak!"*

Grite pounced for Void, and he pulled the trigger wildly. Another flash of green exploded between them, throwing off Grite's aim. The blast skimmed Grite's shoulder as it disappeared into the trees.

Grite fell against Void and they tumbled along the ground, Grite coming out on top. Its twisted smile sent a chill throughout Void's body, and its claws raked through Void's face repeatedly. His hot blood covered his face and neck, and the weight of Grite on his chest prevented Void from breathing. But Grite had underestimated Void, and hadn't thought to restrain his arms. With his own claws, Void dug into the side of Grite's face, his claws sinking inches into the flesh, and slammed Grite to the ground. Void climbed on top of him, but Grite bucked him off effortlessly.

Void hit a tree and landed upside down on his head. Grite stepped up to him and proceeded to kick all of Void's ribs in. They punctured his lungs, and he coughed up blood. Kaitlyn's screams could be heard over the ringing in his ears, as well as Grite's sadistic laughter.

Grite picked Void up by the leg, snapping the bone with only the force of its grip. The demon swung Void in an arc over its head and into the ground. Grite knelt on Void's chest again, driving the broken ribs in further. With a knife that Void hadn't seen before, it began to saw through Void's arm just below the elbow.

Void screamed in panic, and flailed wildly underneath Grite. He kicked against the ground, but his strength was nothing compared to the demon's.

"This body isn't even that strong, and you still can't do anything to me. Just like old times, right?" Grite hissed, leaning in to whisper in Void's ear. The knife was taken from his arm and plunged into his chest right beside his heart. He froze as his heart beat rapidly against the metal of the blade.

Grite stood and turned towards Kaitlyn and Cy. There was a high-pitched grinding sound that Void realized was Cy growling. Grite ignored Cy and focused on Kaitlyn. *"Long time, no see, sweetheart. Did you miss me?"*

Kaitlyn was petrified. She had gone completely still, watching the creature with confusion. Her breath came out in a whoosh, barely any volume in her voice as she spoke, "Kraven?"

"Close, but not quite. This—" Grite gestured to its body, *"—hasn't been his for a while. Crestyss took him apart and put him back together with me inside. Needed to make room in my body for that pathetic thing."*

Grite's gaze returned to Void. The sneer Void received only fueled his confusion. He wasn't even given time to think before Grite was kneeling on him again.

Void stared up at Grite, and recognized the pure hatred that was hidden deep within the eyes, the primal snarl plastered on his face. He had seen it before, but not from Grite. On instinct, Void lifted his hand and pressed it to the hole in Grite's chest. It fit perfectly under his palm, and Void dug his claws into the skin around the hole.

Panic swam through Grite's eyes, and it ripped the knife from Void's chest with a yell. The creature threw it away with a sharp movement, and another wave of fear choked Void. Grite leaned forward and sunk its teeth into the boy.

It was the most painful thing Void had ever felt, and the scream that erupted from his throat was inhuman. Behind his closed eyes, there was a bright green flash. Within seconds, the agony was gone, but it had left Void feeling emptier than he ever had before. The weight lifted from Void, and he hoped that the hollowness inside of him meant that he was finally dying.

He opened his eyes and looked around with blurred vision. Grite was curled into a ball beside him, clutching his leg. A large hole had been blown through his thigh, and it refused to heal. It looked as though his leg was barely still in one piece, the bone completely destroyed inside.

Cy was standing over Grite, the gun in his hand. A thin trail of purple smoke drifted from the barrel of the gun, matching the rage in his eyes.

Grite ran from them on all fours, his leg leaving a thick trail of blood.

He's running away, but why is he smiling like that? Void thought in the back of his mind. It flitted from his consciousness as quickly as he had thought it.

Kaitlyn was at his side next, her hands fluttering over his wounds. "Void! Can you hear me? You're going to be alright, I can heal you. I promise, I can heal you," she stammered, tears in her eyes.

"It's too much for you, Kaitlyn. We have to get him back to Theresa, now! It's the only chance," Cy said, putting a hand on Kaitlyn's shoulder.

"I have to help him, or he's not going to make it!" she begged, though her hands had dropped into her lap.

"It's alright, Kaitlyn. I'm already starting to heal, look," Void said dully, holding up his arm where Grite had started to cut through it. He stared in shock as he saw that there was no sign of healing, just occasional spurts of blood spraying from the wound.

"I'm not healing..." he breathed. Hope bloomed in his chest. "I'm dying..."

Panic struck, blacking out his vision. He shook his head back and forth in a daze.

Something snatched up his arm, and Cy's voice cut through the fog. *"Your blood is white,"* he said pointedly before pausing. He then shook Void's arm, ripping the skin at the wound more and more. *"Why is your blood white, Void? Why do you have a demon body? What aren't you telling us?"*

"My blood's always been white. What are you talking about? Didn't you see it before, or was it too dark? Isn't it supposed to be this color? Because I've always had that blood, and I'm not a demon. What color is your blood?" Void rambled on in his daze. He thought back to Kaitlyn, to when the outcasts had cut her. Her wounds had wept red, and he knew she was normal. But the trail of blood that had been left by Grite, that had been white as well.

"I have a demon body? Hey, Cy, I guess we're just like brothers." Void laughed once, and the pain grew to excruciating levels. He tried to open his eyes, hoping to see Cy and Kaitlyn before he died, but there was only blackness around him before he lost his grip on consciousness.

* * *

"Are you ever going to leave this spot?" *Cy whined.*

Void lifted his head, but there was nothing to be seen. He was sitting with his arms resting on his knees in pitch blackness. "Cy?" he asked quietly. His voice was rough, and it echoed somewhere far from his body.

"It's been days now. If you don't eat something, you'll die. If that's what you want, I can think of a few ways that will be a lot less painful."

Void tried to stand, but found that he had no strength in him. His limbs were empty, but free of the pain he had expected. "Where are you, Cy? Where's Kaitlyn?" Void asked the question intently, but it seemed he had no effect on what was going on around him.

"Hey! It's not just you in here, remember? I feel what you feel, and we're dying!" Cy screamed at him.

"But...I'm already dead. Aren't I, Cyllorian?" Void scanned the darkness as best as he could, but there was nothing around him. He could hear Cy, like an echo in his head, but he was nowhere around.

"Is this heaven? No, I don't think I would go to heaven. But this is too nice for hell. Peaceful. Where am I?"

After a moment, Cy spoke up, "What about her?"

An image of Kaitlyn formed in the air in front of Void, but she looked different. She was younger, and wearing a bright blue dress. There was no sign of the pain and worry she had been put through on her face. He cringed away, not wanting to imagine how she would look if she saw him now. "She cares about you."

"*I know. But I want to be here. I want to stay dead. This feels nice, it feels right. Like I'm supposed to be here. Do you understand, Cy?*" *Void tried again, but his voice couldn't even touch the demon.*

Maybe this is my imagination. Or maybe I can hear him from the other side, *Void thought.* Are they trying to bring me back? What about their friend? They have to worry about him first. I'm not worth saving, anyway.

"Do I have to tell you what you already know? What you did? You told her not to come around anymore because of Kraven. And she doesn't want you to get in anymore fights because of her, so she listened," *Cy scolded.*

"*No, I didn't. You're not making any sense! What are you even talking about, Cy?*" *Void yelled, begging for an answer.* "*Cy! Answer me, please! Don't just leave me alone, what's going on?*" *he screamed at the top of his lungs. He stood in a panic, though he didn't remember choosing to. His legs shook beneath him, and his stomach wretched.*

Void lurched toward Kaitlyn on unsteady legs, but she faded into shadows as he touched her. With nothing but silence, Void wandered. There was no floor under him, but he walked on solid ground. There were no walls, either. He was trapped inside what he could only think to be his own mind.

He found that he didn't need to breath, and his heart no longer beat in his chest. The complete and utter silence was beginning to drive him mad, and he tried to scream again, but there was no sound. He was all alone, and that was worse than every torture Grite had ever put him through.

"Look at your hand," *Cy said after a few minutes.*

"Why?" Void spat, though he didn't expect an answer.

"Just do it."

Void stopped in his pacing, and held up his left hand. His jaw dropped, and a cold chill went down his spine. A jagged scar shone brightly in his palm, and a burning feeling engulfed him. Green lightning was crawling over his hand from the edges. Most of the scar looked raw, blood dripping down his wrist.

"That's what happens when you fight it. It's who you are, regardless of what you want. It's either accept it, or let it break you. You pick."

"I still don't know what you're talking about, Cy. Please, just answer me! I don't know what to do! I need your help." Void fell to his knees as tears rushed into his eyes. He had never felt sadness before, but the sorrow in his heart felt normal, as though it had always been there.

"Get me out of here, Cy! You have to get me out! I don't want to die, I promise. You have to save me from this place, and from myself! Cyllorian, please!"

Void yelled through his sobs, losing all control of himself. He pulled at his hair, willing the tears to stop, but they were endless. They had been building in him for as long as he could remember, unable to escape simply because of what he was. And now that it was too late, he finally had found how to express what had been locked away inside.

A light broke through the darkness, a sliver in the distance that lit upon his face. He raised his arm to shield his eyes, but the light wasn't painful. It showed him the way. He sprinted towards it, his left hand outstretched. He touched the light, and the sorrow and pain fled from his body. The wound and magic on his left hand disappeared, and the light filled the space around him.

"Good choice," Cy's voice said as the light drug Void out of the darkness.

CHAPTER 20

Cyllorian

Cy shifted Void on his back. Though he wasn't very large or heavy, he was moving a lot in his sleep. *"Come on, kid, calm down already. How much further, Tuft?"*

The wolf leading them through the woods paused for but a second, then continued. "We were told you'd have another with you, but this is unexpected. Theresa has set a room up in the dungeons, where he can be watched. She plans to treat him well until there is reason to distrust him."

"There won't be one," Kaitlyn huffed, standing up for Void.

Cy nodded once, thinking back to how Void had saved him. He still didn't understand the boy, attributing his odd behavior to his origins. There were still so many questions to ask, but Cy doubted they would get any answers.

"Are you alright, Tuft? You've been acting weird since you picked us up in the woods," Cy pondered aloud. Void twitched

and slapped Cy in the face, and he shook the boy. *"Watch it, kid! I won't say it again. Stop hitting me already!"*

Tuft was silent for a long moment, his feet dragging as he walked. "Arion's death took its toll on all of us," he said finally, his head drooping.

If Cy hadn't been carrying Void, he would have smacked himself when the realization hit him. *Tuft was meant to be Arion's companion, his protector. He feels just as guilty as the rest of us.*

As they walked toward the castle, Cy noticed Tuft looking over his shoulder every so often, aiming suspicious glances at Void. Cy tried to meet his gaze, but he would always turn away once he was caught staring.

The open castle gates came into view, and Cy's impatience won over his logic. He ran as carefully as he could, though Void whimpered in pain. He ran faster than Kaitlyn was able, and Tuft stayed behind to guide her. They had been able to bandage the wounds, and Kaitlyn stopped the bleeding, but he was only getting worse. Like his body was rotting.

"Theresa!" Cy screamed when he kicked the door open. *"Theresa, get down here and help me!"* His voice echoed in the corridor, unanswered.

"Damnit," he breathed. He searched the entire ground floor, but it was empty. He couldn't even be sure they had returned here. He could only hope.

Cy spun on his heels. The library. It was the largest room in the castle, and the easiest place to gather people. He rounded a corner, the grand double doors now in sight, and tripped over something big and heavy.

He clattered to the ground, Void falling from his grip. The boy let out a yell and curled in on himself. The bandages on his arm came loose. The wound there was covered in blood and dirt, the skin underneath cracking.

"Void!" Cy reached for the boy, but the thing he had tripped over moved. Goyik walked with a slight limp as he sniffed Void. His nose twitched at the foul odor, but he seemed much more interested in something else.

Goyik picked Void up by his coat and dragged the squirming boy to the doors of the library. Cy scrambled to his feet after him. He tried to grab Void, but Goyik growled whenever he got near.

They reached the door after what felt like forever, and Goyik let out a sharp, low bark. The doors opened obediently, and he dragged Void inside. He released him in the middle of the room.

Theresa was standing at the head of a long table. Gil, Adoette and Jayr sat to one side of her, while Jemmina and Holten took the other side. They had all gone silent when the doors opened, and Theresa stared at Cy with rage.

"What is this thing?" she asked. Goyik moved to her side and laid on the ground, his eyes never leaving Void's body. Theresa was the only one not looking at Void, as she bore holes into Cy's metal with her gaze.

Cy finally stepped into the room, as though he were waiting for Theresa to invite him in with her voice. *"This is what we retrieved from Talgrin. He's hurt, you need to—"*

"You risked the lives of everyone in this room for an empty and broken shell?" Her words felt like venom that could chew through Cy's metal. He struggled to hold his ground against his mother.

"He's different. There's something weird about him. Whatever it is, Crestyss wants it bad enough to send a demon after us, the one that tortured Void."

"You were followed into the woods by Grite?" Theresa asked. Her eyes had turned into slits, and she looked at Void for the first time. He was clutching his hands to his chest and mumbling incoherently.

"I guess. He nearly killed Void, rambling on about needing him back no matter what. Sadistic thing wouldn't shut up, not about Crestyss, or about you. He even knew me. But I shot him, and he ran away."

"He recognized you. This does not bode well. Holten was able to save those here without being tracked, but if you were found by Grite, there's no telling if he could have followed this far."

Theresa thought for a moment, and Cy shook with anticipation. He glanced around the room for help. Jemmina's eyes were closed as she held Holten's hand tightly. Jayr had already lost interest and was playing with the sword at his belt. Noma was whispering to Adoette. Gil was watching Void, and Cy couldn't make sense of his dazed expression.

"Are you going to help him? He was injured badly, and it was too much for Kaitlyn," Cy pried gently. He knew it was best to deal with her calmly, but damn was it hard. He glanced down at Void, and saw Noma flitting around him and placing glowing leaves over the wounds. He made a note to stop teasing her, even if the pixie was only helping him because of Adoette.

"Was that all?" Theresa asked after a long moment.

Cy grit his jaw when she ignored him. There was too much he needed to sort through for himself, and he decided to give her only the bare minimum, *"I'm pretty sure. Grite was talking nonsense most of the time. I think Crestyss might have switched Grite into another body so he could use his original for Void. He has demon blood, and he can't die as far as anyone can tell, but Grite had a bunch of scars on him, and the gun I used did more damage than I would expect for a demon."*

"That wouldn't surprise me, knowing Crestyss. He'll do whatever it takes to achieve his goals," Theresa muttered, lost in thought.

"He mentioned you, too, Theresa. He said he didn't know what Crestyss saw in you. What did he mean by that?"

"It could be any number of things. Who's to know for sure if it even knew. It is a demon, after all," Theresa answered quickly, avoiding his eyes.

Cy ignored Jayr's smirk at her remark. *"What about Void?"* he urged.

"What about it?"

Cy caught his breath before he snapped. *"You need to heal him. Now."*

Theresa changed. Even the others noticed. She lifted her shoulders and forced a commanding tone, "That thing is not worth my time or energy. You've brought nothing but trash into this place, and put us all in danger. It'll be disposed of promptly."

"Disposed of? What the hell are you talking about? He's alive, and we need to keep it that way. I didn't bust my ass getting here so you can just back out! You already left Arion for dead, I'm not letting you do it again!"

"Do not speak of things you know nothing about, Cyllorian!" Theresa snapped. She slammed her hand on the table, and everyone jumped back.

While most would be embarrassed to have an audience when fighting with their parents, it gave Cy courage. *"Have you even tried to help him yet, or have you just spent these past couple days having a tea party? I've heard about war everywhere for the past month since you sent us out. You had us gather your army, didn't you?"*

He glanced at those around him, but no one would meet his eyes. That was more than enough confirmation.

"The boy is beyond repair. It's not what you want to hear, and I knew you wouldn't listen to me before, so I allowed you time to come to terms with this. It seems that was counterproductive. Let it go, Cyllorian. As hard as it might be for you to accept, this is for the best." Theresa had collected herself easily.

Cy had hoped to reveal her true self to the others, but it wasn't as easy as he had hoped. But he wasn't done trying just yet.

"Best? You seriously think this is best? By whose standards? Who would this be helping, to leave him a rotting heap in here? How can you be like this, treat your own child with such disregard. You know, I really thought I was wrong, that I was just being pissy, but no. You're a terrible person and a terrible mother! You never gave a shit about me, or Arion, did you?"

Cy lost control. Years of anger and pain burst from him, and he screamed until the metal of his jaw groaned in protest. *"Why the hell did you even come back? All of this is just for your own personal gain, you don't give a shit about anyone else in this castle, the whole world for that matter. Kole was a tool, I was a waste of your energy, and Arion was a mistake, right? I'm right, I finally got you figured out. It only took me eighteen years, but I finally figured the bitch out! We were just a means to an end, like Grite is to Crestyss! You're just like him, aren't you?"*

"That is enough, Cyllorian! I have had all that I will tolerate from you. Do not speak of things that you do not understand!" Theresa yelled, stepping around the table towards Cy. She raised her hand as though she meant to slap him, and Cy stood his ground against her.

"If I'm wrong, then tell me so. Put me in my place. You can't, can you? Because I'm not wrong," Cy challenged. He squared his shoulders and stared his creator down, wanting nothing more

than to snuff out the glimmer of hope that still resided in his essence...the hope that she could still be his mother.

"You don't know what you are asking for, Cyllorian. You couldn't even begin to understand what lies in the past," Theresa hissed, a threat clear within her words.

"Like what?" Cy growled in return, losing all caution he had held in regard to her. *"What are you so afraid to say? What are you not admitting? What did you do, fuck the bad guy?"*

Theresa's hand connected with Cy's cheek with enough force to send him sprawling to the floor in shock. Her magic raced throughout his body, shocking him at the joints and rendering him immobile.

Theresa stared at Cy for a long, hard moment. Tears welled in her eyes, but she spoke clearly. Once she had begun talking, it all rushed out in a flood. "I was under orders to serve Crestyss. All Mages were. I gave Crestyss the idea to start the war, to bring the ancient army of our ancestors to life and have them slaughter everyone in this land. We scoured the whole world, searching for someone with a power strong enough to achieve this, stealing their power for ourselves, but it was never enough. No one was ever good enough. Crestyss was driven mad by the constant failures, but that's not to say he changed.

"Then I met Kole, and I betrayed him and Crestyss both, serving both at the same time. I no longer hated humans, but my loyalty was to my own people. I couldn't fool Crestyss. He knew as soon as my resolve wavered. Twisted by anger, he raped me. Arion is more that man's child than mine.

"So I stole Arion's power and hid him away from Crestyss, terrified of what that influence could do to him. He became a monster without ever knowing his true creator. If he were allowed to live, there would be no hope for him. He'd become a monster worse than Crestyss, and I cannot allow that."

Cy looked forward, seeing nothing, feeling nothing, as the information was processed in his mind.

"Is that what you wanted to hear? Is it, Cyllorian? Tell me, do you understand my actions now? Or was I right in assuming you are nothing more than a selfish demon, that nothing could change what you are?" Theresa spat.

"He'll never have to know. We don't have to tell him once he's back. It would be too much for him if he knew. But he's not past hope. You thought I could change, you tried. So why can't he?" Cy said. He was trying to convince himself more than anything, but he couldn't deny his own memories. His gaze flashed to Void, and remembered the look on Grite's face when it attacked him. It was just like Arion's when facing Kraven, when he nearly ripped the boy's heart from his chest.

"Some just can't be helped, Cyllorian. You should know that from personal experience," Theresa hissed before storming out of the room. No one else moved. They didn't even dare breathe.

Her magic had faded from his body soon after she had struck him, but he only just found the strength to stand. With one last shred of hope alive in his chest, Cy scooped up Void's body and ran from the room.

Void

Void shook himself awake, jolting upright. His heart was racing, and he pressed his hand to his chest. *It's beating. I'm breathing.*

"Hey, how are you feeling?" Kaitlyn asked from beside him. She was sitting on the edge of the bed, watching him with sad eyes and a tired smile.

Void swept his eyes over the room he was in, taking it all in quickly. Though the bed he lay in was large and comfortable, it was placed in a dark cell with only a small source of light. "Alive," he replied. His pulse returned to normal within seconds, and being in another cage didn't incite a single reaction from him. *I just nearly died for real, and I still can't feel anything?*

"I'm sorry we had to put you in here. We'll get you out as soon as everything clears up, I promise."

"It's fine. I'm used to it, so it's actually a bit comforting." His gaze wandered around the room. He met a pair of bright green eyes belonging to a wolf in the corner of the room, watching his every move. "This is better, anyway. You can't trust me, and I certainly can't trust me. This makes it easier."

"What makes you think we still don't trust you?" Cy asked, entering the cell. He stood at the foot of the bed, his hands shoved into his pockets. The demon's attire always confused Void. He always wore pants, though Void doubted he needed to, but his chest was bare, suggesting that he didn't like clothes at all. This was all Void could think, despite the haunted look that hinted at a much more interesting conversation.

"We can handle it from here, Tuft. You should probably see to your pack."

The wolf inched out of the corner, his eyes never leaving Void. Reluctantly, he ducked out of the cell with his tail tucked between his legs.

"So, what's the deal with Grite? He seemed to have a major obsession with you," Cy asked, diving straight into the interrogation. His voice was hostile, but his eyes suggested that Cy already knew the answers.

"He was the one that got to torture me. He always says weird stuff like that, so I've just stopped listening."

"Did you know about your blood, or your body?"

"How could I? The only person I ever talked to was a demon, and he certainly wasn't teaching kindergarten."

"Well, would you look at that. Personal growth," Cy mused, barking out a bitter laugh. He was holding himself stiffly, and the light within him was dim. Was he tired, or distressed?

"What are you talking about?" Void inquired, watching the demon with suspicion.

"You made a joke. And here I thought you didn't have a sense of humor. Or a sense of anything, really."

"I blame you," Void muttered.

Cy didn't seem to hear, just went back to his questions. *"What did they want from you? You kept telling us that you're worthless, but they wouldn't chase you all that way if you were. So what are you hiding? What do they have planned for you?"*

Cy leaned forward on the bed and glared at Void. Kaitlyn looked ready to scold him, but Void didn't give her the chance.

Void slammed his hands down on either side of him, Cy's own anger affecting him. "I've told you, I don't know! Do you think if I did, I wouldn't have told them already, and stopped the torture? Or told you to get back at the bastard? As far as I know, I'm as good as nothing! I'm still trying to figure out how to feel the emotions that I know I should. I'm not stupid. I know how I'm supposed to feel and react, but I literally can't! I'm trapped inside this messed up body, and I've got a hunch my mind is even more messed up. Give me a break, already!"

Tears came into Void's eyes and he let himself dissolve into crying. Kaitlyn put her hand on his shoulder, but the gesture was stiff and awkward.

"You're right. I'm sorry, Void. Ignore me, I'm just a self-absorbed demon, myself. It comes with the territory, or so I've been told. Apparently, we can't change who we are, no matter what we do," Cy mumbled, rubbing his hand over his head.

"What are you talking about, Cy? Did something happen?" Kaitlyn asked, her concern shifting.

"Nothing. Come on, we'll take him to Theresa. Not like there's

any other choice. She'll know what to do, because she knows every-thing, and is always right no matter what. This is her castle, and she's the queen, ruling over everyone and everything." Cy marched to the cell door, holding it open.

Kaitlyn helped Void untangle himself from the blankets and led him from the cell. Cy stared at the ground as they passed. For once, Void was unable to read his emotions.

They followed Cy throughout the castle, forced to keep up with his impatience. Void was awestruck by everything in the castle, an odd feeling growing in his chest with every room they passed. Kaitlyn questioned him every time he paused, but the feeling would slip away as soon as his attention was on anything else. Kaitlyn turned her questions onto Cy, though their conversation was forced and uncomfortable.

A feather fluttered in front of Void, and he stopped. His pause went unnoticed by the others. He reached his hand out to them, ready to call out, but a small black and white owl landed on his arm. His chest tightened. He could practically hear the bird telling him to stay silent. He swallowed a lump in his throat and nodded once.

The owl took to the air awkwardly, one wing beating faster than the other. The bird flew back the way they had come, and Void followed automatically. His eyes never left the owl as they went through winding hallways and climbed more stairs than Void could count.

The bird ducked into a small doorway at the end of a thin hall. Void dove in after, but the bird was nowhere to be seen. Void was alone, lost and wondering if the owl had just been a hallucination.

The room was small and crescent shaped, a round table taking up most of the room. Two bare shelves stood opposite each other. A small door was set in the wall that curved inward. Despite the barren state of the room, there wasn't a single speck of dust.

Something about that door seemed... off to him. Before he could place it, his body moved on its own. He approached the door, and his left hand raised to grip the handle. Void held his breath as he swung the door open.

This room was even more empty than the last. It held a single, occupied bed, and an old book that lay in pieces on the floor. It was nothing more than a secret napping room, tucked into the furthest corners of this building.

If it weren't for the ominous chill in the room, Void would have been able to convince himself of that. The air here was heavy with death, and after his recent close encounter, he wanted to stay far away from death. But he couldn't bring himself to leave.

Void gaped at the body on the bed, clearly the one Cy and Kaitlyn had been hoping to bring back from the dead. He looked exactly like Void felt... broken, beaten, and rotting from the inside out. He looked far worse than death.

Void had always thought that the body would be perfect, except for the killing blow. He never would have thought they still had their hopes up for someone that looked like they had died dozens of times.

Void drew near to the bed, entranced by the wounds that covered the boy's body. He gazed into the clouded eyes of the body, and his stomach flipped inside of him. Without fully understanding his own actions, he touched his hand to the hole in the boy's chest.

Green magic sparked as his fingers touched the boy's skin. Void flinched, but refused to pull away. A migraine had set in his head, but he lost all thoughts to the pain. The boy's pale skin regained color under Void's touch, while his own hand started to wither and turn black, creeping up his arm.

Void collapsed to his knees, gasping. Nothing Grite had ever done to him compared to the pain he felt now. His lips parted in a silent scream, and tears burned a path down his cheeks.

"What are you doing here?" a choked voice said behind him.

Void turned as much as he could, his body refusing to obey him. A woman stood in the doorway, her face pale and beautiful.

Theresa.

The name was loud in his crowded mind, and Void doubled over with a shriek. He couldn't move, couldn't resist as she strode over to him. She grabbed him by the neck and slammed him into the wall.

Threats and curses spewed from her mouth, but he ignored her. He watched in astonishment as the healed patch of skin on the boy's chest reverted to its original state.

Void dropped to the ground and crumpled. The woman was pulled from him by Cy. Kaitlyn ran to the bed and fluttered around the body on top of it.

The pain stopped, and Void looked down at himself. He was covered in wounds, some he could remember getting from Grite, and others he couldn't explain. Half of his skin was mottled and black.

A tremor went through him as his demon body started healing, and he fell onto his side. He couldn't breathe, couldn't even think, as his skin smoothed over. Every lash and cut sealed shut, and the burns faded into nothing. The only mark left on his body was the lightning mark from his last dream carved into his palm.

His mind was another matter. It felt more damaged than his body had been. Memories came and went until he had no idea what was real or fake, what was his or... someone else's.

He felt like he was melting from the inside out. Void had never felt more numb and empty than he did with his head stuffed to the brink with incoherent nonsense.

Cy was in front of Void, shaking him violently. Cy was speaking, but he couldn't be heard over the buzzing in Void's head.

"Void!" Cy screamed in his ear. His mind went silent. He stared at Cy, his jaw hanging open.

Void? No, a voice crashed into his mind, and he jerked away from Cy. With the first voice came a wave of others that he couldn't place.

Yes.

No.

Empty. Nothing, nothing, nothing.

Hurts. It hurts. Stop it.

More, more. I need more.

Let me go, let me go!

Void. Void, void, void, void, void, void.

"Arion." That one word from Kaitlyn's mouth cut through everything in his mind. It chased the chorus away, leaving only one voice behind: his own.

Arion? His heart raced as he thought the name. He looked to Cy for clarification, but he was gone.

Cy stood beside Kaitlyn, examining the body on the bed. The woman was leaning against the wall across from him, looking utterly defeated.

"Look at Arion! Just look at him!" Kaitlyn squealed. Her smile was gorgeous.

Look at me. Look at me! he copied. He tried to say the words, but his voice only sounded in his head.

Kaitlyn was shaking the body, speaking in broken sentences. Her smile fell when the body showed no signs of responding.

Cyllorian, look at me. He begged again, but it was no use. Cy looked empty, and Kaitlyn was lying across the body, shoulders shaking. His stomach twisted in pain as he watched them. He wanted to help them, to take the pain away no matter what. If he could, he would take all the pain for himself so they would no longer have to suffer.

"Arion," Kaitlyn sobbed.

"I'm here." The words escaped his lips in an immediate response to his name. All eyes turned to him. He tilted his head back, and he felt dizzy from the pain he had just gone through. Nothing made sense in his head, and for now, he was content just leaving it for later.

Cyllorian was the first one to move. He dropped to the ground, his hand only an inch from the boy's face. Green magic sparked between them, and Cy touched just below the boy's eye.

"Took you long enough, stupid demon." The boy's voice sounded odd to his own ears. The joke was lifeless and he had no clue why he made it. He didn't feel like himself, whoever that was supposed to be.

"Arion," Cy breathed. He snatched the boy into a tight hug that prevented him from breathing, but he didn't mind. He sat frozen, still numb and unsure of what to think or feel. It wasn't until the demon started shaking against him, and the boy's shoulder grew wet from tears made of pure magic, did he move.

Arion wrapped his arms around Cyllorian, gripping onto the plates of his shoulders. In that moment, nothing else mattered. Not the pain that ached in every muscle, not the chaos that was his mind, not even the woman watching them with resentment. The only thing that mattered to Arion was that his brother had saved him.

Arion let himself cry. He let himself feel the pain and loneliness he had been hiding. He let himself be weak.

Theresa's worn voice brought down a sense of dread and exhaustion. She spoke her thoughts aloud, disconnected and foreboding. "There's no time left. War will be upon us. Arion's magic was taken."

"So, you mean to tell me that you didn't capture him, and he got away alive?" Crestyss hissed, pacing in front of his throne. Grite was bowed before him, his nose touching the ground. The demon shook nervously.

"Yes, Master. But I weakened him. I hurt him. And I got a bit of his blood!"

"We've been spilling his blood for nearly a month. What good would it do me now?" Crestyss snapped. The demon flinched, but didn't move away.

"When I bit him, there was magic. I felt it, tasted it. Those two that stole him were waking him up. We have his magic now. We don't need the body!"

"You stupid demon!" Crestyss burst. He kicked Grite in the side, and the demon rolled down the steps to the throne.

"Master, how have I failed you? Why do I anger you so? We have a success! We can use his magic to raise our army. We will wipe out this miserable world, along with that wretch, Theresa!"

Crestyss descended the stairs, and stood menacingly over

Grite. The demon trembled until Crestyss kicked him again. The demon flew into a wall, and crumpled to the ground.

"You'll not speak of her like that. You know better, Grite. Now crawl your way back into your place! You are nothing more than a servant, and you are certainly not an adviser. You know very well why I wanted the boy brought back alive. I was a fool to believe I could trust you with such a task."

Crestyss paced back to his throne, and fell into it. He pinched the bridge of his nose, fighting against the coming headache.

"Not only did you screw up our last chance to retrieve him, you could have gravely wounded him. He could be dead now, for all we know. His magic may have awakened within him, but he does not know how to use it. We have no idea what effect extracting magic might do to a Void child. Who knows what damage you might have caused with your reckless actions."

Crestyss opened an eye and glared at Grite. The demon had pulled himself into a crouch, his wounded leg bent under him at an odd angle.

"You also nearly lost me my most valuable slave. That pathetic excuse for a demon of Theresa's could have killed you, were it so inclined. It's interesting that it didn't, though it might have felt sympathy for one of its own kind. As it is, you're useless to me now. That wound won't heal."

Crestyss gestured to the blackened hole in Grite's leg. The muscles inside the hole had hardened almost to the point of bone, but it couldn't support any weight. Grite was forced to crawl, or walk with a crutch because of it.

"No, Master. I will be fine. My body has never received damage to this extent before, not even by your hands. I simply haven't had the energy my body needs to heal from it. I will be at your side, ready

to serve in no time. While you wait, you can begin preparations for your army," Grite insisted, covering the hole with his hands.

Crestyss stood, and reached for a holster behind his back that he kept hidden within his cloak. "Tell me, Grite, did the sniveling demon shoot you with something like this?" Crestyss exposed a small gun he kept with him at all times. It had a small trigger, and a long thin barrel etched with a pattern of an explosion around the rim. Grite nodded vigorously, shrinking away from the weapon.

"Did you know, Grite, that humans were the first to invent the gun? They had stolen the technology needed for it from the Mages, and created this tiny device with the sole purpose of the complete annihilation of a person's life. It's all it was meant for, and the humans came at us with these, fully intent on destroying us. But Mages defended themselves from these weapons of mass destruction, and the humans deemed us the dangerous ones. This is what sparked the riot. Mages refused to die simply because the humans wished it.

"Mages took the guns from the humans, and created something even more deadly...a gun that fires magic, taken straight from the user. Not only can it kill another Mage, but other magical creatures in this land and beyond. It was always my assumption that it could even kill a demon, but I never had the opportunity to test it. Given how that wound looks on your leg, my bet is that I was right. But I won't know until I pull the trigger, will I?"

Crestyss pointed the gun at Grite's head, and the demon froze. It began to cry silently, terror in its eyes. Crestyss smiled sickly, relishing in the creature's torment.

"Please, Master, I'm not useless, I swear! Don't kill me, I can still serve you! I swore to serve you until my final breath, no matter the conditions. Don't you remember, Master, my oath?" Grite backed away from Crestyss as he drew closer to the demon.

"Oh, I remember perfectly, Grite. And I'm sure if I thought hard enough, I could think of something for you to do. But at the moment, I don't care. You upheld your oath, straight till the end, but I'm done with you. I'd take a deep breath, if I were you. This one's your last after all."

Grite's expression went blank as Crestyss pulled the trigger. A thin bullet of his dark green magic shot from the barrel, piercing through Grite's head between the eyes. The light in the demon faded, and he fell forward onto the ground. Light purple wisps of magic mixed with his white blood pooled on the ground. Crestyss snapped his fingers twice, and two guards rushed to the body and dragged it away.

Crestyss waved the smoke from the barrel of the gun and holstered it, a disgusted sneer on his face. He marched back to his thrown and sat heavily in it. The headache had formed over his left temple, and he pressed his fingers to the origin of it. From his cloak pocket, he produced a small vile of white blood laced with green shots of magic.

"I *will* have my war, Theresa. No matter how hard you try to keep it from me. And those boys of yours will be the first that you will lose."

THE END

The series will conclude in The Void's Lament: Of Magic, Book Three.

Keep reading to experience the first chapter!

The Void's Lament

The First Chapter

Cyllorian

"Theresa's been gone a long time," Kaitlyn said as she paced the large gathering room.

Two months had already passed since Cy and Kait had rescued Arion from Crestyss, but the days had gone slowly. Almost immediately, Theresa had left the castle, taking everyone that Cy and Kait had gathered, ushering them back to their lands to declare war on Crestyss. She had given them express orders to remain at the castle and wait for her. Cy had been all too happy to oblige, and was glad that Arion had been to weak to argue. But they hadn't heard a word from her yet, and her return was looking less and less likely with each passing day.

Theresa had turned most of the first floor of her castle into one room meant for meetings as she was expecting many more to soon join them. Though the room was vast, Kaitlyn never strayed more than a few feet from where they sat.

Cyllorian knew just how much Kaitlyn wanted to explore

and examine every inch of Theresa's castle. In the first week since bringing Arion back, when he had shut himself inside a bedroom and refused to come out, Kaitlyn had tried to wander the castle herself while Cy stood by Arion's room. Hours later, Cy had gone to look for her, and found her lost in a far corner of the castle. She had gotten lost in a secluded area of the castle that held only bare and boring bedrooms. Cyllorian hadn't even known how many beds the castle had held, and he shuddered at the thought of having to share space with so many people.

Even now, Kaitlyn would pause in her pacing to stare in wonder at the tapestries that covered the walls, set high out of reach. They depicted creatures of myth and legend, creatures that Cy had no answers for whenever Kaitlyn had asked about them. There was a beautiful mural of a sunset over an unknown horizon, and one of a darkened battleground. Between the paintings were tall stained glass windows with crystalline patterns. Their colors danced through the room as the day passed.

The paintings disappeared into darkness along the walls, the other end of the room too far to see. Cy wondered if this room was larger than the castle was from the outside. It took an hour just to walk from one end to the other. The large entrance doors of the castle stood ominously in the shadows, ever out of reach of the painted sunlight. Silver metal gleamed on its own, crisscrossed over the wood.

Cy remembered the first time Arion had left his room, he had found Cy and Kait in this room, and Arion had recited passages about the paintings. He had stood far from them, and his voice was rough with the effort to be heard. Cyllorian thought he had glanced tears in Kaitlyn's eyes then, but he too was in shock at the sight of Arion.

Kaitlyn's voice drew Cy's attention back to her. Her gaze

was fixed on the floor again, were feet moving purposefully within the intricate lines of the rug that covered most of the floor.

"Do you think we should go after her? Or check on her, somehow?" she asked as she came to a halt. She didn't address either one of them in particular, but she looked directly at Cyllorian. She tapped the toe of her boot against the ground as she watched him, waiting for an answer.

Cyllorian found himself lost in her eyes, as he had every day since they had rescued Arion. It felt as though he was fighting for her, despite Kaitlyn's awkwardness when around the other boy. Even still, her attention was always divided between the two of them, and Cy could barely control his jealousy.

"She'll be fine. Didn't she say she would be gone this long? She had a lot of people to try to recruit," Cy said, turning away from her. Though he was at a disadvantage in their fight over Kait with his current body, he was thankful that it didn't give away his true feelings. He forced a deep breath into the metal of his chest, and he rattled when he let it out in a loud sigh. Though Kaitlyn already knew how he felt, he was terrified of what anyone else might think. Especially Arion.

"Are you really so sure she's even coming back?" Arion griped. He was laying sideways in a chair, and he bent backwards over the arm to stare at Cy. His dull green eyes showed no signs of emotion.

"Arion!" Cy sniped, staring him down. No matter how much force he put into his gaze, Arion remained unphased and uncaring.

"Think about it. She locked Cyllorian away in a box with no intentions of ever letting him back out, she never liked Kaitlyn. . . and the only reason she even came back for me was to kill me." Arion crossed his arms over his face, and spoke in a monotone. Despite his insistence that he was more Void than Mage, a twinge of sadness could be heard in his last sentence.

"Why the hell would you think something like that, kid?" Cy asked, looking for any chance to change the subject. He looked to Kaitlyn for help, but she was staring at the ground in disappointment.

"Because she said so. Don't you remember? You were there, just before I got my memory back."

"I seriously have no idea what you're talking about. She wasn't making any sense then. Besides, why would she want to kill her own son?" Cy argued. He was scaring himself by defending Theresa, but the last thing he wanted to do was fuel Arion's rage.

"If I had just gotten to you first, taken your life myself, we could have made it. That's what she said, when she was trying to destroy my old body before this one got to it. You must've blocked it out. I only remembered it a couple days ago myself."

"You're sure you're not just confusing it with something Crestyss or Grite might have said? That doesn't sound like Theresa."

"Sure it does. And that's why she left, to get away from us. And if we were made to believe she'd be coming back to give us direction, we'd stay here and never leave. After all that trying, it only took a couple words to get rid of us all." Arion cackled lightly under his breath, as though he genuinely found the whole situation humorous.

"That's not why she left. She went to build up our army before shit gets even worse for us. She told us that it was only a matter of time before Crestyss tries to take over the world, or whatever it is he wants. Now can we just drop the subject?" Cy said between clenched teeth. He was gripping the arms of the chair hard enough for his claws to bite into the wood.

"Then why did the others have to leave at the exact same time, hm? Answer me that," Arion retorted, a smug smile spreading across his face.

"They had to report back to their homes, and talk them into joining the war."

"Let me guess, did *Theresa* tell you that?" Arion bit back, sitting upright in his chair. His movements were so stiff and quick that it looked inhuman. Cy sat back in his chair to put more distance between them. Kaitlyn moved to sit on the floor at Cy's side, grabbing onto the leg of the chair.

Arion's eyes followed her every move, and his mouth twitched into a sneer for a split second before clearing completely. He glared at Cyllorian, a storm rolling deep in his eyes, nearly out of sight.

"They told me themselves why they were leaving, that good enough for you, kid?" Cy leaned forward slowly, holding himself up on his knees. He narrowed his eyes, daring Arion to make a move. They had been getting in arguments nearly every day, some of them escalating into physical fights on rare occasions. Being locked in the castle together was clearly not helping either of their moods.

"Right, because Jayr is *so* trustworthy and Gil has all his wits about him. And what about Adoette, did *she* tell you, Cyllorian? She likes you more than the others, I'm sure she tells you all sorts of things, doesn't she?" Arion taunted, raising his eyebrows suggestively.

Kaitlyn shifted on the ground beside him, and Cy lost his temper. *"She has Noma, remember? As annoying as the bug is, she's helpful to her. She doesn't have to say anything!"*

"No, no, you're right about that. Body language can tell a lot about how someone is feeling," Arion scoffed, turning away. He leaned forward, then pushed off. The chair fell back onto the floor, and he kicked his legs in the air, laughing quietly to himself.

He reached his hands toward the ceiling, and green lightning weaved through his fingers. He closed his fists, then flung his fingers out, sending the lightning all around him. It stretched up into the air, growing with every inch it progressed. With a click of his tongue, the lightning shattered and teal sparks shot out in every direction. They hovered in the air around them, surrounding them with stars.

The only time Arion ever looked alive— really alive— was when he used his magic. It lit up his eyes the way they used to, and Cy's essence twisted in the metal body.

Guilt flooded him, mixed with hope. As much as they fought, Cy held no resentment toward Arion. He cared more for him, worried about him more each day, trying his best to make up for his mistakes. But there was no changing his bitter nature, and he found himself squelching Arion's spirits if they got too high. He told himself it was jealousy, part of their rivalry for Kaitlyn, but he knew he couldn't justify himself forever.

"Just like you used to do, for me," Kaitlyn cooed, reaching out to touch a star. As the magic touched her finger, it burst into flame. Her veins just under her skin became luminous, spreading throughout her whole hand.

Cy snatched up the exploding star before her, snuffing it out. He swat them each down, one by one, gaining a murderous scowl from Arion. *"Careful. He's still getting used to his magic again."*

Cy glared back at Arion, continuing to free the air of the stars. The light in the boy's eyes was gone again, replaced by the distant expression of the Void.

Arion swung his arm out, and each star slowly fell to the ground and died. "I can control it just fine. Better than you," Arion snapped, grinding his teeth. A grim smile overtook Arion's expression, and he taunted, "At least the magic I have is my own, and not some pity gift!"

"That's enough! You guys have already used up your

allotted fight for the day!" Kaitlyn yelled, getting to her feet. She stood between them with her arms outstretched and her eyes shut tight.

While Cy watched Arion carefully for any wrong move, Arion's focus was on Kaitlyn. Sorrow glinted in the boy's eyes, and Cy backed down out of guilt.

Could he really still be there? This is all I can think of to get him back, but he's fighting it. He doesn't want to come back, I can tell. Am I just going about this the wrong way? What else is there for me to do?

In the rare moment of peace, Cy took the opportunity to check on Arion. Arion had found himself in his old clothes easily, and was never once seen without his coat. Tome was tucked into the pocket, though Cy hadn't seen Arion open it even once in the past month. His eyes had regained their color, but not the light that used to define him. If it weren't for the white hair that Arion had been so determined to keep, Cy could've almost told himself none of it had ever happened.

No. He could never convince himself of that. No matter what he tried to force himself to believe, nothing ever felt right about Arion. Not anymore. The boy had only gotten thinner since they had retrieved him, and Cy couldn't remember the last time he had seen Arion eat. Or sleep. Dark circles ringed his eyes, and his hands shook violently most of the time.

His sanity was the most questionable thing about him. Cy had always been able to know everything going on inside the boy's head. Now that he was unable to, he was always on edge. Arion had been unpredictable just before his death, and he was sure he could have only gotten worse from there. The only question was... just how *much* worse?

"Can we get along now?" Kaitlyn asked, exasperated. Cy was broken out of his reverie. Arion was staring back at him with a longing in his eyes that mirrored his own.

"Yeah," he said quietly, lowering his head. His voice was lighter now, calmer. Cy nodded silently, watching Arion as the boy studied his hands. Kaitlyn sat down on the ground between them, letting out her breath.

"Finally. I swear, getting you two to behave is worse than pulling teeth!" Kaitlyn giggled awkwardly, trying her best to make a joke of the situation.

Arion cringed at the comment, and put his hand to his cheek. His jaw dropped slightly, and Cy could see that he was running his tongue over the surface of his teeth. Checking that they were all there.

He caught Cy watching him, and quickly stopped what he was doing. His hands dropped into his lap. Arion's demon body wasn't capable of changing fully, but he could still manifest a set of short, black claws. He'd made a habit of playing with them whenever he avoided Cy. The claws were out now, picking at a loose string on Arion's pants. His expression went blank. Like always, there was no telling what could possibly be going on in his head.

"We're not the only ones who have a shitty situation. We keep forgetting that. Yeah, we're angsty teenagers with massive mental damage all cooped up together, but that's not the end of the world. If something happened to Theresa, or she couldn't get all the people she needs, that's it. Crestyss wins, and Lontorra is destroyed. He brainwashed all the Mages, and most of everyone else, too, for that matter. He's going to kill all the humans, then the species that sided against him, then the ones that tried to stay out of it completely. Without anyone left after that, who knows what he'll do next. Probably go terrorize the rest of the world. So either way, being stuck here is better than being dead," Cy said finally. His accidental speech replaced the silence, and it echoed in the room.

"We won't let him win," Kaitlyn said simply, smiling at

him. Her eyes flashed fiercely, and her pupils narrowed into slits. Dragon eyes.

He smiled back, but Arion's wide eyes staring into the distance caught his attention. He hadn't responded to his speech in any way, and it worried Cy. A bitter comeback or sarcastic remark would have been better than nothing.

"Arion?" he prompted, leaning to the side to try to meet his gaze.

Arion's eyes darted to him for a moment, before he fell backwards onto the chair again.

"Don't tell me you've got absolutely nothing to say to that."

"Nothing at all. At least, nothing you want to hear."

Cy narrowed his eyes, knowing what conversation would follow if he pressed the issue. *"You're right about that, kid. I don't want to hear it. And I don't want you thinking it, either, you got that? Hey, I'm talking to you, stubborn brat!"*

"Yeah, yeah. I hear you. Selfish demon," Arion muttered under his breath, waving his hand in the air dismissively. His lips pulled up in a slight smile, but he avoided Cy's gaze.

"We don't even need her..." Arion whispered slowly. He drummed his fingers on the ground beside him, his mind working anxiously. "We can do it ourselves. Sneak in and kill him without a second thought. He's the only one that wants a fight out of all this, not his followers. If he's dead, there's no threat. We don't need an army, especially not one led by a woman that effectively didn't exist until a few months ago.

"Just the three of us, we can do it. Right, Cy? You and me, we can storm his Tower and kill Crestyss. Just you and me, Cy... like before." Arion turned to Cy and smiled.

Cy readied himself to talk Arion down, worried he had let his mind go too far again. But the smile on the boy's face wasn't cunning or sadistic. It was elated, hopeful as he gazed at Cy.

"I'm not so sure, kid. We barely made it out of there with more people fighting for us, I don't think less is the way to go here. You're not in the best of shape for a fight, either. You gotta get your strength back before we go on any wild adventures. Remember last time we got in over our head?" Cy chose his words carefully, and spoke slowly.

He watched Arion closely, testing him. The boy's face grew dark, tormented, and he looked back to the ceiling. His mouth moved minutely, but there was no sound.

Arion closed his eyes at the silence, and Cy watched him carefully. He knew he wasn't trying to sleep. Arion did everything he could to stay awake. His breathing quickened, and his hand fluttered to his head. He dug into his scalp with his black claws, and his white blood soaked his hair.

"Arion," Cy said softly. Arion's eyes shot open and he glanced at Cy. There was fear deep within them, but the boy hardened his resolve in seconds. He retracted the claws and quickly lowered his hand, wiping the blood off on the side of the chair.

As Cy thought how to phrase his concerns, Arion jumped up from the fallen chair. "I'm going outside," he said pointedly. He marched past both of them before they could say anything. Kaitlyn reached for his hand as he passed, but he dodged her grasp easily.

The door shut behind them with a resounding *thud*. Kaitlyn dropped her head and played with the thin band on her finger. "What does he do when he goes out there?" she wondered aloud. "What if he's..."

"Tuft keeps an eye on him. If something happened to him, or because of him, he would tell us. Tuft won't tell me anything else," Cy answered, chasing her fears away.

She didn't respond. Her expression was uncertain as she spun the ring on her finger.

Cy wanted to comfort her, to reach out to her, but couldn't. Not only did he lack the proper words, he lacked the right. He sighed, and clawed at his head.

In the depressed silence between them, voices could be heard outside the doors. Cy jumped from his chair, stepping in front of Kaitlyn reflexively. She stood slowly, shaking out her arms as they covered with scales. Vyekrin grumbled from the roof in response, and waited. Her own talons extended, and poison dripped from them.

Cy gathered his dwindling magic, and opened the door violently with a sweep of his arm. The voices ceased as Theresa and her small army stood in shock at their stances.

"What do you think you're doing?" Theresa scolded as she marched into the room. The others followed her, and Cy could make out only a couple faces among the crowd. Gil stood on his own, looking as lost as ever and glaring at the small huddle of Draken on the other side of Theresa. Jayr was obviously ignoring him as he pushed Kaliyah in a wheelchair.

Adoette was jumping up and down somewhere in the middle of the crowd, her flowered hair bouncing wildly. She finally pushed her way through to the front, and she beamed when she caught sight of Cy. She waved her arm in a wide arc over her head, while Noma buzzed around her head. Cy noticed the small blue buds that ringed her head were gone, leaving small red thorns in their place.

"Well, are you just going to stand there, or are you going to greet us?" Theresa asked impatiently. Cy realized he was still in an attacking stance, and shifted into a normal position.

Theresa looked around the vacant room as the swarm of creatures wandered into the castle. "Where is he?" she asked irritably.

"He's outside somewhere," Cy answered, defensive at her tone.

"And you're not concerned with keeping an eye on him because..?"

"He's with Tuft, so why should I care past that point? He can do whatever he wants. I'm not his babysitter." Cy crossed his arms and avoided her scowl. Kaitlyn had shed her scales for her preferred human form, and left him to meet their new comrades.

"You should know better than to let him go unsupervised. Goyik, come." With a snap of her fingers, her trusted wolf was at her side, appearing from within the throngs of people behind them.

"Yes, Lady Theresa?" he asked dutifully.

"Find Arion," she said shortly, his name clipping off of her tongue violently, as though she couldn't stand the taste of it. Goyik bowed gracefully, and charged back through the doors.

As they waited Goyik's return, Theresa motioned for her army to step forward. "We've had some new recruits that will be residing with us for short periods at a time. They will attend every meeting and memorize every possible strategy, then report back to their homes so that everyone will be prepared. We must be careful to not draw attention to ourselves. I have a barrier that can keep only so many magical creatures hidden at once, or else we would all be here. But we will just have to make do with what we have."

"Fine by me. Just one question. Do I have to learn all of their names?" Cy asked sarcastically. Over two dozen pairs of eyes turned to him. Most scowled at him, including those he knew. Only Gil smiled at his remark, covering his mouth to hide a laugh.

"It would be helpful, yes, not to mention polite. Acquaint yourselves with each other quickly while I get ready."

With that, Theresa left the group of mostly strangers to talk amongst themselves. Despite her words telling them to mingle, more than half of the army left to explore the castle. As the crowd dispersed, Cy realized their cavalry was smaller than expected, less than fifty. He understood why Theresa had made the entry such a grand room as all the bodies shuffled through toward a large staircase that had formed silently across from the door. All that was left were those that he knew, and half a dozen new faces. Two Droll, two Draken, and two Mages. Adoette was the first to disband from the group, flitting about the room as though it was her first time inside the castle.

Seeing as how none seemed inclined to start, Cy spoke first in a monotone. *"Hi, I'm Cyllorian, and I'm a demon. Get your complaining, bickering, and judging out of the way now, you have three seconds... and time's up, who's next?"*

The Droll chattered amongst themselves, standing a short ways behind Gil. They were clearly older than him, one large and clearly male with his chest bare beneath a thick vest. The other had dominant curves to her body, and the scales along her shoulders seemed larger than normal. They seemed lost in their own world as they pointed to various aspects of the vast room.

Jayr was flanked by two males, similar in size. While Jayr scowled behind a nervous Kaliyah, the other two Draken were smiling idiotically. It was difficult to recognize them outside of their armor, but Cy was certain they were Orthros and Lane, their guards from their time on Mount Draken.

Most of them looked amongst themselves for help. The first to step forward were two Mages, whose eyes burned like fire around the silver pupils. They had thin black hair, and gray splotches on their skin. The oldest, a boy with a thin face and high cheekbones, said, "I am Hunter Vamyr, a Mage. This is my sister, Twila. Crestyss killed our parents many years ago and captured us. He held us captive near the ocean, away from everyone. He experimented on us, tortured us, and turned us into something we still don't understand yet. This is why we choose to fight."

Hunter held himself high, but Cy could see the responsibility of being the oldest weighing on his shoulders. He couldn't be much older than himself, but the haunted look on his face said that Hunter had been through much more torment than Cy could imagine.

His sister couldn't be older than twelve. She had her long hair tied into pigtails. Even restrained, it nearly reached down to her hips. Her long, light pink dress with a red floral pattern reached to her ankles, but left her arms bare. There were dark rings all along her arms, of both bruises and scars. Silver bracelets squeezed her wrists, and when she lifted her hand to wave enthusiastically, a drop of blood ran from underneath the bands. She wiped it away without a second thought, and rubbed the blood onto her dress. It was then Cy realized the dark flowers on her dress were smudges of blood, rather than a pattern. Despite this, her smile was bright and genuine in her heart shaped face.

"Vamyr's, come here a moment, would you?" Theresa called as she levitated a table near the middle of the room. The two turned to look at her, and nodded. Moving as a single unit, they left for Theresa.

Gil stepped up to Cy and Kaitlyn, reading the distress that was clear on their faces. "Theresa told us about them before she left to save them. She said Crestyss had been mixing their blood with that of ancient creatures, a type of demon that got their immortality from the blood of others, and had special control over strong, dark magic. *Otherworldly*, she called it. There was supposed to be four, but the two middle siblings had already passed away by she time we got there. And the little one, Twila, is the strongest. Because her magic as a Mage wasn't fully developed, it was the most malleable, so Crestyss did the most to her. He had those bracelets made specifically to keep her under control, by sending magical charges straight into her blood."

Gil looked after the orphans as they helped Theresa to set the room up. Hunter was using thick black strands of magic to move the furniture. Twila stood with her hands clasped behind her, picking at the bands around her wrists. Her smile was plastered to her face as she watched her brother. Blood dripped to the floor without her notice.

Kaitlyn stepped closer to Cy, and he turned to face her. She was fidgeting in her place, rubbing her arms. Though she had turned away from the group, her gaze was still fixed on one in particular; Kaliyah. The other girl was staring at her hands, refusing to lift her head. The unknown Droll and Draken had disappeared while Cy was distracted by the Mages, leaving them in an uncomfortable silence.

Cy racked his brain for anything he could say to break the tension, but nothing that came to mind sounded right. He knew what kind of trouble he'd be in with Theresa if he started a fight as soon as they arrived, but honestly, what else did she expect? *Does she even know about Kaliyah and Kaitlyn's fight?*

Just as the silence was becoming unbearable, the doors flew open once again, and Arion stumbled into the room. He caught himself on his hands and knees, whirling to glare at a triumphant Goyik. Tome fell to the floor right in front of him. "What was that for? I wasn't doing anything!" he snapped.

"My Lady asked me to fetch you, so I did."

"No need. I'm fine on my own," he grumbled as he picked himself off the floor. He stuffed Tome hurriedly into his coat, and marched into the room. He walked straight past the curious glances, his attention fixed on Theresa.

Cy stepped in his way, worried that Arion would lose control of his temper. *"Welcome back, kid. Meet our new friends, will ya?"* He grabbed onto Arion's sleeve tightly, forcing the boy to meet his stern gaze. Cy held his hand out toward Gil and continued hesitantly, *"They're-"*

"He," Gil piped up, his voice breaking. "I had my birthday while I was gone, so...he."

Cy nodded shortly, though a bit confused. *"Right, he's—"*

Arion let out a sigh, cutting off Cy, and glared over his shoulder at the three that were left. "I don't care who they are," he barked, and went to turn away.

With a groan, Cy grabbed Arion's wrist, but Arion writhed under the touch. He twisted desperately until his fingers touched Cy's arm, sending lightning straight into Cy's essence. Cy jumped back from the shock, releasing Arion. Just as Arion was turning away again, Cy thought he saw guilt in his eyes.

"Arion—" Theresa called, harsher than necessary.

With a stomp of his foot, Arion cut her off. The room filled with thick green smoke, leaving everyone but Cy in a coughing fit. When the smoke cleared, Arion was long gone.

"This definitely won't be a fun group bonding vacation," Cy groaned, staring at the last remnants of the smoke.

TO BE CONTINUED IN

The Void's Lament: Of Magic, Book 3.

About the Author

T. Ariyanna is a newcomer to publishing, but a veteran at storycrafting. After being enchanted by the worlds within books during middle school, she spent her high school years creating her first novel-length story. A few years later she hit the scene with a magical debut, *The Mage's Son*.

Ariyanna's specializations run from realistic fantasy to dystopian steampunk. She juggles writing with being a stay at home mother to a daughter just as adventurous as any heroine. Her hobbies include reading, crafting, and playing video games.

www.ingramcontent.com/pod-product-compliance
Lightning Source LLC
Chambersburg PA
CBHW021336150726
47989CB00005B/2015